NEXT LEVEL LOVE

ALSO BY SHAMEEZ PATEL

Playing Flirty

NEXT LEVEL LOVE

♥ ♥ ♥

SHAMEEZ PATEL

FOREVER

New York Boston

Copyright © 2026 by Shameez Patel Papathanasiou

Cover design and illustration by YY Liak.
Cover image of Pac-Man by ZinetroN / Shutterstock.
Cover copyright © 2026 by Hachette Book Group, Inc.

Forever
Hachette Book Group
1290 Avenue of the Americas, New York, NY 10104
read-forever.com
@readforeverpub

First Edition: January 2026

Forever is an imprint of Grand Central Publishing. The Forever name and logo are registered trademarks of Hachette Book Group, Inc.

The publisher is not responsible for websites (or their content) that are not owned by the publisher.

Forever books may be purchased in bulk for business, educational, or promotional use. For information, please contact your local bookseller or the Hachette Book Group Special Markets Department at special.markets@hbgusa.com.

Print book interior design by Jeff Stiefel

Library of Congress Cataloging-in-Publication Data

Names: Patel, Shameez author
Title: Next level love / Shameez Patel.
Description: First edition. | New York : Forever, 2026.
Identifiers: LCCN 2025035622 | ISBN 9781538768402 trade paperback | ISBN 9781538768419 ebook
Subjects: LCGFT: Romance fiction | Novels | Fiction
Classification: LCC PR9369.4.P39 N49 2026
LC record available at https://lccn.loc.gov/2025035622

ISBNs: 9781538768402 (trade paperback), 9781538768419 (ebook)

Printed in the United States of America

LSC-C

Printing 1, 2025

*Internet friendships are often overlooked,
but isn't it beautiful to think about how your
online friends managed to still be there for you
without physically being there?*

To all my internet friends, this is for you.

AUTHOR'S NOTE

Next Level Love is a fun, swoon-worthy romance, but it also explores heavier themes such as grief, the death of a parent (in the past), harassment, and other emotionally abusive relationships. Please take care, and be kind to yourself.

1

LINCOLN

[110 weeks ago]

@theanswerisno:
Don't go in there

                    @pancakesareelite:
        I don't take advice from strangers

@theanswerisno:
You'll be dead in 3 seconds

                    @pancakesareelite:
    Who are you and why are you in my DMs?

@theanswerisno:
2 seconds

                    @pancakesareelite:
            I don't trust you

@theanswerisno:
1 second

                    @pancakesareelite:
                        No

                    @pancakesareelite:
                        NO!

```
@theanswerisno:
Welcome to the Engineering Lobby
```

Main quest: Pack up my old bedroom. Side quest: Be consumed by nostalgia.

"Donate it all," I yelled down the hallway.

I spun around on the once-black rug, which had faded to various shades of gray. There was too much to do. Growing up, I had nothing and everything at the same time. At least, that was how it felt while sorting through the stacks of used comic books, odd blocks of Legos, and shelves of superhero figurines that were already old when I'd received them.

I swung open one of the closet doors. The white plastic hangers drooped with at least ten crinkled items hanging on top of each other.

There was so much clutter. So many things my mother wouldn't let go of.

I grabbed as many hangers off the rail as I could manage and tossed them into a box. My mother walked through the doorway at that exact moment and gasped. "You're giving everything away?"

The scent of cinnamon reached me before she set down two steaming cups of chai. My favorite. Regardless of the weather, Mom used every opportunity to offer me a warm beverage.

She walked up to the overflowing basket in the corner. "Maybe there's something you'd want to keep." After rummaging through the pile, she pulled out the black-and-brown, homemade pirate costume she'd sewn the night before a kindergarten Halloween party. "You loved this."

I took the outfit and held it against my body, which had more than doubled in height. "I don't think it'll fit."

Mom burst out laughing as though I were the funniest person

in the world. She had always done that, ever since I was a kid—I couldn't resist taking advantage of it.

"I'll bet you want to keep this." She pulled out a box from underneath the dresser before lifting the lid and revealing my old Atari console and a stack of cartridges.

She was absolutely right about that.

"Your children will love this." Her soft, green gaze met mine.

It was like looking into a broken mirror. The same refined nose, wide mouth, and deep brown skin, but I had my father's brown eyes and dark lashes. And every time she looked at me, it was as though I could see her thinking about him.

Which often had me thinking about him too. About his untouched study.

No. Don't go there. Not yet.

Shaking off the thought, I resorted to teasing my mother instead. "Who are these kids you keep mentioning?" I took the console and set it aside. "I haven't been paying child support."

Her hearty laugh filled the room once more. She pinched my stubbled chin, and her gold bangles jingled as they slid down her forearm. "Someday, you will make me a grandmother."

"Humans haven't evolved enough to procreate on our own, so…" I walked over to the other side of the room and cracked open the window. Maybe it had something to do with talking about my love life, or lack thereof, but the room was significantly stuffier than when I'd first walked in.

"Is my child not enough for you?" a voice joked from the doorway. Claire, my best friend for as long as I can remember, tossed a stack of three empty boxes at my feet. "Those are the only boxes I could find."

"These are the only boxes you found before you got too lazy to look any further," my mother said, pulling Claire in for a tight squeeze. "Where is your handsome husband and wonderful little girl?"

"Daddy-and-daughter playdate." Claire kicked off her sandals and glanced around. "Hey, when did you move the bed?"

"Last week," I said, rubbing my lower back, which had paid the price.

The oven timer pinged, and my mother lifted her index finger. "Be right back."

As soon as she was gone, Claire hoisted herself onto the desk and rummaged around in her tote bag before pulling out a novel.

"You don't look like you're here to help." I took off my glasses and cleaned them using the end of my T-shirt.

"Moral support," she said, and placed her finger on her lips. "Now shush, the enemies are about to become lovers."

I stifled a laugh and kept my mouth shut as instructed. I preferred it that way and enjoyed the sound of Claire turning the page, the traffic that had become white noise, and the distinct sound of my mother using her glass cutting board.

With a deep inhale, I continued my quest to clear this room. If I finished early enough, I could squeeze in a gaming session before bed, and maybe, just maybe, Lily would be online to play with me.

But as much as I wanted to throw everything in the donations box, I got stuck. My brain got stuck. Some items stopped me for a few seconds while others pulled me back to a previous life, keeping me there.

Traffic picked up, and instead of the quiet hum from earlier, there was hooting and the jarring sound of different songs and radio stations overlapping. I could hear the birds. I could hear the neighbors talking. I could hear too much.

I stared at the item in my hand. Frozen. I couldn't think of anything except for everything I was hearing.

"Much better," Claire said as the window snapped shut.

Silence filled the room, and the buzz in my brain softened. She offered me a knowing smile before climbing the desk and resuming her reading journey.

My mother reappeared, and Claire shoved her book underneath her thigh. Mom shot her a playful glare and then turned her attention to me. "Lincoln, I forgot to tell you, there's a leaky faucet in the kitchen. Could you check it out?"

"Sounds like a job for a plumber." I straightened to my full height, which put me more than a head above her. "I could call one."

She laughed as if it were the most absurd suggestion before grabbing my wrist and dragging me to the kitchen, where the left-side faucet released a small droplet every few seconds.

"We can fix it ourselves," she said.

I grew up hearing that line, and for the longest time, it was true.

"I design roads and analyze traffic." I leaned in, scrutinizing the shiny faucet.

"Exactly. Roads are like pipes, and traffic is like water, same thing." She waved her hands and left the kitchen, allowing me time to search for YouTube tutorials on the basics of plumbing.

Mid-tutorial, Mom returned. The kettle boiled for our fourth cup of chai, and gathering from the lemony scent, cake would be involved.

She offered me a slice of carrot cake with lemon icing. "Thank you for doing this. You're a good son."

Never knowing what to do when she said these things, I shrugged and smiled. "Well, I haven't completed any of the things I came here to do. So don't thank me yet." I opened and closed the faucet, testing the pressure. "I'll have to stop at the hardware store. I don't suppose you'll hand over this place with this tiny flaw?"

"It has to be perfect."

I shoved a forkful of cake into my mouth, savoring the sweet and sour combination.

"How's work?" Mom stared at me while I stared at the faucet, willing it to stop leaking because there was only so much the internet could teach me in half an hour.

I swallowed the cake. "Oh…um…"

Before I could ramble off my potential news, Claire walked in, her nose still stuck between the pages of her novel.

My mother offered her a slice of cake but kept her focus on me. "When will they let you know about the promotion? You work so hard for this company. They don't recognize your efforts."

Claire's gaze zapped upward. "You haven't told her yet?"

My mouth dropped open, and my mother ran forward and pinched my shoulder.

"Ow," I yelped.

"Really, Lincoln?" Mom narrowed her eyes but couldn't resist smiling. "Why didn't you lead with that? So you got it?"

"Did you just come here to cause trouble?" I asked Claire. "I was about to tell her."

Claire grinned. "Your mom gives me cake in exchange for secrets about you."

"It's hardly a secret…" I shifted on my feet. "They haven't promoted me. They're offering me a temporary post as the acting manager of the Roads division to see if I can handle it."

My mother's eyes widened and then narrowed. "Of course you can handle it. What are they implying? You've been there for over a decade, and you're the best civil engineer there."

"Engineer? Very possibly." I doubted everything in my life but not my technical knowledge. There couldn't be doubt in a field where there was no room for error. "Manager? Very questionable."

"I've never liked your boss. He always seemed jealous of your brilliance," Mom said. If my mother was a cartoon character, a puff of smoke would erupt from her head. "How does he plan on testing you now?"

"Well…I guess I'll find out tomorrow. Obviously, I'll have to work on more projects and"—I threw my head back, groaning—"manage people."

"We know how you feel about people." Claire burst out laughing. My mother joined her.

I glared at them.

"We're teasing." Mom patted my shoulder. "I'm sure all the people you work with will be exactly like you."

"That would be a nightmare." I picked up my phone and scrolled through another step-by-step tutorial on fixing a leak. At the very least, it distracted me from my growing discomfort at the idea of having people following me around at work, asking me questions.

My mother laughed again and pulled me in for a tight hug.

"Do you think you can do it?" Claire asked, chewing on the inside of her cheek.

I shrugged, wiggling out of my mother's powerful grip. "I don't know…I like design and theory. I don't know if I want to or can manage and—" My words cut off the second I spotted my beaming mother. I found myself nodding, fighting the grimace threatening to creep onto my face.

"Oh, Lincoln." She smiled. "You can do anything you put your mind to. You have your dad's brain and all the opportunities he didn't, thanks to how very hard he worked. He always spoke about the civil engineers with such admiration." Her brows bunched, and her eyes grew misty. "Seeing you achieve this is a dream come true. A manager in the family." She walked away and grabbed her phone. "I must tell my sisters."

My throat tightened. All the hesitation I had regarding this promotion was replaced by a strong sense of duty. She was right. My dad had worked himself to the bone for us, and he'd have been so proud. We'd spent countless hours driving through town talking about the buildings he'd laid bricks on or tiles he'd grouted. He was the reason I went into engineering.

The longing settled in my bones, in my chest. Everything ached.

Before my mom could say anything more about me, my tentative promotion, or my father, I turned the questions on her. I moved the conversation to her book club, crochet club (not to be confused with her knitting club), and when the new house may be ready for her and her new family to move in.

"Oh." Mom turned away and wiped the already clean counters. "You know, it's already ready. It's just that it takes time to move and pack and…" She inhaled a shaky breath.

She didn't have to explain how hard it was to leave this place behind.

Despite being as close as can be, conversations with my mom often felt like a game of hot potato. We tossed around the hard topics, afraid of being burned.

Claire snapped her book shut. "Enough boring talk. It's my turn, and I want to tell you about the hot, grumpy pirate who is, obviously, in love with the girl who has nothing but a knife and determination."

I grinned as she recounted the three books before this one. For some reason, I was reminded of Lily. Maybe it was because her weapon of choice—in most of the games we played online—was a knife. Maybe it was her sheer determination to win despite being outranked by most of her challengers. Maybe it was because sometimes it felt as though I were falling in love with her.

Whatever it was, once I started thinking about Lily, it was hard to stop. Because thinking about Lily was the easiest thing in the world.

And I thought about her often.

As if summoned, my phone lit up and her username flashed across my screen. I couldn't resist the smile stretching across my face.

@pancakesareelite:
I'm ready when you are.

2

ELIZABETH

[108 weeks ago]

@pancakesareelite:
What do you do when you're
not playing games with me?

> @theanswerisno:
> Play games with other people

@pancakesareelite:
Traitor!

> @theanswerisno:
> I'm an engineer

@pancakesareelite:
Well, duh. I assumed that much.
This server was created by an SDSU
engineering student for engineering
students, wasn't it?

> @theanswerisno:
> Yep

@pancakesareelite:
You're not going to tell me anything
else about yourself?

> **@theanswerisno:**
> I am also my mother's handyman.
> For free, I might add

@pancakesareelite:
A man of many talents

> **@theanswerisno:**
> What do you do?

@pancakesareelite:
I'm still trying to figure that out

Was there such a thing as too much makeup? Based on how everyone's eyes widened upon meeting me, I must have rivaled the Joker.

Which was less than ideal on my first day of the most competitive engineering internship in California.

Any civil engineering graduate would kill to be in my position. Every year, Simucon would invite only six graduates from across the country to participate in their eight-week internship.

This year, they hired seven. I was the seventh intern, and I know this because they listed us in order of acceptance in their welcome email.

But still, they accepted me. They created an extra slot for me. Whether that was a good or bad thing, I couldn't tell. But now was not the time for spiraling as one of the directors, Mr. Anders, walked me through the office.

He marched around with his chest puffed out. Raised with money, raised to be confident. In theory, so was I. But it never stuck. To avoid being scolded for it time and time again, I became good at faking it, and that took me far enough. Sometimes in the wrong direction.

Parties. Drugs. Men.

Mr. Anders pushed open the next office door, pulling me out of my reverie.

"Carden!" he yelled.

While the room was the same size as all the others, it was far more spacious because it only housed one person, rather than two or three. The man who sat behind the desk scowled at his computer, unbothered by our arrival. Mr. Anders tapped on his desk, but the man, who appeared to be younger than him—perhaps midthirties with a head of pitch-black hair, brown skin, and dark eyes hiding behind a pair of glasses—lifted a finger on his left hand, silencing the director while his right hand clicked furiously. The fierce frown between his dark brows was noticeable from afar. After a second, he sighed, tore off his headset, and looked up.

He was rather handsome.

Like everyone else, his eyes widened for a second as he did a quick take of my suit coat, fitted pencil skirt, and heels—which I would never wear to this office again.

His gaze traveled back up to meet mine. Wait. No. It settled about a quarter inch above my eyes.

Is he looking at my forehead? Do I have a zit?

I lifted my chin, summoning faux confidence, and wiped my clammy palms across my skirt.

Mr. Anders gestured toward me, a coy smile on his face I didn't quite like. "We have fresh blood! Meet Elizabeth." For a moment, I thought he may not use my surname, that perhaps I'd be spared this one time, but it seemed he had only paused for effect. As soon as the man stood, taller than I'd imagined he'd be, and reached out his hand, Mr. Anders added with a flourish, "Elizabeth Gordon-Bettencourt."

If the man was surprised, impressed, or disgusted, he didn't show it.

I took his hand, and it swallowed mine.

"Elizabeth," he said, his voice low and gravelly, as if it wasn't often used.

Before he could introduce himself, Mr. Anders spoke again. "Mr. Lincoln Carden. Acting manager of the Roads department."

Mr. Lincoln Carden's brown gaze dipped to meet mine for the briefest moment, and it knocked the air out of me. I'd never been perceived with such intensity.

My fingertips tingled with nerves. "It's nice to meet you, Mr. Carden."

"Likewise." He glanced at Mr. Anders and raised a brow.

"Elizabeth is one of the new interns."

Mr. Carden rested a hip on his desk and folded his arms across his wide chest. "Another intern? I counted six of them earlier."

The two men shared a look I'd undoubtedly replay in my head and analyze later.

"Well, lucky number seven and all that." Mr. Anders waved a hand around and then gestured toward me. "And uh…Elizabeth here is particularly interested in Roads."

"Okay" was all Mr. Carden said.

Mr. Anders smiled but it came across as more of a grimace. "And with the current renovations, we're tight on space and…"

"No."

My mouth went dry at his quick and curt response. But Mr. Anders sighed deeply and shrugged. "You'll be in charge of her development before the final test."

The final test at the end of the internship was often referred to but never described in detail. The scraps of information I had were the driving force behind my application.

Mr. Carden frowned, falling back into the seat behind him before rubbing his face.

My stomach dropped. I resisted the urge to apologize for being an obvious inconvenience. I shifted on my feet, letting my gaze wander across his workstation. Nothing hinted at his personality. No photos. No trinkets. Not even a little plant.

"You know how I work." Mr. Carden dropped his head.

"It's a few weeks and she'll have to do work for some of the other managers too. Wait, you have plenty of projects currently in construction, don't you?"

Lincoln Carden whispered something that was likely a curse even though I couldn't hear it. His sky-blue shirt stretched across his strong chest as he took a deep breath.

"You should probably take her with you," Mr. Anders said with an almost impish grin. He seemed to be enjoying this.

Both men took in my outfit without looking at my face. I should not have worn these high-heeled boots, but I would not let these men judge me for wanting to look nice.

I tucked a tendril of copper hair behind my ear. "I can go on-site if that's required."

"I assume you don't have the correct PPE with you today." Mr. Carden pursed his lips to one side as his gaze dropped from my *very interesting* forehead to my shoes. "And I doubt anyone has a spare size six safety boot around here."

"Six and a half," I bit out, as if it mattered. But I was tired of being bullied. I was raised by the world's biggest bully. I didn't escape him just so I could be belittled elsewhere. "Just because I'm an intern doesn't mean I'm a waste of time. You were wet behind the ears once."

He sighed as if this hadn't occurred to him. As if he'd been born a fully functional senior engineer. He took off his glasses and rubbed his temples.

This seemed to amuse Mr. Anders. "Don't worry about it,

Carden. It'll be over in no time. That being said, you should probably enjoy your last few hours of peace before this one joins you." He turned to me, stifling a chuckle. "Come on, I need to get you to the others. HR has a whole presentation setup. There'll be little sandwiches and things too."

Mr. Carden slipped his glasses back on and turned to his computer. He didn't say anything else.

All the other managers had greeted me with smiles. Mr. Carden didn't even care enough to fake pleasantries.

He also happened to be in charge of the department I hoped to work in. The one who would determine if I was ready for the final test. The unknown factor standing between me and a future at Simucon.

Crap.

3

LINCOLN

@pancakesareelite:
Help meeeee

@pancakesareelite:
If we teamed up, I would level up so
much faster and then they can all suck
it for making fun of me

@theanswerisno:
I'm already on 987xp.
What's in it for me?

@pancakesareelite:
My eternal gratitude?

@pancakesareelite:
Virtual kisses, xxxxxxx

@pancakesareelite:
Thoughts and prayers?

@theanswerisno:
Hmm...

@pancakesareelite:
Fine. I'll play that
scary game you keep mentioning that
no one else wants to play

@theanswerisno:
You got yourself a deal.

As soon as Anders and the new intern left, I marched out of my office and into his. I sat on the brown leather seat across from his desk and waited.

"Carden," Anders said as he walked through the door and took his place on the other side of the desk. "How can I help you?"

"I didn't want to say any of this in front of the new intern, but I don't appreciate being blindsided," I said, panic and anger heating my chest.

"Blindsided?" Anders scoffed. "What do you mean? Because she's even more gorgeous in real life?"

"Anders," I seethed.

Her beauty had nothing to do with this.

Anders's brows popped up. "Or because she's Douglas Gordon-Bettencourt's daughter?"

"I don't care about that," I said.

He laughed, waving me off. "I sent you an email about the intern with all her details and everything. If you kept up with your new management duties, you'd have been better prepared."

I scanned through my memories. "When?"

"Last week, when I had IT forward all of Saunders's emails to you. The intern was going to be Saunders's problem, until he resigned." He grinned, not bothering to hide the pleasure he took in my pain.

"Apologies," I ground out. My frustration ping-ponged from Anders to me. Catching up on those emails was on my list of things to do…but the list kept growing. "There are hundreds to get through. Did you know all of Saunders's projects are in crisis mode?"

"We think that's why he resigned. Couldn't handle the pressure." Anders frowned and looked down at his steepled hands. "Can you?"

Taken aback by his directness, I flinched but quickly regained my composure. I was careful not to let the mask of confidence slip at work. The version of Lincoln they knew had earned their trust and respect. I planned on keeping it that way.

Anders leaned backward and sighed. "You know, Carden, I was surprised when I saw your application to take Saunders's place. You never struck me as someone who'd want to manage."

I didn't.

But I could almost see my mother's wide smile and hear the excitement in her voice when she spoke about it.

Besides, I didn't like that Anders thought I couldn't do it.

I stood. "It was a natural next step for my career." My hand fell on the backrest of the chair and rubbed back and forth along the smooth fabric. "I'll deal with the intern, but it took me by surprise. I haven't shared an office with anyone since I was an intern."

"Since you were the top engineer in our internship." Anders moved his mouse, waking his laptop. "The only reason we kept you on your own was because you excelled that way, and it benefited the company. Managers can't work alone, so if you want this job…" Anders's gaze fell on my fidgeting hand.

I tucked my fist into my pocket. "I get it."

"Now, off you go. Please read the email. We have scheduled meetings around everyone's calendars to discuss the interns' progress."

With a final nod, I left his office. Thoughts rushed through my mind, replaying our conversation. There were so many other, better ways I could have handled that. I kept my head down and snaked through the hallway back to my office.

Thankfully, the intern wasn't there yet. If this year's internship followed standard procedure, she and the other interns would be stuck with HR for the next few hours as they learned about company policy and cyber safety and were forced to watch what was essentially a Simucon propaganda video about how it was the best firm in the world.

I closed my door behind me and let out a long exhale. On second thought, I should probably keep my door open, as I'd now be dealing with everyone's problems as well as my own.

I opened the door. Nope. Too exposed. Cracked. I'd leave it cracked.

My focus was shattered. I grabbed my noise-canceling headset and slipped it on before reading my dreaded to-do list. My therapist insisted I create one every morning to help get into the right headspace before work or before doing anything that needed my limited attention span to cooperate.

I added a new task at the top of the list: *Catch up on emails.*

But catching up was hard to do when an unread email from my thesis supervisor piqued my interest. Resistance was futile. With a quick click, I opened the email.

Don't forget the International Conference on Traffic and Transportation Engineering is coming up! If you can't make it, I'll present on your behalf, but I'm really hoping you'll come. We need to catch up. I have a proposal for you.

I've also attached a few related papers. I thought you might be interested in my latest research…If only there was someone to help me finish it.

I bit back a smile. Professor Hahn was anything but subtle. After my research in pedestrian safety and social justice gained some attention, she was convinced I belonged in academia. But academia often led to lecturing, and the idea of being responsible for the transfer of knowledge was absolutely terrifying.

Besides, there was no way I could advance in my career at Simucon with one foot in academia. I needed to be more present. Especially if I wanted this promotion.

I opened the link to the International Conference on Traffic and Transportation Engineering in Los Angeles, about a two-hour drive from the office in San Diego. Judging from the sponsors listed, a number of important officials would be present. Those were the people who needed to listen. The ones who could make a difference.

There was no way I could miss this one.

I switched between tabs, back to the email from my professor. Attached at the bottom were the articles I'd have to avoid. If I opened one of them, it would send me on a deep dive about sidewalk widths, and I'd surface hours later. With the tight schedule I was on, there was no room for hyperfixation on the wrong topics.

Minimizing everything, I finally found the email sent to all the interns. And Anders was right, all her information was there.

Elizabeth Gordon-Bettencourt: Roads and Traffic
(Saunders)

I read through her application and results. There was a reason she was last on the list. Her results were good but lower than her fellow interns. She had a strange gap in her studies, but that was none of my business.

All I knew was that Anders would be keeping a close eye on how

I dealt with this. Elizabeth Gordon-Bettencourt was now part and parcel of whether I was promoted.

I tugged at my collar and blew out a few quick, short breaths while scanning the rest of the emails. What else was urgent?

Everything was urgent.

Time for my favorite side quest: *Coffee.*

I grabbed my phone and pushed up from my seat, relieved to be giving my restless legs something to do. I rushed toward the kitchen while opening the app I used to chat with Lily. Maybe I could tell her about this. Maybe she could make me feel better about it all. She was one of the very few people I shared my life with—albeit cryptically.

I navigated to our chat, a smile already creeping onto my face. Drifting around the corner, I slammed into something.

Someone.

My phone flew out of my hands, and instinctively, my arms shot out, curling around the person before they tumbled. "I'm sorry, I…" I started, but the words got stuck in my mouth. It wasn't just anyone I was pressed up against.

It was my intern.

Elizabeth Gordon-Bettencourt met my gaze with gray eyes so striking that it triggered my fight-or-flight response.

4

ELIZABETH

[105 weeks ago]

@pancakesareelite:
theanswerisno is not a name.
What am I supposed to call you?

> @theanswerisno:
> Whatever you want

@pancakesareelite:
All I know about you is that you're
a Legend of Zelda fan. Should I call
you Zelda? Your avatar is a picture of
Link. I could call you Link.

> @theanswerisno:
> I try not to share too much with
> strangers on the internet

@pancakesareelite:
I'll tell you mine if you tell me yours

> @theanswerisno:
> The answer is no, Pancakes

@pancakesareelite:
Okay, Zelda

@theanswerisno:

Big no

@theanswerisno:

Now get back to building our city. We're
running out of daylight!

@pancakesareelite:
I love this game

@theanswerisno:

I'm aware

@pancakesareelite:
By the way, I like being called
Pancakes, but if you want,
you can also call me Lily.

"Watch where you're—" I gasped the second I realized who those strong arms belonged to.

Mr. Carden released me as though I were a live wire. He jumped backward. "Uh…" he started, far more hesitant than he'd been with Mr. Anders earlier. "Sorry. I'm so sorry." Underneath dark, long eyelashes, his gaze met mine for all of one microsecond before giving me a once-over. "Are…you okay?"

"Fine. Perfectly fine," I squeaked out, clocking the *In My Era* burgundy lipstick stain on the bottom end of his shirt's breast pocket. "You have, um…"

He looked downward, and his eyes widened.

I'd left plenty of lipstick stains before, but never in my life had I smooched my boss's (firm) pecs unprovoked. Heat crept up my cheeks, and I was sure they were almost as red as my hair. "I'm so sorry."

He blew out a small, quick breath and pulled at his collar. "Not your fault," he said, his voice lower than it had been. "I was…" He swallowed hard and searched the floor. "Distracted." He bent down and grabbed his fallen phone before slipping it into a pants pocket.

"It's okay. It coulda been worse. If I were taller or you were shorter, we would have…" I smacked my hands together, immediately regretting the decision.

But then one corner of his mouth twitched upward.

Was that the hint of a smile?

Before I could say or do anything else, the HR director popped her head out of the boardroom. "Come on, the next segment is starting, and it's an important one."

"Be there in a sec," I said, and turned around, but Mr. Carden had already disappeared.

I hurried into the boardroom and pulled out my phone. I needed to panic-text someone who knew how filterless I could be. I scrolled down to Link's name and hovered over it, wondering how much I could share. We had an unspoken rule about oversharing. It was a small industry.

And yet, every day I fought the urge to risk it all and tell him *everything*.

• • •

Mr. Carden and I never spoke about the lipstick stain. We barely spoke at all.

As it turned out, Lincoln Carden was a man of few words and far too many projects. After two and a half days of working together, I'd surmised that he liked his coffee with cream and sugar, enjoyed a simple sandwich at lunch, got to the office before sunrise, and lived nearby, because yesterday and today, his soft, black curls were still wet and dripping onto his well-ironed white shirt.

Oh, and that his headset was noise-canceling, which I embarrassingly discovered after having a long, one-sided conversation with him. When he'd eventually taken them off, I'd tried asking him about his life or his friends, but he kept his answers short and to the point, and they were almost always followed with a work instruction.

He may as well hold up a sign that said: BUSINESS ONLY.

"Mr. Carden?" I used the sweetest voice I could muster. Everything I did seemed to tick him off, and I wasn't about to take any chances.

"Elizabeth," he said without looking up. My name was always a sigh on his full lips. "What can I do for you?"

I lifted the Arch D sheet, and he sighed again. He looked at his smartwatch. "I've got five minutes." He pointed at the large desk on the other end of the office.

I laid the drawing flat on top of many other drawings as he walked over.

He wasted no time. His long fingers traced the shape of the road, and his gaze skittered across the design. His dark brows pulled close, a line of thought separating them. Without looking, he reached out for his red pen. My stomach twisted in anticipation. That awful color had torn through my work multiple times over the last few days.

"This needs to be wider." He scribbled, circled, and scratched through things that had taken me all day. "This isn't the correct font. Check our standards."

How much wider? What font?

But he never paused long enough for me to ask a question. Mr. Carden moved at the speed of light. I could barely register everything he said.

"The north arrow is too small. But I'm pleased to see you've included it this time."

I sucked on my teeth as I thought back to the numerous mistakes I'd made in the past few days. "Live and learn."

His mouth twitched upward.

Getting Mr. Carden to smile was a new game I liked playing with myself.

He straightened to his full height, which left him about a head taller than me. "Where's the vertical alignment?"

"I'm not done with it yet," I admitted. Although the truth was that I hadn't started. Everything took longer than I'd anticipated. "I'm sorry."

Instead of being mad, Lincoln Carden nodded.

I couldn't get a read on this man. It was weird. Everything was either a nod or a sigh. He was always stressed and appeared angry, but the anger was different from what I was used to. And it was never directed at me.

But he didn't seem happy around me either.

As a people pleaser, this killed me. People were generally very pleased by me. Well, those who didn't know the real me.

Pursing my lips, I stared at all the corrections I'd need to make. My eyelids drooped. It had been two days of working nonstop. I'd been falling asleep before managing to get into pajamas.

While no one asked me to stay late, I had to. I was already four years behind everyone else after dropping out and starting over years later.

Mr. Carden walked over to his desk and unplugged his laptop. "Go home. We'll deal with that in the morning." He packed his bag and swung it over his wide shoulder.

I tried not to think about how hard his chest had been when we'd collided or how effortlessly he'd caught me. My pale cheeks threatened to expose my inappropriate thoughts, so I turned away. "I'll leave when I finish these corrections."

As soon as Mr. Carden was out of sight, I went to the kitchen. The next revision required a fresh cup of coffee.

"How's it going?" I asked Kimberley, another intern, who was also filling her cup. She was number three on the intern list and the only other woman in the internship. Other than that, I knew nothing because all her social media accounts were set to private.

"Good," she responded with a curt smile.

I waited for something more while adding a generous serving of sugar. "That's great. It's been such a hard transition for me. I don't feel like college prepared us for this."

"Yeah" was all she said before slipping out without a backward glance.

It was no surprise. The sick scent of competition was thick between the interns. Heads were kept low and resources hidden because only two of us would find placement after the eight-week internship.

Another intern walked into the kitchen as I was leaving.

He grinned. "Hey, Seven."

My muscles tensed at the nickname, but I steeled myself and rolled my eyes.

I knew what everyone thought: I was hired because my stepfather, Douglas Gordon-Bettencourt, was the CEO of one of the biggest movie production companies in North America.

Mr. Anders assured me that wasn't the reason. Still, I couldn't help but wonder. Did I earn this? Did I get lucky? Or was it because everyone wanted to be close to Douglas Gordon-Bettencourt in the hopes that his success would rub off on them?

From prior experience, the third option seemed the likeliest.

But if I worked hard enough, I could still ace the test and earn this internship. I could overcome every roadblock Douglas had set up for me. I could prove to him, to myself, and to everyone that I am capable.

Because Douglas Gordon-Bettencourt doesn't get to tell me what I can and cannot do.

Not anymore.

5

LINCOLN

[101 weeks ago]

@pancakesareelite:
Do you ever think about meeting IRL?

@theanswerisno:
No.

@pancakesareelite:
Hearing each other's voices?

@theanswerisno:
Not a good idea.

@pancakesareelite:
What about photos?

@theanswerisno:
Absolutely not.

@pancakesareelite:
Are you real?

@theanswerisno:
Debatable.

@theanswerisno:
I'm sorry. I just like that you kinda
like virtual me. Let's keep it that way.

@pancakesareelite:
I don't *kinda* like virtual you,
I *really really* like virtual you

As soon as I left the office, I shoved work, the pressure of becoming a manager, and my curious intern into one of the many boxes in my brain. Despite my aversion to socializing, game night was the exception.

Never would I have thought that Claire and I stumbling upon a board game group back in college would lead to this. After we graduated, I thought I'd never see them again, but Claire kept in touch and kept dragging me along every Wednesday night.

And I was forever grateful for it. The game night group never expected me to do anything except play.

I knocked once, and the door to Shaun and Neema's apartment flung open.

"You came!" Shaun's hand shot up for a high five. He'd always been cheerful, but ever since marrying the love of his life, he radiated joy at a glass-shattering frequency.

I dipped my head and clapped my free hand against his as I walked inside. I wouldn't leave him hanging. "Hey, man."

Rose, his best friend and soon-to-be sister-in-law, popped up to her feet, eyeing the bag I carried. I held it out between us. "Samosas. The cheesy kind."

Her eyes widened, matching her bright smile. She vibrated as she took it and pulled one of them out of the bag. "Your mom is the best."

"My mom's a feeder."

"And I'm an eater." She took a big bite.

I glanced around the apartment. Claire wasn't here yet. "Where is everyone?" It was a fair assumption that, where Rose and Shaun were, their partners would be as well.

Rose pointed at the bedroom. "William's doing one last stream in his old bedroom before Shaun and Neema convert it into a nursery."

I sat on the couch and took out my laptop. Balancing it on my knees, I navigated over to William's account, *@wheretheresawilliam*, and clicked through. I'd been watching William's streams since he started doing them, before we'd even met. Rose transferred couches and settled beside me, leaning in and smiling at the face of her fiancé on my screen as if she hadn't seen him play games online five thousand times. As if she didn't live with him now.

"Oh, and Neema's asleep because of the energy-zapping fetus," she said.

"Don't talk about my child that way," Shaun said from the kitchen.

"Those were her words!" Rose cackled.

I stifled a laugh and kept my focus on the chat. There was one name I was looking for.

And there she was.

```
@pancakesareelite:
Popping in to say hi, and this game
is too expensive. Back to lurking &
working.
```

I didn't like the way my heart skipped whenever this stranger's username appeared on my screen, and yet it did—against my will and better judgment. I resisted the urge to click on her name and open a private chat.

What would I even say?

It had been three days since we'd chatted or properly played a game together. It was the longest we'd gone without contact. Maybe she'd found other people to play with.

A private message appeared, chasing away my insecurities.

I bit down on my lip as a smile tugged on the corners of my mouth.

> **@pancakesareelite:**
> Hey! Fancy finding you here
> (watching a streamer you never miss).
> Shall we play a game when he's done?

Rose shot upright.

"No," I said to her, but it was too late.

Her face was already lit with mischief.

"It's nothing." I minimized the chat but hovered over it, itching to reply.

"It's not nothing. Claire mentioned something about *the* gaming girl being called 'Pancakes'…Lily, is it?" She tapped the minimized chat as though my laptop were a touchscreen.

"What did Claire, my sworn secret-keeper, tell you?" I grumbled.

Rose fell against me, knocking our shoulders. "Oh, don't blame her. She was worried."

I was too afraid to meet the gaze of the enthusiastic woman beside me. "About?"

"Well, all she mentioned was that you've been chatting with this gamer forever, and she thinks you maybe have a teeny-tiny crush."

Claire, why? I sighed and closed my eyes, removing my glasses to pinch the bridge of my nose before the onslaught of questions followed. While I could trust Claire with my life, wanting her to keep information like this to herself was expecting a lot, and I suppose she could get credit for lasting years.

As if reading my mind, Rose continued. "She wanted to know if any of us knew anything about her, and while I agree that pancakes are elite, we've never interacted. Claire said you found her in your old engineering gaming group. The gaming community is pretty tight-knit. We could find her."

"Idontwanttofindher," I rambled out as though it were one word.

William growled at a troll on-screen. An actual troll in the game, not one of the commenting viewers, which he was also known to growl at from time to time.

"What do you mean? Surely, after all these years, you'd want to meet her. What if you already know her without knowing? You're both engineers." Rose was not going to let this go. Neema, Shaun, and William might have, Claire knew not to press…but Rose? Rose was unstoppable.

"She could also not be a *she*. She could be a man for all I know." I kept looking down at Lily's message. My brain was pinging and would continue pinging until I replied.

Rose hummed for a second before wiggling her eyebrows. "What if she's a hot man? I'd like to see that."

My lips curved upward. Rose was nothing if not entertaining.

"Could we rather focus on your hot man, who is growing angrier by the second?" I pointed at my screen, where William was flashing the camera his most charming smile while a string of colorful and creative curses flew out of him.

"I'll tell William you called him hot. He loves flattery," she teased, and turned her attention back to my laptop screen. A little red ONE appeared at the chat box icon. "She sent another message. You better reply! Don't leave Pancakes hanging!"

"No peeking." I turned my laptop away from her and opened the messages.

> **@pancakesareelite:**
> I've been MIA because of work. And I've
> been working hard. Play with me, Link.
> Pretty please.

> **@pancakesareelite:**
> We could even play League.

She must be as desperate as I am.

Rose eyed me above my laptop screen but made no move to intrude.

I shot back a text: Will you be up in about two hours?
It's game night.

> **@pancakesareelite:**
> Forgot it's Wednesday!
> I feel like I've lived a thousand lives
> since Monday. But yeah, of course. I'll
> be up if you want me to be.

My chest heated in a strange and unfamiliar way.

@theanswerisno:
Snap. See you then.

"I don't suppose you're the type to tell me what she said…" Rose
hopped off the couch and grabbed another samosa.

"Not even a little bit."

"So, we're allowed to talk about Pancakes?" Shaun asked, walking into the living area with three cups of coffee.

Not Shaun as well. Did everyone know?

I slammed my laptop shut and held it in front of my face as a
defense for whatever this was. I would kill Claire. "Where is Brutus,
I mean *Claire*?"

A loud-pitched giggle escaped Rose, and then she paused. "Oh."

Her voice tilted upward in a way that made me lower the
laptop.

"She's not coming. I thought she told you," Rose said while finishing off another samosa.

"My phone died." I dug into my pocket and retrieved the dead thing. I needed an upgrade, but I liked my current phone and all my apps and settings. It was easy enough to transfer data between phones nowadays but I just couldn't bring myself to do it.

Shaun offered me a cup of coffee and a power cable, fueling me and my phone simultaneously.

As soon as my phone turned on, all of Claire's messages came flying through. "Oh. I see now."

I wasn't sure what to do next. I rarely attended game night without her, and to be honest, I didn't know how. Navigating social situations was always a bit awkward for me.

"Well, I, for one, am glad you came, because those are delicious." Rose pointed at the bag of samosas on her way over to the board game shelf.

I tried my best to pull myself into the present and be with the people around me. Some days were easier than others. Today wasn't the easiest. I'd used up all my social capacity figuring out how to speak to my intern.

William appeared in the flesh and dipped his chin in my direction. "Always good to see *theanswerisno* lurking in my streams and then immediately in person afterward. Didn't think you'd come tonight."

I wouldn't have if I'd known Claire wasn't going to be here. But saying that would come across in the wrong way. They didn't understand. They were charming, lovable people, and I was…I don't know what I was. But analyzing every social interaction and figuring out the appropriate way to respond was exhausting.

"Aha!" Rose pulled a box off the shelf and then lifted it in the air. "It's my turn to pick, and I'm picking Jenga."

"That's usually Lincoln's I've-had-a-stressful-day choice." Shaun stood and walked over to their bedroom door. "I'm going to wake Neema, but"—he turned to face me—"everything all right?"

"Um…" I didn't want to talk about the hundreds of open tabs in my brain.

"This game is my pick," Rose said with a wide and gentle smile. "Lincoln's fine."

I nodded, grateful for the save. I wasn't fine. I was uncomfortable and still reeling from discussing Lily. But I would be.

Rose scooched beside me and offered me the box. "I know you like setting it up, and I'm sorry for pushing. I'll never bring her up again unprovoked, okay?"

"Okay."

With each block, my discomfort faded. I snuck a glance at Rose, William, Shaun, and Neema chatting away and giving me the space I needed. I wasn't always good at being with people, but maybe some people knew how to be good with me.

Like Lily, who had no reason to wait up for me other than knowing I'd wait up for her too.

6

ELIZABETH

[98 weeks ago]

@pancakesareelite:
What do you do when you're getting
anxious?

@theanswerisno:
Can't get anxious if you stay anxious

@theanswerisno:
Follow me for more helpful tips

Working with Mr. Carden was challenging, but learning about bridge design was even harder. After a week of assisting one of the other engineers, I was glad to be back with Roads.

Even though Mr. Carden was too busy to assist me.

Today, he rushed around and was pulled in a million directions. From where I sat, it was clear that any question from me would be the straw that broke the camel's back—a well-defined back that I sometimes looked at a little too long when he leaned over a drawing and studied it.

Toward the end of the day, he burst into our office. With panicked eyes, he took in my packed bag. "Are you on your way out? What time is it?"

I glanced at my phone. "It's six forty-five."

"Already?" His shoulders slumped.

My fingers found the zipper on my bag. "I assumed you wouldn't have time to review anything today, but I can stay."

"No. Don't. Apologies. I know I've ignored you all day. I've been dealing with crisis after crisis." He blew out a long breath.

This was the most he'd said to me all week. A winning streak. Could I get it to continue? "Is there anything I could do to help?"

"No. But I'm glad I caught you." He flipped through his notebook and tore out three sheets of paper. "I scribbled down some notes during one of my many mind-numbing meetings. You can read through them in the morning." He placed them on my desk without looking at me and then walked over to his side of the office. "I need to reply to this email, and I'd like to leave in the next ten minutes, so I really have to…"

"Focus." I slid the notes into my bag.

He nodded.

Behind his stern expression were lines of exhaustion. And I wasn't making his life any easier.

"Got it. See you tomorrow, Mr. Carden," I said as I walked out the door and closed it behind me. Maybe if the door was shut, everyone would give him a second to breathe.

•   •   •

By the time I got home, all I wanted was to fall into someone's arms and forget about work. But instead, I heated up a bowl of ramen and pulled out Mr. Carden's notes.

I dropped my head on my desk and groaned. More problems.

More corrections. Mr. Carden detailed why everything was wrong. *How were there even more errors than before? Wasn't I supposed to be getting better at this?*

I wondered what Mr. Carden would say about me in his evaluation of my progress. He's given me a chance with some incredible projects, but I wasn't very good. He didn't seem like the type to pull punches.

Admittedly, my first impression of him was way off. Lincoln Carden was always gentle and kind, even though speaking to me seemed to scare the life out of him.

I scanned through the rest of his notes. After the listed errors and explanations, he offered solutions and a handful of tips and tricks for the software. I read them again, committing them to memory. His handwriting was not easy to read, but it was absolutely gorgeous…much like he was.

Do not think about how handsome your boss is.

Tucking the paper into my drawer, I pulled out my laptop and felt an inkling of relief at the mere thought of playing a game with Link. Being the most reliable person in the world, he was already there waiting for me in the lobby—along with a few other people we sometimes gamed with. Joining the engineering gaming server was a stroke of genius and a desperate attempt to connect to people without having to tell anyone who I was, who my stepdad was…There were thousands of members, both current and ex-students across all the various engineering disciplines, plus a few non-engineers who'd slipped through the cracks. And I loved the anonymity and chaos that came along with it.

I never expected to find someone like Link. I especially didn't expect him to stick around with the scraps of information I shared. Granted, I was being fed scraps in return. It was highly unlikely that the account with a *Legend of Zelda* avatar was truly run by someone named Link. But that didn't matter. What mattered was that Link was there whenever I needed him and expected nothing in return except a gaming partner.

> **@theanswerisno:**
> Good week so far?

@pancakesareelite:
Dreadful. You?

> **@theanswerisno:**
> Nightmarish.

@pancakesareelite:
Winner gets to complain.

> **@theanswerisno:**
> Prepare to hear the whiniest
> whines you've ever heard.

I slipped into my nightgown and curled up on the chair at my desk. The weight of the week lightened as we teamed up against a swarm of zombies—who ended up eating us.

> **@theanswerisno:**
> In a strange turn of events,
> we both lost. What now?

I grinned and replied: I don't remember what I wanted to complain about.
This was my favorite part. After the game. Where we'd just talk.

> **@theanswerisno:**
> Neither do I. So,
> in a way, I'd say we won?

My cheeks were fixed in a smile. It always was with him. Strange how this stranger managed to do that.

What's your weekend looking like? I asked.

> @theanswerisno:
> I have a tedious meeting tomorrow,
> Saturday I need to learn how to
> fix a faucet, and then on Sunday,
> I think I'll have to fix said faucet.
> How about you?

I was hoping we'd spend the entire weekend play-ing together, I backspaced that almost as quickly as I'd typed it. The last time I flirted a little too intimately with Link, it had scared him off. Instead of the embarrassing truth, I said: I'm going out for dinner.

Which wasn't true. It wasn't entirely a lie either. I could end up going out for dinner. I just needed to find a date first.

I stood and stretched my legs. It took three steps to put my bowl in the kitchen sink and three steps to my bed. That was about the extent of my apartment, which was tinier than the bedroom I'd grown up in.

But it was mine, and aside from the outright strange rules set by my landlord, I could do whatever I wanted. My time in what could easily be called a mansion was more claustrophobic than these four walls.

Spark welcomed me back as I opened the dating app and started swiping. I wasn't particularly picky, and I knew how to flirt. Know-ing what to say and how to charm people was something I was taught very early on in my household.

A message popped up in-app: I have a fetish for redheads with great tits.

A sigh was born in the depths of my soul. *I give up.* I closed the app and did something better. I called my grandmother.

"Hello?" she answered with a croak.

"I'm sorry, Gran. Did I wake you?"

"This old bat doesn't sleep, you know that." She cackled. "How are you, my Lily? How's work been? I've been meaning to call, but I'm still sorting through your grandpa's things since his final checkout."

"Gran!" I said, my mouth dropping open. That was how she referred to my grandpa's death. He'd suffered for so long that we'd mourned him while he was alive and his passing was a mercy.

She only laughed louder. "That's what I get for marrying an older man. I should have gone for his assistant, but nope, I went for the boss." I could hear her lighting a cigarette. "Speaking of bosses, how's your new boss? What's he like?"

"He's…good."

"Good…at what?" she asked. "Good in bed?" Another cheeky cackle.

"At his job! Behave!" I couldn't help but burst out laughing too. "I also meant that he seems like, maybe, a good person, because I kinda suck at this job, and he's still nice to me."

"As he should be. If he wasn't, I'd have to have words with him. You're my favorite granddaughter after all."

"I'm your only granddaughter!" My walls crumbled around my grandmother, and I told her everything about work, the managers, and the other interns.

"Why couldn't you apply for a normal job like a normal graduate? This internship sounds like a battle royale."

"First, I love a battle royale. Second, Simucon pays more than other firms. If I get this job, I could pay you back."

"Lily," she said, calling me by the nickname she'd given me.

There could only be one Elizabeth Gray, and I could never live up to how incredible she was.

"I never asked to be paid back," she said.

"I know, but I also know you need it, even though you'll say you don't. I've just discovered how expensive your insulin is. You can't fool me." I swallowed the lump of guilt climbing in my throat, and before she could protest, I continued. "Third, there aren't that many companies hiring junior roads and transport engineers right now."

"And…?"

I took a long, deep breath before stating the next reason, the real reason. "And finally, with Douglas's surname, it's hard to tell what was given to me because of him and what was earned. He'll claim my every victory until I can prove he had nothing to do with it." I blew out a long, slow breath. "And I know I should be grateful. People would kill to be in my position, but it's not fair to anyone. I hate it. But this internship's final test is completely anonymous. It might be the one and only chance to see if I could do something without him."

My grandmother hissed. "I can't wait to see you prove him wrong."

"I hope I don't prove him right," I said, my chest shuddering at the thought of his smug expression. "I never told you about what happened the night I left…How come you never asked?"

"I was so happy, Lily. So relieved. I knew you'd tell me eventually, once you'd processed it all. I didn't think it would take two entire years."

I fell backward onto my pillow and grumbled, "It kind of started and ended because of engineering. I mean, he was always awful, but I didn't see it, I didn't realize. I thought a man with his success and reputation had somehow earned the right to be difficult. He took every opportunity to remind me that everything I had, I had because of him. Until I started studying. He didn't want me to. He said it was a waste of his money and my time because there was no way I was capable. My stupid twenty-year-old self believed him and I dropped out."

My gran tutted. "I bet he was thrilled."

"Oh, yes. He was so kind and supportive after that. He took Mom and me around the world on a de-stressing adventure, and when I returned, he shoved me into modeling. But I didn't enjoy it. Mom noticed and, without telling him, drove me down to SDSU, where we spent the day wandering around the campus. I didn't realize at the time, but she wanted me to get away from Douglas and UCLA was still too close to home."

A whoosh of air came through the line. Gran's voice cracked. "Your mother never told me that."

"She wouldn't, because afterward we drove home and pretended it never happened. When my application was accepted, I broke the news to Douglas and he lost his mind. He reminded me of how I failed the first time around and promised me I'd fail this time too. Mom tried soothing him—she even took the fall—but his rage-filled eyes were focused on me. I was so scared I ran to my room and considered staying there forever. But in the middle of the night, when Douglas was asleep, Mom came to me, gave me a handful of cash, and told me to leave. That was the night I showed up on your doorstep."

"Oh, Lily," my grandmother whispered. "It was one of the best and worst nights of my life. I'd never seen you so devastated." Sizzling rage underlined her next words. "But I'd hoped and prayed that you and your mother would get away from him. He knew and hated me for it." She took a deep breath and coughed. "You did the right thing. And look at you now, participating in a battle royale."

I laughed, but a tear slid down my cheek. "I just don't understand why she's there. Why hasn't she left? Why didn't she leave with me?"

"Do you honestly think he'll let his wife walk out? Lily, he's barely let go of you. Darling, men like Douglas are powerful for a reason." My gran's voice dropped back down to its usual rasp. "Your mother was once a strong and independent woman, but as soon as she fell in love with him, she lost herself and was entirely consumed by it. Despite how complex she is, she's very simple when it comes to love. All the Gray women are. It's our only weakness."

"Not mine," I huffed out.

"Mmm…" From the sound of it, my grandmother lit another cigarette. "Not yet."

7

LINCOLN

[97 weeks ago]

@pancakesareelite:
I don't need your help

@theanswerisno:
Wasn't helping. They broke the rules
and I told them off.

@pancakesareelite:
Is this where you admit you're the
creator of this server?

@theanswerisno:
Does it matter?

@pancakesareelite:
Not really. But as the creator,
could I force you to play a game of
DotA with me or should I assume *the
answer is no*?

@theanswerisno:
I'll never say no to that.

Mornings were my favorite time of the day. Running through the city when everyone else was asleep gave me a moment to clear my head. Perhaps it was the pull of my muscles or the way my heart pumped against my chest, but in those bursts of heavy breathing, my mind was clear.

I leaned against the office gate and swallowed a deep breath before scanning my fob and letting myself into the staff bathroom in the basement. After washing off this morning's jog, I slipped into the fresh shirt I'd hung there and made my way up to my office. I had a few more minutes of silence before my office mate showed up.

The seventh intern always arrived with a bang. An actual bang sometimes. Yesterday, she'd knocked over an enormous vase of flowers, something that shouldn't have been in her path in the first place.

"Good morning, Mr. Carden," she said, a little more enthusiastically than usual. And she was usually very enthusiastic.

"Elizabeth." I kept my head down. Even after almost two weeks of working in close proximity, I wasn't quite able to face the combination of her charming smile and stormy gray eyes.

"Mr. Carden, I have two things to say-slash-ask, and then I'll let you do your morning focus session and won't bother you until you take your first coffee break, which is usually in around an hour and a half, right?"

I glanced over at the time. She was spot-on.

She continued. "Okay, so, first, thank you for the notes. I read them all and only cried a little bit."

Cried?

My head snapped up, only to be met with her laughter. Her smile was as bright as I anticipated it would be. Today, her copper hair was pinned back on either side with blue butterfly clips, showing off her jewel-adorned ears. I never noticed her tragus and helix piercings before.

"Just kidding. I didn't cry. Externally," she said, and a second finger joined the first. "Second, when is my first evaluation or has it already happened?"

Straight to the point. I appreciated that.

"There's a reason that information isn't shared with you," I replied.

"What are you going to say about me? Is it bad? Or is it best I don't know?" She pressed her hands on my desk and tapped her fingers nervously.

I sighed, and using all my learned social behavior, I looked up and met her gaze.

Mistake.

Those eyes were as stormy as I remembered. She bit on her pink-painted bottom lip. "I'm the cat. I'm going to obsess about it all weekend."

For some unknown reason, Elizabeth Gordon-Bettencourt's presence deleted every thought in my brain. "What?" was all I managed.

"That curiosity killed. It's me, the cat." She drew a finger across her neck. "What animal best describes your curiosity style?"

Taken off guard by her ridiculous question, I answered, "In your analogy, probably an ostrich. Head in the sand and all that."

She grinned. "Your brain is way too large."

I shut my eyes, but a smile played on my mouth. The seventh intern was cheekier and far feistier than I expected her to be. "I don't really know what to say to that."

"You don't need to say anything. This is already the most you've ever said to me that wasn't criticism."

"Might be the most I've ever said to anyone here."

She giggled.

It was a nice sound. In terms of all the giggles I've heard, it was a good one.

What type of thought was that?

Shaking my head, I sidestepped her and tapped the drawing I'd marked up. "Stop worrying about the meeting. Focus on improving. You can't change the mistakes you've made, but you can avoid making them again."

A soft breath whooshed out of her, and for the first time since Elizabeth showed up, my office was silent.

I glanced upward. Elizabeth was frozen in thought. Before I could say anything, my phone buzzed against the desk, and the screen lit up with a message from Claire: Come outside. It'll take five minutes.

"Be right back," I said, without looking at Elizabeth. I couldn't risk her trapping me with one of her all-powerful gazes or her words that left me tongue-tied.

I hurried downstairs to meet my best friend. The one I was going to kill.

Cleverly, Claire arrived with defense in the form of caffeine and sustenance. She held up a brown paper bag and a coffee cup, scrunching up her nose. "I'm sorry for abandoning you last week. Was game night without me really so bad that you had to skip this week and avoid me?"

"I wasn't avoiding you. I was busy. I'm drowning with these new tasks." I grabbed the coffee and took a swig. Cream, sugar. She knew exactly how I liked it. "Management is awful."

We walked a few steps away from my office and sat on either end of a nearby bench with the food between us.

"Wanna talk about it?" she asked.

"Nothing much to say. It's just a lot. I'm struggling to keep up. I'm not sleeping enough. Haven't helped my mom pack. Couldn't make it to game night." I looked skyward, thinking of a topic change. "Why'd you miss last week, anyway?"

"Dean and I had a spontaneous date night." Her cheeks flushed, and I was glad to see it. She opened the paper bag. "Peace offering?"

I salivated at the scent of a freshly baked feta and spinach muffin. "Things are…better?"

"Much." Her little smile widened. "Who would have thought taking fewer shifts at the hospital and starting therapy would do wonders for a marriage?"

Seeing her happy again lifted the weight on my shoulders ever so slightly. It didn't even matter that I was mad at her.

"So," she said, running a hand through her auburn hair, "are you still angry at me for telling them about Lily?"

"A little. This is helping." I held up the coffee and muffin.

"Let me explain."

Leaning back, I gestured for her to continue.

"I know how you are." She smiled but shook her head. "You hide your feelings until you're so far gone, you can't come back. And I think you care about Lily way more than you let on. I think there's a chance you've created this perfect idea of her, and it's the reason you're not hooking up with anyone in real life."

The air was knocked right out of me. "That's…not entirely true."

But it was a little true. Yes, I was consumed by Lily, but that wasn't the only reason I wasn't dating anyone. The truth was more complicated than that.

I felt nothing for anyone else. And I'd tried. And failed. And it was awful and uncomfortable, and I had no desire to do it again.

Something was obviously wrong with me.

Claire's brows hugged as she stared out into the distance. "I want to know who she is and whether she has the power to hurt you. Because if she does, I'll have to learn how to fight. Lincoln, do you know how hard that'll be for me?"

I chuckled, but a tightness spread through my chest at the mere thought of Lily hurting me. There was only one way to prevent that. "You don't have to worry. I have a plan."

"Are you sure? What if you meet and it's like an online-friends-to-real-life-lovers situation and then—"

"The plan is simple." I lifted a finger, interrupting her segue into romance novels. "We're not going to meet. We're never going to meet. And I've told her so. I like her where she is, exactly how she is."

"Oh." She scrunched her lips up on one end, and I assumed she was withholding all her questions.

But there was no way to explain why I needed this internet stranger to confide in when Claire was always ready to listen. I didn't know how to tell her that, while all I wanted was for my friends to be happy, it was hard seeing them expand their own personal lives without me, and Lily was…mine and somehow completely unaffected by anything going on in or around my life.

Besides, no real person could ever live up to the Lily I had in my mind, and I didn't expect them to. She was perfect. I definitely wasn't anything like my online persona.

"I'm presenting at a transportation conference in a couple weeks," I said, hoping to change the topic.

Claire's face lit up, despite not knowing anything about the conference or engineering. "Ooooh, when? Where? Can I come?"

"It's in LA, and pretty last minute, so I really don't expect you to join," I said, amused. "I need to double-check the date, but it's on a Friday." I blew out a long breath. There was a mixture of nervousness and excitement at the thought of presenting my research.

"Awesome," she said. "Presentations are your thing. Which is weird for someone who doesn't like talking."

I chuckled and shook my head. It was a little different when I had the opportunity to prepare what I'd be saying.

Claire raised a brow. "So, you said you'd tell me about your new intern in person. What's his deal? Is he awful?"

"*She's* not awful. She's…" How was I supposed to describe Elizabeth? "Interesting."

"How so?"

I bit into the muffin and thought about Elizabeth while chewing. Where should I begin? "She's wearing butterfly clips."

Claire squawked. "Is that a problem?"

"In my office."

"Mmm-hmm. How dare she? A criminal offense, really."

"As an engineer, it…" I said, struggling to find the point I was trying to make.

She shook her head. "You're full of crap sometimes."

I tutted, swallowing hard and taking another big bite. "She hums."

"At least she doesn't sing."

"She doesn't eat."

"What do you mean? Everyone eats." Claire bit into her muffin.

"She doesn't. I've seen her drink coffee, plenty of it. But never eating. At lunchtime, I'm the only one chewing in the office." I crumpled up the brown paper bag. "No snacks, even."

"She could be trying to lose weight."

"She looks great as is."

Maybe that wasn't the right thing to say.

Claire's eyes narrowed, but she said nothing. "Maybe she's trying to save cash. Engineers in these internships can't be getting paid too much, can they?"

"She doesn't need the money."

"How would you know?" Claire crossed her arms.

I stood. My five-minute break had come to an end.

"Because she's a Gordon-Bettencourt."

8

LINCOLN

[95 weeks ago]

@theanswerisno:
You up?

> **@pancakesareelite:**
> Barely

@theanswerisno:
Okay, never mind.

> **@pancakesareelite:**
> What's up?

@theanswerisno:
It's okay, I'm fine. Sleep well, x.

> **@pancakesareelite:**
> I've sent you an invite

@theanswerisno:
Patchwork? This game is for old people
and children.

> **@pancakesareelite:**
> It's cathartic and my brain isn't
> working too well at the moment

@theanswerisno:
You don't have to do this

                                        @pancakesareelite:
                                             It's your turn

@theanswerisno:
Thank you.

@theanswerisno:
Pancakes?

                                        @pancakesareelite:
                                             Hmm?

@theanswerisno:
Today would have been my dad's 57th
birthday.

I blinked, and an entire week flew by.

With the promotion being dangled over my head at work and my mother needing me to fix up her current house, I wasn't coping. Add to that my new office mate, and I should be declared a national emergency.

Despite doing her best to respect my focus sessions and hone her skills, Elizabeth still managed to fail at both by being incredibly distracting and her work requiring a fair amount of correction and guidance.

And I wasn't the only one she was distracting. There were whispers in the office wherever she went.

But that was a weekday problem, and today was Sunday.

The front door at my mother's new home flung open. I hopped out of my truck and met her halfway. She pulled me in for a gentle hug. "Lincoln, it's so beautiful. Even more beautiful than I dreamed."

With those words, every worry washed away. Every hour worked was worth it.

"Are you sure it isn't too much?" She released me and smoothed out my T-shirt.

"I was about to pay for it by myself, but your boyfriend swooped in with the ultimate grand gesture and helped out."

At the mention of her *boyfriend*, she smiled.

"So, in a way, I got a huge discount," I said.

This time, she laughed.

Her misty eyes cleared. "I adore it." She spun on her heel and practically skipped inside. "Come see what I have in mind."

I followed her inside with limbs that couldn't decide if they felt light or heavy. Part of me longed for my childhood home, which was still waiting to be packed up and handed over. It was weird knowing that, in a few weeks, it wouldn't belong to the Cardens—weirder knowing that my mother would be living here with another man.

After nineteen years, I was happy she'd finally found someone.

At some point during a tour of the house I'd already seen twice, Daniel arrived. My mother hurried outside, and I gave them a few minutes to greet each other before joining them.

I walked out to the front yard, where a pickup truck was parked in the driveway next to mine. Daniel stood with an arm around my mother. He jumped away the second he noticed me.

"Lincoln, hi." He shifted his weight from one foot to the other. His cheeks were flushed red as though I were the scary father and he was the naughty teenage boy.

"Daniel." I reached out and shook his hand.

My mother turned to me. "Daniel picked up all the wood he needs for the closet, but he could use some help putting it together."

Main quest: Help mother unpack. Side quest: Bonding exercise.

My mom had been doing this to me for years. It was how Claire and I had become friends. Claire was our neighbor, and

Mom asked her to help me tend the garden. Of course she agreed. And she did it every Sunday morning with me until…I guess until we bonded.

But it was somewhat more awkward as adults. Daniel pushed up his glasses. Instinctively, I did the same thing.

He smiled. "It's really good to spend some one-on-one time with you, Lincoln. Your mom tells me so much about you."

I nodded. I was terrible at small talk. Ask anyone. But I couldn't leave him hanging, because he seemed about as uncomfortable as I was. "Good stuff, I hope," I replied. A cliché, but surely it was a cliché for a reason.

Daniel chuckled. That was a good sign. "Well, she mentioned your promotion. Congratulations, that's impressive."

"Well…it's not…mine yet," I said, my discomfort rising.

"She's confident you'll get it." He offered me an easy smile. The same one I was sure won my mom over. "She's so proud of you. She told everyone. So, you know, no pressure."

I forced out a laugh and glanced away. Uneasiness prickled across my skin. Daniel meant well, but he didn't know me. He didn't know how my brain latched on to things to obsess about. This was one of them. I needed that promotion, and right now, I wasn't sure I was doing a good enough job to get it.

Daniel pointed at wood jutting out of the back of his truck. "Could you help me carry these pieces up to the bedroom?"

I nodded, happy to be put to work.

"Thank you. I'll be there to help in a second. I need to wake my granddaughter." Daniel walked up to the truck and opened the passenger side door, revealing a kid who was fast asleep. "Emily Ann." He gently poked and prodded her.

I'd heard all about the beloved granddaughter but had yet to meet her.

I lifted a large piece of wood before carrying it upstairs to the second floor, where it would be transformed into a closet.

It took a few trips up and down, but eventually we got everything up there.

"Ever built a closet before?" Daniel asked, setting out all the boards. Most of them were already cut to the right size, but there were a few pieces that seemed unaccounted for.

I shook my head.

"I used to be a carpenter." Daniel looked up at me from where he knelt on the floor. "Many moons ago."

I knew that. I wasn't in the least bit surprised Mom paired us on an activity that would highlight his abilities. But Daniel seemed to want my validation.

"Cool," I said, and when it didn't feel like enough, I kneeled beside him. "I'll follow your lead, then."

I enjoyed working with my hands. It helped silence my mind, which is why I never complained about all the little tasks my mother made me do. On some level, I was sure she knew.

This time, my mind couldn't rest. There was one thought plaguing me.

I was betraying my dad.

This was something I'd have done with him. My father was a construction worker capable of building anything. I spent years watching him fix things in our house and sometimes other people's houses.

He should have been the one teaching me.

I didn't blame him, of course. He certainly hadn't intended on leaving behind a wife and an eleven-year-old boy who had even fewer social skills than I do now.

My chest ached. Far less than it used to, but it was like the pain in my lower back that sometimes flared up.

Emily Ann, who was now wide awake and fueled on her half-eaten candy bar, bounced into the room and pulled me from the thoughts that were close to consuming me.

"Ma wants to know if anyone wants chai," she said, and did not even try to avoid staring at me. "Are you Uncle Lincoln?"

Uncle? That was a first.

"Uh, yeah. Are you Kid Emily Ann?"

She giggled and lost her balance but quickly found her feet. "You don't have to say 'kid.' That's silly."

"I'm a bit silly." I shrugged as I fixed the last shelf. "And a bit thirsty."

"Gotcha," she said, finger guns popping in my direction and then toward Daniel. "Pops?"

"I'd love a cup, but could you…" Before he could finish his sentence, Emily Ann was gone.

She whooshed downstairs and landed on the first floor with a big thud. "They said yes!"

With the tea came more tasks, and after we finished the closet, we built a TV cabinet and a few floating shelves, nothing that I had on my list for the day.

I was supposed to be packing up the old place. I'd been avoiding it for weeks.

But after today, after spending this time with Daniel, I craved my old home. Daniel was a stand-up guy, but he'd completely drained my social battery. I needed a moment alone.

"Come back for dinner, okay?" Mom called after I said my goodbyes and made my way outside.

I nodded, climbed into my truck, and drove back to our old house, where I sat outside for a few moments. The coat of white paint I'd put on about four years ago looked a bit grubby, but the buyers had agreed to paint it themselves once they moved in.

I turned off my truck and let myself into the now almost-empty house. None of the rooms interested me except one. I crept to the study and grasped the handle. A part of me almost thought to knock. To call out. To ask if he was in there.

My heart pulsed. This was stupid. He died years ago. I couldn't let it haunt me. I was a grown man with responsibilities, and if I didn't toughen up and empty this room, it would be handed over to the new owners as is because Mom wouldn't be able to do it either. She'd lost the love of her life. Her soulmate. Someone she had shared herself with for almost twenty years before he was torn away.

I pushed open the door, and it creaked as if surprised to see me.

My breath caught at the sight of the PlayStation 2 and the two controllers strewn across the floor. The cushions we'd sat on were still there. Unmoved. And I knew if I turned on the little TV and the console, the game we'd paused and saved all those years ago may still be there. Stuck in a different time. Where dying in Middle-earth was my biggest fear.

With a few deep breaths, I went to the controllers and lifted one of them. I hadn't played on a PlayStation 2 since then. I hadn't stopped gaming, but I'd moved over to PC gaming where I could play alone or with strangers online and not be reminded that I'd lost my Player Two.

9

ELIZABETH

[92 weeks ago]

@theanswerisno:
Thought you'd given up on our farm and
become a respectable adult

@pancakesareelite:
I've had a rough week.
Will you water my crops?

@theanswerisno:
Of course. I'll harvest them too

@theanswerisno:
Do you want to talk about it?

@pancakesareelite:
Not really

@pancakesareelite:
I appreciate the offer.
But I think I need to sleep.

@theanswerisno:
I'm sorry about your week

@pancakesareelite:
Thank you, Link <3

@theanswerisno:
Wait, quick one before you leave…

@pancakesareelite:
Hm?

@theanswerisno:
I like that you call me Link.
Legend of Zelda was one of my
dad's favorite games

@theanswerisno:
Night, Pancakes

@pancakesareelite:
You shared something with me!
Don't go now! Stay! Tell me more!

@theanswerisno:
Ha. Sleep well, xx

When I left the Gordon-Bettencourt empire, I also left behind a life that no longer suited me. And it was heartbreaking to see how many of my so-called friendships relied on my access to fame.

But maybe I was the problem? Douglas always said I was. And right now, the only person who liked spending time with me didn't know me in real life.

It had been three weeks of working with Lincoln Carden, and while he could now occasionally look in my direction, we were still pulling up short when it came to chitchat.

So when Richard, a fortysomething-year-old senior engineer who smiled at me often, struck up a conversation, I was more than happy to engage.

He raised a steaming pot of coffee in my direction. "Want some?"

"Absolutely." I grabbed a mug and extended it. "I need at least two cups before I'm a functional human, three to function as an engineer."

Richard chuckled as he filled my mug. My office humor was improving daily.

"Same here." He set the pot back in the machine and added sugar to his coffee. "How's the internship going? Which discipline are you enjoying the most?"

I grinned. "Roads."

He made a show of rolling his eyes. "Roads. Who needs 'em?" He walked out of the kitchen, continuing the conversation. "That places you with Carden, doesn't it?"

"Uh-huh."

"Interesting." Richard's brows popped up. "You must be rather nervous about your evaluations."

My heart rate doubled. "I'm terrified."

"Carden is a tough one, but I guess you could ask your dad to buy Simucon if it doesn't work out."

I schooled my face, hoping it gave nothing away. The less Richard knew, the better, and there was no way I was about to offload my life's drama on the nice man who always made an effort to greet me in the mornings.

Unlike my boss.

Mr. Carden was already at his desk as I nudged open the cracked door to our office. Hair wet, as usual. The deep frown between his eyebrows let me know I should move with caution.

"Your father's been expanding his portfolio, hasn't he?" Richard asked me while raising a mug in Mr. Carden's direction as a greeting.

Mr. Carden nodded in response.

"Uh-huh, but I don't think he's ready for engineering just yet. Still mostly films and media…" I said, taking my seat and turning on my laptop. I wanted conversation, yes, but I didn't want it to be about Douglas Gordon-Bettencourt.

"If all else fails, you could absolutely become an actress," Richard added.

Mr. Carden's head shot up, and the glare he delivered had the structural engineer retreating back to Bridges. Mr. Carden's gaze dropped without meeting mine, and he tugged his headset over his ears. I tried not to take it personally but failed. Over the last few weeks, there were moments when I felt like I'd decoded him. It was addictive. I craved his validation. I mean…he's my boss. Everyone wants praise from their boss.

Ignoring the urge to say something, I opened my inbox and found seven new emails from Mr. Carden, where at least five could have been done in person through a three-second conversation.

I replied to them since he had his headset on. I wasn't in the mood to swing my arms around and get his attention—which would probably leave him unimpressed.

His gaze lifted from his screen to me. My email landing in his inbox must have drawn his attention. I waved sheepishly, and despite knowing he wouldn't hear me, said, "Good morning."

He slid the headphones down to his neck and swiped a hand across his growing stubble. "Morning. I'll be busy and on-site for the first half of the day, but when I get back, we can take a look at the Poplar and Azalea Road intersection."

"Can I come with you?" I asked, and pointed at the pair of worn-out secondhand safety boots I'd bought online.

He shook his head, and my face must have fallen because something in his gaze softened. "Not today. All we're doing today is fighting. It's not a good introduction, and you won't learn anything except maybe a few new swear words."

"I know I've underwhelmed you with my technical abilities, but I could definitely impress you with my foul language."

He shook his head, and his tight shoulders relaxed for a moment. If I could see his face, I'd bet the corner of his mouth would have twitched into an almost-smile.

He grabbed a rolled-up drawing off his desk and handed it to me. "Focus on fixing this alignment. We'll review it when I get back."

He walked back to his desk, taking a long moment to stare at it. His eyes darted around as he seemed to make a mental checklist of which items he'd need.

Then he gathered his things and was gone. Replaced by Mr. Anders, who was one of those men who were always making jokes that bordered on offensive but wasn't quite enough for you to ever call him out on it. Plus, he was the boss, my boss's boss, and I wanted this job enough to laugh at whatever under-thought-of pun he sent my way. Simucon's reputation and higher salaries would be worth it.

"Working hard or hardly working?" he asked, walking into the office in the one second I took to reapply my lipstick in my selfie camera.

I laughed awkwardly and pressed my lips together.

"Carden hasn't given me an update on you in a while. I've heard from everyone else."

"He's been swamped," I said, unsure if I was defending Mr. Carden or myself. My mouth went dry with that awful feeling of falling behind.

He snickered. "It's not too late to switch disciplines."

For a second, I considered how effortless it would be to get the senior engineer I'd spoken to this morning to provide feedback. Mr. Carden on the other hand…

I accidentally exhaled out loud.

Mr. Anders narrowed his eyes. "I'm aware Carden isn't the easiest person to work with, and if you have any complaints about him, I'm all ears. We, at Simucon, pride ourselves on this internship, and our mentors and managers need to meet the high standards we've set."

"He's perfect," I replied in one quick breath, despite wanting more from Mr. Carden. "I have no complaints."

Mr. Anders nodded. "Well, that's good to know. Carden is the best of the best in traffic and geometric design." He walked around to Mr. Carden's desk. "He single-handedly designed the widening of the highway between Freeland and Disselweed, including every inter-change upgrade along that twenty-five-mile stretch of mountainous road, and he did it in half the allocated time. We made a fortune."

My jaw dropped. I knew Mr. Carden was brilliant, but somehow he kept surprising me.

"If he wasn't so good, I wouldn't have kept him around," he said with a laugh.

"What?" I squawked out.

Mr. Anders leaned down and picked up a framed certificate hanging in the corner, below eye level. "This is an award given to him by the ICTTE for his research for pedestrian safety or whatever he did at UCLA to get that PhD, and look at where he keeps it. It's almost face down." Mr. Anders placed it back with care. "They've invited him back this year, and do you know how I found out? His name was in the mailer sent out by the conference. You'd think he'd tell his boss."

"Wow" was all I'd managed. "I didn't know he had a PhD."

Should I be calling him Dr. Carden?

Mr. Anders walked back to the doorway and turned to face me. "Gordon-Bettencourt, that's what you're up against. Engineers who want nothing more than to solve the problems I give them. Do you have that or are we wasting our time here?"

"I…" I started, self-doubt flooding my bloodstream. Still, I managed to say, "Yes, I do. I can. I will."

He looked back at Mr. Carden's desk. "Granted, if Carden could have an ounce of your charm, that would certainly make things easier." He chuckled to himself as if there was something I didn't know.

Before he left, he turned around. "By the way, I hear your father's bought shares in a new social media platform."

"Seems to be the talk of the town."

I'd seen it on the news like he did. If he was looking for an exclusive, I didn't have it.

"Do you see him regularly?" he asked.

"He's a busy man," I bit out as politely as possible, hoping my pale cheeks weren't reddening with guilt, shame, anger, and all the other awful feelings turning up with the thought of him. Instead, I offered Mr. Anders the smile that earned me many favors. "But when he's in town, I'll tell him to come around to the office."

"I'd love to meet him. Let him know I'd be honored to take him out for dinner and drinks." Mr. Anders narrowed his eyes, his head tilting. It was as though he was trying to calculate exactly how much I was worth.

Not that his guess would be anywhere near the truth. I resisted the urge to squirm.

One of the other interns came rushing into the office, and Mr. Anders stepped back, saluting me before going to bother the next person, I presume.

Cedric, the number one on the intern list, rested his hands on my desk. "Can I see your latest design for the Groveport interchange? I've been working on the bridges, but I need to make sure we're on the same page before that technocrat of yours gets back here and tears me a new one."

"You mean Mr. Carden?"

He nodded, his nostrils flaring. "The man's insane. No one cares for that much detail, and I shouldn't be forced to design to the nth degree. My designs were fine. Mr. Fischer approved it, but Carden took one look and found like fifty problems."

"His attention to detail is pretty phenomenal." I don't know why, but there was an urge to defend him and each of the interns seemed to feel that way about the heads of their chosen departments. It was as though we needed to prove we'd made the right choice and somehow their credibility reflected our own.

That and Mr. Carden's attention to detail was more than phenomenal.

Cedric huffed. "Yeah, whatever. Well, I don't want him to do it again. It was embarrassing enough the first time."

I opened our latest design and emailed it to him. "Just sent it."

"Thanks," he said, and spun around.

"Hey, before you leave," I called, "could you show me how to import your design?"

An eyebrow popped up. "You don't know how? That was like the first thing I learned."

Blood rushed to the tips of my ears, and I imagined they went as red as my hair. "Well, I wouldn't be asking if I knew."

A laugh squeezed through his smug grin. "Well, good luck figuring it out, Seven."

And with that, he turned around and left.

I swallowed the growl threatening and shut my eyes. He was right about one thing, though: now I would figure it out. Without his or anyone else's help.

LINCOLN

[90 weeks ago]

@theanswerisno:
Team up with me

> **@pancakesareelite:**
> You'll be better off teaming up with a
> more seasoned player. I don't want you
> to lose this tournament

@theanswerisno:
What happened to all that talk of "we
are undefeatable together"?

> **@pancakesareelite:**
> When did I say that?

@theanswerisno:
You haven't, but you totally should.

I resisted the urge to lay my head face down on the sixteen-seater mahogany table. The other engineers were late. Or maybe I was a few minutes early. But this was my first meeting with all the managers since taking on this potential role, and I had to make a good impression.

But I was exhausted.

"Rough night, Carden?" Anders asked as he stepped into the room and rubbed his stomach.

"Sure," I replied, frustrated that my frustration was showing even when I tried hiding it.

But it was a rough night. I'd stayed up late in an attempt to catch up on my emails before this meeting. I overslept. Missed my run. Ran out of meds and had no time to refill my prescription. I was completely thrown off.

The other managers filed in and took their seats, some already bragging about their interns.

I sat thinking about what I'd say about Elizabeth. I'd been on-site and in so many meetings that I hadn't been able to properly guide or evaluate her since she started.

When I'd stayed quiet for too long, Anders turned to me. "How's Gordon-Bettencourt coming along? Caught her putting on makeup yesterday when she should have been working. Not that I'm complaining."

Around the table, faces broke into silent smirks.

"Not that we're complaining," the head of urban design said. This earned a quiet chuckle from some of the others.

"Gents, seems like a good time to remind you about Simucon's strict policy against workplace relationships," Anders said, still grinning.

"Simucon also has a no-nonsense approach to workplace harassment." My tone brooked no room for argument. "She's coming along fine. Eager to learn, picking up concepts quickly, although her first attempts are generally sloppy. She seems to be in a rush."

"Probably trying to catch up to the others. She's a few years older than them," the senior engineer in Bridges said before raving about his interns. "She started at UCLA in her twenties, dropped out after a couple years, then took time off. That's when she was all over the tabloids. At some point, for some reason, she transferred to San Diego State and continued her studies. Rumor has it, there was some family drama."

"What happened?" Anders asked, leaning in.

"Can't seem to find the specifics," the engineer continued. "With that much control over the media, they've been able to keep it hush-hush."

"They haven't kept anything else about her quiet. Her entire dating history is online, and it's long. She certainly had fun in those years when she quit engineering," Anders said. "Heard she even dated Rupert Bryan—you know that star from that superhero movie."

Richard nodded. "I heard about that. And Axe Nilsson, the racer. I wanted to ask her about it the other day, but thought it was better not to."

I didn't know any of that, and I didn't need to.

"You're right," I snapped. "Because it's none of our business. Unless you'd like it if we all started poking around your upbringing, marriages, affairs, and divorces."

A few of the men around the table stiffened, but I couldn't stop. Elizabeth was a person whose choices should be respected and kept private, like anyone else. "We need to evaluate her on her technical ability."

"I agree," Fischer jumped in. "Let's move on with this meeting, please. I have another meeting in thirty minutes. In short, I think Cedric is going to be a wonderful addition to our division. He's a shoo-in." He pulled out a scroll of drawings and unrolled them across the desk. "For position two, it's a close call between Haaziq and Peter. Both have excellent results and workmanship. I've been working closely with Cedric, but Richard has been overseeing the other two."

"It's only week three. We have five more weeks before the final test. I don't think we should be discussing final placements. It could create bias," I said, making a note to scrutinize Haaziq's and Peter's work myself. "Besides, I'm not all that impressed with Cedric. You haven't mentioned his inaccuracies."

I was aware that Cedric's mistakes were overlooked by Fischer. But I didn't care if he took offense. His review was as error-filled as Cedric's design.

The engineer huffed, crossing his arms and lifting his nose in the air. "Let's be honest. It's not going to be Gordon-Bettencourt. You're speaking about creating bias as if she isn't wearing short dresses and low necklines to earn favor. Cedric is working on getting this job fair and square. Perhaps you need to remind your intern that placement is based on technical knowledge."

My blood boiled, and I sat up straighter. All the exhaustion from this weekend was sucked out of me and replaced with a simmering rage. "Fischer," I called, meeting his blue-eyed gaze, "I notice you refer to every other intern by their name. Her name is Elizabeth, and your comments are inappropriate."

A strange defensiveness curdled in my chest. Elizabeth was trying, and she was learning. She deserved respect. On second thought, it wasn't that strange wanting to defend her. "I haven't been able to dedicate the required time to properly guide Elizabeth. I'll prioritize her going forward."

"Interesting, since she said you've been a great mentor," Anders said, a twisted smile on his face.

She did?

Fischer raised his hands. "Whatever the case may be, I don't think you should be wasting your time, Carden. You said her work is sloppy. Why is she here?" He turned to Anders. "Is it because of her family influence?"

Anders shrugged. "Maybe."

My hand balled into a fist around my black pen. I shook my head, willing the anger to subside. If there was one thing that drove me up the wall, it was opportunities being granted based on wealth instead of merit. "I hope that isn't true."

Anders turned to face me. "Or maybe I hired her to test you. I can't make you a manager based on your engineering talent, Carden. You need to be able to manage. Manage your intern. If you can do that, the job's yours."

I stood, unable to be around them. My mood wasn't under control. I needed sleep, and I needed my ADHD medication. I needed to get out of this meeting. I could feel myself unraveling, and they shouldn't see that. "Understood. Please excuse me as I have a meeting at the Princely intersection in forty-five minutes, and it takes an hour to get there."

Without waiting for permission, I dipped my head and left the boardroom.

Spinning through to my office, I grabbed the construction drawings and set them down on my desk. Elizabeth arrived with a fresh cup of coffee in her hands and smiled brightly. I kept my head down. Every part of me was already on edge, and her fitted yellow summer dress and sweetheart neckline poked at my annoyance after the meeting I'd had. She set her coffee cup down on the desk and leaned over my construction drawings while I lifted my car keys, hard hat, and reflective vest.

Her loud gasp called my attention. I turned around as her caramel-colored beverage soaked into my construction plans.

The last strand holding me together broke. My fist came down on the desk between us. Elizabeth flinched, and her body went ramrod straight.

"No, no, no," I ground out, along with a string of curse words.

"I'm so sorry, Mr. Carden." Her voice came out as a squeak. "I'll print another set."

"Leave it." I shook my head and left before I could do or say anything else that would make a bigger mess out of this situation.

I made it to the site twenty minutes late and without drawings. The rush of the day continued, but my heightened emotions simmered down. Elizabeth's wide gray eyes and shaking voice sprang to mind. I jumped out of my truck, and while walking to the container we'd be meeting in, I checked my phone, which seemed a couple minutes away from dying. I navigated to my email app, where I typed out a message.

> Elizabeth, apologies for the outburst earlier. Don't worry about it. It's fine.

I hit send. It wasn't fine. They would be expecting the drawings, but I didn't want the guilt eating at her. It made me feel guilty knowing she'd be feeling guilty. I couldn't begin to explain the logic of my feelings. Even my therapist struggled.

"Where are my drawings?" The resident engineer was nearly snarling upon my arrival. Problems. That's what that meant. Always wretched problems.

"Delayed." I pursed my lips in what I hope was a fairly polite smile.

"Just like you, then," he replied.

I learned a long time ago when to fight fire with fire. An apology would do no good here. "What's the crisis? Spit it out."

"We've hit rock."

I sucked on my teeth and turned to face the contractor. "I told you to hire a geotechnical specialist." If everyone could stop cutting corners to save a buck, that would make my job ten times easier.

We explored the site, and I made note of their progress and any potential problems we might face. Saunders left me in big trouble with this one.

As we neared the entrance, a bright red Mini Cooper pulled up. The door flung open, and Elizabeth sprang out.

Holding a scroll of drawings.

And wearing absolutely no PPE.

"Who is *that*?" the resident engineer said.

"My engineer." I shot him a warning glance before he could say anything stupid.

"Mr. Carden." She walked up to me, her still-shaking hands extending the roll of drawings. "I printed a new set. It's the latest ones. I cross-checked it against the coffee-stained plans." Her face scrunched up, and her red cheeks made the small scattering of freckles disappear.

Something inside me softened unexpectedly as I took her in. Her copper-red hair had unraveled from the long ponytail she'd had earlier. Her gray eyes were still wide enough for me to see the whites around them, and the corner of her burgundy-painted lips twitched downward. Gone was the sunny disposition and sassy woman I'd come to expect.

I must have been far angrier than intended.

Stepping closer to her, I whispered, "I'm so sorry about earlier. You didn't have to drive all the way here." I took the drawings.

"Coo can handle it." She flashed me a weak smile and gestured to her car.

Of course she'd named it.

"Thank you." I squeezed my hands around the drawings, grateful for the set. It solved so many problems. I glanced back at her smile. I didn't like that it was unsure. I didn't like the fear still lining her voice.

Sighing skyward, I felt my walls being beaten down.

Manage your intern.

"You can join for the rest of the meeting, but you're only allowed into the container and back into your car. You're not dressed appropriately to go anywhere else on this site."

"Really? Awesome!" she said with a little hop. Far too excited for such a boring meeting, but there was sunshine creeping back into her voice. "Thank you so much."

"Don't thank me. It's part of my job."

Looking at her on a good day was risky, and today was downright treacherous, but I couldn't resist feeding off her enthusiasm. She made me feel some unlabeled feeling I'd never felt before.

I led her into the container and laid the drawings on the desk. Then I talked them through it. Twice. Because the first time, they were all looking at Elizabeth.

• • •

When my meetings were done, I could finally breathe. I took a slow drive back to the office, and on the way, I stopped at the pharmacy where I could refill my prescription. It also happened to have a delicious takeout place next door.

Zoya's Xpress was the home of the best chicken salad sandwiches in town.

"My favorite customer!" the small Indian woman said as I stepped inside. I'd bet she said that to everyone. "Chicken salad? With a bit of heat?"

My stomach grumbled. I nodded and leaned against the doorframe of the tiny but clean hole-in-the-wall cafe. Driving and being on-site always made me hungrier than usual. I shook my head thinking about Elizabeth driving up there in a wild panic with a roll of drawings.

Did she eat today?

I'd seen her eating at the Friday announcements where little sandwiches and cookies were offered. She didn't seem to be allergic to sugar or dairy, and she once mentioned enjoying a chicken salad sandwich.

But she never ate at her desk, and she never left long enough to eat anywhere else either.

Why?

It wasn't unusual that I'd noticed this. I noticed everything. This was a totally normal thing for me to notice.

Especially in the house I grew up in where my mother was always offering me—and anyone around us—food. There was nothing more important to her than ensuring people had eaten.

My mind wandered while the smell of spiced chicken filled the air.

"Two," I said to Zoya. "Please make it two."

ELIZABETH

[89 weeks ago]

@pancakesareelite:
Oops! Sorry! I didn't
know that would happen!

> **@theanswerisno:**
> Ha, it's okay.
> How were you supposed to know?

@pancakesareelite:
You're weirdly patient with me.
My very own Yoda.

> **@theanswerisno:**
> Better you will get

@pancakesareelite:
Oh no. Please don't. You don't
have to text like he would.

> **@theanswerisno:**
> Your turn play, yes, hmm...

@pancakesareelite:
Link! Stop!

> **@theanswerisno:**
> Stop I will not

@pancakesareelite:
YODA CAN'T EVEN TEXT

> **@theanswerisno:**
> The greatest way to learn is to do

@pancakesareelite:
You're an absolute fool

> **@theanswerisno:**
> Love it you do

@pancakesareelite:
Maybe I do

If only I'd thought to take my hideous safety boots along, I could have explored the site. I'd been in such a panic to leave that I rushed out without them. But it was worth it. Worth the long drive. Worth the cost of the gas. Worth the way Mr. Carden's face changed when I'd handed over those drawings. And now I needed to clean up this mess before he returned and remembered that I was the mess beyond saving.

The first email in my inbox was an apology from him, sent around the time he'd have arrived on-site. Well, if I'd seen that before I left, it would have saved me a lot of trouble.

Who am I kidding? I'd still have reprinted those drawings, and I'd still have taken them to him because I knew he needed them. He'd been under so much pressure that I worried he might crack.

I wheeled toward his empty desk and took one of the thick geometric guidelines from his stack of books. After studying it for about an hour, I tweaked the intersection design for the seven billionth time. Quick but soft footsteps drew my attention. Mr. Carden walked in. The frown that had lived between his brows was gone, but his shoulders were still a little tenser than usual.

"Mr. Carden." I gestured at my laptop screen, hoping to catch him before he settled in and sent his focus elsewhere. "Do you have a moment? I think maybe this is the one." I gave him a double thumbs-up.

One side of his mouth lifted in what seemed to be a smile. A lopsided, genuine half smile.

It was like leveling up every time I got that out of him.

"I admire your confidence," he said, and hesitated at my desk. Without looking my way, he dropped his voice low, barely a whisper. "Lunch first. For you."

He put a foil-wrapped square on my desk, which was exactly the size of a sandwich and smelled exactly like a sandwich, and the condensation appearing underneath it hinted at a *warm* sandwich, and while all the evidence pointed at "sandwich," I couldn't bring myself to make sense of the situation.

He tapped the mystery sandwich-shaped parcel. "Wasn't sure if you'd eaten. I never see you eat lunch. But if you're hungry, it's yours. Chicken salad…which I think you like? If not, no pressure. Someone will eat it."

My breath hitched. I didn't know Lincoln Carden listened to me when I nervously rambled on and on. My stomach tingled and fluttered…because of hunger. Probably. Not because my handsome boss was also kind and attentive. Nope. Not that. Just excited to eat.

Before I could answer, he was already at his desk, unwrapping his own foil square.

"Thank you." I tipped my head and took the sandwich, enjoying the way it warmed my fingertips.

I unwrapped it, already salivating. I hazarded a glance his way, but he was in his zone already. His headset fixed across his ears.

Spinning away, I bit into the warm, soft bread with crispy edges, and my tastebuds lit up. I'd never eaten a chicken salad sandwich as delicious as this one. "So freaking good," I whispered to myself as a small moan escaped me. There was a hint of chili I wasn't expecting.

His head snapped upward, his eyes round.

"Sorry. I thought you couldn't hear with the…" I pointed at my ears, which were prickling and hot.

He tugged the headset off and gulped. "Haven't turned them on yet. Sometimes I forget or I just wear them to deter interruptions."

I slammed a hand over my heated face. "Sorry for interrupting you, then. Well, not sorry. It's your own fault for giving me a sandwich so tasty. What did you expect?"

"Nothing less." His gaze dipped to his computer screen, but I enjoyed the underlying playfulness in his tone.

I'd bet Lincoln Carden was a lot of fun to be around when he was in his element.

He was already kind, smart, and ridiculously good-looking. I couldn't add *fun* to that. No, not fair.

Heat kept radiating through my face, my chest, and now my brain felt as though it were being flooded with inappropriate hormones. *Was this a side effect of the chili?* "Thank you. And it's really good," I rambled in an attempt to say anything except what I was thinking. "But I think I said that already. Where did you get them? Did you know they call this a chicken mayo in South Africa?"

His dark brows lifted, giving me the smallest glimpse of his soft brown eyes behind those glasses. But he rarely gave me more than a split second. He lowered his head and popped the last piece of his sandwich into his mouth. "Zoya's. I'll show you next time. It's not too far away." He crumpled the foil, squeezing it until it disappeared in the palm of his hand. "Chicken mayo, huh? I had no idea. But it makes sense." He passed the foil ball from one hand to the other and continued rolling it. "When you're done eating, please print the alignment."

After polishing off the meal and enjoying the weight of it in my belly, I floated over to the plotter, grabbed the drawing, and then spread it across the large desk in our office.

Mr. Carden stood and sucked in a deep breath. He lifted a scale ruler and his trusty red pen as though he were going into battle. He walked over to the desk beside me and leaned over it, placing his instruments down before spreading his long fingers wide, and for a moment, I wondered what it might feel like to be touched by him.

My heart rate skyrocketed.

What am I doing? What am I thinking? It was just a sandwich. Come on, Lily. Get a grip. Focus.

I was probably ovulating. And a handsome man handed me a delicious meal and expected nothing in return. I couldn't be blamed.

Seconds passed and it was the longest he'd gone without making a correction. I glanced up at his face where a deep divot divided his dark brows as he stared a hole through the drawing. His wide chest lifted slowly, and before exhaling, he murmured, "I'm sorry about earlier. It wasn't fair."

"I messed up, so I deserved it. And if you give me a bad evaluation, I can't even blame you, but please don't."

He shook his head. "It was an accident. I'm not going to bad-mouth you because of a spilled cup of coffee. Although I am mildly concerned about how much caffeine you're consuming. The average person shouldn't have more than four cups a day."

I giggled, but for some reason, my eyes stung at the gentleness of his tone.

"I really am sorry about the yelling and the cursing."

"You weren't that bad…" I gulped as memories of Douglas's

tantrums flashed across my mind, keeping me there like my very own horror house.

Mr. Carden paused, taking me in. When I didn't say anything else, he continued. "I was a lot worse than I needed to be. Today was just…hard. I've had a strange day. Stranger weekend," he continued in that low voice he used when he stepped out of being Mr. Carden and let me in to see what Lincoln might be like. He straightened, gnawing on his bottom lip, but kept his gaze on my drawing. "I was at my mom's and out of routine, and then last night, I stayed up and didn't sleep well, or at all, and…"

Something about the tension surrounding him let me know that if he were to say something more, he would say it softly.

"Are you okay?" I kept my voice quiet and took a step toward him, close enough to smell that citrusy scent that always radiated off him.

He gulped, his Adam's apple bobbing. "I think it's only fair, since we're office mates and all, that you know I have ADHD, and probably some other undiagnosed things." He shook his head, still studying the design. "Anyway, on some days like today, I struggle to find my focus, and it irritates me. I get mad at my brain, and you weren't supposed to be on the receiving end. I'm usually better at it."

"Oh." I studied the dark stubble on his strong jaw, which was longer than usual. I worked my way up to the deep frown always in place above his glasses before settling on his soft, and simultaneously intense brown eyes. "I had no idea."

"No one knows." His focus was still stuck on the alignment, or pretending to be. "Well, Anders does…It's why I have my own office. I'm easily distracted."

I groaned and covered my face. "Working across from me, of all people, must be a nightmare. I'm so sorry. I'll ask them to move me."

"No, they'll just put someone else here."

"I feel like anyone else would be better," I sighed. "I'm like a walking, talking strobe light."

He chuckled now, and it may be the first I'd heard it. It was a deep laugh that stayed in his chest. That lopsided smile made an appearance, too, as his shoulders seemed to unwind. "Not untrue. You are possibly the most distracting woman I've ever come across."

My heart skipped a beat. *Distracting in a good way?* I wanted to ask, but managed to stop myself at the last second.

"In the industry," he added, clearing his throat.

"Oh."

My appearance? My personality? Did I talk too much?

He leaned down until he was almost eye level with the end of the long desk. He narrowed his eyes, still reviewing my design.

"I could tone it down while I'm sharing an office with you," I said.

"No, I don't want you to do that." He reached across the drawing. "I'll be fine. I have to figure it out." He cleared his throat again. "Since I'm sharing all my secrets with you today, I may as well let you know I'm meant to prove myself as a manager. I'm only 'acting' manager for now. They're not convinced I can do it."

Secrets? This was a new level.

"What? You're, like, incredible." As soon as the words escaped me, my face heated. Maybe that was too direct.

A slight redness filled his brown cheeks. "I haven't got the best track record at working with people. I've been called abrasive, cold, harsh, uh…" He looked around the office. "Aloof, and those were to my face. I'm sure far worse things have been said behind my back."

I'd be lying if I said I didn't think those things, too, upon our first meeting.

"So now I have to prove myself, and I think I'm already failing." He finally glanced down and met my gaze. "I haven't given you the guidance you need."

"Oh crap," I squawked. "Me? I'm your test?"

He raised one brow, and an unexpected sheepish look spread across his face. "Kinda."

"Let me get this straight—if you upskill me and I ace my final test, you'll ace yours? As a manager?"

He nodded.

"Sounds like we want the same thing," I said with a smile, and then tapped the drawing. "Stop your yapping and teach me stuff."

He burst out laughing. This time, the deep sound extended from him to me, and I shivered with delight.

"No one has ever told me to stop yapping." He shook his head. "But you're right. Let's do this." He dragged his finger along one curve. "What's this sight distance? Looks like seven hundred feet?"

It was weird seeing the mental switch happen as Lincoln settled back into Mr. Carden.

"Seven hundred and ten," I replied, unsure of how easily and accurately he guessed distances. He hadn't even used his ruler.

"That's fine." He stood and scrunched his lips up on one side. "Except for this kink in the road. Smooth it out. Kinks aren't good."

"Depends on the context." I bit down on my lips, heat spreading through my face as all the blood in my body rushed there since none of it was being used by the part of my brain that filters my words. "Like certain hairstyles require it."

Mr. Carden's eyes widened before he started coughing, concealing a laugh. He turned away. Even with his darker shade of skin, I could see the blush creeping to the tips of his ears.

"Smooth it out, Elizabeth. After, we'll start on the vertical alignment."

I nodded and kept my mouth sealed, in case I said something ridiculous again.

Before taking my seat, I noticed so much more. The way his desk was arranged: he often put his cell phone in his drawer, he took timed breaks, and he always wore the noise-canceling headset. It all made so much sense.

I imagined being where he sat and seeing me. Oh no. It must be the worst. I bounced my legs, tapped my fingers, and hummed along to music. I had desk ornaments and trinkets. I stood for a coffee every hour.

This wasn't fair to him.

But I had an idea.

• • •

With my idea packed and ready to go, I was too buzzed to sleep that night. Lucky for me, *@wheretheresawilliam* was streaming. His streams were always incredibly entertaining and informative. Plus, he was rather nice to look at.

But most importantly, I always found Link there.

> **@theanswerisno:**
> I've had a DAY.

His message popped up within a minute of me logging on. *Did he wait for me? The way I waited for him?*

I brought up his chat and replied: Me too. What happened on your side?

> **@theanswerisno:**
> Too much to explain, and it was a big rush. I was not in my element. Took it out on someone who didn't deserve it.

He took it out on someone, and someone took it out on me. Ha. What a coincidence.

I read it again. *Was it a coincidence?*

I drew my brows together while my brain pinched at bits of information.

Mr. Carden did say he'd been at his mom's place over the weekend. Just like Link.

No. No. No. This was outrageous. It absolutely couldn't be. Mr. Carden was my boss, and he was quiet and smart, and I'd go as far as to call him serious and withdrawn. And a little frightening. Everyone in the office seemed to be scared of him.

Link was…soft, funny, and flirty as can be. Link was a charmer. They couldn't be more different if they tried.

But…it was an engineering group….

Link…Lincoln?

It couldn't be. Lincoln Carden would never go by Link. He barely went by Lincoln. He was Carden to the other managers and Mr. Carden to everyone else.

My Link is a Zelda fan. He'd said so himself. It had nothing to do with Mr. Carden. So, no. No way. Nope.

My heart kept racing as I pushed the thought to the back of my mind. I typed up a reply: `It happens. Did you apologize?`

> `@theanswerisno:`
> `Yeah. Of course. I'm not a monster.`

`@pancakesareelite:`
`How?`

I thought I might throw up in the moments that passed.

> `@theanswerisno:`
> `By saying "I'm sorry"? Is there another`
> `way the kids are doing it nowadays?`

I giggled to myself. This wasn't Mr. Carden. Could it be?

I could have told him, and it would have been obvious whether it was Mr. Carden but…what if it was? Did I want him to find out like this? During *@wheretheresawilliam*'s stream of *The Haunting*?

Besides, did *I* want to find out that I'd been flirting and confiding in my boss for years? Heck no. Link knew far too much about me. It wasn't the same person. It simply wasn't. That would complicate everything and even risk my chance of getting this job.

I brought up the search bar on the Engineering Lobby and searched "Link." Eighty-seven accounts came up. I searched *Lincoln* and zero accounts came up. *Carden* led to nothing.

A conversation with Mr. Anders came to mind. Mr. Carden had been to UCLA, and the Engineering Lobby was created by and for SDSU students.

The relief sent shivers up my spine. There was something else, too, another unidentifiable feeling. Disappointment? That didn't make any sense.

Whatever it was, it set me on edge. There was no way I'd be able to play with Link tonight. I stared at his message for a few more seconds and then watched the comments coming in on *@wheretheresawilliam*'s stream.

I should be relieved. Only relieved.

But I was also disappointed.

LINCOLN

[88 weeks ago]

@theanswerisno:
Hey, hey, hey, that's unfair. Stop it.
Stop stealing my loot. And stop teasing
me, you menace

> @pancakesareelite:
> I like teasing you

@theanswerisno:
Careful, I can tease too

> @pancakesareelite:
> Your move, playa

It was weird telling Elizabeth the truth yesterday. Weird because it didn't feel weird at all. Suppose she was one of those people, like Rose. Easy to talk to. The complete opposite of me.

And yet, since then, I'd been obsessing about her. About it. Not her.

I should probably remind her that I'd prefer my confession stay between us, but even as the thought crossed my mind, I knew Elizabeth wouldn't go around telling the rest of the office. She didn't strike me as a gossip because she was the subject of too much of it. I'd heard the whisperings about her family money, dating history, and about how she didn't need this job. Someone went as far as to say she probably did engineering as a fun little hobby.

It wasn't my place to judge her. Hobby or not. As long as she did the work the way it needed to be done. But something told me that wasn't the case.

Other than her clothing and jewelry, she never showed off her wealth. Her car was a few years older than mine. Perhaps it was to avoid being seen as a member and possible shareholder of the Gordon-Bettencourt enterprise.

There was more to Elizabeth than what she let on.

And for the life of me, I couldn't stop thinking about her.

It.

It.

I couldn't stop thinking about *it*. Her situation. Not her specifically. That would be inappropriate. She worked for me, and I was responsible for evaluating her performance.

Main quest: Stop thinking about Elizabeth. Side quest: Stop thinking about not thinking about Elizabeth.

Shaking my head, I wondered what awaited me at the office. *Not* Elizabeth, but rather what she'd come up with for the vertical alignment. I opened the door and stopped dead in my tracks as a large, white accordion divider stood unfolded between our desks. It was covered in flowers and photos and reminded me of what I imagined a teenage girl's bedroom would look like.

Granted, the only teenage girl's room I'd ever been in was Claire's.

"Good morning," Elizabeth almost yelled, a wide grin across her pretty face as she popped up and out of her chair.

"Morning." I eyed the large, troubling thing.

She smoothed out her gray jumpsuit. It matched her eyes perfectly.

"Hear me out." She gestured to the elephant in the room. "This way, you can't see me. And"—she took my wrist—"it's plain white on your side, so absolutely no distractions."

Her fingers were ice-cold and soft, yet forceful lava seemed to spread from the contact point throughout my body.

"This is ridiculous," I managed, staring at the plain white, inoffensive view I'd be looking at, which was completely different from her side.

She let go of me, and my skin prickled in response.

The smile fell off her face and welcomed those clouds that sometimes shadowed her sunshine features.

"No, I mean. It's brilliant, but unusual…" I added in one quick breath.

"I thought it might help you focus…" She looked far more unsure than she had when I'd walked in.

My chest fluttered in a way it hadn't in years. I stomped on the feeling before the butterfly could take flight. "I think so too." I sat down on my side of the office.

She excitedly ran over to hers.

"You can't see me, can you? I'll bet you can't even see my flowers."

I couldn't.

"How will I know if you need me, especially if I'm wearing my headset?" I asked.

She rolled her wheely chair to the edge of the divider, and her grinning face appeared. "Like this." She giggled. It was an undeniably cute giggle.

Oh no. That was not a reasonable or appropriate thought. Perhaps this divider was exactly what I needed.

"All right. Let's give this a chance." I blew out a long breath. "Thank you. I think it's great."

"But," she said, wheeling all the way over to my desk, "before you start focusing, could we take a look at my alignment? Then when you tear it apart, I can get to work, and you can do whatever it is you do while you're frowning so deeply."

"Good idea." I walked around to her side of the office and looked at her screen where she had the design open.

"Zoom in," I said.

She did.

The design wasn't perfect. But I didn't expect it to be.

"It's a decent first try," I said, and even though she'd teased me about tearing it apart, I could see criticism would knock out the last bit of light in that smile. I softened my voice and tried to be as gentle as possible. "We could do better on the grades. These are acceptable in theory, but in reality, the steeper grades could encourage speeding."

"Mr. Anders told me to reduce the amount of cut and fill because it's expensive." She tilted her head upward, and it brought her too close to me. "He said the project is over budget."

Too, too close. It almost made me dizzy. Why did she smell like a cinnamon bun?

I stepped away and nodded. "Um, yeah. He's not wrong. But one should always choose life over money. Anders grew up in a nice area with nice roads and walkways. He probably had everything he'd needed. It's sometimes hard for the rich to see what's happening to those with less."

I slammed my mouth shut. That was personal. Even more so considering her family's wealth. "I didn't mean to imply…"

"It's okay. You're right," she whispered, looking at me and making my chest feel a little tighter. "Up until a few years ago, I had no idea what things cost." Her voice dipped toward the end, and her eyes skittered away from mine.

What happened a few years ago? I cleared my throat, swallowing the question. There was a sadness in the lilt of her voice. I wanted to ask her about it. If I knew the problem…Maybe I could fix it.

She opened a map of the area and zoomed in. "There are no sidewalks in this area, so I didn't think there'd be a high number of pedestrians. Mr. Anders said anyone who walked there would know the risks, and the developer wouldn't be at fault."

Anger stirred in my stomach. Cold and hard. "That's true." I took a deep breath, but before I could stop myself, I said, "But it's not right…is it?"

She shook her head.

It was enough to stop there, but for some reason, I wanted Elizabeth to know more. To know why I felt so strongly about this. "My father was killed in a hit-and-run, and had there been a safe sidewalk with a curbed edge, it would not have happened. But because he should have known the risks, he paid for it with his life. There was no payout because the developer, as you said, was not at fault."

Years of buried feelings resurfaced as I spoke those words for the first time since college.

Her hands flew up, muffling her gasp. "I am so sorry." The pain in her voice was more than my own.

I'd worked through the grief. Well, I'd hidden it away, at least.

"I'm all right." I swallowed hard. "Anyway, Anders always cuts costs. If you're going to be the kind of engineer I'd like you to be, I'll need you to fight him. It's not only about the driver's experience, but also the pedestrian's. There wasn't a sidewalk so, yeah, maybe we were to blame, but why wasn't a sidewalk provided in a suburban area between homes and the closest convenience store? Not everyone has a car, or gas to waste."

Her eyes that often switched between cloudy and clear sparkled with tears. At my expense?

That thing in my chest she seemed to have control over tightened, and I nearly invited her to the ICTTE presentation I'd be giving about pedestrian safety. I had never invited anyone to watch me talk and I couldn't figure out if her presence would hinder or help.

"May I?" I reached out for her mouse, desperately trying to regain my composure.

She nodded, withdrawing her hand but somehow sliding closer to me.

"Why is it sticky?" I said as my palm landed on the plastic.

"I may have moisturized a second ago." She let out a low chuckle. Her breath breezed against my shirt, and the area underneath fluttered in response. "You didn't see me do it because of the divider. I can keep plenty of secrets from you now."

My mouth kicked up into a smile, and I huffed out a laugh. It seemed to travel directly to her. "My palm is going to smell like you do." I lifted the sag curve and mindlessly said, "Edible."

"I smell edible?" she asked in a volume only slightly higher than a whisper.

My stomach flip-flopped, and my face flushed. No, no. I mean, yes. She did smell deliciously edible. But no, she wasn't meant to hear that.

This was why I didn't talk to people.

"Uh…uh," I stammered, my heart beating directly in my ears. "I meant…"

She put me out of my misery by saying, "I'm cinnamon-scented." Her grin widened, and her cheeks were tinged pink. I was sure they matched mine.

In a few fast clicks, I fixed her alignment and then went to my desk and hid behind the divider. I wouldn't comment any further. Wouldn't talk. Maybe to anyone ever again. I obviously could not be trusted around this woman.

13

LINCOLN

[84 weeks ago]

@theanswerisno:
What do you do when you feel like
everyone is moving on without you?

@pancakesareelite:
I start a new game

@theanswerisno:
Good to know we have
the same coping mechanisms.

@pancakesareelite:
Jokes aside, I try to remind myself
that everyone is moving. So are we.
Different paces, different places

@theanswerisno:
I didn't expect such a profound answer
while we're playing a game pretending
to be goats

@pancakesareelite:
You underestimate me

@theanswerisno:
I have to. Because your greatness knows
no bounds and any estimates I have would
therefore be less than what you are.

@pancakesareelite:
Are you flirting with me?

@theanswerisno:
I blasted your goat into the ocean and
now you'll have to swim back, haaaaaaa.

It was Neema's turn to pick a game, and to my surprise, it wasn't Dungeons & Dragons. For years now, whenever it was her turn, she'd pick D&D. Between her enthusiasm and Shaun's love for her enthusiasm, the game went on for hours too long. I enjoyed it on most days, but after a twelve-hour workday, I was relieved when she picked Azul.

"I know, I know." She unpacked the game with a big sigh. "But I'm tired. I've been throwing up all week, and this is all I have capacity for right now. Rose brought along her set, too, so we can have two groups."

I stood and helped prepare the second set.

"We can split up the couples so there's no cheating." William playfully shoved Rose out of his way.

It was hard not to notice that everyone was coupled up. I was the third wheel, then fifth wheel, and now the seventh wheel. There had always been a quiet loneliness, but it was louder now since Claire's husband, Dean, started joining game night and after Rose and William hooked up.

Still, William had a point. Whenever Shaun played beside Neema, he played in her favor. As did Dean with Claire. The only two who fought tooth and nail were Rose and William, and the winner was truly anyone's guess.

Rose, Claire, and Shaun joined me at the board I set up. Neema, William, and Dean took the second set beside us.

The conversation flowed easily between them. I'd always been more of a listener than anything else. I didn't mind it. They lived interesting lives, and I looked forward to their updates.

"How's work going? My office is still boring." Shaun picked up a tile I needed.

"Work's awesome. This set was from them. There are some perks to working for a board game production company." Rose beamed. "How about you? Anything you're not telling me? How's work? Still saving lives, Dean?"

"Uh…" He shrugged. "I treated a child for a fake cough today."

Dean was a favorite doctor among the moms. I swore they brought their kids to his practice just to be around him.

"Hannah runs now. So all I do when I'm not working is run after her." Claire huffed. "I haven't even been able to read." She turned to me, always noticing when I hadn't contributed to the conversation. "Lincoln? How's your new office mate? Still driving you nuts?"

I shook my head before I'd even had the chance to formulate a sentence.

"You're sharing a space with someone?" Rose's mouth made a perfect O.

"I haven't told them a thing. See! Not even about who she is," Claire said, and then squeezed her eyes shut. "Crap."

"Who is she?" Shaun asked as though it were a simple question. I suppose for most people, it was. For me? It felt as though sharing anything about anything would somehow put me at risk.

But this was game night. Game night was safe. I repeated it to myself like a mantra.

"Elizabeth Gordon-Bettencourt," I said, forcing it out of my system…and admittedly, relieved that, when I thought of her now, it was because someone else brought her up. A totally reasonable reason to be thinking about my employee.

"Why's that name sound familiar?" Dean asked, his arm snaking around Claire's waist.

"Already on it," Rose said, whipping out her phone. A second later, her eyes widened. "I remember her. She's the heir to GB Productions. She must be a million—billionaire. Is she awful? I was always jealous because Oscar Lenard admitted to having a huge crush on her."

"Oscar Lenard," William grumbled, rolling his eyes. "Stupid, pretentious vampire."

"She's not awful," I said, ignoring the thing my heart was doing. I should get checked out for pericarditis or something. "She's… uh…actually really nice."

Rose's face lit up like a cartoon cat. I lifted a warning finger.

It didn't stop her.

Rose scooched closer. "I'm trying to find her social media accounts. It doesn't seem like she has any. The only photo of her on the entire internet other than her modeling years is one that is so beautiful it's surely fake."

"Cool," I choked out, trying not to sound too interested. She'd never mentioned anything like that. In fact, she rarely spoke about herself even though she seemed to be talking all the time. "Doesn't matter. I don't like her in, like, *that* way, and I'm only saying that because I know you need to hear it."

"I mean…office romance is my second favorite trope," Claire said. "Weren't you annoyed with her at first? It could totally count as enemies-to-lovers."

Rose tilted her phone toward Claire, whose mouth dropped open.

I grumbled, dropping my head in my hands and hoping my curiosity wasn't showing.

"Oh my goodness, she's gorgeous. Is this her?" Neema turned the phone to face me.

I spotted those now-familiar gray eyes. Her hair was redder, and her freckles bright. But it was her. She was breathtakingly beautiful. And they all agreed, so that was simply a fact. It didn't mean anything. It was scientific if you considered that the majority in this room thought so too.

I nodded.

"No wonder you have a crush on her." Rose let out a failed wolf whistle.

"I don't." I looked at Claire for help. "I said I don't."

She raised her brows and simultaneously narrowed her eyes. "You sure?" She wasn't teasing like the rest of them. She looked… worried.

"I don't. She's nice and smart and kind…and a better engineer than I expected her to be. I misjudged her. I'm the problem here," I rambled. "And besides"—I tried stopping myself but the words came out faster than I could filter them—"she's my employee. Even if I did like her, I can't do anything about it."

I glanced over again and saw the caption on the photo read: *GB Production Princess*. Nausea gathered in my stomach.

"So, you *do* like her," Neema teased.

Shaun leaned in for a closer look. "I get it."

"Stop, okay? Stop, please." I rubbed my hands across my face and all the way to the back of my head. "Talking about her like this is inappropriate."

"Sorry," Rose retracted fast. While she was quick to tease, she also knew when to pull back and never pushed thereafter. She silenced the rest of them with a glance. "We won't say anything else."

William also knew when to fly to her rescue. He grabbed his laptop. "Change of topic."

I blew out a long breath, grateful for whatever it was William would show us.

"Rose and I have game news." He navigated over to the video game he and Rose designed together and double-clicked it. "*Overpower* is ahead of schedule, and Thunderstruck wants us to capitalize on the current buzz around genre-blending and host a huge in-person LAN where local gamers can access an early version."

He opened a saved file, and a dark-haired sorcerer appeared on-screen with a sharp-eared dwarf that undoubtedly resembled Rose.

My eyes widened, and I leaned in. I hadn't seen these updates. "This looks incredible." I'd been following the creation of this game since William had the brilliant idea of surprising Rose with it. "I can't tell you how excited I am to play this version."

Rose beamed, and I could see how she tried her best not to launch herself into my arms. "Really?"

Over the last few years, I'd been updating Lily on *Overpower*'s development, knowing how much she'd love it. And how much I'd love experiencing it with her. In my head, I'd already blocked off release weekend in the hopes she'd be available to play it with me.

"It's sometimes all I can think about."

Wait.

Lily follows William. She could see his announcement. For an in-person LAN.

That means…Lily could be there.

14

ELIZABETH

[82 weeks ago]

> **@theanswerisno:**
> I had pancakes today

@pancakesareelite:
I'm filled with envy

> **@theanswerisno:**
> #pancakesareNOTelite

@pancakesareelite:
Link!

@pancakesareelite:
There must be something wrong with
your mouth!

> **@theanswerisno:**
> Last I checked, my mouth works
> perfectly fine. In every aspect

@pancakesareelite:
Oh.

> **@theanswerisno:**
> Your move, playa

On Thursday morning, I awoke to the buzz of my phone. Not my alarm. A phone call. The grogginess in my brain was replaced by complete alertness the second I saw MOM flash across my screen.

"Hello?" I answered, sitting up straight. My eyes burned. *What time is it?*

"Lily, love. How are you? I'm sorry for waking you but…"

It wasn't unusual for her to call at strange hours.

"It's fine. I should probably be up for work soon." I blinked a few times. "How are you? I miss you."

"I miss you too. How are you doing?"

She always asked in the few seconds we had, and each time I'd lie and tell her I was doing fabulously. I needed her to believe in a life *after* Douglas.

"When will I see you?" I asked.

"Soon."

"Mom," I started, my heart picking up speed. I jumped out of bed. "Why are you still with him?"

"Elizabeth," she whispered. "Not again. We've spoken about this. I told you to stop worrying. I'm fine. Everything is fine. I promise."

"Mom—" I started.

She cut me off. "I gotta go, love." Without another word, she hung up.

I stared at my phone for a few seconds and considered calling her back. She probably wouldn't answer…couldn't answer. That familiar tension twisted my insides. Texting wasn't an option because he had full access to her phone.

Rage burned inside me as the uncomfortable memories of him flooded my mind. That manipulative jerk who always made me feel like I had nothing more to offer the world than my looks. The controlling monster who ridiculed and belittled and shoved me into modeling. The cold narcissist who loved me for one second and discarded me the next.

A scream hidden deep in my chest threatened to escape.

Shut up, sit pretty.

Do what I say and do it perfectly.

There were a handful of Douglas one-liners I could recite by heart and even now, even with years apart and distance between us, a burst of fear and fury was born at the mere thought of him.

I stepped into the shower, reminding myself that I was safe and free. If I didn't need Douglas, neither did my mom. Why couldn't she see that? I was doing everything in my power to make that obvious. And yes, this place was tiny, but if I got the job at Simucon, we could move somewhere bigger.

I was stuck in my mind while getting ready. I opened my closet and considered the handful of outfits I'd fled LA with. Just as I was about to pull out an ordinary pants and shirt combination, my grandmother's voice crept through my chaotic thoughts: *Just because you don't feel good doesn't mean you can't look good.*

Desperate to feel better, I chose my prettiest floral-print dress and hurried out of the house earlier than usual. With enough time to spare, I caught the bus. My wallet was stretched a little too far after accommodating the gas for that site visit.

I took my seat and stared out the window, thinking of all the things I could say to my mom to convince her to leave him.

As if caused by my mood, the clear skies darkened. By the time we reached my stop, the gray clouds had cracked open and rain came pouring down.

I squeezed through to the door, and as soon as my cowboy boot hit the ground, I rushed toward the office. It was a five-minute walk. A three-minute run. But it was three minutes too long.

By the time I stepped inside, I was soaked.

The wet walk of shame to Mr. Carden's office was even worse than I'd expected it to be. Aside from the cold air stinging my dripping skin, the other interns gawked as I walked by. Cedric even spun around in his chair with that awful, smug smile slapped across his face.

But I would not cower and summoned all my grandmother's energy. I pushed out my chest and glided by, despite Cedric's gaze tearing across my every revealed curve. I glanced over my shoulder and delivered a cold stare, sending daggers. He gulped, shifted, and spun toward his laptop screen.

My fake confidence ran out the second I was inside my office. My shoulders fell, and my head dropped. I longed to be dry and safe in my office chair, crouched behind the little divider that would grant me a moment's privacy.

Mr. Carden's eyes flicked upward from his screen, and he took in my appearance. His gaze lingered far less than anyone else's, but I suffered under the weight of it. Embarrassment and self-awareness heated my core. I crossed my arms.

But he didn't stare or say anything to make me feel any worse, only "You should go home and change. It can't be comfortable."

"It's okay." I shivered. "I live forever away. I'm only a little wet."

His dark eyebrows popped up and drew close. He flattened his mouth—something he only did when he was problem-solving. After a beat, he stood and opened the closet in the back corner. With a quick glance my way, he then pulled out an ironed gray shirt. A shade lighter than the one he wore today.

He held it out. "I might have spare pants."

I reached out for the soft, dry fabric and then held it against my body. It landed in the middle of my thighs.

His light brown cheeks reddened, and I bit down on my lip,

stopping myself from smiling. It didn't take much to make him blush.

He spun toward the closet, rummaging through it. He took the shirt I held and exchanged it for a different shirt, which was slightly longer, but not by much.

"No pants. But you can take this." His voice jumped as he spoke while he continued digging, with loud nervous energy, into the depths of the closet. He pulled out a black coat that would go down to my knees.

Unable to resist testing the limits of teasing, I said, "I'll just wear the shirt. It covers all the important bits."

He winced as though he was experiencing pain. "Elizabeth. Please."

"I'm kidding," I said, putting him out of his misery.

He shook his head but offered me his trademark lopsided smile. Victory. Victory. Victory.

I reached for the coat, and his hot hand brushed over mine. A cold shiver danced up my spine, and I almost flinched.

Because I was cold. It must be. It had to be.

He straightened and moved his hand back to his side before scratching his head, then his neck, and then his ear. "Your hands are freezing. You can…um," he said, and swallowed hard before looking away, "take a hot shower downstairs in the basement." He blew out a quick breath. "There's an emergency stairwell out and to your left. It'll take you straight down so you won't have to walk through the office. Um…Yeah." He spun back to his laptop screen and drummed his fingers on the desk.

Lincoln Carden was the most bashful man I'd ever come across. If I changed behind the divider, it may even kill him.

Which was kind of adorable.

"Why do you have so much clothing here? Living out of the office?" I asked.

"Some sites are muddy and dusty, and then the next meeting has me in a politician's office asking them to trust me on a high-risk technical design. It wasn't a good look for me, and they didn't appreciate the mess I'd stomped in." He turned to his closet once more and grabbed a towel before handing it to me. "It's clean."

"Thank you."

Finally, he met my gaze. The office always felt far too intimate when Mr. Carden looked directly at me. There was an intensity behind those dark eyes that held me in place and tugged at my well-kept secrets. If I stayed too long, I'd tell him everything. After living a life avoiding attention, I spent the last few weeks wanting to be perceived by him.

"I'll start bringing in my spare clothing then in preparation for all the site visits you're going to let me do," I said, but it came out as a squeak.

He looked away and gestured to the window behind him where raindrops blurred the view. "Or in preparation for climate change."

Before he could look my way and pin me down with a glance, I spun around and zoomed out of our office. I padded downstairs and found the bathroom in the basement. I locked the door and peeled off the dress that still clung to my skin. After turning on the shower, I stepped inside, warming my cold bones.

Safe from hypothermia, I climbed out and dried off using his cotton towel.

Do I give it back now? Take it home first and wash it? Probably.

The soft black shirt smelled like citrus, but the coat smelled like citrus and something else, sandalwood maybe. Like Mr. Carden. Clean and safe. My hands slipped into the pockets, and I pulled out a lanyard with a conference card attached to it.

Mr. Lincoln Carden—Presenter. Underneath his name was his photo. His hair was the same length with the same unruly, black curls. His deep brown eyes somehow set me at ease and made me nervous beyond my understanding. Based on this, he didn't smile back in 2022 either.

With the cowboy boots on, I was sure this was an outfit that would give my mother a heart attack, but upon seeing my reflection in the full-length mirror…I quite liked it.

When I walked into our office, Mr. Carden's gaze raked along the length of my body.

"Thanks again," I said before clocking the headset he was already wearing. I slipped behind the divider and sent him an email instead.

He replied within seconds.

No prob. Get moving on those corrections. I wanna wrap it
up so we can move onto traffic analysis.

In what had become a comfortable silence between us, I opened the project. I glanced over my shoulder and narrowed my eyes, wishing I could see him. All I heard was furious typing.

When I eventually sent off my design, I heard his email ping on the other side of the divider.

I heard him click through.

And then I heard him sigh.

"That bad?" I yelled, popping up on my side of the divider.

Mr. Carden snapped backward, nearly falling out of his chair. He ripped off his headset, and his hand landed over his heart. "Elizabeth! Don't jump up like that."

"Is it that bad? I heard you sighing."

The frown I always expected crept between his brows. "It's not bad. But it's not done. I don't think we'll get to traffic analysis today."

I resisted the urge to throw myself on the floor and kick my feet like a toddler. I'd worked so hard on it. How was it still wrong? "Permission to come around, sir."

He pressed his lips together. "You don't have to ask for permission."

I circled the divider and stood beside him, glaring at my design. "Will you walk me through the problem? I promised you we'd be the best manager-intern team, and I can't let you down."

He glanced down to my cowboy boots sticking out underneath his long coat but quickly turned his attention back to the design. "Bold," he said, and nodded. "I like it. Let's do it, then." He grabbed his notebook and pen. "I'm going to give you a few pointers and exercises. It's also a great way to keep you busy tomorrow when I'm not around."

"You'll be at that conference?" I asked, and part of me—nay, all of me—wished he'd ask me to join. "Mr. Anders told me about it."

"Uh-huh."

My eyes widened. "I can't believe I'll have to engineer without you."

Lopsided smile.

My heart skipped.

Dammit. Traitorous organ. Behave.

"That's the goal, isn't it?" he said, still making notes. "I'll brief Dade, so any questions you have can go to him. He's not too bad, and if he gives you trouble, let me know and I'll sort him out."

That wasn't meant to be sexy, was it?

I looked away and deflected. "Oh, I'm used to trouble. My current boss has been giving me loads of it since I started."

He broke his focus and glanced upward. "You know what? I'll show you how much of a jerk I can be. Shoo. Back to your desk, menace. Get to work."

He gestured for me to get away, but there was a twitch to his lips and a spark in his gorgeous eyes that confirmed my suspicions that Mr. Carden had a sense of humor, and he seemed to do his best trying to hide it.

"Suuuuure." I stretched out the word and let a wide smile spread across my face. I fell into my chair. I was facing the divider and could still imagine his every expression.

His head peeked out over the top. "Okay, I'll be a jerk. Today, you're getting a grilled cheese instead of a chicken salad."

"I love a grilled cheese." I spun around and opened the drawing on my laptop.

The tut of his tongue carried over the divider. "You're too easy to please."

I sighed and mumbled underneath my breath. "The guys on Spark disagree."

An IM popped up.

L. Carden: The guys on Spark suck. Now, get to work.

I stared at his message for at least thirty seconds. Even though we'd been emailing, seeing an IM with such casual language from Mr. Carden took me right back to my conversations with Link.

And I had the sudden, deep urge to text him and ask him to help me sort through my thoughts.

Because there was never anyone else I wanted to share my secrets with.

Not until Lincoln Carden walked into me and into my life.

15

ELIZABETH

[80 weeks ago]

@pancakesareelite:
How would you go about convincing
someone to divorce the man they love
because you know they're evil?

@theanswerisno:
You always find the weirdest
simulation games to play

@pancakesareelite:
I wish it were a game

@theanswerisno:
If it was, how would you deal with it?

@pancakesareelite:
I think I'd log out and pretend it
doesn't exist.

@theanswerisno:
Sometimes that's okay

My clothing had dried by the end of the workday, but I wasn't ready to change out of Mr. Carden's shirt and coat. It was warm, worn in, and made me feel…safe. At least, what I assumed safety felt like.

The sunset cast a golden pathway toward the bus shelter, and I was lost in my thoughts about Mr. Carden while walking, waiting, and climbing on the bus. He'd been open, and helpful, and… wonderful.

Fine. I've developed a tiny crush on my boss. The tiniest of crushes. Nothing harmful. Nothing illegal. Just the smallest little flutter in my stomach every time he looked my way, or kind of smiled, or grabbed a ruler or…breathed. Totally normal behavior.

With great difficulty, I pushed these thoughts to the back of my mind, where they belonged.

I climbed out at my stop. A familiar voice called out, as if jumping from another corner of my brain. A corner I'd cordoned off. "Elizabeth."

I ignored it.

"Elizabeth," he said again. "Come on. We can chat, can't we? You're looking lovely as ever."

I kept moving. I dug my hands into the pocket of this coat, ignoring my fast-beating heart, and found my keys.

Footsteps followed. "Mr. Gordon-Bettencourt would like to talk to you."

"Leave me alone." I beelined for the stairwell, grabbed the railing, and jogged up.

Alistair kept following.

With my key ready, I shoved it in the lock the second I reached my door.

"I said, Mr. Gordon-Bettencourt would like to talk to you."

"Well, I don't want to talk to him," I snapped, spinning around and finally taking him in.

Alistair was now a thirtysomething-year-old man I'd once fumbled around with as an inexperienced and inebriated teenager. No part of me had expected he would end up working for the GB empire, but I should have known. Everyone in their circle was there by nepotism. "You don't get to say no to him."

I clenched my fists, and my nails poked into my palms. "No," I spat. "*You* don't get to say no to him. But I do. Run home to your boss and tell him that I said he can go to hell."

Without waiting for a response, I slipped inside and slammed the door shut. I locked it and paced the short distance to the sink and back. My heart hammered in my chest, and the grilled cheese I'd enjoyed at lunch threatened to come up.

I grabbed my phone and navigated to my mother's name. There was nothing new. No warning. No explanation.

What did Douglas want?

What could he possibly want from me? He's got everything. He's got my mother.

I entered and exited her chat. I hit the call icon, and after a few rings, it went to voicemail. I tried again. What would I even say to her? It's not like she could get him to leave me alone.

I shrugged off Mr. Carden's coat and slipped out of his shirt. I kicked off the boots and, wearing nothing but my underwear, I climbed into bed and pulled the covers over my head.

My breath steamed up my phone's screen, but I felt safe in here. I scrolled down to my grandmother's name and called.

No answer.

A message popped up from Link.

```
@thenaswerisno:
Where are you?
I thought we were playing tonight.
```

@pancakesareelite:
I can't.

Within a second, three dots appeared. He was already typing.

> **@theanswerisno:**
> No problem. Everything okay?

Without thinking, my fingers were moving.

@pancakesareelite:
I'm not in a good place tonight. I'm
going through something with my mom and
stepdad.

> **@theanswerisno:**
> What do you need? Are you safe?

@pancakesareelite:
For now. I don't want to talk about it
just yet. Not tonight.

> **@theanswerisno:**
> Let me know what you need. I can listen.
> I can talk. I could send you nudes.

@pancakesareelite:
Nudes?!

Seconds later, about six images of different shades of nude filled our chat. I burst out laughing despite the tears bunching at the corners of my eyes.

> **@theanswerisno:**
> There's more where that came from ;)

Feeling more like myself, I sent another message.

@pancakesareelite:
I know I said I didn't want to talk
about it but…my stepdad is awful.
Really, really awful and he wants to see
me and it's a little scary.

@theanswerisno:
If you ever need me to come and get you,
just say the word. Okay?

@pancakesareelite:
And reveal your super-secret identity?
Is this where I find out you're like a
prince or something?

Or…an engineer working at Simucon?

@theanswerisno:
The prince of Genovia, but to protect my
royal privacy, his highness shall wear a
full body suit and mask and won't say a
word.

@theanswerisno:
Although, on second thought, please
don't trust anyone in a full body suit
and mask. Especially one who isn't saying anything.

@pancakesareelite:
Link. I need you to know that I'm
laughing. And it feels really good.
Thank you.

@theanswerisno:
Main quest achieved.
Side quest: In progress.

@pancakesareelite:
What's your side quest?

> **@theanswerisno:**
> I'm buttering you up so you can play
> Starlight with me.

@pancakesareelite:
-_-

@pancakesareelite:
Fine.

Despite my protestations, I was glad he asked. *Starlight* was exactly the game I needed. And I should have trusted Link would know that.

Link. Link-in. Lincoln.

Gah.

Yes, they were both engineers. It was possible, sure. If I was smarter, I would calculate the odds. The only person who I knew who could calculate those odds was Mr. Carden, and well, I wasn't going to ask him.

My anxiety-filled mind was playing tricks on me. This was my Link, and I couldn't risk losing him.

> **@theanswerisno:**
> How bad are you feeling?

@pancakesareelite:
I'm fine for now. Thanks for your
concern.

> **@theanswerisno:**
> I'm only concerned because playing
> anything against me will definitely make
> you feel worse about yourself.

Ha. Mean. And I told him so.

@theanswerisno:
Let's play. But if I stop replying, it
means I've fallen asleep and have not
abandoned you.

Beggars can't be choosers. Right now, all I wanted was to forget about Alistair and Douglas and even the heartache attached to my mom. So, I let myself be immersed in the one hour and forty-two minutes I spent hunting with Link before he stopped replying. There was no part of me that doubted he'd fallen asleep because if there was one person in the entire universe I was sure would never abandon me, it was Link.

16

LINCOLN

[79 weeks ago]

@theanswerisno:
I'm not going to tell you that.

                        @pancakesareelite:
                        You have trust issues

@theanswerisno:
I do. Does that bother you?

                        @pancakesareelite:
                        No, I have them too

I'd fallen asleep playing games with Lily. It wasn't the first time, and I hoped it wouldn't be the last. She was different last night. Something was wrong, and part of me wanted to throw our aliases away and talk. I wanted to be there for her, but we'd been doing this dangerous evasive dance for so long that I worried a single misstep would ruin everything.

By the time I arrived in LA, I wished I'd slept more and worn less.

It was hotter than I'd anticipated, and I was wearing a long-sleeved shirt with a tie. On top of that, my nerves were climbing. I rubbed my palms across my black chinos and finally hopped out of my truck.

It wasn't the presentation I was worried about. These conferences often came with a lot of new faces and forced interaction, which I mentally had to prepare for.

I grabbed my backpack and swung it across my shoulders before making my way to the hotel where the conference was being held.

As soon as I stepped inside, the air-conditioning chilled me to my core. My options were sweating outside or goose bumps inside. I made my way to the welcome desk, where a woman with auburn hair in a tight bun sat.

"Welcome to the International Conference on Traffic and Transportation Engineering. Do you have a ticket?"

I spoke, but nothing came out of my dry throat. Swallowing, I tried again, summoning the persona I'd mastered after years of being in the industry. My now-steely gaze met hers. "Dr. Lincoln Carden, here to present at four p.m. this afternoon."

Her smile widened. "Dr. Carden." She leafed through the box of lanyards. She grabbed the one with my name and face on it and, with her other hand, grabbed a tote bag. "Here you go. The details for your presentation are on the program inside with some other goodies, as well as your room card."

I took the bag and thanked her before slipping the lanyard over my head and turning the card to face in.

According to the program, I'd be presenting in the Ruby Room.

With my gaze floorward, I squeezed through the crowd. It had grown since the last time I attended a few years ago, the first year after finishing my PhD. There were a few faces I recognized on my way to the Ruby Room. A handful from SDSU, a few from UCLA, and, other than me, no one else from Simucon.

I couldn't help but wonder whether Elizabeth would have wanted to be here.

Who was I kidding? Of course she would. Her gray eyes flashed through my mind, eager to learn. She'd be bouncing around from session to session wishing she could clone herself and attend them all.

Without intending to, my mind slipped toward the image of her walking into our office yesterday. Her wet dress clinging to her every curve was something I actively had to remind myself not to think about. In hindsight, giving her my coat was more for me than it was for her.

But seeing her in my much-too-big clothing did something to me too.

An almost-painful heat pulled through me. Perhaps I needed the AC. Even without being around, Elizabeth would be the reason I lost complete control over my body's temperature.

I shoved her from the forefront of my mind, but that only meant she got comfortable at the back. She clearly had no intention of leaving.

I focused on the task at hand and managed to get to the venue I'd be presenting in. There was a session in progress, so I stayed near the door at the top of the stairs and studied the area.

The room wasn't intimidatingly large. I'd presented in larger, but it still meant a maximum of one hundred people could be attending. Although knowing how these sessions often went, I'd predict closer to eighty.

I made my way over to the Emerald Room, where Professor Hahn would be presenting in the next session. I slipped into one of the seats and waited.

When Hahn took the stage, I was transported back to my university days. I learned almost all of my presentation tricks from her.

An engineer I once feared had become familiar over many years of polishing a PhD thesis together.

Professor Hahn's face split into a smile when she spotted me, and I knew I'd have to linger afterward for a chat before I could get to my room.

"I was worried you weren't going to come." She pulled me in for a hug. I hadn't anticipated the physical affection but should have.

"Nearly didn't." I awkwardly patted her back.

She released me. "I have to keep an eye on you. I was gearing up to present your work on your behalf."

"You still can," I teased. "I could sit in the audience and ask all the questions I wasn't able to answer."

She cackled and slapped me on the shoulder. "Oh, it's good to see you haven't changed." She brushed her hair out of her face. She was only in her mid-fifties, but she was almost completely gray. She used to joke that engineering was to blame.

I didn't think it was a joke.

"For anyone else, I might have. But these young engineers need the formidable Dr. Carden."

I shifted on my feet and glanced sideward. She always complimented me. I never knew what to do with it. I shoved the compliment to the back of my mind. Her kind words could reside with Elizabeth in the part of my brain housing all the things that made me feel good but confused.

Professor Hahn checked her smartwatch. "Oh! I want to chat with you about a life-changing idea I have, but not now. Professor Van Zyl is in town and wants to grab a coffee. You're welcome to join us."

My face must have given me away because my professor chuckled. "He reminds me of you. Anyway, I'll be in your session."

"Sure," I said with a curt nod, and escaped before she could invite me to more things. It was her life's mission to introduce me to every transport engineer in the world. I was certain we'd already conquered North America.

I hurried up to my room and set the temperature to exactly what I needed it to be before throwing myself face down on the soft duvet.

Now all I needed to do was kill time until my session.

Despite the nerves, I didn't need to practice my presentation. I'd worked on that research for years. I knew it better than anyone and could recite it in my sleep.

I could work. Elizabeth had sent me a million emails, and after the last few days of working together, I could hear them in her voice when I read them. I could see exactly what she'd look like. She had the slightest frown line between her perfect brows when receiving critique on her designs. Her eyes would narrow when she pushed back. And then there was that easy smile whenever she saw an opening for a joke—which was often. She'd bite down on her bottom lip when she focused and…

Be professional. Be professional. Be professional.

I needed a release. Or a distraction.

And there was only one person who could distract me from Elizabeth. One person who managed to make me laugh and question my every thought.

I swapped out my work laptop for my gaming laptop.

```
@theanswerisno:
What are you up to?
```

17

LINCOLN

[78 weeks ago]

> **@pancakesareelite:**
> How do you make friends?

@theanswerisno:
Accidentally

> **@pancakesareelite:**
> That doesn't help me

@theanswerisno:
Well, you accidentally became my
friend. Didn't that help?

> **@pancakesareelite:**
> More than you'll ever know

Instead of preparing for my presentation or attending other sessions, I hid away in my room and lost myself to a few hours of gaming. With every click and every pixelated arrow released, my anxiety lessened until all I could think of was how much gold I'd make in-game after selling everything I'd found.

But I'd had to do it without Lily, which hindered my enjoyment by at least thirty-five percent.

I never double-texted anyone unless it was an emergency, but with Lily, it always felt welcomed. I sent her another message, despite my previous one being unread.

```
@theanswerisno:
Caught THE golden beetle while hunting.
Would consider trading it for your
presence. Ps. Are you okay? Been
thinking about you lots.
```

If I could unsend it, I would. *Aaaaahhhhhhh.* Regret flooded my stomach.

The platform we chatted on didn't allow message deletion. I shoved my phone face down, feeling a little exposed, vulnerable, and then all at once, stupid too.

Every now and then, something in my brain would snap and remind me that Lily, while a real human being, was not *real*.

She wasn't real enough to be here. To attend events with me. I couldn't see her or hear her voice. I couldn't, maybe, kiss her.

I shut my eyes and ran a hand over my face. *Why am I thinking about this?*

My phone buzzed, and I grabbed it at a speed fast enough to almost send it flying out of my grip.

Not Lily. It was the Game Night group chat.

```
Rose Marie Jones (SDSU Board Game Society):
@Lincoln come down to the parking area.
```

I should probably update the way I saved their contacts all those years ago.

I texted back: I'm in LA. Didn't Claire tell you?

Claire: So are we.

Shaun Ashdern (Rose's coworker): I hate that I'm missing out :(

What? I replied.

William Ashdern (Shaun's brother): @Shaun sucks to be you. Hey @Lincoln, come get us. We have no idea where to go. This place is filled with people who look really smart.

I left my room and walked downstairs in a complete haze. They couldn't really be here, could they? This was all some elaborate prank.

But when I stepped outside, Rose, Dean, William, and Claire were there. Waving. Smiling.

My mouth dropped open. "Hey?" With my brain attempting to process the situation, my hand managed a small return wave. "What are you doing here?" A grin crept onto my face. I wasn't an idiot. There was no other reason they could be at this conference, but I still needed to hear them say it. I wouldn't believe it otherwise.

"Here to watch your presentation. Duh," Claire said.

"I may fall asleep, but that's only because I was up all night working on *Overpower*," William said.

"But he only needs, like, a twenty-minute nap. He's like a giraffe," Rose chimed in.

"In more ways than one," I added.

This elicited a giggle from Rose. "You know, we've always wanted to see you present but you never tell us in time." She lifted her tote bag. "By the way, I wasn't sure if us plebs were allowed in since we're not engineers, so I have a hard hat and a reflective vest just in case."

More PPE than Elizabeth, I thought to myself, and chuckled. "Why do you own this?"

"I dressed as Builder Barbie for a party once," she replied. "Do I need to gear up?"

Not at all surprising.

I shook my head. "The public is welcome, but it's not often anyone wants to pay and register to hear us talk about concrete and trains."

"Sounds thrilling," Claire said. "But tell me you have a swanky hotel room with room service?"

"I sure do," I replied.

I led them inside and chatted with reception about getting them registered, and then we went upstairs to my room.

William went straight to the desk and set up his laptop beside mine. "We could jam a quick game if you wanted?"

"William." Rose playfully whacked him over the head. "Why would we drive all the way here to watch you play games? Besides, he might need to prepare for his presentation. Pretend we're not here. Or use us as a practice audience."

I chuckled and woke my laptop from sleep mode. "I'd have picked the game, but this thing's about to die, and I forgot my—"

"Charger," they said together.

I shrugged, heat rising to my cheeks. My devices were always dead or dying, and I hadn't realized they'd noticed this.

A message popped up on-screen.

> **@pancakesareelite:**
> THE beetle? Oh, please give it to me. I
> can't play now though, I'm heading out.
> I'll be free later. Much, much later.

She sounded like herself again. I typed a reply without waiting a second: I'll keep the beetle. I caught it for you.

Unsure of how tonight'll go. You might be on your
own, Pancakes.

> @pancakesareelite:
> Boooring.
> It's way more fun when you're involved.

Blood rushed to my ears. Claire squeaked beside me, her gaze fixed on my screen.

"Don't," I said to her, and before I could reply to Lily, my gaming laptop died. I grabbed my phone, but it was dead too. I grumbled and shoved my laptop into my backpack, enviously looking at William, who still had power.

Before Claire could say anything about what she'd seen, I put my phone on charge and changed the topic. "How's the *Overpower* LAN planning coming along?"

William spun on his chair and faced us. "Oh, it's awesome. I posted the details for the LAN event about an hour ago." His smile was wide, and his dimple deep. "Please repost and share, and do whatever you need to do. We want a big turnout. The event of the century."

"That is *a lot* to ask from a LAN," Dean said, and was met by unimpressed stares. As the only non-gamer in the group, he must be used to this.

Rose hopped over to William's side. "Dean's right. It's a bunch of nerds getting together to play a game. Maybe you should lower your expectations."

"Let me rephrase," William said, and I couldn't help but notice how his arm curled around Rose's waist with such ease. "I want it to be the gamer event of the century. Every gamer we know on this side of the world needs to attend."

William's words struck that already worn chord in my head.

"Every gamer?" I mumbled to myself.

"Do you think Lily will come?" Claire asked, reading my glitching mind.

My stomach dropped. "Uhhhhhh…"

"We've spoken about this before. Did you not consider it?" Claire twisted and glanced at my face.

"Uhhhh…" Words escaped me. Thoughts escaped me. Lily could be there. Lily *would* be there.

"Would you know who she is?" Dean asked without looking up from his phone.

"Uhhhh…"

Say something useful.

But would I? Would she know who I was? Had I ever described myself to her? My avatar was a pixelated beloved fictional character.

"What does she look like? I'll keep an eye out," Rose said.

Everyone knew I chatted with a woman online while gaming. All of a sudden, in front of these people who had real relationships, it felt rather childish.

But they were waiting for me to say something. I sucked in a deep breath. "I don't know. Probably not." I exhaled and should have been relieved. But I wasn't. Everything inside me was twisting.

"If she registers and logs in using her gamertag, I'll be able to see which station she'll be gaming at." William lifted his dark eyebrows at me. "If you want to know."

"I don't," I said quickly, unsure if it was true. It was. I think.

"I know you've said you don't want to meet her, but don't you even want to know who she is, like, from a distance?" Claire asked, trying to make eye contact with me, but I resisted.

I shook my head.

"Do you think she's a weirdo? Will it break the fantasy you have of her?" Claire asked.

A scoff broke out of me. "It'll ruin the impression she has about *me*." I huffed out a breath and hopped to my feet with an energy I didn't know what to do with. "I'm the weirdo. I'm nothing like the person I've portrayed myself to be."

"Lincoln," Claire started.

My stomach churned, and I ran a hand through my hair. "No, don't. You don't get it. None of you get it. Claire, you have a warmth people take to. Rose? You're an anomaly; people trust you within seconds. Children who aren't even sick want to see Dean"— I pointed at him, and then my finger swerved to William—"and don't get me started on that unlawful charmer."

They froze. Like my words had snapped a photograph of this moment, and we'd all be trapped there because I hadn't fully explained myself. But I wasn't good at this. I didn't know how to explain it. So I kept rambling. "Claire was forced to be my friend growing up. Then she forced me on you guys too. If it wasn't for her, would we even be friends?"

Claire stood, but I continued. "No, we wouldn't. Because I don't know how to make friends. I don't know how to do this…" I gestured between us, but my movements were jerky. I shoved my hands into my pockets. "I'm really bad at it, which is obviously why I've never been in a real relationship."

"I wasn't *forced*," Claire said, a deep frown forming on her face.

"Right now, I can plan my responses. I can think about them. I can backspace. But in real life? She'll see how incredibly awkward I am and…" I turned around, not wanting to talk about this anymore. "And she'll be disappointed."

The sympathy on their faces let me know how pathetic I must have sounded.

"I need some air. I'm fine, okay?" I walked out of the hotel room and meandered through the hallway, dodging other engineers who may or may not recognize me. I went down to the pool area, but it was too full of people.

I slipped into the emergency stairwell and went up. And kept going up and up until I reached the roof.

As I pushed open the heavy metal door, a fresh breeze slapped against my heated face, followed by the thick and heavy stench of cigarette smoke.

Regret curled inside me.

I wish I could rewind to before my outburst and erase it. How was I supposed to face them now?

Someone with their head down low stepped onto the roof. Judging from their height, it was Rose, or a child.

She marched toward me. "Hey."

"Hey." I took a breath, preparing my apology.

But before I could say anything, her knuckles slammed right in my gut.

I doubled over, clutching my stomach. "What?" I coughed, catching my breath even though her punches weren't that hard.

She angled her head to look at me properly. "How dare you insinuate we aren't friends?" She threw another punch, and I jumped backward, but she ran up to me with her tiny, powerful fists. "How dare you insinuate we don't know and love you as you are?" Another punch.

Dodged it.

"Rose," I started.

She grunted. "You're my friend, Lincoln. And I love my friends. And I know Claire is your best friend, and well, she's one of mine too." She threw another punch, but this time I caught her hand.

I'd never seen her this furious.

She wrenched it back. "So are Neema and Shaun, and guess what, you are not just my friend—you're one of my best friends. I will be so mad if you don't feel the same way about me. If I was ever in trouble, I'd call *you* before I called Claire, because she's a terrible driver."

This time, her punch landed because I'd been distracted by the laughter bubbling out of me. "She is awful." My body shook so hard that I struggled to breathe.

"But don't tell her I said that," Rose replied, bursting into a fit of giggles. "She'll be so angry." She finally dropped her fists of fury.

We kept laughing, and with each inhale, our laughter grew louder until I worried it would be heard in the presentations below.

"You'd call William first, wouldn't you?" I asked.

"William? Are you out of your mind? He'd kill everyone in his path to get to me, including possibly himself."

I stumbled backward and fell onto my backside, the last of the laughter still squeezing out of me. Rose attempted to pull me up but failed miserably and ended up beside me on the hot concrete.

Footsteps sounded behind us. I turned around as Claire whacked me across the head. "I heard all of that, you idiots."

"When did this group become so violent?" I asked, rubbing my scalp, though it didn't hurt.

"You're Claire's emergency contact, too, because I'm terrible with my phone when I'm at the hospital," Dean said, stretching out a hand to pull me up.

"Shaun's mine, but now I think I should change it to Lincoln." William lifted Rose to her feet and pulled her against his chest.

"Even though you don't talk much"—Claire nudged me—"we're listening when you do."

I looked down at my feet and mumbled, "I'm sorry for not noticing."

The adrenaline seeped out of me, clearing my mind and leaving me shuddering.

"Not entirely your fault. I've been neglecting you a little," Claire said. "Dean and Hannah have been preoccupying me."

"As they should," I said, and smiled. I never wanted Claire to feel guilty about being happy. "You don't have to worry about me."

Claire came closer and whispered, "I do worry…a lot. But I'm a worrier. One thing I'm not worried about is whether you'll find someone. Maybe Lily is the one. URL to IRL is a less popular romance trope, but it's a pretty good one."

Maybe Lily is the one.

I'd had that thought multiple times over the last few years.

"I'm scared," I breathed, my stomach sinking at the admission.

"It's okay to be. If it's not her, it'll be someone else. You'll find your person, Lincoln. Someone who understands you. Who sees you."

Despite the secrets and evasiveness, I knew that, on some level, Lily saw me. She always knew what I needed.

Unprovoked, my mind jumped to the divider in my office, to the subtle changes Elizabeth had made to increase my comfort. A strange guilt crept in but was quickly overpowered by a new and different feeling…one that recurred with every thought of Elizabeth. Which was happening more and more.

And there was nothing I could do to stop it.

18

ELIZABETH

[77 weeks ago]

@pancakesareelite:
Sometimes I don't think I'm smart
enough to be an engineer

@theanswerisno:
Nonsense

@pancakesareelite:
I mean it.

@theanswerisno:
I mean it when I say NONSENSE

@theanswerisno:
We don't talk about the engineering
stuff often, but when we do, I can see
you're smart. Your gaming strategies
are smart. Smart mouth, too

@pancakesareelite:
If I ever find you, I'm keeping you.
Finder's keepers and all that.

@theanswerisno:
That's a little creepy

In a strange twist of fate, I was on my way to Los Angeles.

Mr. Anders had told me, in the nicest way possible, that there was very little for me to do without Mr. Carden around, and I may as well attend his presentation and learn something.

Ignoring the passive-aggressiveness, I'd leaped at the offer.

The familiar buildings came into view, and I was transported to a different life. LA had been my home since I was a child. I barely remembered the life we had before my mom married Douglas. And I wished I could forget a lot of it since then.

I willed his image out of my mind and pulled into the parking lot. Nothing made me feel faster than reaching my destination before the estimated time on Google Maps.

I exited the app and checked my notifications. One voice note. Gran. I hit play and let her voice fill my car.

"Lily, I'm sorry I missed your call. I think I may have reached the maximum amount of turmeric I should be having. I fell asleep earlier than usual and only woke up now. Pity. Really. A younger version of your grandpa had just entered the dream, and I could have used a few extra minutes. Anyway, call me when you can. Love you."

My head dropped backward with a laugh before I sent her a voice message letting her know I'd call her tonight.

I sent another message, this time to my mom: I'm in LA. Maybe I could see you later?

There was a slim chance she'd reply. She hadn't been answering my calls either. I didn't know what else to do except text and hope for the best. Douglas was probably having one of his anger episodes or maybe a love-bombing episode—either would keep her occupied.

Ignoring the longing in my chest, I scanned through the other notifications. *@wheretheresawilliam*'s channel was flooded with messages. I scrolled up and up until I found out what the noise was about. *@wheretheresawilliam* had finally announced the promised LAN for his and *@theresarose*'s video game. A wonderful mixture of pride and excitement burst through me as if I knew these people. Sometimes it felt as though these online connections meant more than my real-life relationships.

It seemed as though everyone else felt that way too. Hundreds of replies filled the chat and more were coming.

Strangely, *@theanswerisno* didn't say anything. He hadn't even reacted to the announcement. Maybe he hadn't seen it yet.

The timestamp on his last message to me wasn't that long ago. Although he did say he was busy. Possibly even too busy to play with me tonight.

But it begged the question: If he wasn't going…was that a good or bad thing?

My heart fluttered wildly. I knew what I wanted. I wanted to meet Link. I wanted to be able to hear his voice and see his face when he said these ridiculous things. I wanted…There was so much I wanted from him. It was almost unfair.

But what if I went and was faced with Mr. Carden? What would I do?

The heart fluttering turned to panic.

I swapped over to my email app. There was nothing from Mr. Carden after I'd let him know I'd be coming to the conference. Either he felt no need to acknowledge my email or he was also too busy.

Was it a coincidence that both he and Link were busy tonight?

You're reaching, Lily. Settle down.

With a deep breath, I made my way over to the hotel's main entrance. Behind me, there was a line of cars looking for parking. I seemed to have snagged the last spot. You'd think a transportation and traffic conference would have ensured enough parking spaces for the anticipated number of attendees.

Security took one look at my Simucon pass and let me in. I grabbed the two-day program, scanning for the surname seared in my mind.

4 p.m. Ruby Room.

A number of other sessions drew my attention. There were talks on pedestrian-oriented development, high-speed rail, and so many other topics I had spent hours researching. But my pass only allowed access for today, and there was no way I was missing Mr. Carden's presentation.

I could possibly attend another talk after his. Maybe, just maybe, he'd want to join me.

My mind flooded with images of us sitting side by side in the auditorium. He'd definitely have insight into each of the speakers, and I bet I could get him to laugh out loud. He'd be a little mad, but not really. Maybe we'd grab coffee after. Maybe we'd choose to stay here overnight. Maybe…

Heat rushed through my veins at the thought of it.

"Elizabeth," someone yelled.

I looked up and resisted the urge to sigh. "Matthew, hi."

Matthew, a burly man with a brain as big as he was, pulled me in for a hug. "Fancy finding you here. I didn't know you were still an engineer."

"What do you mean?"

He shrugged. "Dunno."

I smiled, hoping it softened the bitterness in my voice. "Did you hear something about me?"

"Nah. But you know…"

I did know, but I still hated it. Before I could defend myself and remind him that my relation to Douglas Gordon-Bettencourt doesn't determine my career, his gaze dropped down to my chest.

No, down to my lanyard.

His mouth fell open. "Why do you have a Simucon pass?"

I lifted my chin. "I'm part of their graduate internship."

"No way." His bright blue gaze met mine. "How?"

"I applied."

"So did I."

I shrugged. "That sucks. I'm sorry."

His face reddened, and he scoffed. "Be honest. Did your dad help you out?"

Every time someone threw that at me, I wished I could say something and put them in their place, but it never worked. I always froze.

Matthew tutted and smiled, as if he'd hit the bull's-eye. "Well, whatever. They only take two people from the internship, and everyone else gets tossed. By then, none of the other firms will want to hire you because they already have enough graduates on their plate."

I blocked everything he said from my brain. I did not need that on top of all the stressors already ruining me.

Beyond Matthew's head, a far-too-familiar face caught my attention. And I couldn't place him. Dark hair, dark eyes, and a sharp nose. He looked at me but there was no recognition in his gaze.

He slipped into the Ruby Room, which reminded me: I needed to get in there too.

"I have to go. I can't miss this talk," I said, and walked off.

But Matthew followed. "Same. Dr. Carden's research inspired mine."

"He's my boss." I bit on my lip, resisting the smug smile threatening to burst onto my face.

Even if I didn't get the job at Simucon, Matthew's crumpled expression made it all worth it.

I took a seat as far away from Matthew as possible and stared at the empty podium. In a few minutes, *Doctor* Lincoln Carden would be up there. I couldn't imagine it. He was so quiet. How would he speak loudly enough to command this room?

Looking around, I recognized one lecturer and one old class-mate. The dark-haired man was seated a few rows in front of me.

Did we study together? Did we hook up? I'd have remembered that…Maybe we matched on a dating app.

He stood and twisted, revealing a Pokémon T-shirt. He waved at someone. Two people joined him. One of them, a brown-skinned woman who looked oddly familiar too.

Hold on.

Was that *@wheretheresawilliam*? What was he doing here?

Was he an engineer?

No. He was a full-time game developer.

But he could have studied engineering.

No, I'd read an article about him. He studied computer science. Unless…

My head snapped toward the stage. Could it be?

@wheretheresawilliam and *@theanswerisno* were always friendly…Really friendly. Link was the one who introduced me to *@wheretheresawilliam*'s streams. Could they be friends in real life?

I shook my head again.

Was he here for Mr. Carden? Here for *@theanswerisno*? Here for Link?

At that exact moment, Lincoln Carden took the stage, his chin raised high, his wide shoulders squared. Every thought escaped me and was replaced only by his strong, calm presence.

He pushed his glasses up the bridge of his nose and dipped his gaze to the podium, where I was sure he had notes ready. He'd prob-ably anticipated everyone's questions too.

"Good afternoon, everyone." He glanced upward, and his gaze met mine.

I couldn't help but grin and offer him a double thumbs-up.

Then he smiled.

Not the half-lopsided one I was used to. A full smile. *Milestone unlocked.*

He was happy to see me.

My traitorous heart fluttered as though it had grown wings.

"I'm Dr. Lincoln Carden," he said. His voice was still quiet like it always was but somehow he managed to capture everyone. "Listen closely, because I'm only going to say this once, and if you ask me a question I've answered in my presentation, I will call you out for it."

Mr. Carden was handsome and unintentionally sexy, but Dr. Carden was something else. I didn't expect the sass. It tickled me. Blood crept to my cheeks and I was grateful for the darkened room.

A few latecomers shuffled in and filled the gaps. His session was almost at full capacity. He straightened his tie and clicked through to his first slide.

THERE IS NO AMOUNT OF MONEY THAT COULD JUSTIFY THE LOSS OF LIFE.

"If you disagree with that, this presentation isn't for you." He walked across the stage and eyed the crowd, who remained seated.

He launched into the intricacies of his work and I was fixated. If my mouth was open, I'd have to mop up my drool.

There was something so incredibly powerful about him up there. A deep wanting spread throughout my entire body. I was in big, big trouble here.

And it wasn't only because of his deep voice or large, capable hands. With every passing word and well-timed joke, my admiration grew more and more until I could barely stand it. I considered fleeing. But how would I explain that to him? Or Mr. Anders? I could pretend to get sick.

But he'd probably worry about me.

"Thank you. That's it from me." Lincoln's deep, serious voice grabbed my attention. He bowed his head and gestured to the slide on-screen, which read: *You've got questions? I've got answers. Ask away, but do remember my warning.*

He was so incredibly impressive, I clapped my hands together. Thankfully, at the very last second, I managed to stop myself from giving him a standing ovation. Another woman near the front joined in, and soon the entire hall filled with the cacophony of applause.

This was my chance to make a swift escape. I hopped up, and before I could spin around, his brown gaze met mine.

And he smiled again.

That smile.

Even if I wanted to leave, I couldn't. Even if every logical cell in my body told me to, I was frozen, clinging to every second of attention he gave me.

A group of engineers flocked around him, and I hung back, waiting my turn. I glanced over my shoulder to where the dark-haired man had sat. If it was *@wheretheresawilliam*, he was gone now.

When Matthew approached Mr. Carden, I stepped closer, giving in to my petty feelings and mimicking the smugness he'd shown me earlier.

"That was amazing," I said.

"Thank you and thank you for the uncomfortable applause. They don't usually clap at the end of presentations." His smile was now on show for me and everyone around here to see. They had no idea how lucky they were or how hard I'd worked for it.

"They should," I said.

"I do wonder how my intern could be in LA and simultaneously finish all the work I left behind for her."

"Mr. Anders said I could come." I grinned. "Work can be done on weekends."

Matthew opened his mouth, but Mr. Carden didn't even seem to notice. With all the unnecessary aggression of a mediocre white man, he pushed past me, and I stumbled forward, bumping into Mr. Carden.

He caught me, his hot hands sending a shiver up my spine. My legs nearly gave in. "Sorry," I said with a nervous giggle, and took a step backward. "Actually, I'm not sorry. Now we're even since you bumped into me last time."

"It's not fair. I didn't leave lipstick on your shirt," he replied, and his gaze dipped to my mouth before traveling lower to where my breast pocket might be.

My heart was beating so hard that I wondered if he could see it. "I don't understand," I said, and glanced away. This time it was me who couldn't hold eye contact. "You seem different here."

He looked down at the floor. "I like conferences. A merging of minds…" He shuffled on his feet more like the awkward boss I'd come to know. "Are you sticking around?"

I wanted to. Speaking to Mr. Carden outside of the office was exhilarating. I wanted more of it. I wondered what he did at home, what he wore, what movies he liked watching. I didn't just want Mr. Carden.

I wanted Lincoln too. Because it wasn't just a crush…it was something bigger. Something I was struggling to ignore.

Panic struck, slamming me back down to earth. "No," I said, hating each word as it left my mouth. "I can't stay. I have to go."

Because if I didn't, I'd throw the internship away for a chance with him. One night. One moment. One kiss.

But that would jeopardize everything I'd worked so hard for.

I'd promised myself. My mom. My gran.

Lily, don't fall in love with your boss.

19

ELIZABETH

[74 weeks ago]

@pancakesareelite:
Do you flirt with all the girls you
play games with?

>   **@theanswerisno:**
>   I don't flirt with any of the girls I
>   play games with

@pancakesareelite:
Wait, what? You're always
complimenting me.

>   **@theanswerisno:**
>   I'm always telling the truth

>   **@theanswerisno:**
>   Oh. I see how that could be flirtatious

@pancakesareelite:
No backsies

As soon as I was sure my car door was shut, I checked my phone. Nothing from my mom. I wished I could talk to her right now.

Instead, I called my grandmother.

"Lily, love," she said upon answering, her voice coming through my stereo.

"Gran, I think my long-time internet crush might actually be my boss," I rambled out in one long breath.

"The boy you play games with? Well, what are the odds of that?"

"Probably just above zero. And now that I've said it out loud, I hear how ridiculous it sounds."

She burst out laughing, and I could picture the twinkle of mischief in her eyes. "Don't doubt your gut that easily, my darling. Nothing is impossible."

"No. It isn't. I mean…Yes, it could be. No. I…" My hands curled around the steering wheel at the mere thought of Link and Lincoln.

"What's the problem?" she asked. "I think it would be wonderful. You keep telling me how handsome your boss is."

"W-when did I say that?" My stammer rendered me guilty of her accusation. "That's beside the point. Didn't you hear me? He's my boss, Gran. My boss. I report to him."

"Makes for some interesting dynamics in the bedroom."

"Elizabeth Gray!" I yelled her full name like my mother used to yell mine when I was in trouble. Laughter burst out of me as I made it onto the highway.

"Hold on, hold on. Let me make a cup of tea." The bed groaned in the background. "I want the whole story, but most importantly, I want to know this: Do you want it to be him?"

I opened my mouth, and the answer bottled up in my throat. Before I could say anything, panic prickled my chest. "I…I don't think I should actually talk about him or either of them. I just needed to tell someone, and unfortunately for you, I tell you everything because Mom doesn't answer my texts or calls. Now I've said it, and I never have to think about it again because it could ruin everything."

"How?"

The panic grew, spreading with each spoken word. "If it isn't him, then I'd have embarrassed myself in front of my gorgeous and incredible boss. If it is him, there's a chance Link doesn't like the real-life version of me. What if I'm not his type?"

"You're everyone's type. You're a Gray woman."

I slowed down the car, but my heart continued racing. "On the slim chance that he is interested in me, we can't do anything about it anyway. During orientation, Simucon gave us a forty-five-minute lecture on forbidden relationships in the workplace, and a manager evaluating an intern is going to be a problem."

"Didn't you say this evaluation was anonymous?"

"Only the final test. Mr. Carden still has to give continuous feedback on my progress. And if I get the job, he'll be my boss. Permanently."

"I used to call your grandpa Mr. Gray." A teaspoon clinked against the inside of a cup. "Those rules didn't exist in my day. If they had, you wouldn't exist either."

"Gran, I just…" I kept my eyes fixed on the road, but images of Mr. Carden and his rare full smile flashed in my memory. I wanted to picture Link, but there was no face to his username. Link was a feeling, and that feeling meant everything to me. "I'm trying to sort through the mess in my mind."

I could hear her take a sip of her tea. "Why don't you start at the beginning and tell me everything."

For the next couple hours, I did.

• • •

By Monday morning, I wanted nothing more than to confirm whether Link and Lincoln were one and the same. I couldn't live with the uncertainty. My grandmother wanted me to confront him and get it over with, but I didn't have the guts. Not yet. I needed more information. I couldn't make this decision based on an unconfirmed sighting of *@wheretheresawilliam* at the conference. A lot of men are tall with dark hair and dark eyes. And maybe a lot of them would wear Pokémon shirts.

These were the thoughts that kept me up almost all weekend, and instead of getting proper rest, I rushed to work as early as the bus would take me.

The lights were already on at the office. No surprise. The early engineer catches the…I don't know, what were engineers obsessed with? They were working all the time.

I zoomed through to my office, doing my best to keep my mind clear.

Think about intersection design. Do not think of Lincoln Carden. Do not think of Link.

Only intersection design. Every other thought was too dangerous.

But the second I opened the door, I was in peril.

Total body shutdown.

I forgot what an intersection looked like or the reason it existed. Right now, I couldn't spell the word *road* if you asked me to.

Because my boss, Mr. Carden…Mr. Lincoln Carden, stood before me. Wet. Shirtless. With a fresh black shirt dangling in his hand.

A curse escaped his full lips as he spun around, eyes wide. I turned around too. But it was too late. I'd seen the way his pants hung low on his hips, the way the defined muscles on his chest were still shiny with water droplets. I'd seen his Adonis belt.

My entire body clenched with desire.

He stammered behind me. I could picture his panicked eyes and how flustered this would make him. "I was, um, I went for a run and…" He swallowed, his voice shaking.

Before he could freak out, I put him out of his misery. "Mr. Carden," I said, thinking of something that would make him laugh or smile like he did yesterday, "at least we don't have a stopping sight distance problem because that sight stopped me immediately."

The chuckle coming from behind me was foreign and wonderful, and it flowed right through my body and settled in my chest. "Elizabeth," he said, his voice low and still wobbly.

I giggled. My cheeks were hot. Even my fingertips were buzzing with a need to touch him. Right now, I would trade anything to trace my finger along the center of his chest, all the way down…

No, Lily.

"I didn't think anyone would be here this early," he eventually managed. "I dropped the shirt I had with me downstairs onto the floor, and it got wet and dirty and…" I heard him flop into his chair.

"Permission to turn around and look at you, sir?"

"Elizabeth," he grumbled.

I spun around, pursing my lips to stop the smile from spreading.

He was buttoned up, and his face rested in his hands. "Unfortunately, I had to come up for the spare."

Unfortunate? Maybe, I don't know.

My only defense against this man was unfiltered humor, and before I could stop myself, my mouth spewed words I had no time to retract. "I mean, if I were you, I'd look for reasons to walk around shirtless, but sure, your dropped shirt story works too."

"Get to work, menace." His deep brown skin was tinged red.

"Yes, sir." As soon as I said it, my cheeks filled with heat. I'd seen that phrase being used far too often in relation to a certain subgenre of romance.

As much fun as it was teasing him, I couldn't focus. I curled into my chair, grateful for the divider between us. I stared at my computer screen and tried shaking off the image of my boss half naked. Glistening.

I needed to know what he'd feel like underneath my hands. An unruly blend of panic and want coursed through my veins.

"I'm off to site." Mr. Carden hopped up from his chair. He had no site meetings scheduled for today.

"Mr. Carden," I said.

He froze at the doorway but didn't look at me.

I fidgeted with the clicker on my pen. "Your presentation was incredible and inspiring, and I would really like to know more about your research. I'm sorry I left so quickly…I, um, I had to go…"

He shrugged, gnawing on his bottom lip. "Yeah, um, thanks, and no problem. I figured you'd probably have, like, family to see or something."

I nodded, even though it wasn't true.

"Okay, bye," he said, more awkwardly than usual, reminding me of our first couple weeks working together.

I longed for the familiarity in his tone at the conference, the knowing looks, the rare smile. But, with him gone, I could think a little clearer. If I wasn't going to get any answers out of him, perhaps I could get them out of someone else.

I'm ashamed to admit that, during my many coffee breaks, I snooped and asked anyone who would listen a few casual questions about Mr. Carden. I needed to know if there was any chance he was Link because it was all I could think about…well, that and his deliciously defined chest.

"He's a brilliant engineer."

I already knew that. I wanted to know more, but there weren't many ways to ask questions without seeming suspicious, or worse, interested in my boss.

"He's rather strange."

Kinda picked up on that too. But I liked it.

"He's a bit of an asshole."

That I refused to accept and took a moment to set them straight. Janine wouldn't be leaving this kitchen until she accepted that Lincoln Carden was a delight.

I trudged back to my desk somewhat despondent and wired only to find Mr. Anders and Cedric standing there.

Mr. Anders drummed his fingers impatiently on the textbook they landed on. "Gordon-Bettencourt," he said, "I need you to work with Cedric on the Stringent interchange. He needs input from Roads. He's basically designed everything else already."

An interchange. I hadn't done an interchange yet.

"Unless you're incapable?" His voice lifted with one of his brows, and it triggered the pettiest, most self-destructive part of me. Beside him, Cedric's smug face glowed.

"I can do it."

Crap, crap, crap. I can't do it. Why did I say that?

"Good. He needs the drawings by tomorrow morning."

Okay, now I definitely regretted it.

20

LINCOLN

[72 weeks ago]

> **@pancakesareelite:**
> What do you look like?

@theanswerisno:
Like the character in this game

> **@pancakesareelite:**
> I love an 8ft, blue-skinned
> man with elf ears and fangs

@theanswerisno:
I aim to please.

@theanswerisno:
How about you?

> **@pancakesareelite:**
> Before I tell you, please answer this
> totally unrelated question: What does
> your dream girl look like?

⇔

I'd spent the entire weekend thinking about my presentation, about Elizabeth being there and how badly I'd wished she'd stayed after.

Now I might have to resign because I could never face her ever again.

I pressed my forehead against my steering wheel and blew out the breath I may have been holding since fleeing the office. Fleeing. I freaking fled. Because no part of me anticipated being half naked in front of an employee today. Of all the employees, it had to be the prettiest one with the smartest mouth who took every opportunity to say something cheeky.

My entire body heated at the memory of the exchange. At the redness of her pale cheeks and the grin she wore when she teased.

But the jokes were good. I think. It meant she wasn't too uncomfortable, and perhaps I hadn't ruined the only real-life relationship I'd formed with anyone outside my small circle of friends.

I looked out of the truck at the intersection that was slowly being built. There was absolutely nothing for me to do here. Maybe I should head over to my mom's and help her pack. I'd been promising her.

But I still didn't have it in me to do that either.

I'd have to sit here until the fluttering in my chest stopped, and by then, hopefully, Elizabeth would have forgotten all the extra-mischievous comments she could muster in my time away.

Fat chance.

•   •   •

By the time lunch swung around, I was hungry enough to find my way to Zoya's, where I grabbed two sandwiches. Offering Elizabeth food would keep her mouth busy. Being cheeky and chewing didn't go all that well together. And if there was one thing I knew about her—based on the hard-to-ignore sounds coming from the other side of the divider—it was that she got lost in her meals.

What I didn't expect to walk in on was Elizabeth red-faced, not with an awkward encounter but with frustration.

"Mr. Carden," she said with such relief in her voice I had to believe she was pleased to see me. Then she started rambling. Interchanges. Cedric. Anders. I don't know, it was hard to focus when she spoke sometimes because, when she was all riled up, her animated expressions and speech speed reminded me of gaming characters who'd taken a booster potion.

She was so much crammed into one person that it amazed me she managed to get anything done.

I sucked on my teeth, and she took a big inhale, puffing out her chest.

"Okay." She raised her hands. "I'm going too fast, aren't I?"

"Way too fast. But I gather something is due, and you need some help?"

"Stringent interchange, and they want the horizontal layout by tomorrow morning." A deep line formed between her brows.

I didn't think I'd seen her frown that hard before.

After dropping my bag at my desk, I turned around and peeked at her over our divider. "Do you want me to do it for you? I could have it done in a couple hours."

I held out the sandwich, and she launched out of her seat—her hand stretching out to receive the foil-wrapped square.

She unwrapped her sandwich and made way too intense eye contact with me. "No, I want you to teach me how to do it. I want to show them I can do it."

A strange sense of pride bubbled up in my chest. "Atta girl," I said before I could stop myself. I made my way over to her side of the office and scrutinized the drawings. Cedric's initials were in the bottom left corner.

It was remarkable Cedric had learned how to design this by

himself over the last few weeks, but it wasn't uncommon. Every few years, they would find an engineer with a natural ability to pick up technical design and tricks.

Many moons ago, I was that intern.

I bit into my sandwich, glancing at Elizabeth, who, in all honesty, did not have that talent. She'd have to work incredibly hard to prove herself against him. It was a pity her year had a Cedric. Had she been part of the internship last year, she'd have easily been one of the best. She'd leveled up since starting and shown her dedication to the craft, to improvement, and sometimes, that was more important. Engineering was ever changing, and Elizabeth had already proven she could roll with the punches.

That was part of the evaluation comments I'd sent to Anders. He'd seemed surprised, and I didn't ask whether it was because of how well she was doing or because I'd actually started managing her.

Elizabeth hovered around me while eating. Her gaze flicked between the drawings and my face. She spent a considerable amount of time trying to read me. Everyone did that. She was one of the few who succeeded.

"You're comfortable with intersection upgrades, yes?" I asked, leaning in to read the contours while she stammered in the affirmative. "Interchange design incorporates many of those aspects. We'll start there and build up to the entire interchange. What you can do, in the meantime, is tell me which kind of interchange would work best?" I walked over to my desk and leafed through the stack of drawings until I pulled up a few other layouts. "The options are endless, but these are the popular ones."

She stared at them in silence. Her sea-blue painted nail traced along the curves of the four-leaf clover interchange. "They're beautiful. I've driven on this one."

"I designed it." I shoved the last piece of the bread into my mouth to shut myself up.

Usually I wouldn't tell anyone, but the genuine awe in her voice made me want to claim it.

"It's art," she said, still nibbling on her own sandwich. She ate with her mouth closed. Not a single crumb fell on her clothing or to the floor. She was like a princess.

"Yeah…for the birds," I replied, pulling my gaze away from her. I crumpled up the foil and aimed for the wastebasket in the corner of my side of the office. I tossed it, and it ricocheted off the rim and onto the floor.

She giggled in a way that was gentle, warm, and caused flutters for whoever heard it. Probably. I'm sure it wasn't only me.

"Diamond, I think?" Her voice peaked at the end in question.

"I'd have chosen that too." I started scribbling on the drawing.

From the corner of my eye, I spotted her crumpling up her wrapper. She bit on her tongue as she aimed. When she released the silver ball, it landed inside the wastebasket. My mouth dropped open, and she spun around, her expression as shocked as I was.

"I'll increase your evaluation by one point based on that alone." I walked over to pick up my missed ball and tossed it inside.

She almost collapsed with the laughter that bubbled out of her. She leaned across the desk and watched me draw. If I hadn't spent years doing this, I may have had some performance anxiety. But this was something I knew how to do. One of the very few things about myself I didn't doubt. I explained everything as I went along, reciting guidelines from memory and enjoying how intently she listened.

Having her full attention was alarming. It made me feel somewhat…invincible. Like what I said mattered.

"I don't recall them teaching this in college. I mean, the idea of it, yeah…but maybe I missed that class," she said as we moved to her computer and opened the design software.

"There's no way they can cover everything in the few years you spend there. You'll learn as you go along. Or you can go wild in your postgrad."

"I'd like to do mine eventually, but part-time. I don't think I have the luxury of full-time studies considering I'm already behind." She navigated to Cedric's design and imported the data as I'd previously taught her to do.

Without saying anything, I waited to see if she'd perform the checks I always recommended.

She did.

I grabbed my laptop and wheeled my chair into her office space. Her desk wasn't that large, but before I could change my mind, she scooched over and shoved everything out of the way to make space. For me.

This was a completely normal thing for people to do for their bosses. Just because she laughed at my jokes or listened to me when I spoke didn't mean anything. She was Elizabeth Gordon-Bettencourt. Aside from being my intern, she was way out of my league. We weren't even playing the same game.

After going through all the design principles and some trial and error, she hit PROCESS on the software and leaned back in her seat, her chest dropping with a heavy exhale. She undid the giant bun that held her red waves out of her face but then redid it. Her glance fell toward her phone. "Oh my goodness, it's already after nine. You probably need to go."

Time had flown.

"I'm fine. Do you need to go? We can carry on tomorrow morning."

She shook her head. "I really appreciate you doing this. I feel like…maybe I stand a chance of acing this internship. I really, really need this job. Am I being delusional to think I could get it?"

Despite what everyone said about her and her wealth, Elizabeth genuinely seemed to need this job. There was a desperate panic behind those eyes whenever she spoke about the internship ending.

"Not delusional, but you're not there yet. We could get there in time."

"We?" She smiled.

I had to look away. Sometimes her beauty overwhelmed me. "We," I managed. "Best manager-intern team at Simucon, remember?"

She hopped up. "Damn right. In that case, could I make you a cup of coffee?"

My gaze, now eye level with her waist, swept upward until it met her face. Something foreign tightened in my abdomen. "I can make my own coffee."

She crumpled up a scrap piece of paper. "Loser makes coffee."

I grinned, activating muscles that didn't often get used. "Okay, but we have to stand farther back than last time."

"Deal." She danced around and then tossed the ball. It hit the edge and fell to the floor.

I collected it and took her spot. I focused on the center of the wastebasket and threw it. Somehow it landed even farther away. I turned to face her. "I clearly didn't play team sports."

Her laughter was contagious. "I think I expect you to be good at everything."

I nearly choked, even though I had nothing in my mouth to choke on. But getting a compliment like that from a woman like this was too much for my esophagus.

On the next throw, I got it in. Sheer luck.

"Fine," she huffed. Less playful than usual.

I hadn't expected her to be so competitive.

"I didn't expect you to be so competitive," she said.

"Likewise," I said, stretching. My muscles were loose and light. It was weird.

"Sugar and cream, right?"

I nodded, unable to hide the smile creeping onto my face. I wasn't a stranger to working late, but I'd never worked late with someone else. Not even during my studies on the tightest deadlines. I'd always send the rest of the group home and finish the assignment by myself; they never minded.

But this was…nice.

"Mr. Carden," she said as she entered a few moments later with two cups of coffee. Her mug had cat ears. Obviously.

"You can call me Lincoln, if you'd like…" I heard myself saying even though no one called me Lincoln around here. Not even Anders. "We'd need a retaining wall here." I changed the topic and pointed at the large amount of fill required on one side of the on-ramp.

"Do I have to design that?"

"No. Mark it up and send it off to the structural engineers. They'll take a look and give it to the right person." I took a moment to observe her before asking my next question. For someone who had been concentrating for more than twelve hours, she didn't look tired at all. "Do you want me to tell you about the basic retaining wall structures often used alongside roads?"

"I thought you'd never ask." She flopped into her office seat and kicked off her shoes before tucking her feet underneath her. "If you can take off your shirt in here, I can take off my shoes, right?"

And there it was. Cheeky little thing.

21

ELIZABETH

[70 weeks ago]

@pancakesareelite:
I can't play tonight. I have a call with
my gran. She's my favorite person in
the world. IRL.

> @theanswerisno:
> What's she like?

@pancakesareelite:
So sassy

> @theanswerisno:
> Oh, I'm so surprised. I never would
> have thought anyone related to you
> could be sassy

@pancakesareelite:
Ha ha ha. I'm actually named after her

@pancakesareelite:
And it's an honor to resemble her in
any way or form. What's your gran like?

> @theanswerisno:
> They both passed away when I was little

@pancakesareelite:
I'm so sorry

                              @theanswerisno:
          I feel like I'm always sharing sad
          stuff. I'm a sad boy, not a bad boy

@pancakesareelite:
You have that in common with all the
hot TV villains I end up falling in
love with

My brain was liquid. Mush. I couldn't follow a coherent thought. After a bajillion hours of engineering design, I was ready to drain it through my ears into a jar and stick it at the back of my kitchen cabinet never to be used again.

But I wouldn't. Because that would mean forgetting everything else about this evening. Seeing Mr. Carden—*Lincoln* in his element. The intensity of his face while designing, the excitement when levels lined up. Better yet, the pride when I had a good idea.

Honestly, at some point in the night, he started feeling like my Link, and the design felt like one of the games we played. It reminded me of the early days where Link was the one who walked me through many games after most of the other players had lost their patience.

My chest ached in the strangest way.

Was I mistaken? Was it wishful thinking? If he wasn't Link, would I be disappointed?

Yes.

I knew that to be true now.

It didn't make either of them any less perfect.

I was in trouble. Big trouble. With Lincoln's unforgivable sculpted body, gentle manner, and brilliant brain, I couldn't handle him—if I was forced to add *my* Link, my safe space, to this Lincoln, I wouldn't stand a chance.

But I needed to know. Now. Before I fell even deeper. Before I drowned.

And it was this flurry of thoughts that had me reaching for my phone. If I could call Link, I would, and I'd know from the depth of his voice whether he was Lincoln.

But I didn't have his number. We only ever chatted in-app, and his settings had calls disabled, or at least disabled with me.

So I did all I could and messaged him instead.

```
@pancakesareelite:
Let's meet at the Overpower LAN.
```

• • •

It didn't matter that we'd been up for most of the night working, Lincoln looked fresh the next morning in his well-fitted white shirt and gray chinos. His focus was on his phone, but when I walked in, he looked up. As soon as those brown eyes met mine, he smiled.

Yes, it was that lopsided grin, but still my breath caught.

I had once lived a life in the limelight where I was photographed at award shows and stalked by journalists and young actors, yet nothing compared to the adrenaline that flowed through me in the moments of rare attention I got from Mr. Lincoln Carden.

"Good morning, Link-in," I said, pausing ever so slightly between the two syllables. My blood stopped as I analyzed his every micro facial expression.

But there was nothing. Just a sideways glance at his phone.

"Good morning, Elizabeth," he said with his usual sigh, except his frustration didn't seem linked to me. "Anders and Cedric want to meet with you to discuss the design."

My stomach jumped into my throat, and any inkling of peace that once resided in me disappeared into thin air.

He stood, taking two quick steps toward me. He lifted his hand as though to touch me but then decided against it. "Do you want me to come along?"

I wanted him to. Desperately. But I had to learn to do these things on my own. I shook my head, and he flopped back into his seat.

"You already wasted an entire evening with me yesterday. You can do your work. I'll survive. Probably."

"I don't mind." He lifted his noise-canceling headset and paused.

I could swear his soft brown gaze raked across my body, even just for a second before settling on my eyes. Much better than when he avoided looking at me.

A touch of red covered his cheeks before he added, "I also didn't mind last night. It was fun. I guess I'm never beating the dweeb allegations."

I grinned. The anxiousness in my belly was joined by something else. "Careful. I may ask you to do it again."

"Let's," he said, the headset half on his head, half off.

"Seriously?"

"Yeah. You have so little knowledge, there's a lot of room for improvement," he said, and while the comment had my mouth dropping open, it wasn't an insult. Lincoln Carden was *teasing me*.

Crackles of excitement went off in my chest. This was new.

"But go off to your meeting. We'll talk after," he said.

I nodded, grabbed our drawings, and went upstairs to where Cedric, Mr. Anders, and the senior structural engineer waited in the boardroom.

"Gordon-Bettencourt," Anders said.

Cedric mouthed, *Seven*.

I greeted them with my best smile and willed the nerves out of my hands as I unsteadily laid the drawings on the desk for them to scrutinize. Cedric sneered while the other two looked through it.

"I don't see any red flags. Has Carden checked it?" Anders asked.

"It was probably designed by Mr. Carden," Cedric huffed out.

Anders and the other engineer looked up at me, eyebrows raised. "Was it?"

I swallowed hard, unsure of what the correct answer would be. "He assisted…a bit."

"Oh," Anders said, the impressed look he wore earlier disappearing. "It was your task."

"I know, and I did it."

"Obviously. There's no north arrow," Cedric said, and if I was a violent person, now would be the time I'd punch him.

"Mr. Carden wanted to ensure the design was sound before we finalized the presentation." I then ran through the guidelines we'd used and assumptions we'd made.

"All right." Anders sighed. "But if I wanted Carden to do it, I'd have asked him."

The heaviness of his tone tightened around my words. I stood frozen for a second before choking out, "Understood. I'll add the arrow and get Mr. Carden to sign it, unless you have any other changes you'd like me to make?" I steadied my voice as best I could, but I was defeated and exhausted. I'd slept for around two hours, and this wasn't how I planned the morning to go. Regardless of what they said, I was proud of this design. That stupid north arrow.

"That's all from me." Mr. Anders looked at the other two, who shrugged.

I rolled up the drawing and walked downstairs to the office.

Lincoln pulled the headset down to his neck as I entered. "And?"

"And the design is fine, but um"—I struggled to keep the shake from my voice—"they're disappointed that I couldn't do it on my own."

"What? Did they say that?" His brows drew close, and that familiar frown returned.

I nodded and shook it off. "Whatever. I don't care anyway." I didn't want to discuss it anymore. "I'm going out for a short coffee break. Do you want anything?"

"No, thank you," he said, his voice clipped. Perhaps he was also disappointed in me. Well, he could join the club.

Keeping my head down, I stomped out of the office building while avoiding everyone.

I hadn't spent much time walking around, but today I would find a coffee shop, order the most delectable drink on the menu, and gulp it down before going back to the office to figure out whether I had what it takes to be an engineer.

After about ten minutes, I spotted a neon sign that read THE ARCADE CAFE and wandered into it. The smell of freshly ground beans was already soothing, and on one side of the store stood old arcade machines.

Coffee shops were some of the best places in the world. Aside from being an essential service, it was always hot with steam and filled with chatter and satisfied people getting their fix. And baristas were always friendly with me. Even though it was superficial, it was nice.

"Could I get a cinnamon mocha, please?" I asked.

The handsome barista nodded and offered me a somewhat suggestive smile.

It had been ages since I'd hooked up with someone. Perhaps I needed it. Maybe it would help with all the big feelings fighting for attention in my head and heart. Maybe it would get Link and Lincoln out of my head.

Yeah, right.

Sitting at one of the tables, I dropped my head into my hands and listened to the sound of the arcade machines. I was tempted to join them and play a few rounds, but if I did, I feared I may never leave. I would stay in this store and dedicate my life to *Puzzle Bobble* and drink a worrying amount of coffee.

"Here you go." The barista's gaze danced with charm and flirtation.

Generally, I'd reciprocate. But when I searched for that feeling, it wasn't there. I smiled at him nonetheless and sipped on the overly sweet but delicious coffee. With each sip, the warmth of the beverage melted the ice within me. And by the time the mug was empty, I was ready to go back to the office.

It was one task. I could do better next time. I could overcome this.

I'd overcome so much more.

"Anything else for you, love?" the barista asked, returning.

"One coffee to go. Sugar and cream. Please."

Even though Lincoln said he didn't want anything, I owed him for all the sandwiches.

With his coffee heating my palm, I hurried back to the office. I was out longer than the allowed break, but after spending so many hours working overtime, I needed it.

From the corner of my eye, I spotted Alistair. I sped up but already knew he would keep following. My hand shook around the cup of coffee. Had it not been for the white plastic lid, it would have spilled. "I told you to leave me alone."

"I've come to deliver his message, seeing as you won't see him."

I reached my free hand into my pocket and fished out my fob as I neared my building. Ahead of me were two engineers having a chat outside the door. I stopped and spun around. No one else needed to see this happening. "I don't want to hear it."

Alistair leaned against the wall and shoved his hand into his jacket pocket. "He knows you're bad-mouthing him to your mother and giving her ideas of a life without him. She won't survive on her own. Neither can you. And you'll see that soon enough."

I tore my gaze away from him as his words splintered my heart. I could hear Douglas saying it, and I relived every moment he had belittled me. My self-esteem plummeted. *What if he was right?*

The engineers left, and the entrance to the office stood empty. I hurried toward the door and tapped my fob against the scanner. It clicked open, and I slipped inside, but not before hearing him say, "You can't keep ignoring me. I'll be back until you agree to leave her alone."

22

LINCOLN

[69 weeks ago]

> **@pancakesareelite:**
> I'm struggling to understand something
> and it's making me mad

@theanswerisno:
Do you wanna tell me about it?

> **@pancakesareelite:**
> It's very niche. But thank you

@theanswerisno:
Hm…Unsolicited advice from an internet
stranger: Take a break and then start
at the beginning, even if the beginning
isn't the problem.

> **@pancakesareelite:**
> Internet friend*

> **@pancakesareelite:**
> Favorite internet person*

> **@pancakesareelite:**
> Internet soulmate*

@pancakesareelite:

And thank you.
In that case, I'm off to bed

@theanswerisno:
You got this and good night, Pancakes

@pancakesareelite:

I'm waiting for you to say something
about how I'm your favorite person too

@theanswerisno:
Good night my B&FP2
(best and favorite player 2)

@pancakesareelite:

That's better, night, Link

As soon as Elizabeth stepped out of our office, I launched to my feet, already knowing where I was going even though I hadn't fully figured out what I'd be saying. A flare of adrenaline rushed through me—I never did anything like this. I liked emails. Planned sentences.

But this was different. It wasn't fair to punish her when I'd offered to help. Heck, I'd basically insisted. She was the one who wanted to learn and do it herself.

The defeat in her eyes and the lack of bounce in her step had me entering Anders's office without knocking. It wasn't like Anders ever gave me the privilege of welcoming him in.

"Carden." He looked up from his lavish desk chair that was anything but practical. It didn't even have wheels or proper back support.

"Elizabeth tells me that you're unhappy that I assisted." I walked up to his desk and threw myself into the seat across from him.

"That's right," Anders said, his eyebrows high as he studied me.

"According to one of the other engineers, you were here with her, at her desk, working. Unless there's another reason you're staying behind. You don't do it with anyone else."

Now only one of his eyebrows remained cocked.

I swallowed the grumble wanting to escape me. "Cedric was correct in what he saw. I stayed late to supervise her. You told me to manage my intern, and that's what I'm doing. It's an interchange design, Anders. What did you expect from her? Last year, the interns barely did anything more than road widenings."

He leaned forward, resting his elbows on his desk before steepling his fingers. "Last year, all we had were road widenings, but things are changing, and I need engineers who will add value. I'm not paying overtime if it was spent teaching her."

"Then how do you expect her to learn?" I balled my hands into fists underneath his desk. "You're making no sense. One minute you're telling me to manage her, and the next you want me to let her figure things out on her own."

And then it struck me. This wasn't about engineering design and Elizabeth's progress. They wanted to see Elizabeth fail because her failure would be mine too.

My mother had warned me. But I would be damned if I let an insecure man stand between me and the promises I'd made to my family.

"I know what I said but I don't know if Elizabeth's got what it takes—" Anders started.

I raised a hand, stopping him. "There needs to be a transfer of knowledge; otherwise Simucon will be left with a bunch of clueless engineers when we retire." Clenching my jaw, I continued. "Elizabeth has shown improvement and a willingness to learn. Plus, technically, her design is sound." The fire in my voice was foreign, but I liked it. "A good engineer knows their limitations." I leaned forward, dropping my voice. "Otherwise, we have structural engineers who think they can design roads and vice versa."

Anders blinked twice, his mouth opening and closing with a sharp inhale as I'm sure the memory of a multiyear, multimillion-dollar court case came to mind.

"This isn't a school assignment," I said. "I needed her to know and understand what she was doing, and now she does."

Anders considered me, swallowing once before regaining composure. His eyes narrowed, but my emotions were running high and rational thought had all but left me for dead as I stared him down.

"Has she gained any site experience?" he asked.

I shook my head. If Elizabeth was going to struggle in any aspect of civil engineering, it would be the site work. At least at first.

"Put her on Disselweed with you. We don't have much more for her to do here."

"Why is that?" I asked. "Why hire seven interns when we've only ever had work for six or less?"

He ignored my question and said, "No more mistakes."

"I'm certain she won't make any," I said, entirely uncertain because it was impossible not to make mistakes and he knew that.

I huffed out a breath, but it did nothing to arrange the thoughts zooming through my mind. Instead, I shoved myself upward and made for the exit.

As I reached the door, Anders spoke. "Carden, you know relations between senior engineers and their employees are against company rules. There's an imbalance of power, and I'd hate to see a pretty face ruin a career you've been building for years. I wouldn't put it past her to use the assets she's been blessed with."

"Careful." I clenched my jaw until my teeth hurt. "I am well aware of the rules. My statement stands."

I left his office, and when I passed by Cedric and the other graduates, I considered giving them a piece of my mind and letting them know they had no place watching my movements or deciding who I could and could not help.

But I wasn't looking for a fight. Confrontation was at the bottom of the list of things I enjoyed doing.

A sense of calmness hit me the second I walked into my perfectly curated office, but I immediately noted Elizabeth's absence.

I peeked at her side of the divider. It was personalized with flowers, hearts, and glitter. But like my side of the office, there were no photos or ticket stubs, and her trinkets gave me very little insight into her mind.

Although there was a sticker of Zelda. *She likes* The Legend of Zelda? A chuckle escaped me, along with some of the residual anger.

Elizabeth Gordon-Bettencourt would keep surprising me in the best of ways.

But Zelda reminded me that I'd left Lily's message unread. Well, not unread. I could see the preview, but I was too afraid to open it, too afraid to reply.

I'd been up most of the night staring at it, and this morning, I'd have stared at it more had it not been for Elizabeth, who stole my focus so effortlessly.

Pulling out my phone, I looked at the message again. Lily wanted to meet me. My chest caved under the pressure of living up to the idea of me she may have. I wasn't anything like Link.

And what if she was nothing like Lily? Then what? Would I lose the person I had whenever life got too noisy?

I nearly dropped my phone when Elizabeth barreled into the room in a blur of copper curls and a beige coat. Her chest heaved, and her eyes darted around in a way I hadn't seen before. Her hand shook around a takeaway coffee cup. I took a step toward her instinctively, and she held out the cup.

"For you." Her voice was uncharacteristically small.

I took the cup. "I spoke to Anders."

She grabbed her phone, uninterested in what I was saying.

"Elizabeth?"

Her stormy gaze met mine. I didn't like what I saw.

Fear. Shame. Anger.

She looked away, her chest rising and falling as she blinked away tears. I nearly reached for her chin to tilt it upward. Instead, my hands pressed against my chinos. "What is it?" I asked, my voice low so only she could hear me.

Her mouth opened and shut. I could see the wheels turning in her head as though she were trying to decide whether she could tell me.

Whatever it was, I could fix it. I would fix it.

"Uh…someone from my past," she eventually said, swallowing hard and pulling her hair up into a tight bun.

An ex-boyfriend?

Jealousy climbed my throat. I did all I could to keep it out of my voice. *What the heck was it doing there in the first place?* "Is everything okay?"

She shook her head and blew out a few quick breaths. "It's fine. I, um, told security not to let him in, so it's fine. I just…I don't like that he's here. I don't like that he found me."

"Who is he?"

"It doesn't matter." She sat down at her desk, but her skittering eyes and wringing hands let me know that was untrue. Whoever this person was had left her frazzled.

"Elizabeth." I walked up to her and knelt beside her chair. I needed to see her face when she answered. "Are you in trouble?"

Again, she shook her head. "No. He's just an irritation, and I want him to leave me alone." She inhaled deeply, finding some of her calm, and the light energy that generally surrounded her returned. "But thank you. Anyway…you mentioned speaking to Mr. Anders?"

I wanted to know more, but it was none of my business. "Yeah." I took a seat at my desk. "He was being petty, and I've seen to it."

"Oh." Her voice was so soft. "You didn't have to do that."

I took a beat and thought of how I'd phrase the next bit. "Unfortunately, he's going to keep testing you, and I think it's because he's testing me."

She popped up, her head sticking above the divider. That little frown returned. "That's not fair."

"I'm sorry."

"No. It's not fair to you either," she grumbled, her eyes darkening with anger. "I'm sick of these petty men in power. You deserve that promotion, and if it's up to me to be better, then I'll be better." She let out another little grumble and spun around to face her computer.

I turned my focus back to my laptop, actively trying not to think about how cute she looked when she was angry.

I lifted my headset, trying to straighten my thoughts, but her voice carried over to me.

"Lincoln?"

"Hmm?"

She wheeled sideways to the end of the divider and looked at me. "Will you help me become as good as you are?"

The seriousness of her voice and the blush on her cheeks sent heat flowing through me. "Impossible," I teased, "but I'll try."

She disappeared again, and I heard her chuckle.

Wretched divider. It ruined my view.

23

ELIZABETH

[65 weeks ago]

@pancakesareelite:
Am I annoying?

> **@theanswerisno:**
> Username

@pancakesareelite:
What?

> **@theanswerisno:**
> My username

@pancakesareelite:
Oh, you're my favorite

"I'd love a cup of coffee," Lincoln said from the other side of the divider.

"Oh. Me too. I'll make it," I replied, spinning around in my chair. "I think it's my turn."

It had been about two weeks since I begged Lincoln to teach

me, and he had. Every night. And every night I imagined what would happen if we were alone. Most times we weren't. But next week, we'd be on-site together for three entire days.

I needed to constantly remind myself that Lincoln was still my boss for at least a week and a half, and if all goes well, he'd be my boss for a lot longer. I couldn't let this crush consume me. I couldn't give in to the Gray women weakness Gran had warned me about.

"Do you want it in your plain white mug or your other plain white mug?" I hopped to my feet and peeked over the divider.

Lincoln's shoulders shook with quiet laughter. His soft brown eyes, now bright, glanced upward. "Um…Claire, I'll call you back."

My eyes popped wide. "No. No! You weren't talking to me?"

He tugged down his headset and shut his eyes. His mouth twisted in a concealed smile. "Not this time."

I threw my head back. "I hate your stupid headset. I didn't hear you say hello or anything, so I assumed…" I covered my face.

"I'm sorry. Claire jumped straight in with a question."

Claire? Who was Claire? A girlfriend?

Nauseating jealousy swirled in my stomach.

A warm hand grazed my elbow. I lowered my palms, and Lincoln's fingers shot into his pocket. He offered me that bashful half smile and looked away seconds before my legs went weak.

If an elbow touch did that? A kiss may kill me.

Link or not, Lincoln Carden was everything I wanted.

And while he was shy and blushed generously, he didn't want me. I knew what desire looked like. I'd been on the receiving end of it plenty of times. Lincoln Carden studied me like a project he needed to master, not a woman he wanted to devour.

It didn't help that my Link (was he *my* Link?) hadn't replied to me after I'd asked him to meet up. He'd barely been online since I'd asked, and the *Overpower* LAN was two days away.

I wanted to be one of the early players, but I wasn't sure I wanted to be there with him, without being *with* him.

The sting of rejection was painful. Link and I lived in our own world, with our own games, and being ignored wasn't part of any of the levels.

But maybe our world never existed.

Or it did. And I ruined it by bursting our bubble and trying to make real-life contact.

I'd considered, multiple times, whether I could delete the message or send him a game request and pretend I'd never asked to meet. I also considered lying and saying that I sent that while being deeply medicated…or I suppose I could come clean and confront him and tell him that it was okay, that we didn't need to meet or put pressure on this thing we had going on.

But I needed to know if he was Lincoln Carden.

Still, I wanted my friend back. Even if that was all he wanted to be.

Even virtually.

Turning away from Lincoln, I pointed at the drawings on my desk. "Are we working on these tonight?"

His smile dropped, and he sighed. It reminded me of when I first got here. "Shoot. I forgot to tell you. I can't stay late tonight. I have somewhere to be."

"Oh," I said, ignoring the solid stone of disappointment landing in the depths of my belly. "That's okay. It's not like you have to."

"I know." He dropped below the divider, and I could hear him packing up his laptop and other belongings. "To be honest, I wish I could stay. I don't know what this says about me, but I kinda enjoy it. I've never really taught anyone before. I feel like I'm learning something new as well." The genuine excitement in his voice made my heart swell.

"You're really good at it," I said. "Both the teaching and the doing."

He stood, holding his mouse in his left hand and his wallet in his right. "You should go. It's pretty late."

I glanced over at my task list. There was still plenty to do. But I was exhausted.

"We're visiting the site tomorrow just to check a few things before we stay over next week." Lincoln kept his gaze on his backpack and spoke far too quickly. "It'll be a good opportunity to see the processes. It's a greenfield project."

Was he as nervous as I was to be alone together?

I followed suit and shoved everything into my backpack. "Absolutely, I've looked at those plans. It's such an interesting concept. You designed the entire thing, right?"

He shifted on his feet, an awkward but bashful smile curled onto his mouth. "Um…Yeah." He walked over to the doorway. "Anyway, I'll send you the details as soon as I get my laptop back on. But I am in a bit of a hurry."

I followed after him. "Fun plans?"

My pathetic little heart stilled in the seconds that passed.

He sighed, then smiled, and I couldn't figure out if it was a chore or something fun. "Yeah, it'll be fun."

"A date?" I squeaked out as we reached the front door.

My body curled in on itself as I cringed. It seemed I really couldn't control what came out of my mouth anymore.

His eyes widened, and he let loose a short laugh. "No, no. I'm heading to a friend's place. We'll probably play some games." He scanned his fob to unlock the door and gestured for me to walk ahead of him.

I stepped outside and the night air cooled my heated cheeks. Dammit, if my cheeks were this hot, could he see it? I spun away from him and froze. My stomach jolted with discomfort and annoyance as a familiar black Mercedes stood parked right outside the building.

Without thinking, I stepped backward, wanting nothing more than to retreat into the safety of the building. But I slammed into something hard.

"Elizabeth?" Lincoln's hand gripped my shoulder, steadying me.

I turned around and looked up at him, but his gaze was fixed above my head.

"Is that the guy who has been bothering you?" he asked in a low, threatening grumble.

"Um, yes."

I was ready to push past Lincoln and rush upstairs. I could use the emergency exit at the back.

But Lincoln's warm palm dropped to my waist. His fingers pressed into my side with intent, but it was gentle. All he did was shift me to the left.

Lincoln squeezed past me and walked straight up to the car. He tapped on the window hard enough to make me flinch.

"Who are you?" Lincoln asked. Not in the voice I was used to, but in another, deeper, firmer voice. The one that had all the engineers scurrying out of his path.

Alistair lowered the window and glanced between Lincoln and me. Even in the dim lighting, I could see that laser focus in his eyes that had always made me uncomfortable.

Lincoln looked over his shoulder and met my gaze for a second before turning back to Alistair. Whatever he'd read on my face had him growing in size and authority as he said his next words: "Stop pestering her, or I'll call the police." His voice was low and gravelly, filled with a threat even I believed he'd act upon.

"I'm not doing anything wrong, Mr. Carden," Alistair's voice broke through the quiet night. "I'm here to chat with Ms. Gordon-Bettencourt."

Lincoln blew out a harsh breath, misting up the side of the car. He pressed his hands on the open window and leaned inward before whispering, "Consider this a warning and leave her alone."

Alistair, who had retreated within the car, locked eyes with me then and threw me a knowing glance that said, *I'll tell him about this.*

Within a second, he was gone, leaving me trying to steady my breathing while Lincoln straightened. For a moment, he just stood there, watching the Mercedes blend into the night. When he turned around, the angry energy was still alive around him, making his black curls seem wilder.

"Would you like me to take you home?" His voice was controlled and careful, but his chest rose and fell like mine.

I shook my head. "I'm fine, thank you."

"If you're concerned about him coming back or following you, I could—"

"I'm fine, Mr. Carden. I won't be alone."

A blatant lie. But I didn't want to explain all of this. My messy life. Lincoln Carden, my *boss*, didn't need to hear any of it. And more importantly, he didn't need to be involved. It wasn't lost on me that Alistair knew his name. Alistair had been watching him too.

"Okay" was all he said, but still he waited until I was in my car before he got into his.

And I was grateful. Even though I wasn't in danger. Alistair, that awful weasel, had been doing Douglas's dirty work for years.

While driving, I checked my rearview mirror every other second. It seemed Lincoln Carden's threat had worked, for now. As soon as I was inside my apartment, I locked the doors. Then, without showering off the day, I climbed under the covers and pulled them over my head.

I couldn't go on like this anymore. It made no sense. Running away hadn't worked. And no matter how hard I tried to forget everything and create a new life that was my own, it was all pretend. Douglas would always find a way to be there, haunting, hunting, hurting whenever he could, however he could.

It was nice having someone there to defend me. Lincoln Carden was my boss, and he didn't have to. He had plans. He had friends. He…

He was going to play games with his friends.

On a Wednesday night.

That was something my Link did too.

24

LINCOLN

[61 weeks ago]

@theanswerisno:
BRB mom is calling

@theanswerisno:
Don't go into the mines without me

@pancakesareelite:
I won't. I'll die. Instantly

@pancakesareelite:
Mommy's boy?

@theanswerisno:
Yeah, kinda

@pancakesareelite:
That's nice

My adrenaline was high as I pulled up to Shaun and Neema's apartment. What just happened? Why the heck did I defend Elizabeth? I don't even know the whole story.

I should not be getting involved. But she was scared.

Her bright red cheeks against her pale complexion were etched into my mind. Her rigid body. Her high-pitched voice. I had known something was very wrong since the first time she'd brought that man up. Why was he still following her? It had been weeks.

I'd acted on instinct. I didn't regret it one bit.

"Lincoln, you're mumbling to yourself in a strange, beautiful, genius kind of way." Neema let me in. She rubbed my back and leaned in for what could possibly be termed *the idea of a hug*. "Also, it's nice to see you. We've missed you."

"There was a man stalking Elizabeth," I announced to the room, which got the attention of everyone. I wouldn't usually do such a thing, but I was still processing.

"We're going to need a little bit more," Dean said from one of the couches.

I paced the living room, rattling off exactly what had happened.

"Poor girl. That sounds horrible." Neema rubbed a hand on her growing belly.

"What would he want from her?" I asked. My brain wasn't going to let this go until it made sense. Until I could figure out how to stop it. I got the sense my threat was only a temporary solution.

"Could be anything, I guess," Rose said. "Ex-boyfriend, scorned business partner, influencer gone wild, a stalker! I mean…she's a Gordon-Bettencourt. It could even be a journalist looking for dirt on her dad."

On autopilot, I found my way over to the leather armchair, the only single-seater in the room. "She was terrified."

"Is she okay? Did you make sure she got home safely?" Claire's brows furrowed.

"I offered, but she didn't need me…She's, uh, she's got someone else," I said, and my heart banged unpleasantly against my rib cage at the mere assumption she'd been referring to a partner. "Obviously. Why wouldn't she? She's…" I stopped midsentence as they all stared at me.

I shook my head. *Elizabeth = employee = losing promotion or even losing job. She's too beautiful and funny and smart for you anyway.*

I turned my phone around in my hands, and it unlocked upon recognizing my face. Lily's message remained unread.

Lily.

I intended to reply. But I hadn't figured out my move, and with the late nights tutoring Elizabeth, admittedly I'd kind of forgotten.

My throat thickened. *Was I cheating?* No. How could I be cheating when nothing had happened with either of these women.

I was working with Elizabeth. I could hardly be blamed that she was so…immersive. I lost myself in her, around her. Working was hard. Focusing was harder.

And tomorrow we'd be alone in my car while we visited the site. But what really worried me, the thought I'd been denying, was that next week we'd be staying over on-site together for a few days as part of Elizabeth's training.

Alone. At night. Sleeping in one cabin. In not-work clothes. Oh no. I needed a distraction before I combusted at the thought of it all.

I opened Lily's message. A pang of guilt hit me square in the chest. Lily wasn't just a distraction either. For a long time, Lily was my only person.

How did I get myself into this mess?

At the very least, I needed to honor her request.

"I think I want to meet Lily," I said, wondering, not for the first time tonight, why I kept announcing everything. And judging from the looks on their faces, they were as surprised as I was.

"Are you sure?" Claire leaned forward, but her husband's arm curled around her and she fell backward against him.

Beside her, William scooped Rose into his arms before kissing her, and while I considered myself a private man…I wanted that. I wanted to love someone so much I couldn't stay away from them. I wanted to be loved by someone in a way that made us forget there were people around.

But I didn't want it with just anyone.

I wanted Lily to be the person I hoped she was. I wanted her to love me the way I'd already fallen for her.

But somehow at the same time, in a way I didn't understand, I wanted Elizabeth. In every way possible. I wanted everything or anything from her.

But that would never work.

I nodded. "She wants to meet, and I think I need to know who she is…whether she's real and whether…" I trailed off, knowing they'd know what I meant without the pain of me having to dig any deeper.

Claire grinned. "And we'll all be there."

"Oh my gosh, I'm excited!" Rose squealed. She turned to William, who had been nuzzling against her neck. "*Overpower* brings people together."

"How will you know it's her? Are you going to arrange a meeting spot?" Neema asked at the same time as Shaun joined us in the living room with a tray of coffees.

I looked down at our open chat and the small silhouette of a woman with pink hair. "I feel like I'll know."

I finally typed out a reply.

```
@theanswerisno:
I'm sorry it's taken me this long to
message you. It's a long, complicated
story that I think I owe you at some
point but for now, yeah. Let's take it to
the next level.
```

• • •

Sleep evaded me.

I kept thinking about the message I'd sent, and apparently checking your phone one hundred times does not increase the likelihood of a reply. It may even decrease your chances.

It was marked *read*.

Maybe she was angry at me for leaving her hanging for such a long time. Which was understandable. Maybe I didn't deserve a reply.

The sun peeked through the gap in the blackout curtains, and my phone started making noise for all the wrong reasons.

I slammed the snooze button even though I wouldn't fall asleep again. The twisting and turning in my stomach weren't slowing. I was too anxious.

Lily. Work. Elizabeth. Meeting Lily. Promotion. Man stalking Elizabeth. Final internship test. Moving house. Mom. Dad. Work with Elizabeth. Lily not replying. Elizabeth being scared.

I was unraveling.

When I got to the office, Elizabeth was slumped over her desk. Maybe she had a rough night too.

"How are you?" I asked, freezing at the doorway and taking her in.

Her copper hair was tied back, revealing her pretty but tired face. Her gray eyes were hidden under lowered brows.

"I'm fine. You can stop worrying about me. I'm ready for our site visit." She lifted one foot to reveal her clunky site boots, which didn't look as though they fit properly.

Without making eye contact, I made my way to my closet, where I kept my boots, vest, and hard hat. "Just so you know, you can call me if you ever need me…"

"Thank you," she whispered.

The sincerity in her voice only further pulled the last thread holding me together. I grabbed everything I needed and changed the topic. "There's a really good bakery along the way."

Her bright smile returned. "You know the way to my heart."

That's something people say all the time.

Ignoring the urge to obsess over everything she said, I gestured for her to follow me downstairs, and once we got outside, I unlocked my truck. The lights on my black Ford F-150 flickered.

Her eyes widened in my direction, and I got the sense she was back to her usual self.

"Is this yours? Or a company car?" She made her way over to the passenger side.

"Mine."

"You know what they say…the bigger the truck, the—"

"Elizabeth," I almost yelled, and it was all I could do not to choke on the laughter she summoned. Her cheeky grin made my chest feel as though it were being put back together.

I didn't know it needed to be.

"The higher the gas consumption," she finished with absolute delight. "Get your mind out of the gutter."

Shaking my head, I opened the passenger door and kicked the step at the bottom so she knew to use it. I stayed near in case she needed assistance, but she held on to the grab handle and pulled herself inside.

I closed her door and hopped in on the other side. When I turned the engine on, the vibration provided the perfect amount of white noise, helping to quiet my thoughts.

She clipped in her seat belt, her cinnamon bun scent intoxicating me and covering all of my truck's regular leather and coffee smell.

I turned on the radio before maneuvering out of the parking bay. Elizabeth went completely quiet, her gaze fixed on me.

If I wasn't reversing, I'd give her my full attention to figure out why she was staring.

The radio automatically connected to my phone's Bluetooth, and Blade Olive's "Another Time, Another Place" echoed through the cabin. My insides cringed, but before I could change it, Elizabeth swiped my phone.

"You're a Blivvy!" she shrieked, scrolling through my music app. "A *Blivvy*?"

"Yeah, a huge fan of Blade Olive's music." She grinned.

"I wouldn't say I'm a *huge* fan. I just enjoy listening to every single song Jane Adams has ever created."

"You even know her real name!" Elizabeth burst into giggles. She kicked off one of her shoes, slid her water bottle into the cup holder, and laid her phone in the console between us.

Within a few minutes, she fit. In my truck. But then again, she'd taken over my office, too, after I'd kept it just mine for years. Perhaps that was one of her many talents.

She then twisted and threw her coat across the back seat. "Every time I learn something new about you, it makes you even better."

I'd need to turn up the AC if she kept saying things like that.

"Blade's talented; there's no denying it." I turned onto the highway.

"Oh, you don't have to tell me," she said. "I saw her live a few years ago, and I had VIP tickets." She squeaked, closing her eyes. "It was incredible. Can I show you my favorite song?"

"Of course." I gave up on fighting the smile that came when she was around.

Elizabeth navigated to the song and hit play, but as it started, it stopped. My phone vibrated in her hands with my mother's smiling face popping up on the screen. She panicked, tossing it into my lap.

I managed to catch it and answered, trying and failing at disconnecting the Bluetooth.

"Hi, Mom, you're on Bluetooth," I said as quickly as humanly possible.

"Hi, my boy," she replied. "Aren't I usually?"

"Uhhhhhhh…" I glanced at Elizabeth, who stayed as still as a mouse. Probably for the first time in her entire life. "I have someone with me."

"Who?"

"You don't know her."

"A woman?"

"Mom," I said, and if I weren't driving, I'd be covering my face with my hands, but now I was forced to see Elizabeth stifling a grin. "A coworker. What's up? Are you okay?"

"I'm fine, darling. But Daniel is a bit worn out, and we've got all the furniture standing on the front lawn. I know you're working, but you're always working, so I thought I'd ask…"

I peeked at the time and looked at Elizabeth. "I could drop you back at the office, then pick you up after. We should still have enough daylight to walk the site."

"Bring her along," my mom said.

A strangled sound escaped me, and I leaned over my steering wheel. "Um," I said, my voice weaker than usual.

"I don't mind either way, as long as we get to stop at the bakery later," Elizabeth said, and I could picture my mother wanting to analyze her voice.

"Darling girl, what do you like? I can make anything. Cheesecake? Carrot cake? Brownies? Are you Indian? I can make jalebi, laddu—"

"Mom…" I started and gave up. I'd already lost the battle.

"Any of the above!" Elizabeth yelled, clapping her hands together. Her turquoise nail polish glimmered in the sunlight.

"See you in ten minutes." I hung up.

Blade Olive's voice filled the car once more but all I could think about was that Elizabeth Gordon-Bettencourt would be the first girl I'd brought home to meet my mother.

25

ELIZABETH

[60 weeks ago]

@pancakesareelite:
Do you think we know each other in real
life?

> **@theanswerisno:**
> Possible

@pancakesareelite:
Maybe we talk every day

> **@theanswerisno:**
> Impossible

@pancakesareelite:
Why?

> **@theanswerisno:**
> Because the only woman I talk to every
> day is my mother and that would be the
> worst outcome I can imagine

I was going to meet Lincoln's mom. I hadn't met another person's parents in ages. No friend or lover had been close enough to invite me home, and now I was on my way to meet my boss's mother.

And Lincoln was nervous. Did I need to be nervous?

He worried his bottom lip, and his gaze was fixed on the road. Every few seconds, he'd make an attempt at saying something like, "My mom…" Then he'd pause and rethink it. "She's great but…" Sometimes he'd start all the way at the beginning. "Elizabeth, my mom is…" Cue the long exhale. The sigh. The hand sliding to rake through his beautiful, black curls.

What a lucky hand.

I glanced away. Maybe if I couldn't see him, it would be easier to shut out these thoughts. "If it makes you too uncomfortable, then you don't have to take me. I could even wait in the car, and you could hand-deliver me a snack."

A peal of laughter burst out of him. "Yeah, right. As if my mom would allow that. She'd drag you in herself."

Summoned by his laughter, I turned to face him.

He smiled now, one I'd never seen before, and I imagined it was reserved for his mom. "She's nothing like me. She's chatty and welcoming. She never quite understood where I came from."

"She sounds wonderful," I said. *Of course she was wonderful. She made you.*

Leaning my head back, I shut my eyes for a second. I hadn't been sleeping well, and right now, in this giant moving vehicle, with my favorite music and my favorite boss, I felt a warm calm take over. "It's nice that you're close."

"What's your mom like?" he asked, and sucked in a deep breath. "It's okay if you don't want to answer. I didn't mean to pry. I know everyone is always curious when it comes to your family."

I kept my eyes closed, knowing if I opened them, I'd find him studying me. "My mother is…She's beautiful and funny and…" *Trapped in a relationship with an evil man.* "And…busy. She's really busy, so I don't see her much."

He didn't ask any more questions, but I found myself wanting to tell him things.

"She was a model. Her name's Charlotte."

"Oh," he said, and the surprise in his voice was genuine. Everyone else who'd met me had already known.

"I kind of…followed in her footsteps for a while."

I didn't miss the flashing lights, the way the clothing didn't fit, and the unhealthy competition with the other girls. I'd mastered the value of a flawless fake smile before I'd mastered multiplication.

"Did you like it?" Lincoln asked, almost a whisper.

My eyes flew open, and I turned to face him. His gaze moved between me and the road.

"Not really." Tears pricked at the corners of my eyes. I blinked them away. It was that time in my cycle where my emotions were a little more heightened than usual.

The low grumble he failed at swallowing went straight into my belly, untwisting me in the process.

"It's okay," I said, noting the way his knuckles whitened around the steering wheel. "It was Douglas's idea. Not hers."

"Douglas?"

"Douglas Gordon-Bettencourt, my stepfather. Surely you've heard of him."

Lincoln looked at me with narrowed eyes. "Of course I have. But…I thought he was your father."

"Most people think so. That's what he wants people to believe, I guess. I don't know. I don't try to understand the workings of his mind anymore."

Lincoln's brow furrowed, and he tilted his head.

I swallowed the unwelcome lump in my throat. My hormones were wreaking havoc today.

A few seconds later, we pulled up in front of a bright yellow house. The garden sprawled out in front of it was filled with furniture and bordered by lines of beautiful roses. In the corner, there was a small vegetable and herb patch.

The door flung open, and a woman, who had Lincoln's rich brown skin, straight nose, and black curls, walked up to the truck, her arms already spread wide.

Lincoln did what I called the *yikes* face before hopping out. I reached for the handle, but he somehow sprinted around and opened the door for me before I could get to it. I slid out of the truck, even though Lincoln was there, ready and waiting with an elbow extended. But it was better not to touch him. Every accidental office brush had my body malfunctioning.

"Mom, this is Elizabeth. Elizabeth, this is my mom, Irene," Lincoln said after being released from his mother's tight hug and kisses.

"Nice to meet you, Ms. Carden," I said.

She pulled me into a hug too. "You can call me Irene." She extended her hands, pushing me away before looking at my face. "You are stunning." She gasped and looked at Lincoln. "Look at her fiery hair, and those eyes. Lincoln, look!"

"I've seen her, Mom. Every day at work," he replied, and looked skyward. He offered us a smile before stalking off. I couldn't hear him, but I knew he was sighing.

"Come inside. I'm baking for you." She pulled me into the house.

The living room was completely empty. All the couches, tables, and chairs out front probably needed to be in here. In the middle of the floor sat a child on a blanket.

"That's Emily Ann, my future grandchild," Irene said. The little girl didn't even look up from the iPad she was busy with. "She doesn't hear anything when she's watching those shows." Irene kept leading me through the hallway until we got to the kitchen.

"Sit." She gestured at the small table and chairs. "Do you eat biryani? It's not very spicy. My white colleagues can handle it."

I had never had it in my life, but I nodded anyway.

"Good." She walked over to the stove, where she dished spoonfuls of rice, meat, potatoes, and lentils into a plate. The oven light clicked, and she leaned left to grab a cake dish filled with batter. She slipped it into the oven and turned the timer on before reaching for the food-filled plate and putting it into the microwave. The kettle on the stovetop called for her attention, and while I'd expected water, she poured a caramel-colored, cinnamon-scented tea from the spout and offered it to me.

Watching her in the kitchen was mesmerizing. She could write a book about multitasking. I'd never seen anything like it. Even the professional cooks we had back home didn't move like this.

Lincoln walked into the kitchen at the same second the now-heated plate of food was placed in front of me. The steam pressed against my face, followed by a most delicious smell.

"Mom, give her a second to breathe before you feed her." He smiled at his mother and turned to me. "Feeding people is her love language."

"It's yours too," his mother said.

I sipped on the hot tea in an attempt to disguise the flurry of heat traveling through me at that single comment.

Beside me, Lincoln threw his hands up. "Okay, well, I don't have all day, so I'm gonna help Daniel move the couches and shelves into the living room, then I'm off. Deal?"

She nodded, and he looked at me. I gave him a thumbs-up. He took that as permission to leave me alone with his mother.

I expected an awkward silence or, at the very least, an awkward pause once left alone together, but Irene launched into conversation. "Lincoln and my soon-to-be husband, Daniel, surprised me with this house." She placed a hand on her chest. "I don't mean to brag about my son, but I can't help it."

After dishing up a plate of her own, she sat across from me and used her hands to eat, scooping up the rice between her thumb, forefinger, and middle finger on her right hand.

"Lincoln is really thoughtful and kind," I said without any hesitation. "He deserves to be bragged about."

I tried mimicking her, but the rice kept slipping out. Enough of it went into my mouth, and the spicy food packed a heat I wasn't prepared for. My cheeks must have burned bright red, because Irene scooted the tea closer to me.

"He's always been thoughtful," she said. "Since he was a child. Soft, and thoughtful. My guess is that all that thinking had him realizing the world needed someone who listens, rather than speaks. Someone who gives, rather than takes."

"That is the perfect description." The warmth in my heart reserved for Lincoln spread. It grew every time I found out something new and wonderful about him.

Lincoln's mother tilted her head and observed me. I scooped another handful into my mouth to stop myself from confessing all my thoughts about my boss to his mother. I'd need a few bottles of water after this meal, but it was delectable.

Irene polished off her plate and put it into the sink. As she washed her hands, the little girl ran up to her.

"Look what I found." She handed a thick photo album over to Irene.

After drying her hands, Irene sat down at the table and tapped the chair for the young girl to join.

"Hi, I'm Emily Ann." The kid waved and climbed onto her seat. "Are you Uncle Lincoln's girlfriend? You're very pretty."

I choked on the rice.

But Irene came to my rescue. "She works with Uncle Lincoln." She pulled the attention away from me by opening the album. The first photo was of a brand-new baby in the arms of a much younger Irene and a man who looked nothing like Lincoln, aside from the soft brown eyes I could see despite the aging photograph.

She turned the page, and Lincoln was starting to look like himself. "How old was he here?" I asked, starting at the top left.

"He must have been around five."

"I'm older than that." Emily Ann huffed. "And this is kinda boring. I'm gonna go play outside." She walked over to the fridge, grabbed a juice box, and then skipped out of the kitchen.

I turned my focus down to the grinning boy. There were so many photos of him having fun. And being happy. Dancing. Dressed up. Baking. Running. Playing.

On the next set of photos, his smile wasn't quite as wide. But the half smile was something I was used to. Something I adored.

"This was around eight or nine." She pointed at the boy in a school uniform. "He was so brilliant, the teachers would force him onstage and test him in front of everyone."

"Oh" was all I managed, because the Lincoln I knew would have hated that.

"He started feeling isolated from his peers. They pushed him over a grade. My little genius." She sighed. "I didn't know how to slow him down or protect him, so he did it himself."

She turned the page, and Lincoln, a few years older than the previous set, wore the same grumpy expression he wore now. Beside it, another photo of Lincoln, this time with half a smile as he held a deck of cards with a little girl standing next to him.

"Who is that?" I asked, pointing at the girl.

"Claire."

"Claire?"

"His friend. They've been friends since he was a child. One night, I prayed to God my boy would come out of his shell, and the next day, she moved in next door. I may have orchestrated a friendship after that," she said with a chuckle. "And I'm so glad I did. She was the only one who could pull the occasional smile out of him."

There were two strange pangs in my chest. Jealousy and heartache. I stared into the sad eyes of this boy who resembled my boss. The man who spent countless hours helping me in more ways than one. And even though he was only a few feet away, I missed him.

Irene pointed at another photo of Claire. "But I knew she'd be able to handle him. He was a lot more back then, and the kids weren't always sure what to do with him."

"He's perfect as is," I clipped out, without intending to. I brought the cup to my lips and shut my eyes.

"He is," she said with a smile. "I wish more people would see that. But judging from the way you look at him, you have."

I gulped down the scalding tea.

She patted my back. "Don't worry, your secret is safe with me."

The timer went off, and she pulled open the oven door, letting the scent of freshly baked carrot cake engulf me. "Let's take our boys a slice of cake, shall we?"

Our boys. *Our?*

Lincoln wasn't mine. He was my boss, and I should probably tell his mother that, but then why was I carrying a slice of cake? Why did I want to be the one to hand it to him?

And why, why is it that, when his shirtsleeves were rolled up and his hair was all messy, I lost my breath? Why is it that when he took the slice of cake and thanked me, his smile seemed to control the blood flowing in my veins?

Danger, Elizabeth. Danger.

26

LINCOLN

[58 weeks ago]

@theanswerisno:
I am plagued by wondering if every
pancake-eating woman is you

> @pancakesareelite:
> Every pancake-eating woman IS me

@theanswerisno:
Well, that certainly doesn't help

> @pancakesareelite:
> I am plagued by wondering if every
> pancake-hating man is you

@theanswerisno:
I don't HATE pancakes. I'm not a
monster. I just prefer cake

> @pancakesareelite:
> You don't have to choose. You could
> have it all, Link

> @pancakesareelite:
> Ooooh, let's bake a cake next!

Main quest: Help move furniture. Side quest: Don't fall in love with Elizabeth.

Having Elizabeth at my mom's house, making my mom laugh and handing me a slice of cake, was really not helping the side quest.

Elizabeth, Emily Ann, and my mother picnicked on a blanket in the center of the mostly empty living room while Daniel and I carried in the last of the furniture. There were more items than I'd bargained for, and even though my back started complaining, I didn't want this to end.

From here, I could hear Elizabeth laughing, and now and then she'd tease the way she often did and glance in my direction. Those beautiful gray eyes knocked the air out of me.

I couldn't have her. I knew that. She was far out of my league, not to mention my employee. But maybe I could enjoy her. Right? Like this. It wasn't against company policy.

Mom walked over to me. "You better get going. I didn't mean to keep you."

"I don't mind." I took one last look at how comfortable Elizabeth was. Her safety boots had come off, and her feet were curled up underneath her. She and Emily Ann were taking rock, paper, scissors very seriously.

"Because you're the most wonderful son." Mom gave me a squeeze.

Elizabeth glanced upward and studied me as she often did. Over the last few weeks, she'd started reading me and acting without me having to ask her to. Right now, she knew I was ready to leave. She stood, walked over, and stretched out her hand toward my mom. "It was wonderful to meet you. Everything I ate was delicious. I wish I could cook like that."

My mom swatted her hand out of the way and pulled her in for a hug. "I'll teach you." She released Elizabeth and winked. "Come over, anytime."

Elizabeth squirmed.

Why? What did she and my mother talk about? I'd need to ask.

My mother edged closer, her eyes wide. "Lincoln…" Her brows hugged. "There's one other thing. We need to hand over the keys to the new owner in just over a week."

I knew what was coming, and yet I waited for her to finish in the hopes it would be something else.

"If you can't finish the last of the packing…" She looked downward and fidgeted with the hem of her blouse. "I can do it."

A violent pang slammed the inside of my chest. "I'll do it," I barely got out. She remained unconvinced, so I mustered up all the confidence I had before adding, "I'm busy this weekend, but I promise it'll be all cleared out before next weekend."

"Are you sure?"

My thoughts turned to noise. "Yes," I said through the mess of feelings swirling inside me. Packing away my father's things would make it hard to forget that he'd died. "It's no problem."

As fast as humanly possible, I left. I wasn't interested in thinking about it any longer, but now it was the only thing I could think about. If Elizabeth hadn't been quick, I may have driven off without her in my distracted state.

But there she was, in the passenger seat, observing me without saying a word. I should explain to her why I went from hot to cold, but I couldn't find the right sentences.

"Your mom showed me photos of you as a kid. Apparently, you were really into pirates."

An unexpected laugh pushed out of me, and the sweet sound of hers joined. I glanced over at her, grateful for the subject change. "I should have known she'd show you all the embarrassing things she's kept of mine."

The naughtiest grin crept onto Elizabeth's face. It was the one I enjoyed most. I think. It was hard to choose.

"She told me about Bianca too."

If I wasn't driving, I'd have thrown myself out of the vehicle. My mouth dropped open while I searched for something to say. *How am I supposed to defend the imaginary friend I'd held on to for longer than I cared to admit?*

"In case you haven't guessed," I deadpanned, and kicked the truck into the next gear, "I was a strange kid."

Elizabeth relaxed in my passenger seat, and I savored how different she was outside the office. "I had an imaginary friend too—Noah." She twisted in her seat to face me, her eyes alight. "I'll tell you about mine if you tell me about yours."

A smile I could no longer resist spread across my face. The grief and longing were still there in my chest, but it was hard to sit with it when I could be here instead. Listening to the most beautiful woman in the world tell me wonderful things about herself.

•　•　•

As we reached the project location, heavy fog rolled in, accompanied by a chill. I should have brought a headlamp. I slipped on a jacket and offered Elizabeth my spare before gearing up.

Seeing her in my clothing was a level of torture I apparently enjoyed.

"Thank you." She zipped up and folded the long sleeves, freeing her hands.

Maybe it will smell like cinnamon when she returns it?

"No problem." I cleared my throat and focused on the task ahead.

Walking through the site, I gave her a quick rundown on what was happening and introduced her to everyone along the way. As I imagined, even with Elizabeth's hard hat, the reflective vest, the oversized jacket, and the ugly shoes, they all did a double take. Because it was hard not to with those eyes and her smile that gave flight to butterflies.

"When will this pipe be placed?" I asked the construction manager while peeking into one of the deep trenches.

"First thing tomorrow morning. There's been a bit of unexpected drizzle, hence the mud."

I nodded. "Manhole locations?"

He gestured for me to follow him. Behind me, Elizabeth appeared completely enthralled with what someone else was showing her.

I opened a set of drawings and reminded myself of what we'd recommended here for the layerworks. That would happen next week when we were placed here and could supervise.

We. Me and Elizabeth. Elizabeth and I. Placed here. Together. At the same time.

I searched for her through the dense fog and found her about fifty yards away chatting with one of the other workers. She waved, and I gestured for her to join me.

On her left, one of the construction vehicles revved up. Elizabeth flinched. As quick as a flash, her foot slipped and her eyes widened. She screamed at the same time as I instinctively leaped toward her. But it was too late. She disappeared into the trench dividing us.

With a deafening ringing in my ears, I jumped in.

Elizabeth was on her backside in the mud. "Don't come in here, you'll get all muddy!"

I kneeled beside her. I didn't care about the mess. "Are you okay?"

She nodded, but her eyes welled up.

"Are you hurt?" I gripped her shoulders and slid my palms across her arms, tempted to investigate every part of her.

She choked out, "I'm…I'm sorry. I wasn't concentrating, and my foot slipped on the edge, and now I messed up." She gestured at the curbs that had fallen along with her.

"Don't apologize," I bit out, and cupped her face. I couldn't stop myself. I tilted her chin upward, an ache ripping through me at the sight of her tears. "That doesn't matter. You matter. Are you sure you're okay?"

Her mouth turned downward, and she nodded. "I'm okay. I'm sorry for crying. I'm having a weird day. Family stuff. Work stress. I got my period, and I'm not prepared. I didn't mean to cause trouble on my first day on-site, and I can't lose this job and…your mom is really nice and I miss my mom…I don't know why I'm telling you any of this. Oh, and my ankle is kind of hurting." She flinched as she tried pushing herself upward.

Her lip trembled, and without any input from my brain, my arms scooped her up. My left hand slid under her knees, and my right arm cradled her back.

"What are you doing?" she said, but a laugh and one of those small smiles followed.

That's how I knew I was doing the right thing.

"Getting us out of here." I trudged through the mud to the shallowest side of the hole before climbing out.

The construction manager was at my side. "Is she okay?"

"She's fine," I answered for her while she composed herself.

She leaned against my chest, and I could feel her short, warm breaths. If I thought about it too hard, I may forget how to walk. Or breathe. Or exist.

My back protested with each step, but I ignored it. We were almost back at the truck.

"Follow me. I'll show you how to get to the cabin," the construction manager said, and pointed at his car.

Without letting Elizabeth go, I managed to open the door of my truck and place her inside, mud and all.

"I'm sorry," she said. "I'm getting everything dirty."

"Stop apologizing." I climbed into the driver's seat.

"Sorry." She huffed out a soft giggle. "I mean…" She swiped at her face with the back of her sleeve. But it only put mud there. "I'm a recovering people pleaser."

I reached into my cubby, my fingers grazing her knees as I grabbed a box of tissues. "You've got mud"—I gestured to her face—"everywhere."

She smiled, and for a second, I could almost ignore the crippling pain flaring through my back. Between the work at my mother's and my valiant attempt at getting Elizabeth to the truck, I seemed to have summoned trouble.

I wasn't planning on going to the cabin today, but I was left with little other choice.

There was no way I'd be able to drive all the way home like this.

27

ELIZABETH

[57 weeks ago]

> **@theanswerisno:**
> Can't play for a few days. It's game night and then a work event tomorrow evening

@pancakesareelite:
Ahh yes. That's awesome. Enjoy it!

@pancakesareelite:
Is it weird that I'll kinda miss you?

> **@theanswerisno:**
> Yeah, it is weird

> **@theanswerisno:**
> But I'll kinda miss you too

You matter.

That was what he'd said, and I'd started crying. There weren't many ways I could explain why without offloading years of trauma.

But I didn't care about any of that now. Because Lincoln Carden had carried me out of a trench and all the way to his truck, despite people watching, despite me being able to walk or at least limp, if I tried.

And I should have protested.

But the second he'd pulled me against his strong chest, I never wanted to leave. Lincoln's chest smelled like coffee and citrus. And I imagined he tasted that way too.

I shut my eyes, releasing a long breath that would hopefully help me draw my thoughts back to something more appropriate.

"Detour," he said.

I nodded, not trusting myself to speak. When the loud vibration of the truck stopped, I cracked an eye open. We were parked in front of a drugstore.

Lincoln dropped his keys in my lap. "Be right back."

As soon as he left, I took out my phone and navigated to my chat with Link.

My gaze fell on Lincoln's phone in the center console. If I texted Link right now, would it light up? Had I imagined all of these connections? Were they coincidences?

Wishful thinking. That was it. Because if Lincoln was my Link, it would mean he knew me on a level deeper than anyone else, and it would mean he stayed anyway.

I glanced at his phone and, with trembling fingers, typed out a message.

```
@pancakesareelite:
I'm really, really scared of meeting you.
```

My eyes were fixed on his screen as I hit send.

Nothing happened.

I lifted his phone and touched the unlock button, but the screen stayed black. My head rolled back, and I grumbled. It must have died.

Lincoln returned, and I dropped his phone back in the console. His wide eyes and red cheeks made a smile curl onto my mouth. *What did he buy?*

He climbed in and handed me the large paper bag, grimacing.

"Are you hurt?" I asked.

"A little," he replied. "Most of that stuff is for you." He started the truck and zoomed back onto the main road.

I opened the bag to reveal plastic wrapping and little cardboard boxes of every color. Pads. Tampons. Every size. Every brand. Scented. Unscented. Wings. No wings. Thin. Thick. Maxi. Night. "Did you buy the entire aisle?" I couldn't control the giggle even if I tried.

"Maybe," he said with an awkward chuckle. "I didn't know what you might need. I also got…um…ibuprofen and chocolate."

Lincoln Carden was the most perfect man to ever exist. Even though he couldn't look at me while discussing period products.

"Thank you," I whispered.

Come on, Lily. Don't cry in front of him. Not again.

After successfully getting my emotions under control, we pulled up to the cabin where the construction manager and his assistant had been staying. Lincoln climbed out first. I opened my door before he got to me and swung myself out, landing on the foot I was sure wasn't injured. I tested the other foot tentatively, and a pinch of pain lingered. It didn't seem too bad. Maybe I didn't need to be carried.

Even if I wanted to be.

"Don't put pressure on it. I can…uh…" He glanced away and rubbed a large hand across the back of his neck.

"It's fine, I'm fine," I said, and limped inside.

A deep frown embedded itself onto his handsome face and his breath struggled while Luis, the construction manager, gave us a tour of the small cabin.

It was a cozy two-bedroom cabin with one bathroom and a large living room with a fireplace and open-plan kitchen. It wasn't unlike the cabins I'd visited for quiet holidays away from LA.

But knowing we'd be sharing it, alone, in a few days made it feel tiny.

Lincoln and I took turns to wash off as much mud as we could.

"Um…so…Anders wants you on this site next week, with me. I know not everyone likes…uh…being away from home, or…uh…living with someone else, so if you don't want to be here every day, you don't have to, like…stay over." He rambled. A wince still marked his features whenever he moved.

"Are you okay?" I asked.

"Honestly?" He huffed out a heavy breath. "Not really. My back is killing me, and I need to lie down."

Luis pointed at the bedroom. "Go ahead. That's the spare room, no one's in there. Mark's taken off for the rest of the month." He then walked toward the front door. "I need to make a few calls. I'll be out front if you need me."

Lincoln walked—with much effort—to the bedroom, and I followed, wishing I could carry him instead.

He lay down on his back and shut his eyes, but it did nothing to soothe the lines of pain across his forehead. His fists were clenched at his side.

I crawled onto the bed beside him. "What can I do to help?"

"Ibuprofen helps, heat or ice helps, too, but mostly I need to rest."

"Is it because you carried me?"

He chuckled and winced. "No, Elizabeth. It's because I carried my mother's piano."

"Ah, yes." I got off the bed and went to the kitchen. In the bag filled with tampons, I also found a pack of ibuprofen. I poured a glass of water and returned with my offerings outstretched. "Take this."

He struggled to sit up and drink it, but once he was done, he dropped back down with a groan. "It should subside in a few hours. Luis can take you home."

"And leave you here on your own?"

"I'm on my own all the time," he said with that half smile.

"Do you get this often?" I asked as the soft warmth of the bed called to me. I slid down until I was lying flat on my back too. Our shoulders were almost touching.

Lincoln was quiet for a while, and I thought perhaps he'd fallen asleep, but when I pulled my attention away from the wooden ceiling, I saw his eyes wide open and staring ahead.

He looked away. "When I overdo it. It's…from an old back injury I like to pretend I don't have when I offer to help my mom move furniture, or carry women around, apparently."

I laughed and that seemed to bring out a smile on his face. "How'd you hurt your back in the first place?"

Lincoln sucked in a deep breath and frowned. "Uhh…remember I told you about how my dad died?"

My heart already ached at the hesitation in his voice. "Hit-and-run?"

"Uh-huh." He swallowed. "I was, um, I was with him. We were walking to the store to get stuff for dinner, and he, uh…he must have seen the car coming. I didn't. He pushed me out of the way, and I fell into a concrete channel and hurt my back. I didn't even register it at the time." He swallowed again, his Adam's apple bobbing.

I moved closer, wanting nothing more than to give all the comfort I had. "I'm sorry."

"Yeah. So am I." He blinked a few times, but a rogue tear still escaped.

I reached out and dabbed it with my thumb. His lids dropped closed.

He removed his glasses, setting them on the bedside table before rubbing his palms across his eyes. "That's the most I've spoken about it in years."

"You can talk to me about it whenever you want."

With great effort, he turned around, shoving his face into the pillow. "Thank you," he mumbled, his voice muffled. "Could you tell me something else? Another interesting and random fact I wouldn't have guessed about Elizabeth."

Lincoln rarely used my last name. I don't know how he knew not to.

"I'm a masseuse."

He turned his face to look at me, and it was an entirely different experience seeing him without his glasses. His brown eyes were even softer, warmer. My heart skipped over itself.

"No, you're not."

"I am."

"Elizabeth, you were a model, you're an engineer, and now you're a masseuse?" His amused smile and still-shining eyes lit a fire inside me.

"I mean, it was just for fun. I did it as part of a three-month wellness program in Thailand. But I remember some stuff. I'll prove it." My blood turned to lava at the mere suggestion.

Lincoln swallowed but said nothing.

"It could help with the pain," I added, breathless as if I'd been working out. *Why am I doing this?*

I opened my mouth to retract the offer, but no words came out. The logical part of me screaming about the inappropriateness was gone, replaced only by the need to make him feel better.

And the intense desire to touch him.

He turned his face back down to the pillow, and his muffled voice said, "Okay."

Okay?

Okay. I gulped in a mouthful of air, but there seemed to be no oxygen in it.

I could do this. I could totally do this. I kneeled beside him and pushed up my sleeves.

"For what it's worth, you don't have to prove yourself. I believe you," Lincoln mumbled at the speed of light.

But it was too late now. I laid my palms on his back, and he arched away but then came back again. My breath hitched, but I was already surviving without oxygen, so I dug the heel of my hand into his hard muscles and pushed it upward.

A soft groan escaped him, sending goose bumps across the back of my neck.

My hands slid downward, and my fingertips worked across the tight knots. Again, he breathed a low and guttural breath. I shifted closer until my knees were pressed against his side.

The heat of his skin passed through the light fabric against my palms. My hands shaped the contours on his back, and everything tightened within me.

I let my hands roam upward across Lincoln's shoulders, gripping both of them and resisting the urge to play with the hair at the back of his head, the way he often did.

Below my touch, Lincoln moved against me like a cat would while being petted, and I used all the restraint I had not to lean down and kiss his exposed neck. I couldn't help but imagine what my mouth would feel like against his firm body. What it might feel like to bite him. Just a little.

With each stroke, with each groan that escaped him, my need grew. Until I could barely stand it anymore.

There was no denying it. I had fallen prey to the Gray woman weakness.

28

LINCOLN

[56 weeks ago]

@theanswerisno:
Wanna play?

> **@pancakesareelite:**
> theanswerisyes

@theanswerisno:
You're agreeing and you don't even know
which game.

> **@pancakesareelite:**
> Link, by now you should realize I'll
> play anything with you, at any time

> **@pancakesareelite:**
> Except DotA

@theanswerisno:
Well, now that's all I want to play

> **@pancakesareelite:**
> ffs

At some point, the pleasure started to feel like pain.

Wanting Elizabeth to touch me when it felt like I may die because of it was masochistic.

"Do you want to turn around? I could do your chest." Her voice was filled with the playful flirtation I dreamed of. Or imagined.

"No." The word came out clipped and fast. I couldn't look at her. She'd see the flush of my cheeks, the craving in my eyes. I didn't need her to see that. Not at all.

Her hands pressed against my lower back, sliding down to my sides where her fingers applied a pressure that nearly had me combusting.

"That's enough." I panicked and shifted away ever so slightly. My heart raced, and my thoughts were fuzzy. I could not do this with my intern. *No. No. No.* "Luis should take you home now. It's getting late, and you need to be in the office bright and early with those corrections."

"Um…" She stumbled on her words. The mattress dipped as she moved away. "Okay."

I wouldn't dare look up. Never in my life had I felt this way. I didn't know I could feel this way.

As soon as she was out of the room and I was sure I'd heard the door close, I hopped up and sat upright. I grabbed my glasses off the bedside table and put them on so everything could come into focus. Maybe it would help focus my brain too.

The pain in my back had been helped by the meds and her surprising set of skills, but it still threatened to return.

I had to take more medication and sleep it off. But not in these jeans. I undid my pants.

Elizabeth burst back into the room. "Lincoln, I'm sorry if I—"

"Elizabeth!" My hands frantically wrenched the zipper up. I spun around. My skin burned. My chest tightened. Everything was impossibly hot.

"Sorry!" she yelled, and swung the door closed with a loud bang.

I collapsed onto the bed and remained there unmoving, wondering how difficult it may be to find a new job and never return to my old one.

• • •

"I wasn't expecting you," Claire said when I walked into Rose and William's apartment. "You're usually running or working extra hours no one's asked for."

"Took a personal day" was all I said. They didn't need to know that I was scared of seeing Elizabeth after yesterday. Mixed in with that anxiety was knowing Lily was scared of seeing me. I needed a distraction. "How can I help?"

There were keyrings, stickers, coupons for the *Overpower* video game, and themed T-shirts scattered across the floor. Rose sat in the center with a bunch of gift bags.

"For me?" Rose glanced upward. "You've never taken off work for any reason. I won't flatter myself into thinking it was to come over and get a head start on *Overpower* promo."

"Does it matter why I'm here? Or does it only matter that I'm here and your bags will get packed?" I sat on the edge of the circle, and Rose tossed a bag at me.

Claire's eyes narrowed. "William said you two were playing *DotA* all night. Which is why he's still asleep. You don't have kids, you should be asleep." Her expression turned to concern. "Something's off. Are you sick?"

"Everything's okay," I said. A lie. Everything was not okay. "I, um…needed some time off."

"Tell me the truth." She sighed, dropping her gift bag in her lap.

"No."

"Tell me."

"No."

"Lincoln." Claire crawled over and poked my ribs. "I'm your best friend. We have no secrets."

I shoved a T-shirt into the bag, and the truth spilled out of me. "Elizabeth gave me a massage; then she left the room and wasn't supposed to come back but she did, and I was busy taking off my pants…"

They gasped.

"Because the pants were uncomfortable!" I groaned and dropped my head into my hands. "I was going to sleep, and I can't sleep in jeans, but I don't know how much she saw or what she's thinking. I panicked, and she panicked, and I…"

There was a beat of silence before shrill laughter surrounded me.

"I hate both of you," I said. "You tell me that I never open up, and now I'm opening up, and I don't know what is and isn't appropriate to share. That's why it's easier not to."

"I, for one, am happy to know you get as flustered as I do when I have a crush," Rose said as she composed herself, only to start giggling again.

Claire dropped her hands from her mouth. "Oh my goodness, wait, what? Backtrack. She was giving you a massage?"

"Uh, yeah. My back was hurting." My face was hot and I was deeply uncomfortable, but a part of me, for the first time ever, wanted these two to weigh in. To help me make sense of…their own kind, I suppose. I don't know what women want. I never cared but now…I did.

With this one woman, at least.

"So, you're worried she saw your hobnob. That's not so bad." Rose lifted the oat cookie she was eating.

"I had underwear on, of course. Who doesn't wear underwear?" I said, and that made everything worse. *Did she see my boxer briefs?* "She's my intern."

"Who willingly gave you a massage." Claire folded her arms across her chest. "Unless you instructed her to do that, which would be creepy. Please say you didn't do that."

I grabbed an empty gift bag. "No. Of course not. She offered." I inhaled a deep breath. "Because of my back. I think she felt guilty because she thought it was hurting after I'd carried her."

Rose squeaked. "*Carried?* Lincoln Carden, go back, go back, go back."

"What?" Claire's jaw dropped. Had we been in a nineties cartoon, I'd have had to lift it up from the ground and reattach it.

"She fell." I groaned. "Never mind. Forget I said anything. I'm going to resign. It's fine. I don't need that job. There are others."

Rose laughed so much that she leaned against Claire for support. But it was no good because Claire was laughing too. I nearly joined in.

Claire cleared her throat and reached out to squeeze my arm. "Personally, I wouldn't offer my boss a massage unless I was attracted to him or I was like…a masseuse or something."

"She is a masseuse," I replied, and pulled the paper gift bag over my head.

They may never stop laughing.

One of them pinched me. "Listen," Rose said, "if she came back into the room, it means she wanted to see you, and that probably means she was looking at your face. I bet she didn't see anything."

Another pinch. This time softer. Must be Claire. "Lincoln, I swear, she's not going to make a big deal out of it unless you get weird. Don't get weird. Taking off work after that is a little weird."

"I panicked, and I think it may have come across as mean." I removed the paper bag so I could attempt to breathe.

Claire and Rose both sat with their arms crossed in front of me. "Apologize, then."

I stared at them for a second. Was it really that simple?

Claire nudged me. "So we weren't wrong? You do have a crush on her?"

"It's not a crush," I choked out, and considered hiding in a gift bag again.

"It's more?"

"It's everything." I stood, the admission knocked the stupidity out of me. "I have to get back to work. I have to see her and apologize." I grabbed my keys and wallet. "I'll see you tonight." Panic zoomed through me, and my hand shot up to my face. "Oh no. Tonight. The LAN's tonight."

"Whoop. You've just remembered Lily, haven't you?" Claire asked.

Fear set my bones in place as I thought of her last message. She was scared of meeting me. And I was chasing after another woman on the day I'd be meeting her?

This wasn't right.

I nodded.

"Oh," Claire said.

"Oh," Rose repeated.

"Go, go," Claire said. "Go and see Elizabeth."

"But Lily?" I choked out.

"One at a time, player." Rose threw herself around my neck for a tight hug. "Good luck. If you miss the launch because you're confessing your love to someone, I'll forgive you."

"I'll be there." I paused and mumbled to myself, "I have to be."

"Hey, Lincoln," Claire called as I reached the door. "Take a breath. Follow her lead. Be yourself."

29

ELIZABETH

[55 weeks ago]

@pancakesareelite:
What's your dream girl like?

                    @theanswerisno:
Mystery face. Mystery personal life.
Loves gaming and laughs at all my jokes

@pancakesareelite:
Hahahahahahaha

Lincoln was missing. No one had heard from him, not even Mr. Anders. People around the office were placing bets on whether he'd died.

Death by unsolicited massage.

A mixture of shame and sadness swirled in my stomach.

I sent multiple emails. Only work-related. Because I had no idea how to say *Sorry for getting handsy with you; I forgot you're my boss.*

Or maybe he didn't want me to apologize? I hadn't imagined

the way he'd unwound under my touch or the sounds of enjoyment that had vibrated through him and against my fingertips.

I saw the intense look in his eyes before, the soft blush in his cheeks afterward.

Lincoln Carden was attracted to me. I knew what attraction looked like, and I'd been searching for it in his eyes for a long, long time.

But it would ruin me to risk it all for him. Still, I would. As pathetic as that may be. Because every part of me wanted to be with him in any way he'd take me. One night, even one kiss from him, would be better than anything I'd experienced with anyone else. The few seconds I spent in his arms feeling safe and cared for were already better than so many years of my life.

I did not imagine his enjoyment. But I also hadn't imagined his sudden discomfort.

And to make matters worse, Link hadn't replied either. Maybe I'd scared him off with my last message. Maybe he wasn't Lincoln.

But if he was...Would that be better or worse?

I looked down at the drawing in front of me. It was covered in red pen, as though someone had bled over it. In Lincoln's absence, one of the urban engineers had taken to giving me work, and I had no idea how to complete it. I made error after error, but he never helped me. He only told me it was wrong.

Was I meant to know all this stuff? Was Lincoln going above and beyond every time he taught me something?

I dug my nails into my scalp. *Think, Lily.* Figure it out. Now. Because if you don't, you won't get this job, which means no money, which means Mom did all that for nothing, and in the end, Douglas would be right.

There was only one week left of this internship, and I was deep in my self-imposter era and couldn't figure out whether I was any better or worse than when I'd started.

I could already hear his voice: *Waste of time.*

But another voice came through, louder and real.

"Elizabeth?"

Someone neared. I shook the heaviness from my head.

"Elizabeth?"

My head snapped up, and I met Lincoln's soft brown gaze—the one that melted away so many of my fears. And now, seeing him here after thinking about him nonstop since I last touched him exacerbated them.

"You're here," I said. "Thank goodness, you're here."

He leaned his hip against my desk, his brows hugging. "You look upset." His gaze shot down to the drawing in front of me. "Oh."

"It's awful," I whined, but I couldn't help it. Lincoln was back, and that made me feel like it was okay to dig into my insecurities and lay them open for him to see. "Just when I thought I was getting the hang of it, this happens. I have no idea what I'm doing. I need to rethink my career choice."

Lincoln lifted the drawing and brought it close to his face. "When did you graduate?"

"You know I've just graduated."

"And you think someone who just graduated is meant to know everything about being an engineer?" he asked in the calmest voice. He lowered the drawing until he could look at me over the top of the Arch D sheet. One dark eyebrow popped upward. "Cocky, are we?"

"N-no," I stammered. "But…"

He tossed the drawing aside and turned his full attention on me. "But what, Elizabeth?"

"I feel like I'm wasting everyone's time and resources," I admitted, swallowing the lump and hearing Douglas's voice over and over.

Lincoln slid along the desk, scooting closer. "Jameson, who I assume marked that up, is an urban engineer. There's no way you should have known this stuff. Besides, Jameson can't draft to save his life. He used to do everything by hand and then gave them to me to draw up digitally. It's a pain and costs the company double for any task."

"Seriously?"

"Uh-huh." Lincoln shifted even closer, his thigh brushing against my forearm. "Fischer failed first year and third year."

I craned my neck and took him in. His disheveled hair, his rolled-up shirtsleeves. He wasn't wearing a belt today.

"Your boy Anders." Lincoln coughed out a laugh and leaned closer. "Anders failed engineering math." He held up a hand. "I know many engineers fail it, but he also came here and lost the company an incredible amount of money because he signed off on a road design when he didn't know enough about it."

My mouth dropped open. "No way."

I enjoyed how close he was. How relaxed he seemed to be.

"Name anyone in this firm," he said.

All the tension in my stiff shoulders slipped away with every playful laugh I earned from Lincoln. Every shared joke. I loved this level of our relationship. Of whatever we were.

"Sarah Mbali?" I asked, thinking of the only senior female engineer in Traffic Analysis.

"Qualified as an engineer, didn't want the stress, left the industry, and went back to South Africa, where she became a music teacher for, like, ten years, then returned to engineering later on." He grinned now with both sides of his mouth.

A mouth I wanted to kiss.

"Why do you know this?" I managed.

"They didn't give me any work on my first day, and that was a bad move on their behalf. I spent the entire day in a hyperfixation spiral researching all of their credentials and college results."

There wasn't anything more Lincoln than that.

"You?" I said softly, knowing he'd hear me because of how close he was now. "I'll bet you don't fail at anything."

He pursed his lips. "Not any of my engineering courses, no. But I landed Simucon in some hot water after ignoring a client. I was working on their report, and I didn't realize clients needed so much reassurance. Why waste five minutes on an update email when those five minutes could be spent on the design report?" He let loose a soft whistle. "Well, they were our biggest clients at the time and dropped us for our competitors."

"No!"

"Simucon forced me into a communications course, which I nearly failed."

I didn't mean to giggle, but I couldn't help it.

Lincoln pushed himself off my desk. "I think you get what I'm trying to say…It's not easy doing this work, but it isn't meant to be. Especially at first. We're supposed to be problem solvers and all. It's tough." His gaze was so soft. "You've got the knack, Elizabeth. You're incredible and far from useless. You need to cut yourself some slack…" He pointed his finger at the drawing. "When's this due?"

"Before I leave. And…" I paused. "I can't stay late tonight. I need to leave before seven p.m."

Lincoln looked over at the clock. It was already 4:30 p.m.

At that exact moment, Mr. Anders zoomed inside. "Ah, you're here. Cedric said he saw you come in. Thank goodness. We have a meeting tonight with Mitchell Herman at around six."

"I can't tonight."

"Hot date, Carden?"

Lincoln delivered an unimpressed glare. "I have a really important event to attend."

"I won't keep you longer than seven. It's Mitchell Herman."

"Fine."

"Great. I'm off to grab some dinner, but I'll be back before then." With a final thumbs-up, Mr. Anders disappeared.

"Who is Mitchell Herman? He sounds important," I said.

Lincoln let his head fall to one side and rolled his eyes. "Mitchell Herman is one of the biggest developers on this end of the world. He always hires me to do traffic studies for developments in countries I've never been to. I keep telling him to hire someone locally."

"It's because you're the best."

Lincoln's lolling head snapped straight, as did his entire body. "Stop it, you."

I bit my tongue to resist saying something I might regret.

He peered at my drawing again. "I assume he wants you to do it by hand."

"You have got to be kidding me." I stood and looked at the drawing from the same angle he studied it at.

"Print a long drawing. We're going to work over there." He pointed at the bigger table in the corner.

I hit print, and while I walked over to the plotter, the dimmed office lights lit up. The office went into standby mode at 5:00 p.m., and tonight, the floor was emptier than usual. Granted, it was Friday night.

I stepped back into the office and laid the drawing down on the long table. Lincoln set his tools on the desk: his pencils, scale rule, and a variety of French curves.

"While you'll never be expected to do this for anyone else, I do believe it really strengthens the foundation of the knowledge you'll use to design things in the future." Lincoln's large hands pressed down on the drawing.

Was I jealous of a drawing?

Maybe.

He lowered himself closer to the drawing while fitting the curves.

This may be the sexiest thing I'd ever seen.

"But how do you know what's right?" I asked, my breath a shameless squeak.

"Fundamentals." He leafed through his textbook to horizontal alignment. "Come here."

Summoned, I went closer. As close as I could reasonably be. I inhaled his fresh scent and watched his deft fingers handle the rulers and pencils with a grace that had me thinking about other things he could handle.

"What's on your mind? You look distracted."

My heart jumped to my throat. "Nothing."

His lopsided grin returned. "If you say so." He gestured for me to come even closer. "Now, calculate the k-value manually."

I took the pencil, my hands shaking.

"About yesterday, I hope I didn't come across as angry or rude. I'm sorry. I was in a lot of…pain, and I was trying to get comfortable." Struggle underlined his words.

I followed the curve he'd laid out and made notes on the drawing. "Oh, um, a little, but it's okay. I may have overstepped and shouldn't have barged in." I looked up at him, and my breath escaped me. He was closer than I'd anticipated. His deep gaze raked across my body underneath those long lashes.

"How's your back?" I managed.

"Much better," he replied, now focused on my mouth.

Shaking off my nerves, and maybe delusion, I turned my attention to the calculation and finished it before handing the pencil back to him. He drew the rest of the intersection, edging closer to me. I twirled in and out of his reach until I was sure he was playing along.

I hadn't imagined all of this.

Lincoln walked me through his design, ensuring I understood every last bit of it. We leaned over the drawing, his shoulders pressed against mine. He reached for the pencil, trapping me between his hard body and the edge of the table. My breath hitched, and I stayed there, unmoving for a few seconds while he crowded behind me.

He didn't move either.

With my heart rate soaring, I arched my back ever so slightly, and my body pressed against his for a brief moment. The heat between us was enough to make me lightheaded.

A heavy breath escaped him, caressing my neck, leaving goose-flesh in its place.

His right hand dropped the pencil and landed on my waist at the same second I spun around. His fingers squeezed my side, and my desperate gaze met his. Equally desperate, if not more.

He wet his lips while he focused on mine. I tilted my chin toward him. Those soft, brown eyes filled with fire. He slid his hand around my neck, cupping the back of my head before pulling me toward him.

And then he finally kissed me.

His soft mouth pressed against mine, and my knees buckled. I curled my arms around his neck for support and found the hair I'd been wanting to play with, tug, and rake my fingers through for weeks. His hand slid from my side, around my waist, and I arched into his embrace without breaking the kiss. I never wanted to break this kiss.

I parted my lips, licking the edge of his bottom lip. He groaned, throwing his head back and sucking in a deep breath. "Elizabeth," his voice deep and filled with desire.

I wrenched him back down and kissed him, parting his lips with my tongue. Now his groan vibrated through to me. He gripped my waist and lifted me onto the table. I opened my legs, and he pushed between them. I threw my head back for air, finally. I could breathe. I needed Lincoln Carden to be able to breathe. "Don't stop," I whispered.

His mouth left hot, wet kisses down my neck, where he lingered and licked, sending electricity sparking through me. My nails scraped across his scalp as his teeth nipped at my collarbone. I wanted him lower.

He came back up, leaving me twisting with tension. The speed of my beating heart rivaled the quick breaths I took before crashing our mouths together. His hot palms explored the dip of my hips with a fervent passion I could replicate.

A soft moan escaped me, and I bit down on his full bottom lip.

He groaned into my mouth. "I've been wanting to do this forever."

"More," I begged. "More kissing. Please."

And he gave me more, because Lincoln Carden kissed with the same intent he did everything else. To be the best.

And he was.

Until we heard voices.

30

LINCOLN

[54 weeks ago]

@pancakesareelite:
I've uploaded a Sim for you,
check it out

@theanswerisno:
The one called Lily Pancakes? Is this
what you look like?

@pancakesareelite:
Uh…I don't think that hip to waist
ratio is achievable, Link

@theanswerisno:
Well, now I guess I need
to give you a Link.

@pancakesareelite:
As long as you can't
see what I do with him

@theanswerisno:
Lily!

@pancakesareelite:
removes pool ladder

> @theanswerisno:
> I regret this

> @pancakesareelite:
> Fine. I'll undo it

No, no, no.

Elizabeth and her inviting mouth pulled away from me. She scrambled off the desk and fastened the button on her blouse that had become undone, which should be a crime against humanity.

I spun around, sucking in a deep breath, but it did nothing to stop the pulsing in my ears or the buzz in my fingertips. My lips tingled where hers had been, and my tongue? It wanted more. So much more. I couldn't even risk a glance in her direction. I paced away seconds before Anders and Mitchell Herman walked through my office door.

"I told you we'd find him here." Anders glanced between Elizabeth and me.

She leaned across the long drawing, her left palm pressing onto the French curve and her right hand shakily sketching.

"Although I didn't expect you," Anders said to Elizabeth.

She looked at them, her cheeks pink. I now knew how soft and warm they were against my mouth.

What have I done?

She stepped forward with an outstretched hand. That hand had been in my hair seconds ago. I wanted it back. *Ahhhhh.*

"Hi, I'm Elizabeth. I'm part of the internship program."

Elizabeth was my intern. What the heck have I done?

Mitchell took her hand as Anders added with a knowing glance, "The Gordon-Bettencourt."

Mitchell's brows popped up as he considered her with a mixture of expressions, none of which I enjoyed. She curled away from their greedy, wanting eyes.

I stepped between them, shielding her and stuck out my own hand. "Mitchell, it's good to see you."

He took my hand. "You work far too hard."

"I have to when you're around," I said, and we laughed. I'd learned what I called *corporate humor*, a careful mix of flattery and passive-aggressiveness. Land it, and you're in with the big bosses. Go too far, and you're excluded from all the important decisions. "How can I help you?"

"You know what, boys? How about we have this discussion over drinks," Anders said.

Mitchell cheered in response, and I offered them a quick nod, despite wanting to stay here.

"I suppose we'll continue on Monday," I said in Elizabeth's direction, but I was too afraid to look into those eyes. Not when her beautiful, emotive face was likely doing everything to remain neutral.

A face I'd touched—kissed—only moments ago.

A heavy arm swung around my shoulders. Mitchell was an overly physical man. He slapped me on the back when laughing. Shook my hand for a moment too long, and if it wasn't a business meeting, he'd probably challenge me to a wrestling match.

"Your team lost this weekend," he said with one of those loud laughs.

A team I only picked to be able to converse with him. "We'll get you next time," I said, and before we rounded the corner, I peeked back and caught Elizabeth's bewildered gaze. Her lips still swollen from the intensity at which we'd kissed.

That kiss, that delicious kiss that undoubtedly rewired my brain, could put our jobs on the line. If Anders had walked in one second earlier, he'd have found me flush against her body, my hands savoring the piece of exposed skin between the hem of her shirt and the waist of her pants.

It would all be over.

She'd lose her shot at permanent placement.

I'd lose the promotion.

And everyone would know why.

If Mitchell wasn't dragging me along with him, I'd have stayed frozen in place, paralyzed with the awful decisions I was faced with.

Logically, I knew we couldn't do this. We *shouldn't*.

But my racing heart said otherwise. It longed to be near Elizabeth. To shut out the world and carry on where we left off.

Anders led us to a nearby restaurant. The second we stepped inside and Mitchell finally let go of me, I searched for my phone. It wasn't in my pocket. No. No. I left it on charge in my office.

My office, where Elizabeth may still be.

Although she did say she had to leave. But that was before…before I kissed her. Not to assume that would change her plans…I just…

I needed to speak to her.

"How's the Gordon-Bettencourt's work coming along? Is she working independently yet? Or is she still using you?" There was an accusatory edge in Anders's voice, and I wasn't sure if I projected my guilt or whether he'd seen something.

"She's learned a lot. We were working on the basics of urban engineering before you arrived. Doing it by hand."

"Ah, Jameson got to her while you were away. I couldn't stop him."

I shrugged in my best attempt to remain casual. "It's a good lesson."

"So she's smart, too, huh? Some people have really been blessed on all fronts." Mitchell opened his menu. "She's already drop-dead gorgeous. Think she's looking for a newly divorced man?" He lifted his left hand and wiggled his ring finger, where only a band of lightened skin remained.

"She's out of your league," Anders teased, and made direct eye contact with me. "She could get anyone she wants. Actor, superstar, or maybe she'd like that handsome tech genius everyone is after… What's his name? Viktor something."

Whatever had been fluttering in my chest since leaving the office was knocked out, leaving a hollowness I was more familiar with. He wasn't wrong. She was out of my league. I had no doubt about that.

"Volkov," I said firmly. "Viktor Volkov."

Mitchell's guffaw shook the table. "You're right. My money won't win her favor."

"You wanted to discuss a new development company you're opening in South Africa? Why not consult with a local firm?" I turned my attention to Mitchell and hoped they would take the bait and lead the conversation elsewhere.

"Stop trying to give our work away," Anders chided. "Otherwise we'll have to get rid of you."

"Oh, if you do," Mitchell said, turning to face me, "I could have a full-time traffic engineer on my team."

I dropped my head and inhaled, finding the part of me that learned how to behave in these situations. When I located it, I offered them a smile. "I don't know if you can afford me."

And with that, the negotiations for our fees on the next few projects commenced.

• • •

By 7:00 p.m., I bolted out of the restaurant. I couldn't be late for the *Overpower* LAN. I also needed to speak to Elizabeth. And I needed to do it before I saw Lily.

The multiple coffees I'd consumed during that meeting were not helping my anxiety.

Lily and I weren't in a relationship. I hadn't technically done anything wrong. *But why did it feel this confusing, then?*

I ran up the stairs of my building while thinking about all the years of gaming with *@pancakesareelite*. All the nights spent confiding in her when I wasn't brave enough to tell anyone else. The jokes I dared to make, knowing we'd never meet and I would never have to own up to them. She laughed with me in the hours when I'd forgotten how. Lily. Lily. Lily. Who, without a face, without a real identity, was one of the only people in the world I looked forward to talking to.

Because a part of me loved Lily.

Storming into my office, I found it empty.

And another part of me was falling in love with Elizabeth.

I grabbed my phone from the charger and the low battery alert beeped.

It hadn't been charging. My frustration grew. I was so distracted by Elizabeth that I hadn't bothered to check.

Notifications popped up. Several from Rose and William. One from Claire.

There were no messages from Elizabeth.

Maybe she'd come to her senses and clocked the risks. Her risks were different from mine, and there was no doubt she'd be accused of pursuing her boss to climb the ranks. She'd fall right into the box they wanted to shove her into.

Although…I was the one in the position of power. Did I manipulate her into this?

A foreign pain coursed through me, rendering me useless for a few seconds. I stared at my phone, replaying that kiss in my mind. She'd kissed me back. I was sure of it.

Another notification popped up.

```
                        @pancakesareelite:
      Promise me we'll still be friends after
                                    tonight.
```

And this…this pulled me from my stupor. I replied without thinking, doing what I always did when it came to Lily.

```
@theanswerisno:
I promise.
```

31

ELIZABETH

[53 weeks ago]

@pancakesareelite:
How the hell did you see that coming?

@theanswerisno:
I'm rarely taken by surprise

@pancakesareelite:
Doesn't that make life kinda boring?

@theanswerisno:
Nope. I like it this way

I could still feel the desperate way Lincoln had gripped my chin as he guided my mouth to his. His hot lips on my neck. His hands on my waist. I could still feel everything.

With a long exhale, I paced my apartment wondering if I should have stayed at the office and waited for him. But if I did, I'd be late for the LAN. Late for Link.

Wait.

He had plans too.

It couldn't be a coincidence, right?

I grabbed my phone and spent a solid hour scrolling through my chats with Link. Some of which had been lost as games ended, depending on which medium we chatted on.

I ran through the similarities for the millionth time.

Link…Lincoln. The names were similar.

They both spent a lot of time with their moms. Which maybe wasn't unusual for normal people. Maybe I was the only one who rarely saw mine.

Lincoln and Link were both engineers.

Um…what else?

I thought I saw *@wheretheresawilliam* at Lincoln's presentation, but I could have been mistaken.

How was it possible that I spoke to Link almost daily for years, and yet I knew so little about his private life?

I stumbled upon the message Link had sent me a couple years ago about how it would have been his father's birthday. Lincoln had lost his father too.

Even though the information was scarce, I was sure. I could feel it in my bones, in my gut. I could feel it the first time we met, and I ignored it. I knew Lincoln Carden before I met him. My heart knew Lincoln Carden before I'd fallen in love with him.

Now I needed to confirm it. And confess.

And if Lincoln was my Link, he'd be at the LAN tonight, waiting for me.

I could text him, but what would I say?

Hi Mr. Carden, it's me Elizabeth, aka Lily, aka Pancakes.

Oh gosh, please let that not be the thing I say.

Maybe I shouldn't go at all. That was an option. But regardless of whether Link and Lincoln were the same person, neither of them deserved to be stood up.

I was going to that LAN, and if I was wrong, then I'd get to meet Link and I'd tell him everything. He'd laugh at me. Maybe forever.

My mouth twitched knowing how he'd tease me.

Lincoln was everything, so all-encompassing, that I'd almost forgotten about Link. About the late nights and the early mornings. The soft prods and check-ins. He was even there for me when Alistair had left me unsettled.

So was Lincoln. Alistair hadn't shown his face since Lincoln threatened him. I hadn't received any messages or emails either.

This worried me because I knew it wasn't the end. Douglas was up to something. Scheming. Planning. Whatever it was would be worse than the stalking.

I flung open my closet. Over the last few years, for every date I went on, I'd been rotating the same few outfits and thrifting.

But this wasn't a date. *Was it?*

What does one wear when meeting the possible love of their life who may or may not be their boss?

As I threw every single item I owned out on my bed, it struck me that I had no idea how I'd identify him if he wasn't Lincoln Carden. We hadn't discussed anything like where we would meet or an identifiable outfit to wear.

Or…

Had we?

I had an idea, but I needed a permanent marker.

Here goes everything.

•   •   •

The LAN was being hosted at Thunderstruck's office. My heart was beating so intensely that I thought I may not make it there in one piece. I'd taken a higher dosage of my anti-anxiety medication, and even then, I wasn't sure it had worked. Or maybe it was, and if I hadn't taken it, I'd simply have expired from a heart attack.

On wobbly legs, in my worn-out Converse sneakers, I made my way toward the building entrance. The front glass doors were open, and I stepped inside, being immediately engulfed in upbeat music and excited chatter.

I'd never been to a LAN before. I had no idea what I actually needed to do, so I clutched my backpack straps as if letting people know I brought a laptop along would somehow make me more acceptable to them.

A woman and man, dressed in *Overpower* T-shirts, sat beside a doorway at a small table. "Hi," the woman said with a wide, toothy grin. "Are you here for the *Overpower* LAN?"

I nodded, my eyes scanning every man who passed me.

The problem was there were lots of men here who had slightly darker shades of skin, and plenty of the people here wore glasses too.

But none of them was Lincoln Carden.

Crap.

"Username?" the woman asked, pulling me from my daze.

"My username?"

"The one you signed up with." Her eyes studied me and softened. "Your identity stays anonymous. We know how these things go."

I nodded again. "Pancakes are elite. Lowercase, no spaces."

The woman chuckled, as did the man beside her. "Would you like a name tag or username tag?" She gestured to the blank stickers and markers in front of her. I considered using my name, but it would then connect my identity to anyone else with an interest in the Gordon-Bettencourts.

And I couldn't have that.

I didn't want to think about that at all.

Tonight, I wasn't Elizabeth Gordon-Bettencourt.

Tonight, I was Lily.

The woman strapped a bright blue band around my arm. "You can go on in. Table F12. A plug point will be available, and the Wi-Fi password and all other details will be stuck on the table's surface. You'll see it."

The main gaming area seemed to be the company cafeteria. There were rows of desks and chairs set up, and almost every table had a laptop on it. Some even had desktop computers. There were small groups bunching together chatting in high-pitched voices and plenty more gamers who were already in the middle of some game.

I navigated the aisles to Table F12 while looking around. At the front of the hall, a small crowd had gathered, and something told me that in the center I'd find the creators of *Overpower*, *@wheretheresawilliam* and his fiancé, *@theresarose*.

Would it be the same people I saw at the presentation?

"I'm so pumped," a girl muttered to herself beside me.

I, on the other hand, was on the edge of throwing up. *Deep breaths, Lily.*

I pulled out my laptop and logged in using the details on the desk. I accessed the group and scrolled through the members looking for the name that controlled my heartbeat.

@theanswerisno was online.

He. Was. Here.

My head shot up to people-watch, nay, person-search.

If he was friends with *@wherestheresawilliam*, he'd probably be near him. I stared at the group surrounding the power couple until person by person the crowd thinned.

A dark-haired man who looked a lot like the man from the presentation and a lot like *@wherestheresawilliam* leaned down to speak to someone seated at the desk beside him. A side profile so familiar to me by now, I could spot it from anywhere.

A shiver danced down my spine, contradicting the heat flooding through me.

I could barely breathe.

Lincoln Carden was here.

Lincoln Carden was my Link.

32

LINCOLN

[52 weeks ago]

@pancakesareelite:
Spontaneous personality test: What's
your take on Twilight?

@theanswerisno:
Vampires shouldn't sparkle, but for
some reason, I found myself enjoying it
more than I'd like to admit

@pancakesareelite:
Team Jacob or Team Edward

@theanswerisno:
#TeamBedward

@pancakesareelite:
No one calls them that

@theanswerisno:
By the way, I'm deleting this
conversation. No one can ever know

@pancakesareelite:
I'll always know

My mind was everywhere except here. If this LAN wasn't all about *Overpower*, the game my closest friends poured their hearts into, I'd have skipped it. I'd have gone home and told Lily I was ill.

Because I genuinely felt ill.

But I couldn't do that to them; I couldn't do that to Lily. I needed to meet her. I'd made a promise even though I couldn't stop thinking about Elizabeth.

And I'd probably have to tell Lily. I told her everything else. Albeit indirectly.

She'd never let this go.

I took out my phone and stared at it. Not a single message from Elizabeth. I clicked on her name.

No chat history available.

Perhaps I'd imagined everything. All of it.

Every smile. Every glance.

It was possible. I spent a fair amount of time inside my head. Creating a world where Elizabeth Gordon-Bettencourt was interested in me wouldn't be the strangest fantasy I'd had.

Anders had insinuated that I was being used but it didn't feel that way. We'd kissed. Not a peck-on-the-lips, accidental kiss. I couldn't have fabricated her warmth, her urgency, and that sweet mouth.

With a low sigh that seemed to come from the depths of my heavy soul, I hid behind my laptop screen and continued setting up the game.

Main quest: Enjoy Overpower. Side quest: Don't end up in love with two women.

Incognito wasn't really an option when you were friends with both game creators. It was even harder when they were both show-men. Rose and William were approached by admiring gamers for the longest time, and their excitement was palpable, deliciously so. William wanted to brag about his fiancée, and if Rose could convert her happiness into electricity, she could solve the energy crisis.

Despite everything, a smile found its way onto my mouth as I eavesdropped on their conversations.

"Thanks, yeah. I think it'll be a good follow-up to *Walk of Death*," William said.

"It's way better," Rose teased.

The gamers laughed. "You two are Couple Goals."

While I knew it was soundless, I could *hear* Rose blushing; her love for William and his for her was one of the most intensely public displays of affection I'd ever come across.

I logged in and set up my controls. I'd played *Overpower* a few times to help with the testing since William and Rose were too close to the project and Shaun, Neema, and Claire hadn't gamed in years.

`@pancakesareelite` has entered the chat

My hand shot out, clutching William and pulling him to my screen. He took one look and grabbed Rose, who leaned in and widened her eyes. I wanted to survey the area without the search being too obvious, but what was I looking for?

I dropped my head in my hands. I couldn't do this. This was a terrible idea, and I regretted every single decision I'd ever made, including being born.

"Come on, man." William gripped my shoulder.

"I don't want to meet her anymore," I whispered. "I don't want to ruin whatever fantasy she's got of me. I'm not Link. I'm not flirty and suave and…" I blew out a shaking breath and pushed myself upward.

My heart banged against my rib cage.

And the sound of the game, the music, and the chatter echoed inside my skull, making me dizzy.

"I'm sorry, I need to go for a walk," I said, and without waiting for an answer, I dashed for the exit. I needed more air, more than this room had to give.

Someone ran up behind me. Probably Rose.

But that delicious cinnamon scent reached me as a hand curled gently around my wrist. "Lincoln?"

"Elizabeth?" I breathed, knowing it was her before I spun around and took her in.

She was beautiful. Somehow more beautiful than she'd been when I'd left her at the office. Her eyes shimmered like silver. Her lips were painted red. I don't think I'd ever seen them that way before—it did ungovernable things to my already frazzled brain. Her mouth was slightly open as if her thoughts were sitting on the edge of that cupid's bow.

Her long, loose hair curled around her soft features and landed on her cleavage, over which she wore a very, very tight T-shirt that seemed to have been scribbled on with awful handwriting.

#teambedward

I stared at the word. At the hashtag. I repeated it back to myself, mumbling it. *Team Bedward.*

Had my heart not already been racing, it would have skyrocketed now. The oxygen in this place completely ran out.

My head spun.

I'd only ever said that to one person. One person who was supposed to be here. And that one person randomly brought it up at every opportunity.

Lily.

But…My gaze shot up to meet Elizabeth's worried, stormy eyes. I couldn't breathe.

"Link?" she whispered, quietly enough for me to wonder whether I'd imagined it.

No. No. No. It couldn't be. There must be a misunderstanding. Surely.

She swallowed with much effort. "Link?" she said, louder this time, but it came out scruffy.

There was only one way to describe what overcame me: sheer panic.

I took a step back, stumbling over someone's outstretched leg but catching myself before I hit the ground.

"I can explain," she whispered.

I kept moving backward. I couldn't stop. I didn't want to hear it. I couldn't, even if I wanted it to, I couldn't because the noise in my head grew louder. I took another step back, needing space.

I shook my head. It was the best I could do in an attempt to clear it of the fog setting in. But when it was no use, I spun around and moved forward this time, as quickly as I could. Dodging people, cables, legs, and tables, I needed to get out. I needed to get out of this oxygen-stealing building. I needed to breathe before the tightening around my lungs killed me.

This could not be happening.

Elizabeth? Lily? No.

"Link?" A foreign name with her familiar voice. "Lincoln, please," she begged, nearer now.

I sped up. The bright red light of the exit sign was in sight. I slipped through the crowd shuffling at the doorway.

"Let me explain." She ran up to me.

"Explain what?" The words burst out of me. "That you're…

Lily?" My mouth was completely dry. I struggled to even speak. "This doesn't make sense. It can't be. It…"

She nodded, her mouth opening but saying nothing.

With enough effort, I managed to swallow and spit out, "Have you been lying to me this whole time?"

"I…I…" she stammered, her arms curling around herself.

My hand shot up to my chest as it physically ached. "I confided in you, Elizabeth. Lily. Whatever the heck your name is."

"I—" she started again, her arms tightening.

"Did you know it was me?" My voice trembled.

Again, her mouth opened, but nothing coherent came out.

She knew.

I spun around and walked straight into Claire and Dean. They looked between Elizabeth and me as I pushed past them.

"I need to go. Please let me go." My eyes stung with unwanted tears. I hadn't cried about anyone, not since my father.

I don't know what happened next because I was already in my car and driving out of Thunderstruck's parking lot.

33

LINCOLN

[51 weeks ago]

@pancakesareelite:
Come on, Janine is the best character!

@theanswerisno:
Nope, she's a liar

@pancakesareelite:
She didn't murder anyone, like Lisa.
There are worse things than a little
lie

@theanswerisno:
I struggle with lies

After spending exactly thirty-five minutes pacing my living room, I needed to get out, as far as I could…even if it was just for a few days. And maybe, maybe when I returned, I'd be able to sort through the hurricane in my mind and the mess I'd created.

I considered going to my mother, but if she got the slightest idea this had anything to do with a woman, especially the woman she'd met, she'd want me to fix it, and I wasn't ready. I didn't know how.

On the other hand, if she knew it all jeopardized my career, I don't know what she'd say. But I didn't need another voice in my head right now.

I turned my phone on and shot Anders a text letting him know I'd be in Disselweed a few days early. My phone exploded with notifications, and I shut it off again. Maybe I never needed to turn it on ever again.

A loud bang on my apartment door was followed by Claire's voice. "Lincoln?"

I trudged over, knowing I'd have to talk to her sooner or later, and let her in.

She pushed through the doorway with Dean behind her. "Couldn't you send a text letting me know you were okay?"

"Phone's off." I held up the dark screen and shifted on my feet.

Her brows drew close. "Are you okay?"

"What do you think? Elizabeth is…Lily is…" I said, unable to keep my emotions contained. I felt incredibly unregulated.

"I think you should talk to *me*, your friend."

"Like you spoke to me when you two almost got divorced?" I gestured between her and Dean and immediately regretted it.

She flinched but didn't waver. "Exactly. That is exactly why I should have spoken to you earlier. Dean and I were so busy trying to parent and juggle work that we didn't even realize how far apart we'd drifted. What did you do when I eventually opened up to you?"

I shifted on my feet, my anger falling.

Claire answered for me. "You practically knocked our heads together and told us to talk it out. You changed everything, Lincoln." She looked at Dean. "I went back to therapy because of you."

"I'm glad it worked." I gulped and walked away. Dammit, I was pacing again. "I'm not in a good space right now. I needed to get away from that moment, and the crowd, and the noise. I need time to process."

"That makes sense," Dean said, and offered Claire an apologetic sideways glance. "A lot of the problems Claire and I had were because I didn't have any time or space to process. Space could be good. Clear your mind."

Claire fell onto my couch. "You're going to have to speak to her."

"No."

"You work together," she said.

I pulled a face. Of course I knew that.

"Are you going to skip work on Monday?"

I nodded.

"You can't stay out forever."

"I'm going on-site for a few days." I walked up to my closet to grab luggage. I haphazardly threw things inside the bag. Generally, I had a list and a luggage divider to help me compartmentalize my belongings.

If only I had those for my brain.

"Wasn't she supposed to join you?" Claire asked, studying me.

"Yes, but I'll tell her not to." I made a mental note to send Elizabeth an email in the morning. I couldn't do it tonight. I wasn't even sure I could type out her name right now.

Claire sighed. "And after that?"

I tossed a pouch of coffee beans into my bag. "By then, I will have processed."

Hopefully.

They stayed quiet while I moved around my space collecting items: toothbrush, toothpaste, moisturizer. I needed clothing.

In the smallest voice, Claire asked, "So, she's really Lily? What are the odds of that?"

Dean elbowed her. She winced but kept her gaze on me. She wouldn't retract the question.

I dropped my head again. "I don't know how to deal with this."

"Did she know it was you all this time?" Dean asked. His curiosity seemed to overtake his gentle and un-prying demeanor.

I nodded. "Seems so."

"Whoa."

Again, I nodded.

Claire made her way to my kitchen, where she tossed a few snacks into my bag. "Maybe she's got a reason."

"Anders has been insinuating that she's using me," I said, facing the words as they left my mouth but keeping my eyes fixed on the bottle of shampoo in my hands.

"But you've been chatting for years. You can't tell me this was a multiyear scheme?" Claire said. "Have you packed towels yet?"

I shook my head, and she threw a few towels my way. I caught them with one hand and jammed them into my bag.

"Anders is wrong," she said.

Elizabeth could seduce anyone if she wanted to. But she didn't want to seduce me. I knew it wasn't just that.

"This is how I process. I have to look at every option, every scenario, even the unlikely answers. I have to play them out in my mind over and over against my damn will, okay? I don't want to be this way. This is how my brain works." I could feel my lip quivering. "I wish I could let things go. I wish I didn't ruminate."

I replayed the look in Elizabeth's eyes when I'd asked her if she knew.

With growing frustration, I added, "But I am sure she kept it from me when she figured it out and she kept…flirting with me. As Lily *and* Elizabeth. I wasn't imagining it, and now I don't know what happened when. When did the lie start? She'd given me a fake name. How much of what we shared was real?" My voice cracked open along with my heart. "Every night after spending the entire day with me, alone, she chatted with me like nothing was different…" I massaged my forehead. "Why didn't she tell me?"

"Maybe she was scared of this."

I sat on the armrest of the couch. "Maybe I should apply for some positions abroad."

"I'll die without you."

"Fine, but at least survive the next few days, okay? I won't be very accessible. The signal up there is pretty terrible."

Dean drummed his fingers on his thigh. "William's got your laptop, by the way. I can pick it up if you need it."

I zipped up my moss-green bag. "No, thanks."

The very last thing I wanted to do was play a game with a stranger. Or worse, someone I knew and loved.

● ● ●

The site agent who had been staying at the cabin in Disselweed was pleased to see me. Even if it was in the middle of the night.

"You could have come in the morning. The woods are far less creepy with the sun coming in." He shifted around in his long johns and T-shirt.

"I'd like to get an early start on-site," I said. "I'm sorry for disturbing you. Please go back to bed and feel free to go home in the morning if you'd like. I don't plan on leaving for the next few days."

His face lit up. "Are you sure?"

I nodded.

"I get to surprise my baby girl tomorrow morning, then. Thanks, Mr. Carden."

I offered him another nod, and he disappeared into one of the two rooms. I walked into the other. The second bedroom was exactly as I remembered it, despite my efforts to forget it and forget the feeling of being touched by Elizabeth on that large bed.

Did she already know who I was back then? Is that why she felt comfortable doing that?

Why didn't she say anything in the many hours we spent together? Or online?

These questions would kill me.

I set my bag beside the tall closet and placed my work laptop on the desk, which had a small window overlooking the back area. I went outside and sat under the overhang, but I couldn't see anything ahead of me because the forest was covered in mist. My eyelids dropped, and I focused on the rasp of the tree leaves being blown by a gentle wind. If ever there was a time I needed to master meditating, it was now.

My therapist had promised it would help my anxiety.

She didn't say anything about healing a broken heart.

But time should.

I hoped.

34

ELIZABETH

[50 weeks ago]

> @theanswerisno:
> My therapist wants me
> to try mindfulness

> @pancakesareelite:
> Don't they know the goal is
> mindlessness

> @theanswerisno:
> You get me

> @theanswerisno:
> You might be the only person
> in the world who gets me

It was already Tuesday, after 10:00 a.m., and Lincoln still wasn't at his desk. *Where is he?*

After he skipped work yesterday, I'd put all my hopes on him showing up today and being open to letting me talk. But he wasn't here, and I was too afraid to message him on any medium.

I'd ambushed him. And in hindsight, ambushing someone who had told me, in more than one way, that he couldn't handle surprises was probably not my finest moment.

He had wanted to get as far away from me as possible. For a man who was generally unreadable, *hurt* had been spelled across his pained expression.

My eyes prickled with tears while I struggled with the lump in my throat. I'd been through some awful things, but this…this was unbearable.

I knew why this was worse. I knew it the second I'd realized that he was *my* Link. It hurt because I'd fallen in love with him in a way I didn't think was possible. I'd fallen in love with the same person *twice*.

My email pinged. Lincoln Carden!

I scrambled to click it.

> Elizabeth,
>
> I should have let you know that I'm on-site already. Perhaps this project is too far out for you. I will arrange construction work for you on a site closer to the office.
>
> If there's an emergency on one of the other projects, take it up with Anders. If he's not around, you can email me.
>
> Regards,
> L. Carden

I read it and reread it. He'd used my name. There was no reference to Lily. Had he cut *her* off?

Despite how excited I was to be on that project, I was far more excited to be alone with him. To learn from him. To exist around him before and after working hours.

Was I supposed to reply?

A fresh wave of tears threatened, but I'd dehydrated my eyes after spending most of the weekend crying. It hadn't been the meeting I'd hoped for. Far from it. I wanted him to be as happy as I was. I wanted to pick up where we left off in his office. Instead of pain, I had expected that warm, decadent brown gaze filled with unspoken, overwhelming passion. I hadn't just imagined it. He'd felt it too. He'd kissed me…

But I'd been kissed before by men who wanted me and didn't want *me*. Elizabeth Gordon-Bettencourt.

Maybe Lily was who he actually wanted. He'd gone to meet Lily.

Maybe Elizabeth was what Elizabeth was to everyone else. Maybe Douglas was right.

A pretty face everyone will get bored of.

Maybe he kissed me because he found me attractive. Because I'd started the physical aspect of our relationship by flirting with him, practically throwing myself at him when I'd massaged him.

Douglas often reminded me how everyone only wanted to be around me because of who I was connected to, and once they realized I no longer had anything to offer them, they'd run. Up until now, I hadn't wanted anyone to stay.

But this was different. I wanted Lincoln Carden. I wanted my Link. I needed him. He was kind, as handsome as could be, and smarter than anyone I'd ever met. Was there any reason he'd need me? Lose his management role because of me?

"Gordon-Bettencourt." Mr. Anders walked into my office with a rolled-up drawing. He dropped it on my desk and sighed with the exhaustion of a man who'd lived a thousand lives.

I didn't like the sound of that. At all.

"I used the correct color table and fonts, included the north arrow, and my design is sound," I rambled off.

He pointed a finger at the edge of the road. "This is incorrect. Sidewalks aren't part of the brief."

"Oh." I exhaled a shaky breath of relief. "I know...but I added it in case there was any wiggle room in the budget. Then the design would already be done."

"Wiggle room in the budget?" A mirthless laugh escaped him. "You live in a different world, don't you?"

"What's that supposed to mean?" I folded my arms across my chest.

"We beat around the bush here plenty, but," he said, and leaned back, "we can't keep pretending your understanding of a budget is the same as the rest of ours."

I blinked a few times, stomping on the fire of annoyance and shock growing in my belly. He had no idea of the budgeting gymnastics I'd had to do to stay alive.

He didn't stop. "Is this really what you want? To be an engineer and work here every day for the rest of your life? Because if I'm going to invest in you, I need to know that's your plan. You can't flee back to your glamorous life once this becomes old news."

I shuddered with each stinging word.

"No offense, Elizabeth. I'm aware I come across as rude or crass. I like to think of myself as honest, and more people should be honest. I'll bet everyone walks on eggshells around you."

I had nothing to add. I sat there, pathetically taking it all in.

"Like I said, this is a serious profession, and Simucon is looking for a lifelong commitment from their engineers. You've been at the Friday lunch announcements. We hand out long-service awards regularly. Ten years, twenty years, thirty years even. Is that a future you see for yourself?" He blew out a long breath. "Because from where I'm sitting, I'm unconvinced. You can't follow basic instructions." He pressed his forefinger on the drawing. "I did not request a sidewalk."

"But you should have," I bit out, Lincoln's words and research echoing through my mind. "We need to create a safer environment for pedestrians and people who don't have access to their own private vehicles. The city's planning to build a school half a mile from here."

"Remove the sidewalk. That's an order." Mr. Anders nearly rolled his eyes. "Either you've got a savior complex, which would make sense, or Carden's gotten to you."

I narrowed my eyes, swallowing the vicious and unprofessional things I wished to say.

"Speaking of Carden, any idea why he's on-site already? As far as I know, you're both supposed to be starting there today."

I could physically feel the blood draining from my face.

Anders narrowed his eyes. "That's the problem with Carden. He's not a team player. How is he meant to manage you if you're not with him?"

"I'm fine here. He's left me with plenty of work and a perfect set of instructions. Consider me managed." If Lincoln lost this promotion because of me, I'd never forgive myself.

"Not good enough. You should still join him there. All the other interns have already completed their site experience. Once you're done with these corrections, we can review them, print them, and you can take the set along with you."

This could not be happening. It could *not* be happening. Please, please tell me it wasn't happening.

"Um, Mr. Carden emailed to let me know that he doesn't think this will be a good project for me to join him on." I swallowed hard, hoping the shame, guilt, and longing were kept out of my voice.

"No, ignore him." Mr. Anders folded his arms. "Carden would do everything alone if I let him. He forgets his giant brain is one of the biggest keepers of knowledge and it needs to be shared. He did a good job with you on design." Anders shuffled and met my gaze for a second. "I may have been a bit harsh with you just now, but you have improved. When Carden said you'd impressed him, I wasn't entirely sold."

Warmth cut through the chill in my chest. I *impressed* him?

Mr. Anders took out his phone and typed. A few seconds later, my laptop pinged. "I've emailed you the location pin. Stop upstairs at Construction. They've got a few things they'd like to send as well."

"I don't want to go if Mr. Carden doesn't need me there, Mr. Anders. I don't want to upset him…"

"If you only went where you were needed, would you go anywhere at all?" he said with a laugh. He was still typing into his phone. "There, I've just let him know you'll be joining him."

My mouth hung open at the implication.

"It's a tough industry, Elizabeth, and there will be many roadblocks ahead of you. When an opportunity comes along, take it." Mr. Anders rarely used my first name. For some reason, it made his advice hit harder.

This was work. Lincoln would have to accept that. It wasn't only about his promotion. I fought my way through this internship. I needed the money. I needed this win. And if I had to face up to my mistakes and see Lincoln, I could do it and apologize and be professional.

I'd faked more for longer. If I tried hard enough, I could pretend he wasn't my Link. I could pretend I wasn't in love with him.

Maybe one day I'd believe it.

35

LINCOLN

@pancakesareelite:
I thought I had enough power to take
him on my own but he finished me within
a second. I should have waited for you

@theanswerisno:
Don't worry about it. We live and learn.

@pancakesareelite:
You're too nice to me

@theanswerisno:
Everyone else is too mean

By Tuesday afternoon, I was a little concerned that Elizabeth
hadn't replied. Even though I wasn't ready to speak to her about…
everything, it was worrying that she hadn't asked for my help on
any of the tasks I knew Anders must have given her in my absence.
I would imagine, by now, the other senior engineers would be

taking advantage of her by giving her all the chores no one else wanted.

Not my problem. Not my problem. Not my problem.

But that wasn't true. Professionally, she was my problem. She was my intern, and I should have put my personal feelings aside and ensured that this…whatever this was…wouldn't negatively impact her chances of getting employed.

I walked across the site as everyone continued working frantically. The days were spent pushing hard, as fog was expected to roll in in the late afternoons.

The thoughts and emotions I hadn't dealt with twisted into live energies within me, flowing through my veins, fighting for my attention. I did all I could to ignore them.

One of the men digging a trench inhaled a hefty breath and leaned on the handle of his shovel while staring out to the distance. Exhaustion was marked across his face when he wiped his brow and caught me watching him. "Sorry, Mr. Carden, just needed a second."

"Give me that." I hopped into the hole and grabbed the shovel. "Take five."

"Are you sure?" the worker said, frown lines creeping onto his face. "Could I get you a coffee or something?"

"Sounds good." I turned my attention to the trench he'd been digging. It had been years since I'd done physical labor myself. It was never required, but I did it on occasion for the same reason I ran every morning.

The exertion of my muscles, the tightening of my lungs, and the ache in my back squeezed thoughts out of my mind and drew all my focus away from the turmoil in my heart. Lifting and shifting soil, that I could do.

I kept digging and digging until Rowan, one of the construction workers, called my name. "Anders wants to talk to you."

Stretching, I took the phone and held it to my ear. "Anders," I huffed out, taking what felt like my first breath in a while.

"You're not answering my texts," he said.

"Yeah, my phone's off. What is it?" I replied.

"You can't turn your phone off when you're on-site, Carden," Anders sighed. "Never mind. Gordon-Bettencourt is going to be joining you shortly."

The shovel slipped out of my left hand and landed with a thump on my foot. I winced and coughed out, "What? Why? I told her to stay behind."

"She mentioned that, yes. But this is a greenfield project. It's the perfect opportunity for a young engineer, and she's worked on the project with you. You know it makes sense. She'll be coming up after she's printed a new batch of construction drawings."

"No," I groaned, fighting off the panic. "Absolutely not."

"Carden."

"I don't need her here." I moved my foot. It was fine. Luckily. My steel-toed shoes were wearing out, and the new pairs I'd ordered hadn't been delivered yet.

I suppose I could return the other pair I'd bought for Elizabeth. I couldn't give it to her now. Could I?

"She needs the site experience, and she may as well be there with you. I don't think it would be a good idea to send her off to a site without supervision. What do you think?"

The idea of Elizabeth on a construction site alone sent a brand-new concern blitzing through me.

"I prefer working by myself, Anders."

"I'm well aware. Everyone is. But you've managed to make some magic happen with Gordon-Bettencourt. There are only four days left of this program, and that includes today. Need I remind you of what that means for you?"

I stayed silent while I mentally sorted through my thoughts, separating Elizabeth from Lily and shoving them into different corners of my brain. Professional. Personal. Promotion. Internship.

Anders sucked on his teeth. "It's a two-bedroom cabin, Carden. There'll be more space than sharing an office with her. Unless you're uncomfortable for a different reason? She seemed fine with it."

"Anders."

"She's leaving after work," he said. "Anyway, I don't want to keep you. See you on Friday." And before I could argue, he hung up, and I was left in a ditch I'd literally dug myself into, wishing the earth would do its part and swallow me whole.

$\bullet \quad \bullet \quad \bullet$

I hurried back to the cabin and plugged in my phone. I took a deep swig of the coffee that had been handed to me at some point. The hot liquid burned down my throat.

As soon as my phone lit up with enough battery power, I turned it on and called Claire, but the line dropped. I went outside to the back deck, where the reception was stronger.

"Lincoln, what's up?"

"I'm in trouble," I rattled off. "Elizabeth is on her way here."

"What?" Claire said. "You asked for space, and she needs to respect that." I could picture the little frown on her forehead. Claire was as soft as they came, but if her friends were hurt, she transformed into a protective bear.

"Not her fault. Work," I said.

Claire sighed. "What can I do?"

"I don't know. I just needed to tell someone. I'm freaking out a little. Honestly. We'll be alone. I don't...know how to deal with this. It's too much." I pressed my hand against my forehead.

"Do you want us to come there and be a buffer?"

"Are you really going to drive for hours to get here? And then what? Stay for the next few nights?" I asked, and smiled at her determination to help.

She whined on the other end. "Maybe not today."

"She's leaving later today. I'm sure she'll go straight to sleep when she arrives. I know I will. It'll be late, and I'm already exhausted. I may make it an early night and miss her arrival entirely." The fog wrapped around the trees ahead of me.

"You sound really, really tired," she whispered.

"I don't want to do this," I said. My battery beeped in my ear.

"It's going to be okay. You're so much braver than you give yourself credit for. And if you don't want to talk to her, don't. No one can make you, least of all her."

In the background, Hannah shouted, "Mama." Cute couldn't begin to describe it.

"I'm fine, I'm fine. I gotta go. Give that kid a squeeze for me."

"You sure you're okay?"

"Go, go, go. I'm fine. I'll see you soon," I said, and only finished my sentence after she hung up: *If I survive this.*

36

ELIZABETH

[46 weeks ago]

@pancakesareelite:
What do you do when you don't want to
do something but you also have to?

> **@theanswerisno:**
> Oh, it's simple really.
> I let it consume me until I become a
> husk of a person who can't do anything,
> including the thing I need to do, but
> not excluding all the other stuff I
> could have been doing if I just did
> that one awful thing

> **@theanswerisno:**
> How about you?

@pancakesareelite:
Oh, I dive in headfirst and almost
always regret it, but then I get to
tick it off. I like to get stuff done

> **@theanswerisno:**
> You'll get me killed

I sent the drawings off to the printer and rested my aching head against the desk. I'd been staring at my screen nonstop for almost ten hours. But it was better than facing the hurricane of emotions fighting for attention inside me.

I grabbed my phone. *Should I text Lincoln and apologize that I'd be imposing,* or *should I message Link and apologize for ambushing him?*

Once again, I decided on neither. I had to do this face-to-face.

A message popped up from an unsaved number.

> Elizabeth, could we get your comment on this? Moonlight
> Media would love to hear about your experiences as a
> working girl.

There was a link attached, and my heart dropped down to the depths of my abdomen. I could see the preview, and with every read word, an old, cold presence seemed to circle me.

> Douglas Gordon-Bettencourt's daughter Elizabeth has left
> Hollywood and is pursuing a career in engineering. The
> CEO of GB Productions tells us about the hard decisions
> parents have to make in order to help their kids, no matter
> how old they get.

I exited and slammed my phone face down on the desk. I couldn't read it. I didn't want to read anything he'd said about me.

I stood, straightened my skirt, and wobbled over to the printer. *Was everyone watching me? Had they seen the article?*

There was no reason to believe they'd see it. It was fine. It was all fine.

But when my gaze accidentally met Cedric's, I knew it wasn't fine. His smug smile was now locked and loaded, and there was nothing I could do to protect myself from the words that would be fired.

"I made fun of you for placing seventh, but considering how screwed up you are, it's actually impressive."

Ignoring him, I grabbed the drawing and motored toward Mr. Anders's office. The sooner he could approve everything, the sooner I'd be out of here.

But when I entered Mr. Anders's office, I knew the last of my luck had completely run out.

"Gordon-Bettencourt…" He shook his head. "You lived quite a colorful life before coming here, didn't you? It's not a great look for Simucon, but there's no such thing as bad publicity. I just hope you know we're not as forgiving as your father. Mistakes in this industry kill people."

"I'm aware," I said, my mind spinning. I should have known that awful man would have retaliated when I turned Alistair away.

Anders scrutinized the drawings in total silence and then rolled them up. When he looked at me, the modicum of respect I'd earned was gone. "Off you go."

I mumbled my thanks and rushed home, keeping my head low.

By the time I got home, another message came through from another news outlet. It wouldn't stop there. Every time Douglas mentioned me publicly, my phone would light up for days. There was a reason I couldn't have any social media accounts.

Pushing all of this out of my mind, I focused on packing my bag as quickly as I could. I couldn't think clearly. I just needed to get away. It reminded me of the day everything changed, and I'd fled with the few things that could fit in my trunk.

Shaking the thought, I grabbed my bag and hustled downstairs. The sun was already setting with an orange haze peeking through the gray. I turned my headlights on and listened to the voice on my navigator. Even though I'd driven this route with Lincoln last week, I hadn't been paying attention to the road. I'd been looking at him. At his silly smile and messy black curls. I'd stared at the small mole he had on his neck. The one I'd since kissed. How was I meant to care for the route when inches away was Lincoln's large hand tightened around the stick shift?

These were not the thoughts I was meant to be having. But they were better than everything else I could think of.

The night grew darker, and streetlights became few and far between. I turned on my high beams and widened my eyes as though it would help me see better.

It was hard to tell where I was. Tall trees lined the roads and now and again there was a small cabin. It would make for a wonderful resort. But beyond that, the moon was the only thing guiding me.

At some point, the tarred road gave way to gravel. I'd forgotten a good portion of this drive was on unpaved roads that were much easier to navigate in Lincoln's truck. Coo was capable but not happy to drive across it for long distances. Plus it shook the living daylights out of me.

I took a bend, and the car skidded. Panic rose up my spine.

Slower. I needed to go slower.

Only another six miles. It wasn't much. According to my maps it was…okay, my maps were offline. That wasn't great, but before I'd lost signal, it didn't look that far away.

Instinctively, I accelerated, wanting to get there quicker. The car slid underneath me, sending the icy grip of fear up my spine. Okay, okay, okay, I would crawl there. Slow and steady. At this rate, it would take an hour to get there, but I'd rather be late and be alive.

The winding road seemed endless, and my eyes were focused on the small area lit up in front of me. The blur of a brown rabbit flashed across the road, and I swerved. The sharp, quick movement of my car threw my stomach in one direction and my body in another as it shifted across the gravel once more. I held on to the steering wheel, doing my best to control the unwanted movement. I screamed. Even though no one would hear it.

I shut my eyes and my body froze. The sensation of falling pierced my gut while the car dipped unexpectedly.

I slammed the brake and everything stopped.

Except my racing heart. I had no control over my limbs, everything was shaking, shivering, and all I wanted to do was curl up and have someone else take the wheel. Literally.

But there was no one else here and I hadn't seen any other cars on this road for miles.

I opened my eyes to the small area my headlights illuminated and blew out a long breath. Extending my foot, I tentatively pushed down on the accelerator. The car roared, groaned, and grunted, but it didn't move.

No. No. No. Panic swirled in my chest. I took out my phone to call someone. Anyone. The list was slim.

I scrolled down to Lincoln's name and hit call.

But I had no service.

37

LINCOLN

[45 weeks ago]

@theanswerisno:
You're surprisingly good
at racing games

> **@pancakesareelite:**
> I like to go fast

> **@pancakesareelite:**
> You're surprisingly bad. I thought you
> were good at everything

@theanswerisno:
I like to go slow

> **@pancakesareelite:**
> We really are as different as can be

@theanswerisno:
Opposites attract *wink wink*

> **@pancakesareelite:**
> Are you flirting with me? Link!

> **@pancakesareelite:**
> You scumbag! You used your seductive
> words to distract me so you could win

@theanswerisno:
You snooze you lose

@theanswerisno:
But my previous statement stands

I spent the rest of the afternoon watching *Overpower* streams to soothe my guilt for missing most of the LAN. Rose and William had assured me that it was okay. They needed hype and reviews, and I could do that from here. I commented on every video and blog post I could find.

Gaming generally helped me regulate, but I'd left my laptop behind, so this would have to do.

But it wasn't enough. At some point, I went outside to breathe in the chilly air. Once Elizabeth was here, I'd probably stay locked in my room because I might pass out if I got too close to her.

I went back inside and climbed into bed. As a last resort, sleep would help. My muscles turned to jelly as soon as they hit the mattress. The window I'd left open let in a breeze and the quiet sounds of the outside. My pulse seemed to *tap-tap-tap* along with a branch hitting the roof of the cabin.

I'd have to say something to Elizabeth. But what? When? Tonight?

I grabbed my phone and checked the time. It was late. Later than it should have been. Where was she? I pushed myself upward. She could have stayed at work an extra hour or two or grabbed dinner first. But even so, she should have been here by now.

I hesitantly dialed her number and waited. It beeped. I stared at my screen. The reception along these roads was awful. The road was awful, too, even with my giant truck and its giant wheels. Despite being capable and as determined as can be, Elizabeth's small car would struggle with the unfinished roads and bad weather.

Something unpleasant swirled in the depths of my stomach.

I pulled myself out of bed and grabbed my waterproof jacket and a flashlight. It wouldn't hurt to check. If she was on her way here, I'd find her. There was only one road in and out of this place.

I rushed out of the cabin before hopping into my truck and bringing it to life. I reversed out of the driveway, spinning the truck around, and drove onto the gravel road.

I rang Elizabeth again, but the call still wasn't going through. I drove down the zigzag road, looking along the sides. *What if she wasn't coming at all?* I wouldn't, if I were her. In which case, I'd find the roads quiet and empty and probably hear from her in the morning.

Gravel shot sideways as I tore through it. In the distance, two small yellow lights flickered in the darkness at an angle a car shouldn't be.

Elizabeth? An accident?

I sped up. My heart pounded so fast I thought I may throw up. Panic ripped through me, and I hit the brakes and jumped out onto the gravel, nearly slipping.

My father's accident flashed through my mind.

I stumbled toward her red car through the fog. The driver's side was empty. "Elizabeth!" I yelled, my chest burning with concern.

"Lincoln?" she squeaked from behind me.

I spun around, finding her standing there, her arms wrapped around herself. Her body shivered and shook. My anxiety snapped, and a downpour of relief washed over me.

"Lincoln?" she said again, and leaped into my arms, spreading heat throughout my body.

Thank God. Thank God. Thank God. Thank God. Thank God. Those two words kept echoing in my head, and with the raging gratitude in my chest, I could barely hear her.

In a second, she withdrew, her chest still rising and falling too quickly for that oxygen to be useful. "There was something in the road and I didn't want to hit it and then my car—" She paused, taking a few shaky breaths. "And, Lincoln, I'm—"

"Are you okay?" I said, interrupting what I thought may be an apology I wasn't ready to hear, and right now, it was less than important. A cold breeze whipped by and sent me shivering too.

She nodded.

I wanted to touch her, hold her. I wanted to tuck her into my jacket. But I tried my best to regain control of my still-beating heart.

"I'll pull you out." I walked over to my truck and stepped on the tow bar, lifting myself into the bed. I rummaged around until I found the tow rope. Elizabeth stood exactly where I had left her.

"Get inside." I pointed at her car as I fastened the rope between our vehicles.

"Do you need help?"

I stepped away from her; if I got too close, I'd grab her and never let her go. "You need to steer." I reached my truck. "I'll tow you all the way there, just in case."

I climbed in my truck, and as soon as I closed the door, everything I'd worked so hard on suppressing bubbled up to the surface. I remembered the exact moment that took my dad away from me.

Elizabeth could have been hurt.

For the first time in a long time, I sobbed. I rested my forehead on the steering wheel and cried for a few seconds while Elizabeth climbed into her car and waited.

She was okay.

She was alive.

And I was undeniably in love with her.

38

ELIZABETH

[44 weeks ago]

> **@theanswerisno:**
> Thanks for saving me

> **@pancakesareelite:**
> That's twice now. You owe me

> **@theanswerisno:**
> I'm storing them up for one big save

Lincoln came.

Even without calling him, he came. My body shuddered as the adrenaline wore off and the fear finally settled. I gripped the steering wheel and stared at the rope tying my car to his and thinking about all the threads that bound us. I knew, without any doubt, that wherever Lincoln went, I would follow…if he let me.

How I hoped he'd let me.

At the very least, he didn't hate me. Well, not enough to leave me stranded in a forest overnight.

But enough to stiffen when I'd hugged him. *Why did I hug him?* I cringed at the memory. I'd been so relieved to see him that I even thought I'd imagined him. But he was real. He was there. Strong and tall and warm.

Lincoln's truck revved. I snapped out of it and turned the ignition. Seconds later, I jerked forward as my car was pulled out of the ditch. I turned the wheel, following his movements as we straightened my car.

What should I say when we get to the cabin? Would we talk?

Multiple scenarios played out in my mind. Would he be nasty? *No.* That wasn't in his nature…even though it was something I was accustomed to. Would he ignore me? *Maybe. Probably.* Would we go back to the way we were before last night?

I paused there, wanting a different answer, but all I could think was: *Absolutely not.*

Pain zapped through my already aching heart. *I'd lost Lincoln. I'd lost Link.* My hands tightened around the steering wheel, and my eyes stung with tears. The road ahead of me blurred, and I blinked the mistiness away.

I blew out a long, shuddering breath.

Lincoln Carden wouldn't let his personal feelings affect the way he treated me professionally. But Mr. Anders would. The other managers might. And by now, I'd bet they'd all seen that article.

Lincoln drove off the road to an even narrower path. The growl of his truck stopped, but the lights stayed on. His door flung open, and he hopped out, lifting the hood of his jacket as he walked over to my side of the car. I pulled out my key and opened the door. Before I could say anything, he asked, "Are you sure you're okay?"

I nodded again. "Just a headache."

"Did you hit your head? Are you bleeding or anything? I can call a doctor or take you to the hospital."

"No, I'm fine. I'm…I was just scared," I managed, wanting to say so much more, but my voice cracked.

A softness spread across his hard features. He shut his eyes and walked over to my trunk. "It's locked."

"It's okay. I can manage." I joined him at the back of my car.

He grabbed my bag and swung the backpack across his shoulders. "Go on in. It's open. I've got this. Please."

I didn't deserve his kindness. It made my heart ache as much as my head did.

Following his instruction, I walked ahead until the cabin came into view. Flashbacks of our last visit lit up my brain. Things were completely different between us. So much had happened since I'd pressed my hands against his body.

Warm air slapped against my cheeks. The gentle smell of woodsmoke reached me, but there were no flames in the fireplace.

Lincoln walked past me and up to the first door. He pushed it open. "Yours." He dropped the bags outside the door and walked into the kitchen. He took out a small bottle of ibuprofen and put it on the counter. "We have a site meeting at seven thirty. Be ready at seven if you plan on driving with me," he said with a deep sigh. "Which I'd recommend."

I nodded, aware of how exhausted he looked. Of the pain he carried while wearing a massive jacket and a pair of pajama pants and sneakers.

Lincoln Carden had come looking for me because he was worried. A longing I didn't know what to do with consumed me. Did he care about me? About Lily?

Or was he just the kindest, most wonderful person to have ever existed? Because I could believe that.

He disappeared into his bedroom, and before anything else, I grabbed my pajama pants and a T-shirt and walked into the bathroom. I climbed into the tub and turned on the attached shower. As the water heated, I let it wash off the mud that had settled underneath my nails when I'd attempted to dig my car out by hand. My fingers hurt, and my headache was relentless.

As my body recovered from the shock, tears streamed down my face and swirled into the brown water until it eventually ran clear.

When I left the bathroom, I heard shuffling from the room at the back, which I assumed to be Lincoln's. I dragged my luggage into my room and sorted through everything. With everything aching, I opened my door and scanned the kitchen for the bottle of ibuprofen.

It sat beside a grilled cheese sandwich and a glass of water.

My pathetic little heart fluttered.

• • •

My alarm went off the next morning and shocked me awake. I stumbled out of bed, ignoring the significance of the date, and put on my site-appropriate clothing.

My bedroom was adjacent to the kitchen, and when I stepped out, I was faced with Lincoln sitting at the island in a T-shirt and pair of jeans. He looked at me and nodded; I nodded back. His eyes landed on my ugly shoes and self-consciousness flooded through me, but he didn't say anything. He turned back to his cereal and put another spoonful into his mouth.

I walked up to the coffee machine. "Do you want something to drink?"

He lifted his mug. "There's enough left over for you. I made a pot."

Oh, of course. Idiot. I poured myself a cup and grabbed an apple, but by the time I turned around, Lincoln had walked over to the couch in the living room.

My blood stung like acid at the distance he created between us. It reminded me of the first few weeks we'd spent together. And even back then, before he knew me, he was still open to teaching me.

He'd still teach me now. He still came looking for me when I didn't arrive. Without me even asking. And I could be professional. I needed to be professional because, if I didn't get permanent placement at this firm after this internship, what then?

It would mean Douglas had won.

39

LINCOLN

[42 weeks ago]

> **@pancakesareelite:**
> Link. I miss you. Come back soon, okay?

@theanswerisno:
Hey, sorry. I know I've been quiet…my
anxiety's been getting the best of me

> **@pancakesareelite:**
> Do you wanna talk?

@theanswerisno:
I never know how

> **@pancakesareelite:**
> Do you want to visit my farm and fight
> monsters in the mines with me until you
> forget about it?

@theanswerisno:
Where have you been all my life?

⇄

This was going to be impossible. The only way I'd survive would be to keep our conversations as brief as possible and create as much space between us as I could manage while still doing my job and allowing Elizabeth to do hers.

She didn't make it easy with her soft voice and even softer eyes. The stormy gray was lighter, almost blue. Too easy to get lost in.

I sent all my focus into my bowl of cereal. I didn't want to ignore Elizabeth. I wanted to lift her up onto the kitchen island and kiss her like I did in my office. I wanted to step between those legs again and stay there, feeling her tug at my hair and tasting her skin.

But she wasn't just any woman.

She was Lily.

And she was also Elizabeth Gordon-Bettencourt.

And she was my intern.

And I was…*I don't even know.* I wasn't Mr. Carden, nor was I Link.

Work ethics aside, what were the chances someone as amazing as she was would want to be with me? Because if I let myself love Elizabeth, if I fully acknowledged that she was also my Lily, I wouldn't survive without her.

If I could stop those feelings now, I could recover. Probably. If I kicked her out of my mind and heart. But I couldn't.

I slipped into my PPE and walked out of the cabin, assuming she'd follow when she was done eating her inadequate breakfast. I climbed into my truck and took out my phone while I waited.

Claire wanted to know what was happening. I shot her a text explaining the eventful night.

Elizabeth appeared next to my truck rather suddenly, and I leaned across and opened the door from the inside. She climbed in and looked at me the same way she did when we had started working together. Soft, pleading eyes that gave me the sense she'd lived a life waiting to see people's reactions to her.

I gave her what I hoped was a neutral look because there was no way I could show her my true feelings. Not yet. Not now. We had only three days to go before her internship ended, and then we'd know what our futures at Simucon held. Then, and only then, would it make any sense to dive into everything we've been feeling.

I needed to sort through this mess before breaking my own heart or risking our careers.

The uneven ground shook a gasp out of Elizabeth as we ventured onto the gravel roads. She smiled almost sheepishly. "Glad I didn't try and drive my car here."

"I don't know why Anders didn't give you the company car," I grumbled under my breath.

"Maybe he offered it and I didn't hear…" She looked out the side window.

Every now and then, her confidence wavered. She doubted herself even though the opposite should happen since her abilities had improved.

I wanted to tell her this, but that would go against the rule I'd set for myself. Bare minimum.

We pulled up to the site, and I climbed out. The other workers surrounded me. They'd somehow managed to find questions to ask me overnight. Elizabeth stood on my left, not as close as she used to but close enough for me to smell the subtle cinnamon scent that magically followed her around. Even here, in the middle of nowhere.

We walked over to the container that would be used as a site office for the next few months, and inside, the rest of the team was already bent over drawings. I laid out the new drawings Elizabeth had brought along, but their gazes stayed fixed on her.

Much as I expected.

"Kevin, Radley, Elise," I said, and rattled through the rest of their names, "this is Elizabeth. She's part of our graduate internship." I purposely left out her surname. If she wanted to let them know who she was, she could.

She reached forward and enthusiastically shook everyone's hands.

"It's her first time on-site. Please feel free to explain any interesting concepts to her as you go along. Before assigning any tasks, run them by me," I said, using the voice people obeyed.

They nodded.

After the meeting, we made our way on-site, and I slowed my pace to meet Elizabeth's. "By the way," I said, "your nights are yours. Overtime is not required. I'm not opposed to house guests, but please keep them away from my room, as I tend to stay up working."

"I don't think I'll go anywhere tonight. Do you want me to?" Her brows jumped toward each other.

"You're welcome to be wherever you want, Elizabeth," I said, struggling to even say her name.

"Oh," she said, her voice soft. "Thank you, Mr. Carden."

Mr. Carden.

I wanted to be Lincoln again.

But if she wanted me to be Mr. Carden, I could be. So I launched into the history of the project as we walked across the site, gravel sticking to our shoes and climbing up our pants.

"How come you never wear site boots?" she asked.

I nearly laughed at the irony. I wasn't entirely sure what I'd do when the new boots arrived. I lifted up the formal shoe I wore. "They're steel-toed."

The surprise on her face was obvious and almost irresistible. I turned away before I was sucked in by her presence and the way she lit up. She made me light up.

I seemed to have reached my limit on how much I could interact with her before I started fawning. So I did what any respectable man in my position would do—I grabbed a shovel.

• • •

Thankfully, the rest of the afternoon had been easier. Elizabeth stayed out of my way, which was both a good and bad thing. Good, because I'd technically asked her to, and bad because, well, I didn't like it when she was away. I kept searching for her, waiting for her, and listening to hear her voice.

We drove back to the cabin in silence while I tried reconciling that Elizabeth and Lily were the same person. My scurrying thoughts only got worse as night fell, because by now, I'd generally be texting Lily or playing games with her.

And I craved it. I missed her, her jokes, and the chatty comfort she brought me.

Knowing there was someone who wanted me to come online.

I was addicted to Lily. And now she was here, in this cabin, and I still couldn't face her.

Because every time I reflected on it, I wanted to touch her and hold her. I wanted to kiss her until we forgot our names and identities. I wanted to make her smile, the way she used to smile at me. There were so many things I wanted from her, but I wasn't sure I could have it. It tormented me.

A bang at the front door drew me from my bedroom.

Elizabeth and I entered the hallway at the same time. She stood before me in a pair of pajama shorts showing more thigh than I could handle. She tugged them downward, but it barely made a difference.

I ignored the heat flooding to every organ in my body. Her disheveled hair wasn't helping.

I averted my gaze and gestured to the door. "Is that for you?"

"Um, no. I haven't made plans. Maybe it's for you."

Laughter rang through the door. A familiar cackle.

"Lincoln!" Rose yelled with another knock. "There could be wild animals out here. Open up!"

I took a few quick steps to the front door and swung it open. Rose and Claire fell inside with William and Dean following.

"What are you doing here?" I asked.

"It's game night!" Claire said. Then her eyes narrowed. She was my greatest defender. "And we wanted to make sure you were okay."

I gave Rose the side hug she bounced around beside me for. "Hello."

Since the outburst we had in LA, our relationship had shifted for the better.

I grew up with no real friends, bar Claire, and now, somehow, I'd inherited people who would drive for hours to get to me.

Dean walked by, slapping me gently on the back as he did and giving me the wide smile that had won over my best friend's heart.

"Shaun and Neema are really upset they couldn't join." Rose released me and fell into William's arms behind her.

"Especially Shaun," William said with a loud laugh. "It's killing him. I'm gonna text him and say we're having the best time."

Such a troll. Always has been. And it was rubbing off on Rose too.

William raised his phone and snapped a selfie of his wide grin, my smile clear in the background and Rose and Claire pulling faces at the last second. "He asked for photos," William said with a big sigh.

"Is she here?" Claire whispered.

I looked over my shoulder to where Elizabeth had been standing, but she was gone.

ELIZABETH

[41 weeks ago]

@theanswerisno:
I think I dreamed about you

@pancakesareelite:
You don't even know what I look like

@theanswerisno:
It was more the feeling I woke up with

@pancakesareelite:
Oh

@theanswerisno:
NOT THAT

@theanswerisno:
I meant like...a nice feeling

@pancakesareelite:
Well, now I'm a little disappointed

⇦⇨

The last time I'd seen those people was at the *Overpower* LAN. They'd witnessed what was, undoubtedly, one of the most awful moments of my life.

I could never face them again. Especially Claire. Her glare was fixed in my memory.

Staying in here and working seemed like my best bet. I plonked onto the edge of my desk and leafed through the drawings we'd be using tomorrow. Working on-site had been nothing short of exhilarating. At one stage, I was in a ditch, digging a hole alongside Lincoln. The only reason I was in the ditch was to escape the way my body reacted to watching him dig. His biceps flexed and rippled as he shoveled. As far as I knew, engineers never did any of this, but he was so hands-on, actively engaging every muscle at every opportunity and driving me up the wall with a desire I worried may be unhealthy. It had been a while since I was intimate with anyone, and watching Lincoln dig a ditch had reminded my body of that.

Actually, watching Lincoln do anything didn't help. A second ago, he stood in the living room wearing gray sweatpants and a loose T-shirt. It made him even more irresistible. I thought the shirt and tie did it for me, but off-the-clock Lincoln was intoxicating.

His friends' laughter echoed through the cabin. I thought maybe I heard him laugh too.

I glanced upward, catching my reflection in the mirror. I was a complete mess. But Lincoln's gaze had paused on my mouth. Maybe it didn't mean anything. A lot of men stared at my mouth. Some even had the audacity to speak their thoughts out loud.

Not Lincoln. Lincoln was different. He was kind, gentle, and caring. Even when I didn't deserve it.

Which made this entire situation worse. Couldn't he be mean to me instead? I was used to that. But this?

I grabbed my phone, and despite knowing I shouldn't, I texted my mom: I could really use some advice. The internet up here is a little iffy but I can go outside if you're planning on calling later.

Even though we hadn't seen each other in years, she wouldn't let me down when I needed her. Especially not tonight.

The message wouldn't send. I stomped out of my bedroom and into the living room, where all Lincoln's friends had gathered. Their eyes zoomed in on me.

Especially Claire. The fire in her gaze was an indication of how badly I'd hurt Lincoln. Her mouth flattened into a straight line.

Lincoln glanced her way before turning to me, his face fixed in a hard expression. "William, Rose, Claire, Dean, this is Elizabeth."

"Nice to meet you," Rose chirped up with a warm and welcoming smile I didn't expect.

"Nice to meet you too." I lifted my hand to wave, relieved she wasn't sending me daggers like Claire. While I was generally unbothered by things like that, my composition was weaker today.

William didn't seem too concerned by my presence, nodding in greeting, and Dean, the other person, simply smiled and raised his hand.

"Are your texts sending?" I asked Lincoln.

He frowned, taking out his phone.

"Mine are," William said. "I've sent Shaun a few photos."

"Has he replied?" I asked.

William nodded, smiling widely. He had a deep dimple in his one cheek that I'd never noticed before because his streaming camera faced his other side.

"Thanks," I said, and took out my phone again before walking to my bedroom. Still unread. I hit the call button and held it to my ear.

Voicemail.

I did it again.

Voicemail.

Turning around, I found Lincoln in the doorframe, his brows drawn close. "Everything all right?"

I nodded, swallowing the lump growing in my throat. Lincoln couldn't see me cry. I wouldn't allow it. I'd already ambushed him once; crying would force him into comforting me. And he *would* comfort me. At his own expense.

"Okay," he said, unconvinced.

"Are they staying over?" I asked.

He shook his head. "Leaving to a nearby cabin." He pulled on the drawstring of his gray sweatpants. Casual Lincoln was an entirely different experience from formal Lincoln.

My mind locked away every detail for safekeeping because a part of me worried that every time we spoke could be the last.

"You don't have to hide in here," he said.

The striking sound of something sizzling drew my attention, and Lincoln glanced over his shoulder. His soft smile returned. He stepped out of the way, revealing William in the kitchen frying onions in what smelled like a generous amount of garlic.

"Do you have pepper? We didn't bring any since I assumed the two of you weren't living like savages," William said without turning around.

Lincoln shook his head, and a chuckle slipped out. He left my doorway and retrieved the pepper from the cupboard underneath the microwave. William hoorayed, and again, Lincoln laughed. He hadn't laughed since I'd arrived here. I'd thought he'd forgotten how.

There was excited chatter coming from the living room, and my heart twisted in the strangest of ways. I looked back down at my phone where my text was left unsent. My eyes stung, and I reached out and closed the door before any of them could see I was about to cry. Again.

I didn't need my sadness to drown their party, and besides, these were his friends and they all knew I'd hurt him. I couldn't go out there, and thankfully I hadn't drunk much so I wouldn't even need to use the bathroom. If I were quiet enough, they would forget I was even here.

I'd just have to ignore my grumbling stomach. Whatever William was cooking smelled delicious.

One of the girls shrieked, and it was followed by William's loud laughter. I could bet Lincoln was chuckling in his soft and bashful way.

A new and unexpected longing curled inside me. I'd never had that. And I wanted it. Desperately.

In a moment of defeat, I finally opened the article and faced my punishment for turning down a conversation with Douglas Gordon-Bettencourt.

41

LINCOLN

[40 weeks ago]

@theanswerisno:
I don't know how to comfort my best
friend who is currently going through
some trouble

@pancakesareelite:
Ask her what she needs

@theanswerisno:
That actually makes sense.

I could cook. But William? Man, William was a magician. I've told him. We've all told him. I grabbed ingredients he needed from the cabinets and from the bags of things they'd brought along with them.

"You don't have to do this," I said, giving him a block of Parmesan.

He offered me one of those smiles that had all the women weak in the knees. "Yeah, it's really convincing when you tell me that when I'm nearly done."

I chuckled. If they'd asked me if they should come all the way here, I'd have told them it wasn't worth the drive, but I'd bet that was why they didn't ask me.

This friendship thing was weird but nice.

The same couldn't be said for my oldest friend, who seemed to be experiencing some negative side effects of our friendship. I walked up to Claire, who was seated in the living room where Rose had set up Dixit and Pictionary.

"Hey." I sat next to her. "I'm okay."

She looked at me with what had become a permanent frown. "I know how hurt you are and how difficult this must be. You don't seem angry."

"I'm not. I'm confused and shocked and scared," I said. "Why are you so angry?"

Claire took a deep breath. "Because I worry about you. I know you take forever to trust someone, and when you do, you give them everything. Does she know that's what she's getting? If she's not ready, I…I don't know, Lincoln."

Did Elizabeth want *everything*? Would my *everything* be enough for someone like her? Or too much? She's Elizabeth Gordon-Bettencourt, and I'm just Lincoln Carden.

Dean walked in carrying a pile of wood and made his way straight to the fireplace. Claire's frown turned into an emotion I'd rather not see.

William walked up to us, a bowl in either hand. "Buon appetito." He offered the first bowls to Rose and Claire.

Elizabeth hasn't eaten.

As if reading my mind, William leaned in and whispered, "I made some extra. In case she's hungry. I know she lied and stuff, but…I don't like it when people are hungry."

"Me neither," I said.

I walked to the kitchen and prepared another bowl of spaghetti bolognese. I took the two short steps to Elizabeth's bedroom door and knocked once.

There was a quiet sound of shuffling before the door cracked open. It was as though I was meeting an entirely different person. A red-faced, red-eyed, red-cheeked woman whispered, "What's up? Everything okay?"

I extended the bowl, which couldn't even fit through the tiny gap she'd allowed. I wanted to ask her what was wrong. I wanted to know what she needed to feel better. To not cry. But I didn't know how to find the right words and the right way to say it.

She swallowed and reached out a shaky hand. "For me?"

I nodded.

"Thank you," she squeaked.

"William makes the best spagbol," I said, stupidly, as a replacement for what could very easily be a love confession.

Half a smile graced her puffy face.

I searched her eyes, but she avoided mine. In a desperate attempt to make her feel better, I said, "We're about to play Dixit...Do you want to join us?"

"I don't want to intrude." She swallowed hard. "Plus I look like crap."

Crap? I wish I could tell her otherwise. Instead, I gestured down to my sweatpants. "This is a no judgment zone. Plus, uh, it takes up to eight players..."

"You don't mind? Are you sure?"

I nodded, and she finally met my gaze. Her gray eyes sparkled silver under the light.

"Can you give me a minute to, um"—she blinked a few times, clearing the storm—"freshen up?"

I nodded again, and she smiled, a small smile, but it was a smile.

I pulled the door closed and made my way over to Claire, who was not going to believe what I'd done.

"So…heads-up," I whispered loudly enough for everyone to hear but not loud enough for the sound to reach Elizabeth, "I invited her to join us."

"Interesting." Claire's dark brows popped up. "Why?"

I shrugged. "I wanted to."

"Lincoln," she said softly. Her concern was obvious, and without it, I'd have gotten into a lot more trouble growing up. "If you're okay with it, I am."

"It's just a game, and you're all here. What's the harm?"

Rose clapped her hands together. "I think it's an excellent idea. Especially after that article by her dad. Did you see it?"

"What article?"

Elizabeth walked into the living room still wearing the same pajama shirt but exchanged her shorts for a pair of sweatpants. I didn't realize sweatpants could look that good. She sat on the floor across from me and lifted her bowl. "This spaghetti is the best I've ever had."

"You should taste his stir-fry." Rose rolled her eyes back. "Because of him, I'm insatiable." Her eyes zapped open. "I'm talking about his food, obviously."

"Is that what we're calling it nowadays?" Dean teased, and to my absolute relief, we all burst out laughing. Including Elizabeth.

William smiled mischievously. "She wasn't only talking about my food." Rose pinched him, and he yelped. "Don't wound me now, woman. We have an important date coming up."

"What date?" Claire asked.

"Comic-Con!" Rose shrieked, looking at William with all the love she could muster. "Thunderstruck and Fun&Games have booths, and William and I will be competing to see whose booth gets more customers, so you have to come."

"I've never been to Comic-Con," Dean said, and I sometimes forgot he wasn't raised a geek like the rest of us. "I'm game. Let me know when it is so I can schedule some time off."

"It's months away, but we get comps, so you're all on the list. We're telling you now so no excuses. Put it in your calendars!" Rose was practically vibrating with excitement. She then did what only she would do and asked, "Elizabeth, would you like me to put you on the list?"

And just like that, Elizabeth was here to stay.

42

ELIZABETH

[39 weeks ago]

@pancakesareelite:
So you have game night every week?

> **@theanswerisno:**
> I sometimes skip them

@pancakesareelite:
And you play board games together?

> **@theanswerisno:**
> Yep

@pancakesareelite:
Sounds like a dream come true

> **@theanswerisno:**
> Well, it's kinda like what we do

@pancakesareelite:
And that sometimes feels
like a dream come true too

I wasn't sure if I'd misheard her, but *@theresarose* seemed to be asking me if I'd like to be on her guest list for *the* San Diego Comic-Con. As if we were friends. As if we hadn't only just met.

"I've never been either," I admitted, relieved to see that I wasn't the only one in this little group. "Isn't it impossible to get tickets?"

"Not when you're engaged to Thunderstruck's favorite employee." Rose threw William a loving smile. She then turned to me. "My mission in life is to get everyone to go to Comic-Con, at least once. Come over to the dark side." She curled her hand toward herself and then reached to her left and swiped something from her bag before offering it to me. "We have cookies!"

I burst into a fit of giggles and took the offered cookie. "If you really don't mind, and if it isn't costing you or taking up someone else's spot, then yes, I'd love that."

She waved a hand. "No, not at all. The more the merrier." She slid her phone across the floor to me. "Give me your number and email address, and I'll send you the comp tickets." She looked around at everyone. "There's only one catch." She paused for effect. "You'll have to cosplay!"

"Nope," Claire said. "You know I don't cosplay."

Rose laughed, seemingly unaffected with how unimpressed Claire was. "Meh, worth a try."

Claire's tense shoulders softened. She scooched over and gave Rose a little pinch. "What are you going as?"

"A hobbit, for old time's sake."

"Aw," Claire said, her lips pouting. "And you're…?"

William nodded even though she hadn't finished her question. I was so confused.

"My Gandalf," Rose said, and I couldn't help but chuckle as I pictured a hobbit and Gandalf looking at each other the way these two did.

"Will it be the first time you're both in costume since you met?" Claire asked.

They nodded.

"Ah, my heart." Claire clasped her hands at her chest. "Your love story is one of my favorites."

I wanted to ask what it was, but these weren't my friends and their lives were none of my business.

Taking me by surprise, Lincoln leaned in and whispered, "Rose and William met at Comic-Con while she was dressed as an unnamed hobbit and he was dressed as a suave Gandalf. Years later, they met again and didn't recognize each other. It's kinda like they were meant to be. Like they'd always find each other. One way or another."

His soft and pained gaze dragged up until it met mine, stopping my heart.

"Can we count on you all being there?" William asked, pulling Rose onto his lap as though she were a rag doll.

They nodded. I didn't. It depended on whether Lincoln was okay with having me around. I'd already gate-crashed his office, his cabin, and now his game night. I didn't want to overstep. Again.

Dixit began, and while I'd played it online, the real-life game experience was so much warmer. Perhaps it was the crowd, but I found myself laughing. Actually laughing. At one stage, I'd snorted my coffee and nearly spat it everywhere. Very graceful.

At the end of the game, Claire won but no one was upset about losing.

"Before we start the next round," Dean said, standing, "I brought dessert. I'll heat it."

"I'll make more coffee." Lincoln joined him in the kitchen.

"How are we going to divide the teams?" Rose packed away Dixit and set up the Pictionary. She rolled out sheets of construction drawings, face down, and then looked up to grin at me. "I get Lincoln to give me all his outdated drawings to play on."

A smile spread across my face, matching hers. It was so easy being around her.

"I love Rose more than anything in the world, but she's so bad at this. Please don't let me be paired with her," William said.

Even though this had us in stitches. I was nervous about being paired up with Lincoln.

"Claire and I are both awful at this, so it won't be fair if we're on a team," Rose said, and turned to me. "Are you good at drawing?"

"Let's make it fair," William said before I could answer. He tore off a few pieces of paper and scribbled everyone's names on them. He crumpled them up and shook them around in his large hands. I thought Lincoln was tall, but William was something else.

He walked over to Rose. "My love, you first." She pulled a face and picked out one of the folded names. She unwrapped it and looked at me without any apprehension. "Elizabeth." Then she opened a second piece of paper. "And Claire!"

"Excellent," William said. "This'll be easy."

"What did we miss?" Dean asked, returning with freshly heated brownies and a tub of ice cream. Lincoln carried a tray of coffees.

"You're both teamed up with William for Pictionary," Claire said, and the two men looked at each other and smiled.

Rose scooted up next to me, and we leaned over the big sheet of paper. "Okay, as you heard, I'm not good at sketching…but it was William's turn to pick a game, and he picked this evil game. Do any of you want to go first?"

Claire and I shook our heads.

"Fine," Rose said. "I'll go first."

When the game finally started, Rose scribbled on her side of the paper, and hand on my heart, I had no idea what she was meant to be drawing.

"Chicken!" Claire yelled.

Rose shook her head, and William leaned over with a snicker. He wasn't even focusing on whatever Dean was drawing.

"Squirrel!" Lincoln said in that deep, wonderful voice of his.

"Yes," Dean replied. A point to the boys, then.

I scrutinized Rose's *squirrel*. She really wasn't good at this. She huffed and handed the marker to Claire.

Surprisingly, I deciphered Claire's "leak" before the boys got their answer. She nodded at me, which seemed a lot better than the scathing looks I'd endured pregame. At one stage, I even made her giggle.

When it was my turn, my heart raced. I picked my clue. *Subway*.

A train! I could draw a train. When the timer turned, I started sketching, and Rose and Claire guessed pretty much anything but a train.

"Sausage!" Rose yelled.

"Sausage dog!" Claire said.

I growled, adding windows.

The timer ran out, and Lincoln laughed. I looked up, and our eyes locked for a second. "Subway," he said quietly. "I'm well-trained in reading Elizabeth's drawings."

"You would have drawn a sandwich," I said, savoring the few seconds that felt familiar with him.

That lopsided smile came out, and my insides melted. It was like seeing it for the first time. He nodded. "I would have."

The game raced on, and even with our indecipherable drawings, we managed to win. The losers were sent off to the kitchen for another round of hot beverages.

After they returned, Rose curled into William's chest. He wrapped his arms around her. "Even when I lose, I still win."

"We better get going," Dean announced after everyone finished their drinks. "We have to be up early tomorrow morning to get back to the kid."

Rose stood and gave Lincoln a tight squeeze. To my surprise, she gave me one too.

It had been a while since I was hugged so fully and genuinely by someone. I squeezed my arms around her and wished I could bottle this moment. Tonight was the most fun I'd had in years.

"It was nice meeting you." Being hobbit-sized, Rose craned her neck and beamed up at me. "Tonight was so much fun. I can't wait to see you again."

Again. As though we were friends. Maybe one day we could be.

43

LINCOLN

[36 weeks ago]

@theanswerisno:
What can I buy a woman who
really loves board games

> @pancakesareelite:
> A board game

@theanswerisno:
Smartass. She owns them all.

> @pancakesareelite:
> Hmm

@theanswerisno:
It has to be really good

> @pancakesareelite:
> Do you *like* her?

@theanswerisno:
She's one of my closest like…friends I
guess. She's a close friend of a close
friend.

@theanswerisno:
She's not a generic gift kinda gal. For

```
my birthday she got me a mouse with my
username engraved on it.
```

```
                              @pancakesareelite:
              A personalized 30-second timer
```

```
@theanswerisno:
You're a genius.
```

It was unreal watching Elizabeth laugh with my friends, more unreal knowing she'd managed to coax a smile out of Claire. I felt better about letting my walls drop. If Claire couldn't actively maintain distance, no one in the world could expect me to. Not when Elizabeth had her beautiful copper hair curled into a messy bun with strands escaping to frame her gorgeous, freckled cheeks. Throughout the night, her gaze searched for mine, and I wondered what answers she found there. Would she tell me? Because I still had no idea what to do with everything I was feeling. I knew what I *wanted* to do.

I walked outside with my friends, leaving Elizabeth behind. Even though Rose had hugged me goodbye, she managed to sneak in a second hug before climbing into William's car.

"Bye, you." I patted her head.

She smiled guiltily. "I'm sorry if I was overly familiar with her. I didn't want her to feel left out…"

"Yeah, I kinda rely on you for that," I said.

She let out a small laugh. "I won't be her friend if you don't—"

I pulled her in for a bonus hug, which to her would be gold. "I know, Rose. It's okay. She's hard to resist. That's kinda how I got into this mess." I huffed out a long breath.

"I can see you've already forgiven her."

"Of course I've forgiven her. I'll always forgive her." My heart raced at the mere thought of Elizabeth. Of Lily.

Rose bit down on her bottom lip in a weak attempt to resist a smile. "Lincoln, what's the problem, then?"

"Aside from her being my intern? We could lose our jobs."

Rose waved me off as if that wasn't important. "That's an external factor. If you removed that, what then?"

"It can't be disregarded but without it…" I thought for a moment. It never occurred to me that I could consider us without thinking about our futures at Simucon. "There are at least four outcomes, and I don't know if I can handle the other three."

"Engineers are problem solvers, are they not?"

"Not this kind of problem. I don't think you're supposed to use a spreadsheet for love stuff," I said with a sigh as the word *love* slipped out of my mouth. I looked up at the night sky, where clouds covered the sparkling stars. All I saw was Elizabeth's eyes. The exquisite way the gray blended in with a pale blue, the shimmer and sparkle behind them when she teased.

Everything beautiful in the world reminded me of her.

"I, uh, kinda used a spreadsheet with William. I needed it. Even though I already knew how I felt." Rose stood on her toes and wrapped her arms around me for one last hug. After this, I wouldn't be hugging her for at least a year. She'd used up her hug quota. "You're having doubts about something, and I don't think there's anything wrong with letting yourself solve it the way you need to. Make your spreadsheet, Lincoln. Trust your process."

I walked with her to the car, where the others were already buckled in and waiting. Claire's concerned expression had budged but not disappeared.

"I'm fine," I said.

"We left some treats and essentials." Claire crinkled her nose. "And good luck."

By the time I went back inside, Elizabeth was elbow-deep in

washing the dishes and giving me the same strange guilty look Rose had.

After a game night with my friends, the sight of Elizabeth helping me clean up afterward sent me to a near state of delusion. This could be our life.

It was the thought I'd been trying to ignore every time I looked at her, but tonight made it especially impossible. She'd been at my side while we played, ate, and laughed. She wished my friends good night. In another life, I'd have her to myself afterward. I'd have walked up to her and curled my arms around her from behind, letting my hands explore her soft waist. My mouth would be on her neck in an instant, tasting her freckles. She'd chuckle, and it would only make me want her more. Her sudsy hands would probably end up on my T-shirt, and I wouldn't care. I would kiss her. Love her.

A deep pain flashed across my chest. If I kept thinking about her, I may need a visit to the ER.

"Your friends are amazing." She glanced at me for a nanosecond.

"They really are." I collected some of the dishes that had been left at the now-dying fire. "Rose is very excitable."

"She's like a windup toy," Elizabeth said, and quickly added, "but in a good way."

The laugh that escaped me was louder than I'd intended. I had, on more than one occasion, thought the same thing about Rose.

Elizabeth took the mugs from me and submerged them in the soapy water.

"Need help?" I asked.

She shook her head. "You do enough around here."

Good. Because I had a spreadsheet to make.

• • •

I sat at my desk and navigated to a blank spreadsheet while playing every interaction I'd had with Elizabeth over in my mind. Every word spoken, every smile shared. No part of me doubted the sincerity in her touch and how intentionally she accommodated me, despite what everyone thought of her and the stereotype of seducing your boss to climb the ranks.

I pushed my laptop aside and grabbed an old drawing, turning it face down. I'd need to start at the basics to untangle the web in my brain.

And then I started scribbling.

Unknown variable: At what point did she realize I was *@the answerisno*? How long had she chatted with me as Lily in the evenings and Elizabeth in the daytime all while knowing I had no idea?

Unknown variable: *Why didn't she tell me?*

I switched to a different color pen for the possible answers: *Because I was her boss.*

A valid answer. She needed this job. She knew my promotion was tied to it too.

My pen hovered above the page, afraid to write: *Could her feelings be as real as mine?*

Theoretically, they could be.

But the likelihood of it was yet to be determined.

I put ink to paper, making a list of all the reasons why it wasn't possible. Because Elizabeth was the most beautiful woman I've ever seen. Aside from her flawless physical features, she was also smart, funny, kind, caring, thoughtful, and determined as can be.

There was also that one thing we rarely discussed or acknowledged: She was rich. Again, in theory. Something told me otherwise.

I thought back to the article Rose had mentioned. I should read it, but not now. Not while I was hyperfixated on this.

Next question: *What exactly could I offer her?*

Protection from unwanted attention like the man who had waited for her outside our building.

Blowing out a long breath, I listed the things about me she might like. She called me smart—I shut my eyes and scribbled it down before my brain rejected the compliment.

I think she liked that I kept her well-fed. I could do that forever.

But as I sat there reflecting and ruminating, there was one thought playing over and over in my mind: I was in love with her.

I was in love with Lily's mind, with Elizabeth's wit, with Lily's humor, and Elizabeth's smile. I loved Elizabeth, and I loved that she was my Lily.

More than anything, I wanted her to be happy, and right now, she wasn't.

I could see it in her eyes, in the way the corners of her mouth tilted downward, even for a second. I could see it when the room didn't light up like it used to when she was around.

And I wanted to fix it. Because the one thing I was sure of is that I would love her in the way she deserved.

That should count for something.

• • •

I was ready to speak to Elizabeth.

My eyes burned from staring at my screen. I'd transferred my mind map to the spreadsheet, and even though I hadn't concluded it, I already knew what I wanted. Knew what I was willing to risk. I was focused. Hyperfocused. And there wasn't a subject more fascinating to me than Elizabeth. And if she let me, I'd get lost in her, over and over for the rest of my life.

My eyes flicked down to the time in the corner of the screen: 11:35 p.m.

Waking her to receive a love confession may not be the best way to convince her to love me.

I stretched upward and opened the window above the desk for some fresh air. The sounds of crickets chirping tickled my ears.

With my decision made, I continued pounding away on the keys. It would be nice to have an answer, even if it didn't matter anymore.

Footsteps sounded from behind me, outside my room.

Was Elizabeth awake? Was she walking toward me?

The soft padding of her steps moved past my bedroom. My heart dipped. Bathroom trip, perhaps.

I stood, wanting to check on her. But the sound of the back door cracking open had me freezing. Her footsteps were clear now. The wood of the patio deck creaked right outside the window.

"Mom," she said in the quietest voice, "I'm so glad you called."

In the still of the night, it felt as though I could hear my own heart beating.

"I'm not in trouble," she said, her movement still creaking along the wood. Farther away, then near again. "I…" She paused. "I'm going through something, and I need someone to talk to…Gran's awesome, but she's so chaotic." She laughed, but it wasn't a full one. Something was missing. "I miss talking to you. I miss you. When will I see you again?"

Her voice was so meek, so unlike the feisty woman I now knew I loved.

This was private. I reached out for the window and paused. If I closed it now, she'd notice and maybe feel even more uncomfortable knowing I'd heard some of it. I paced away from the window, but her voice still carried through.

"I could come up to LA, if you could sneak away for a little bit," she said, her voice turning upward at the end.

The hurt in her tone drew me closer. I knew very little about her relationship with her mom and stepdad.

"It's okay. Sure, yeah. I understand," she said. "I know he's mad. I saw the article."

That article.

"I know you asked me to trust you and I do, but I don't understand why you're still with him. You don't need anything from him. Just leave him and come to me. Or go to Gran. If I get this job, I could move into a bigger place."

Alarms went off in my head.

"I know it's not that easy. It wasn't easy for me either. The last few years have been awful but it's better than the hell he put us through." She stopped pacing. "Trust me, Mom. Please."

The wood creaked under her weight again before she spoke. "I trust you, I do. But it's been years." A mirthless laugh escaped her.

I never wanted to hear it again. I couldn't eavesdrop any longer. I made my way over to my bedroom door, unsure of what I'd be doing, but knowing I'd be doing something. My need to defend her, to protect her, ate me up inside.

When I got to the door, I heard her say in the smallest voice, "Thank you. It's been an eventful birthday for sure."

I sucked in a quick breath.

It was her birthday today? If I'd known, I'd have done more. I'd have baked a cake. Invited her out earlier. I'd have done something, anything.

The hurt in her voice left thousands of tiny cuts across my heart.

"I know it's not easy for you." She stopped walking, and for some reason, so did I.

My feet were planted as though stuck to the wooden floorboards.

"Do you have time for my problems? It's a long story." She neared the back door of the cabin now. "Okay. I understand. Was that him? Okay. Go. Go. I love you," she said, and it squeezed my chest that those words were followed by a heartbreaking whimper before she reentered the cabin and took the first left into the bathroom without even seeing me standing there.

44

ELIZABETH

[34 weeks ago]

@pancakesareelite:
What do you do when you're really sad?

@theanswerisno:
Ignore those feelings

@pancakesareelite:
Sounds reasonable

@theanswerisno:
On occasion, it'll bottle up and you'll
explode for seemingly no reason, but
other than that, it works

@pancakesareelite:
I'll have to give it a go. Seems better
than crying.

@theanswerisno:
I don't like crying

@pancakesareelite:
Because you're a big, tough man?

@theansowerisno:
Nah, because I get really snotty

My mother couldn't even say *I love you*. Douglas had found her, so she hung up without a word.

I washed my face in the bathroom and then walked to my bedroom, trying to keep the uncomfortable feeling in my stomach from wreaking havoc on the rest of my body. I climbed onto the bed and pulled the pillow over my head, letting it swallow my tears. With a heaving sob, my lungs emptied.

Would we ever truly get away from him?

I'd been running for so long, but I was tired. I wanted to go home. I wanted *a home* to go to.

Breathing became difficult, and I lifted the pillow. A light clatter came from the kitchen. I sat up and listened. It sounded like Lincoln was awake and doing something unusual for this hour. I'd washed up, dried everything, and packed it away. I'd made sure of it because last night he still found items needing to be packed away after I'd cleared up.

To be fair, for most of my life, I didn't have to clean anything.

The tick of the gas stove drew my attention.

Was he cooking? Why?

I could go and look, but that would mean facing him in this state where a breeze could knock me over, and Lincoln Carden wasn't a breeze; he was an all-encompassing hurricane, sweeping me away with every thoughtful gaze and tentative touch.

Falling backward, I stared at the wooden trusses, studying them as I did on the first night to ensure there weren't any spiders. Tonight, I studied the structure, finding some peace in geometry.

Something crashed in the kitchen and shattered. I hopped out of bed and swung the door open. Lincoln was folded over, picking up broken pieces of mossy-green ceramic.

He glanced up from underneath those ridiculously long eyelashes. "Hey." His voice was thick and low. "I didn't mean to disturb you…yet."

"Yet?" I asked, taking him in. His eyes were wider than I'd ever seen before and he still wore the gray sweatpants and plain white T-shirt. His curly hair was a messy flop.

He stood and threw some of the chunks of sharp edges into the bin. "I'm almost done." He gestured awkwardly to his left. To a plate of…pancakes.

Lincoln Carden made pancakes.

Before I could stop myself, I ran forward. Needing to be closer to him, needing to be held.

Instead of holding me, Lincoln caught me and lifted me before placing me on the kitchen island. Then he pulled back. The lines on his face were drawn deep in shock.

"Sorry," I choked out. "I shouldn't have tried to hug you. I…I…" I flinched, but his horrified expression softened and twisted into something that stirred the old flutter in my stomach.

His hand curled around my neck, his fingers warm against my skin. "Oh," he whispered. "Don't apologize for that." He pulled me close until my cheek pressed against his warm chest. If there was ever a place I wanted to be, it was here.

"You're not wearing any shoes, and you tried running over a shattered mug." His chest vibrated as he spoke. He wrapped his other arm around me in a tight hug that squeezed out the remaining air in my body.

But I could breathe.

I unfurled, lifting my face and finding a new comfort in the shape of his neck. His hand stroked gentle lines up and down my back while the other was knitted in my hair, keeping me close.

"You made pancakes?" I squeaked out, arching as his fingers sent tingles up my spine.

"I didn't know it was your birthday, Elizabeth." His voice was barely loud enough for me to hear as his lips grazed the tip of my ear. "I'm so sorry for running away from you. I'm sorry about your mom."

My heart cracked open. *He heard all that?*

"You made pancakes," I said again.

"According to someone I know, they're elite."

My heart slammed at the acknowledgment of my username, at this moment where Lincoln was my Link and I was his Lily.

We stood in silence for a few seconds as if in another world. Lincoln's mouth pressed against the top of my head, and I wanted to tilt my face upward and catch his lips on mine.

But he leaned back, cleared his throat, and offered me a boyish smile. "I have cinnamon sugar, which, for some reason, you smell like."

My cheeks heated.

"And maple syrup because Rose decided that was an essential."

He grabbed the broom and swept up the last of the ceramic pieces. I looked at the pancakes. A crooked *H* and *A* were spread across the top of two of them.

"What's this?" I pointed at the letters.

He stood, grimacing, before turning around and emptying the shards into the bin. With a voice so deliciously bashful I nearly leaped on him again, he said, "I was in the process of writing *HAPPY BIRTHDAY* but the mug had other ideas. Also, it's not that easy to write with cinnamon sugar."

"And you call yourself an engineer," I teased, unable to add even a playful bite to my voice. "You could have made a stencil."

He turned his head upward to look at the ceiling, his mouth

curling into a full smile. "I was a bit distracted by the thought of the beautiful woman I was doing it for."

My insides melted and I worried I'd slip off the table, onto the floor, and right through the cracks.

"Can I eat it?" I asked.

He nodded and shrugged and did a weird sort of shimmy thing with his body. "Yeah, but I don't know if it's any good. I've never made pancakes before."

I took one.

"Wait, you don't have any toppings." He raised the jar of syrup.

But I already had it in my mouth. I chewed it, the soft comfort of a warm pancake washing over me.

"It's perfect." I picked up another. "Come here." He walked over and I opened my legs, hoping he'd step between them.

He did.

I offered it to him, and the smile playing on his lips was more delicious than the thing I was eating. He took a bite and his full lips grazed against my fingertips. I envied my own fingers. Heat spread all the way to the tips of my ears and my toes curled with the desire to kiss him. I leaned forward and gently pressed my lips against the underside of his jaw.

He jumped away and gulped. His eyes wide in horror. "Are you out of your mind to lay your lips on me while I'm eating? I nearly choked. I could have died."

I dropped my face into my hands in an attempt to contain the hot, unbridled joy sparking through me. But it didn't work. Laughter burst out of me as stars exploded in my chest.

And it was that moment that Lincoln leaped toward me and crashed his mouth onto mine with a desperation I'd longed for. I tightened one leg around him, and he leaned into me. His breath came out in heavy pants as he whispered against my lips, "I can't believe you're my Lily."

"And you're my Link." I glanced upward, meeting his gaze. From this close, I could see the depth of those brown irises that I thought about way too often.

I closed my eyes, and he took this as permission to kiss me again. His arms slipped around my waist, and I resisted the urge to bite down on his bottom lip, which I teased between my teeth. I wanted all of Lincoln Carden. Unrestrained. Unfiltered. I wanted Lincoln in whichever way he was comfortable being. His coffee taste filled me as our tongues finally met. I felt the low moan from the back of his throat and snaked my arms around his neck, pulling him as close as he could get. His hands settled on my hips but it wasn't enough. I needed more.

Even if everything crashed and burned, I wanted one night with Lincoln Carden. One night where I was desired and loved and cared for. One night where I was touched carefully and with intent. One night where I could finally give myself to someone I trusted. Loved.

But this wasn't only about me.

With another, unwanted voice creeping into my mind, I panicked and pulled away. The words flew out of me before I could stop them. "I don't know if this is a good idea."

45

LINCOLN

[33 weeks ago]

@theanswerisno:
Favorite food for dinner?

> **@pancakesareelite:**
> Username

@theanswerisno:
Dinner. Not breakfast.

> **@pancakesareelite:**
> Username

@theanswerisno:
Seriously? Even dinner?

> **@pancakesareelite:**
> When I love something, I love it in all
> its forms at all times.

"I'm sorry." I flinched back. "I read that all wrong. I thought you wanted me to…"

Elizabeth's lips, plump from the way I'd kissed her, were down-turned on the edges. "I did. I do, but…" Her wide eyes welled up. "I'm not…"

"Not what?" I cupped her face and used my thumb to swipe at the tear escaping her left eye.

"Worth," she started, her voice unraveling in the worst of ways. "Worth it. I'm not worth you losing this promotion over. Your mom…Lincoln, your mom is so excited, and I can't be the reason…" She inhaled a shaky breath. "But I still want you. How selfish does that make me?" Her hands fisted the fabric of my shirt as if letting me go meant losing me.

But I was hers. Always.

"As selfish as it makes me," I breathed.

Despite the way my heart ached at the underlying and unspoken issues she had, my body still filled with heat at the idea of Elizabeth wanting me. Lily wanted me.

Main quest: Prove Elizabeth's own worth to her. Side quest: Try not to scare her away.

My brain struggled to figure out how to respond to that, so without saying anything, I pulled her off the counter and twirled her around so I could cradle her in my arms. I would not go any further without this woman understanding how much she meant to me. How *worth it* she was.

While walking, I dragged her as close to my chest as possible and was pleased when her lips placed a soft kiss on my collarbone. Shivers spread from that very spot right through my entire body. It was a relief knowing she was struggling to resist me as much as I struggled to resist her.

When we got to my bedroom, I laid her down on the bed, and she tried dragging me toward her.

I pulled back. "No, no, no."

Her crestfallen face crushed me. Elizabeth had been hurt in the past. I could tell that much from her behavior, but it ran deep. She hid it well and managed to keep up that sunshine personality everyone adored.

"Oh, then why bring me here?" She curled up, lifting her knees to her chest.

"I should have said, 'not yet.'" I placed a soft kiss on both knees.

The smile was returning, and I spun around to grab the scribble-covered Arch D sheet. My stomach turned with embarrassment, and every part of me wanted to hide it away and never show her how deep my neurosis ran.

I extended my hand with the drawing. She took it in and first looked at the road layout.

"Other side," I choked out.

Her gaze fell on her names written in the top center.

ELIZABETH AKA PANCAKESAREELITE AKA LILY AKA THE ONLY WOMAN I'VE EVER TRULY BEEN IN LOVE WITH

"Don't you ever call yourself unworthy of my love when you're the only reason I am sure I can feel that sort of affection," I managed to say when my words returned.

Her beautiful, soft pink lips parted while she stared at the mind map I'd given her.

"You don't know the power you hold." I turned around, unable to watch her eyes when I said this. "Only you can control a room by just walking into it. And I don't mean that because you're a Gordon-Bettencourt. I didn't even know you were a Gordon-Bettencourt when we first met and neither did the team on-site or my mom. Okay, my friends knew, but that's different."

I was rambling and pacing, but I couldn't stop either. "It's not even because you're stupidly gorgeous, even though, you know, it helps, but…" I shook my head, trying to clear it. "But you're you. You shimmer and shine, Elizabeth. You're like the stars on a dark night. Something to make a wish on." I sighed before looking at her. "Elizabeth, I think you've experienced awful things because someone gave you these complexes and…"

Her eyes were wide, brows drawn to the center.

She was exquisite.

My chest was heaving at this point. "You do have weaknesses. No one's perfect. I've had to rewash certain dishes."

She giggled, and it was all I needed to finally meet her gaze.

"Lincoln," she whispered, "what is this?"

I dragged my hands over my face. If there was a chance Elizabeth could love me, I may as well let her know what she was getting herself into. "I was in the process of calculating the likelihood of you falling in love with me and staying in love with me. There were four scenarios I wanted to explore." I pointed at the bottom row.

1. *No contact, and I stay in love with her*
2. *Stay friends online and in person, and I stay in love with her*
3. *We fall in love, break up, and I stay in love with her*
4. *We fall in love, get married, do all the things, and I get to love her forever*

My cheeks were on fire, and I resisted the urge to grab the sheet of paper, throw it through the window, and claim that it was all a joke. But her painted pink fingernail dragged across the fourth scenario.

The one I had my heart set on.

"What about work?" she asked.

"I included it at first. It complicated things, and ultimately, it came down to the same answer." I looked at her, ensuring she knew how serious I was when I said, "Whatever the outcome is, it won't affect your chance of being offered a permanent position."

"And yours?"

"Don't worry about it."

I wasn't worried. Because through the mapping process, I'd not only worked through my feelings for Elizabeth but also inadvertently solidified my feelings about Simucon and about being promoted. But now wasn't the time for that distraction.

"Would we keep it a secret?" she asked.

My heart flip-flopped at the insinuation that she wanted this as much as I did. I nodded. "For now. For the next two days."

Her deft fingers traced another portion of my mind map. "What's going on here?"

"I tried matching our traits"—I turned away while she deciphered the scribbles calling her beautiful, smart, kind, thoughtful, funny (the list went on)—"and when that didn't feel comprehensive enough, I assigned weights to the things about my personality I thought may win you over based on what the internet tells me are desirable traits for a man to have."

I paused here in the hope that she'd giggle and not make me want to bury myself in the various holes I'd been digging on-site.

But her eyes stayed fixed on the map.

A chill ran through me. I overdid it. I showed too much of my true intensity.

"This is a weird thing to tell you. Never mind. I was trying to, like…explain that I think you're amazing, and I can't believe you'd ever think of yourself otherwise but…um…I'm sorry."

I moved closer to take the sheet away from her, but instead, she leaped into my arms, nearly toppling me over. The paper crinkled between our chests.

"Tell me more. What was the result? Did you do a sensitivity analysis?" She wrapped her legs around my waist, and it short-circuited my thoughts.

With no other option available to my love-flooded brain, I kissed her. My legs shook with anticipation, and I sat down, pulling her onto my lap. Heat spread from her body onto my thighs. My mouth skimmed across the freckles on her exposed shoulder.

Elizabeth sighed, letting her head roll back and giving me full access to her neck.

My laptop screen lit up, capturing our attention. Her eyes jumped across the spreadsheet, and she grabbed the mouse and scrolled. My stomach was a mess; even the butterflies were in knots.

"Lincoln," she whispered.

"I know, I'm *unusual* and *weird* and those are understatements, and yes, I've rated those traits negatively." My left hand curled around her waist and rested on her soft stomach.

Her free hand found it and entwined our fingers.

"You didn't finish it," she said when she got to the bottom.

"I didn't need to because, even if my preferred scenario, number four, was ranked on the lower end, I was going to change it. Become the man you need me to be or just drop down on my knees and beg you to give me a chance and prove to you how perfect we'd be together. I know I freaked out at first, but that's because…you liked Link. I'm not Link. You also liked Mr. Carden, and I don't know if I'm him either. I…I mask so often, I don't know who I am, and I…panicked because you're you. You're Lily." I took a breath. My chest was awfully tight, and I did not have an inhaler nearby. "You're everything I want."

She turned around, straddling me on the chair, and I'd never been happier to be locked in somewhere.

"You're Lincoln." As she pinned me with her intense gray eyes, my adrenaline rushed. "You're Link, you're Mr. Carden, Dr. Carden, you're your mom's handyman and the person your friends will drive forever to see. You're a coffee drinker, a sandwich buyer, an ADHD-riddled genius who loves Blade Olive, and yes, you're anxious and closed off, but you're you. We don't need this spreadsheet. I'm already, and will always be, in love with every version of you."

My heart sprang into my throat, and before I could reply, her mouth was against mine. Softer than before. She mumbled against my lips, "And I'm so sorry for not speaking up sooner. I started suspecting it weeks ago but I wasn't sure." A soft kiss. Another. Another. More words came out of her mouth, directly onto mine. "All I knew was that you were both engineers, mommy's boys, and like…your name, I guess. But I genuinely thought it was only because of *Zelda*."

My chest opened. That was the best answer to one of the plaguing questions I'd had. I cupped her red cheeks.

"And I kept thinking about how I could be wrong and how awkward it would be if I was, because you're my boss, but there was this giant panic, like, what if you're Link. My Link? Statistically, that's unlikely, isn't it?"

"Your Link," I repeated, stuck there. *Hers.* I kissed her again. I couldn't do it enough. "And you're my Lily." A breath whooshed out of both of us. "Whoa."

"Exactly!" She pulled back and looked into my eyes. "It's a little terrifying to think of it…of all those times I enjoyed the lobby more than the game. I went back daily to talk to you, to play with you, Link…" She flushed bright red. "Lincoln."

"You can call me Link." I kissed her perfect cupid's bow.

"My mom and gran call me Lily. Link was the only other person who called me that."

"Can I?" I whispered.

She nodded, and then she looked away, her eyes glistening with unspoken pain. Pain I hoped she'd let me help her carry one day. "You saved me. Link was all I had for a really, really long time and then we started working together and you became the only other person I had. But you are Link, so you saved me twice? It was so confusing."

My chest ached, realizing the total mind trip it must have been. Had the tables been turned, I never would have spoken up. I never would have even gone to the LAN. I don't know what I would have done.

But this was Elizabeth, my Lily, and she dove in headfirst and asked questions later.

46

ELIZABETH

[32 weeks ago]

@pancakesareelite:
It's been forever since I've been on
a date

> **@theanswerisno:**
> Same

@pancakesareelite:
Two birds, one stone

> **@theanswerisno:**
> You are so cheeky

@pancakesareelite:
Are you blushing right now?

> **@theanswerisno:**
> No

> **@theanswerisno:**
> Okay, fine. I am

⇨

I couldn't believe it. The formulas Lincoln used, the lengths he'd gone to. The only thing unlinked to a calculation, the only known factor, was the solid one hundred percent next to my name. Lincoln Carden believed I was the unachievable number of perfection. According to *science*. Despite knowing all my flaws. Despite everything. And when I looked into his eyes, I knew, without a doubt, that he really believed it to be true.

I scrolled to the bottom of the spreadsheet where the conclusion lay blank, but the spreadsheet was already set up to auto-populate once the rest of the cells were filled in. I changed a few things, marked myself down (which led to an error) and then marked him up instead. The final percentages jumped around. I needed the fourth scenario to be on top.

> *4. We fall in love, get married, do all the things, and I get to love her forever*

Lincoln Carden wanted to marry me?

He wanted to love me *forever*?

And while I continued playing around with the numbers, his arm circled my waist and stroked the not-so-flat stomach I'd tried hiding. His mouth pressed against my shoulder, sending a buzz of electricity to my brain.

And then I did it! Sort of.

"There we go." I twisted toward him. "There's a one hundred and seventeen percent chance we'll fall in love, get married, do all the things, and you'll get to love me forever."

"One hundred *and* seventeen percent?" He bit down on his lip in the most adorable way. "That hasn't been peer-reviewed."

I pressed my mouth against his, and he chuckled before scooping me up.

"Careful," I said, already grinning. "With all this carrying, you might hurt your back."

"Your smart mouth should have been a dead giveaway." He burst out laughing.

I vibrated at the sound.

When he set me on the bed, I looked up into those gorgeous eyes and said, "Hey, Lincoln, I love you." Then I pulled my top off.

He froze.

I should have timed my confession better.

Taking off my shirt in front of the man who blushed when I looked at him for anything longer than a second was a risky move.

He almost comically adjusted his glasses.

I reached out to take them off. They'd get in the way of me kissing his eyelids, his eyelashes. I wanted my mouth on every part of him.

But his hand shot up to stop me. "No, no, I need to *see* first."

"Did you even hear me?" My hands dropped onto the waistband of my pajama shorts.

This time, he launched forward, stopping my hands again. "Not yet." He inhaled and closed his eyes. "Give me a second to compose myself. I've wanted to hear you say that for so long."

I gnawed on my bottom lip to keep from having the laughter spill out of me. "Link." I crawled to the edge of the bed, where he stood staring. "Lincoln." I slid my hands up his shirt, and a shiver shot through me as my fingers traced over the strong, lean body I'd spent far too many moments thinking about.

"Permission to touch all of you…everywhere?" He straightened and gestured up and down my body.

"With all of you and everything you've got." I leaned forward and kissed his Adonis belt, which peeked out between the hem of his shirt and the top of his pants.

He pulled off his shirt, and I planted my lips on his skin, biting and licking as I moved upward until I was standing on the edge of the bed. I leaned downward and kissed him.

Lincoln's strong arms circled me and then I was on my back. His weight pushed down on me like I'd dreamed of. I wrapped my legs around his waist, wanting to be even closer. A low groan escaped him, and his touch, which had been gentle and hesitant, turned sure and desperate.

He whispered my name against my lips and dipped his head, but I pulled him back up.

"Stay here. Kiss me," I managed, even though I wanted him everywhere, all at once.

"Lily." His eyes were filled with excitement and desire and…love.

He wet his lips and placed his mouth on mine in a deliberate, slow kiss that had I been standing, would have knocked me over. "I think you should know…I…haven't been with anyone."

I leaned in for another kiss, desperate to keep my mouth on his. "Same."

He pulled away, his eyes darting around. "No, I don't think you understand." He gulped. "I've never been with anyone."

Lincoln Carden was a virgin?

My heart raced, filling with warmth and love at the intensity of this moment. I cupped his jaw until his gaze met mine. "Oh. Are you sure you want to do this now?"

His brown eyes darkened. "Yes."

"If you don't…"

"Elizabeth," he said, his hands gaining confidence as he pressed his fingertips against my skin, "I want you so badly that I fear I'll devour you entirely. So you're going to have to tell me when to stop." He lowered his mouth to my neck, trailing his tongue down my collarbone.

"Devour me, then," I breathed, unable to say much else as the little jolts of electricity kept sparking through me.

And so he did.

Slowly and intentionally. Lincoln Carden made love to me in a way no one else had. We fell into a tangle of limbs between the thin sheets and heavy blankets, our skin hot and glistening. My heart cracked open, overflowing with the love he so openly had for me.

His mouth stayed on me. Keeping me there. Grounded with him.

Lincoln Carden was the first man to love me. I knew that to be true. And he showed it in every way he could. I let go in the safety of his arms. Something I hadn't been able to do before.

"I never want to be apart from you," I admitted.

"You never have to be." He captured my mouth in a sweet kiss as his hands crept toward mine, entangling our fingers. "And by the way, I love you too."

"You love me?"

He smothered me with kisses. "Now you're just fishing to hear me say it again."

My heart sang. I'd been hoping someone would say those words to me, but I had no idea I'd be lucky enough for it to be Lincoln.

LINCOLN

[31 weeks ago]

>   **@pancakesareelite:**
>   Have you ever been in love?

@theanswerisno:
Maybe

>   **@pancakesareelite:**
>   What do you mean?

@theanswerisno:
Just…maybe. I don't know.
I haven't been in love with
any of the women I've tried dating

@theanswerisno:
You?

>   **@pancakesareelite:**
>   I think I'm maybe,
>   kind of, falling in love

⇦⇨

Being with Elizabeth was different from any experience I'd had before. Her lips were entrancing. Her skin, inviting, and the sounds she made letting me know she was enjoying me were something I'd crave forever. I pulled her against my body, pressing my mouth on her pink cheeks. If there was a way I could get even more of her, I would.

"I love you," I said again.

"It took you a long enough time to say it back," she teased, and the soft yellow light flickered across her beautiful gray irises.

"You distracted me, woman."

I kissed her because that was something I was allowed to do now. Her delicate but deft fingers tilted my jaw upward before trailing down my neck and over my shoulders. She kept touching every part of me she could reach. I lifted her up and wrapped a blanket around her before carrying her to the living room, where I set her down on the couch.

"Pancakes?" I asked.

"Yes?" She looked up at me.

I chuckled. "I mean, do you want some pancakes?"

She grinned and nodded but stole a few more kisses before I could leave.

I grabbed the plate of pancakes but then had a thought and detoured to my bedroom. When I returned, she extended her hands and took the plate while I set up the old Atari console I'd brought along.

She gasped, crawling to the floor and wrapping herself around me as I did it. It only meant I had to carry her back to the couch, which she seemed to enjoy, judging from her giggles.

"Where did you even get this?" she squealed, taking the now-faded controller into her hands.

"My mom found it when packing up our old house." At the

mention of packing up, the soft carpet turned coarse under my knees. I still had more to do at our old home, and I had to do it this weekend. The pit in my stomach grew.

"I can't believe you brought this along," her sweet voice said, a medicine to my bitter thoughts.

"Well, I thought I'd be alone and bored, and the internet sucks."

"Sorry for intruding." She bit down on her bottom lip.

I kissed her.

"*Pac-Man*!" she squealed as we separated.

"You are the woman of my heart," I said.

Her cheeks flushed even redder than they'd been. "Link?" she said after we'd been playing for a few minutes in what I thought was a comfortable silence. Panic and guilt spread across her features. "There's still a lot you don't know about me, and I should have told you everything before we…"

"Before we confessed our undying love for each other and I basically proposed?" I said, hoping to lighten whatever blow was about to knock me over.

She smiled, but it didn't reach her shiny eyes. "I don't want to keep a secret from you ever again or break your trust or…"

I curled my arms around her. "You don't have to tell me everything. If you want, I'll be here, and if you don't want…guess what?" I kissed her nose. "I'll still be here."

"I don't want to ruin tonight."

"Nothing can ruin tonight," I said.

Her slumped shoulders riddled me with concern, but I knew not to push. So I did what I'd been doing for years. I nudged her. "How about all we do tonight is play this game, and when you're ready, you can tell me?"

After about an hour, when Lily was more pancake than woman, she mumbled, "My mom got knocked up as a teenager by some random guy she'd met at a concert. He disappeared, and she became a single mother, with big dreams of becoming an actress. At some point, she crossed paths with Douglas." Her nostrils flared, and she ground her teeth. "And I suspect he saw how vulnerable and desperate she was, so he plucked us from obscurity and molded us into the submissive family he needed to complete his near-perfect image."

I kept my gaze on the little TV screen, where I imagined she wanted it to stay.

"He gave us everything money and fame could buy, but it wasn't free. My earliest memories of him are good. He loved me, and I loved him. But at some point, I learned that love wasn't unconditional. In fact, he only loved me when I agreed with him." She blew out the softest breath. "Two years ago, when I was at my lowest point and Douglas only pushed me lower, my mom encouraged me to leave even though it meant leaving behind the mansion and the money. I'm so grateful she made me do it, but I don't understand why she stayed."

Rage seared through my chest, setting everything alight. If Douglas Gordon-Bettencourt ever found me, he'd regret it.

"And I wonder if I should have stayed with her." She stopped playing and held the controller loosely in her hands.

I took the controller from her and entwined our fingers, letting Pac-Man get eaten by the little ghosts. My anger was growing but the last thing she needed when talking about an angry man was another one. I took a deep breath and chose my words carefully. "No wonder he's threatened by you."

She squeezed my hand. "What?"

"Why else would he be writing nasty think pieces?"

She glanced my way. "You read the article?"

"Nope. I'm not interested in what other people have to say about you. I only want to hear about you from you. But…I heard about the article. And it's pretty clear to me now that he's scared of you, and he should be."

She climbed onto my lap and pressed her face against my chest. After a second, I felt a wetness seep through my T-shirt. I wrapped my arms around her shoulders and held her while she cried, years of pent-up frustration and sadness dripping out of her shaking frame.

She sniffled, leaned back, and wiped her eyes. "I shoplifted when I was eleven, and when I was a kid, I had a crush on a cartoon lion, and when I was fifteen, I told my mother I slept over at Kaia's house, but actually I went on a date with her brother, who I wasn't allowed to see."

"What are you saying?" I asked, lifting her chin to gaze into those puffy eyes.

Her lip trembled. "Those are all my secrets. I'll never keep a secret from you ever again. I am still so sorry I didn't tell you I was Pancakes. I just want you to love me, Lincoln. I really, really want it."

"Is it not strange to want something you already have?" I kissed her forehead and her cheeks. Every part of me was on edge, piecing together the challenges she must have been through and how much effort it had taken for her to get here. To excel, despite having one of the richest and most powerful men standing against her.

Going forward, I would do everything in my power to help her in whichever way I could, but there was one more solo obstacle. She'd have to ace that final test all on her own.

48

ELIZABETH

[29 weeks ago]

@pancakesareelite:
I see girlbotxo is flirting with you

> **@theanswerisno:**
> Jealous?

@pancakesareelite:
Maybe

> **@theanswerisno:**
> Then I'll tell her to stop

@pancakesareelite:
I'm only joking

> **@theanswerisno:**
> Told her you'd challenge her to a duel

@pancakesareelite:
Link!

> **@theanswerisno:**
> Be ready at dawn

I awoke against a hot body (both in temperature and physique) and turned onto my side before looking at Link's gorgeous profile. So many things replayed in my mind. The way it felt to be touched and loved by him and finally feeling safe enough to tell someone everything. He'd listened without judgment.

I peppered his face with kisses.

"This has never happened to me," he mumbled. "Best..." His eyes dropped closed before he could finish his sentence.

I pressed my mouth against his and gently bit his bottom lip. One of his large hands pulled me on top of him and stroked along the length of my spine. "Time?"

Sleepy Link was too adorable for words. "Five thirty," I said.

"That's an entire thirty minutes earlier than my alarm," he groaned.

"Yes, that was intentional," I whispered before pushing my body against his.

"Oh." His eyes shot open. "Am awake. Wide. Awake. But we're doing it my way." He flipped me over and climbed on top of me. His lips fell onto my neck, and every thought I had disappeared, replaced by how soft his mouth was. My hands found his curls, and I raked my fingers across his scalp. He groaned, dropping his mouth from mine, before dragging his tongue down my chest and lower still. I arched my back as he did all the things I'd hoped for.

I was right about one thing: Lincoln Carden was the most capable man to have ever existed.

And he'd have proven that again if someone didn't knock at the door.

He pushed himself up onto his elbows and glanced at me, his eyebrows low and close. "I might kill the person at the door."

I chuckled and rolled out of bed behind him. I pulled on his sweatshirt while he opened the front door.

I made my way into the kitchen and prepared a fresh pot of coffee. "Who is it?"

He spun around with a huge grin on his face and a box in his hands. "For you."

"A birthday present?" I squeaked. I hadn't received a gift from anyone except my grandmother in ages.

His grin turned lopsided. "The timing is lucky. I got them for you a while ago. They're late."

I tore open the package, revealing two white shoeboxes. Lincoln grabbed the larger one. I took the other, confused. "A boot?" I looked at the picture of the black ankle boot on the top of the box. "It's cute, and a bit random."

Lincoln pointed at the very important hyphenated word I seemed to have overlooked. "It's steel-toed, Lily."

Lily. My nickname. Our nickname.

"My attention to detail is something you can add to your weaknesses list along with the dishes," I squealed while taking them out and slipping them on.

"Without socks?" Lincoln shuddered. He ran off to the bedroom and returned with a pair of his socks. He kneeled before me and took my foot in his hands. He slipped the sock on and kissed my ankle before sliding the boot on. He did the same with the other foot. The socks went all the way up to my knees.

I hopped up and danced around, appreciating how perfectly the shoes fit. "I didn't even know they made cute site boots. I'm ready to be the best site engineer ever, even though I have to leave in a few hours."

He groaned. "I don't want you to leave."

"I know. I don't want to leave without you." I wanted to throw myself on the ground and kick and scream every time I thought about leaving Lincoln here and facing the final test on my own.

"We should probably get a move on. I'd like to show you some stuff on-site before your test tomorrow." He kissed my forehead. "And don't worry about it. You're going to do great. Just believe in yourself."

Once we were on-site, we surveyed everything together, and I had to use all of my willpower not to touch him. When I nearly did, he withdrew, and my soul flinched at his hesitance before remembering why. We couldn't do this in public. Not yet.

"I guess I can't let them know I'm dating the boss," I whispered once we were alone in the site office.

"We're *dating*?" he replied as we crouched over a drawing.

I bit my bottom lip. "Aren't we? Last night you said you wanted to marry me."

He threw his head back and sighed before offering me that lopsided smile I would never get enough of. "I do. I know it's weird, but I am an absolutes guy."

"And I absolutely love you," I said, letting my pinkie finger graze against his thumb where he pressed down on the desk. "I don't suppose you'll tell me anything about the final test tomorrow?"

"Unfortunately, I don't know anything. It's different every year to keep it a surprise. The only person who has that info is Anders, and he won't tell a soul."

"Even if you did know, you wouldn't tell me, would you?"

He shook his head. "Speaking of, you better leave. I think it's best if you're not on the road alone in the dark."

"Would you come find me again if you had to?" I asked.

He leaned his hip against the desk and drank me in with a gaze. "Lily, it appears I'll find you without you calling, without intending, without us knowing. I'll always find you."

• • •

By Friday morning, I was a mess of nerves. I got to work earlier than usual, as did the rest of the interns. I walked into my office and stared at where Lincoln should be. Last night, his signal was choppy, but he still managed to call me when I got home because, for the first time in my life, someone was waiting to see if I arrived safely.

Excitement joined my nerves at the thought of seeing him later.

"Good," Mr. Anders said, walking into my office. "You're here. How was your experience on-site?"

I nodded. "Great. Wonderful. Informative."

"Excellent." He gestured for me to follow him. "Come on. It's time."

I grabbed my laptop, pen, and paper and walked behind him while he gathered the other six interns. We formed a straight line as he led us into the big boardroom on the second floor.

The sixteen-seater table was transformed into seven cubicles. I took my seat, and Cedric sat across from me, but thanks to the dividers, we couldn't see each other.

I set up my workspace and fidgeted with my office supplies.

"Interns," Mr. Anders announced, "welcome to your final test." He gestured to the presentation on the wall. "Please navigate to the folder location shown and use the password on the screen to access the resources."

I did as I was told, and the folder exploded with drawings, location pins, and bills of quantities.

"This year's final test requires each intern to prove their holistic knowledge on a very basic level. You're all fresh out of college, so I assume some of the things you learned still reside in your brains."

He clicked over to a new slide, where an abstract area was

highlighted. "You have the next six hours to prepare a conceptual design of the infrastructure required for a multipurpose development. Considering the time limits and how many of you are specializing in different disciplines of engineering, detailed designs are not required."

The next slide had our names ranked underneath different headings: technical correctness, neatness, theoretical knowledge, professionalism, and others.

I was in position four or five for most of them.

"These ratings are based on your weekly evaluations, but as you all know, this final test will be the largest factor determining your future at Simucon."

My heart pounded in my chest. I thought I might throw up.

"Good luck, and remember that all reports and plans submitted have to be anonymous."

49

LINCOLN

[27 weeks ago]

@pancakesareelite:
Peanut butter and honey is an elite
combination

@theanswerisno:
I don't know if you know what "elite"
means

@pancakesareelite:
I know you don't trust people, but
trust me on this

@theanswerisno:
Okay. Fine. I'll try it.

@theanswerisno:
Here we go.

@theanswerisno:
You're right.

After my morning site meeting, I rushed back to my truck, ready to get to the office even though I wasn't allowed to interfere with the final test.

I scrolled through my messages and found one from *@pancakes areelite*. A strange feeling burst in my chest when I opened it.

> **@pancakesareelite:**
> Hey Link, I have to do something big and scary today. Will you play with me tonight? (Play can be interpreted in whichever way you desire)

Elizabeth would never cease to amuse me. I replied in a way *@theanswerisno* would: Of course. There are many ways to play with you, and I intend to do them all.

Heat crept up the back of my neck as if I hadn't already spent all night with her in my arms.

I turned my truck on and started the journey home.

My phone pinged, and I grabbed it, eager to see if Elizabeth had replied, but the naughty thoughts I had quickly disappeared. It was my mother texting me that the professional cleaners would be at our old home tomorrow afternoon.

Somehow, amid all the chaos, I'd forgotten about the room that both haunted and comforted me, and I still didn't want to face it.

I had little choice but to pack up my father's office tonight, but I wanted to spend tonight with Elizabeth. I'd promised her.

Technically, I could do it now. I wasn't needed or allowed to be involved in the final test, and Elizabeth wasn't likely to leave the boardroom before the end of the day.

My phone rang, and I answered on instinct. Professor Hahn's voice connected to my radio. "Lincoln, you answered!"

"It was accidental."

She laughed. "Listen, I have a meeting at SDSU. Are you in

town? We could grab a cup of coffee. There's an opportunity I want to tell you about that I believe you'll be perfect for."

"Is there another conference coming up that I don't know about?" I said.

"No. But I'll be at SDSU for the next few hours, and I'd really like to talk to you. If you can't make it today, we can arrange a video call for whenever you're free, but it has to be as soon as possible."

My curiosity piqued. "Why?"

"Well, how will I lure you into an in-person meeting if I give away all my secrets?"

"Fine. I'm on my way."

Maybe it was because I wanted to know what secrets she held… or maybe it was because I would choose to go anywhere instead of to my father's office. I would do anything instead of unplug and pack up our unfinished game.

• • •

I pulled up at my first university and hopped out of my truck. While my postgraduate research at UCLA had given me the world's best supervisor, it was SDSU that gave me the opportunity to study engineering. It also gave me Rose and Neema, which led to Shaun and William too.

It was also where I created the Engineering Lobby.

I checked my phone a couple of times, only looking for the names I'd answer to. The list was very small.

I texted Professor Hahn, letting her know I'd be in the commons. She replied with a triple thumbs-up.

Within minutes, she was at my side. "How's my favorite non-communicative ex-student doing?"

"I communicate just fine," I replied.

"Sure, you do." Her eyes shined the same way they did when she had first invited me to the meeting where she offered me the scholarship to UCLA. "Coffee?"

I gestured at the small stall in the corner, Coffee and Things. It wasn't the best coffee, but it was the cheapest. I had a lifetime of gratitude toward it as the only stall open twenty-four seven.

"What is this opportunity you want to tell me about?" I asked while waiting on our order.

Professor Hahn sighed, but there was a smile on her lips. "Straight to the point, huh?"

I pressed my lips together in what I hoped was a smile. Professor Hahn, while one of my favorite people in academia, was chatty and easily distracted.

The old man handed me the cups of coffee. "It's been a long time since I saw you."

Surely he couldn't recognize me from all those years ago, could he?

I paid and tipped him generously before following Professor Hahn to a small two-seater table. She sat down, and the wide grin on her face meant she was about to explode with whatever news she had: An upcoming conference. A research grant. A new idea she wants my input on.

"It's a job opportunity!" she announced.

Well, I didn't see that coming.

"Uh…I have a job," I managed, but gooseflesh prickled across my skin.

"I know you do, but you're wasted in the industry!" she almost yelled. "And your heart has always been in research. Lincoln, you single-handedly changed the guidelines on traffic calming."

A muscle fluttered in my abdomen. I shifted on my seat.

"I know you love design, and working here wouldn't stop you from freelancing as a technical advisor or engineer. But it'll allow you to pick and choose which projects you want to be involved in, leaving more time for research and conferences. More young engineers will get a chance to be inspired by your mind."

The flutter only grew stronger as I churned the idea over in my head.

"Wait"—I set my cup on the counter—"working *here*?"

"The dean, Professor Eldridge, let me know that SDSU is looking for a transport lecturer. He tried poaching me first, but I'm quite happy where I am, so I recommended you. He was more than open to it." She raised her hands in surrender. "I know I'm coming on too strong, so that's all I'll say."

SDSU. I could work at SDSU.

I glanced around the commons, where students shuffled in and out. Some of them chatted excitedly; others looked on the brink of collapse. A couple in the corner neglected their food to stare at each other instead.

I was transported back to my younger years. Late nights and early mornings. Ride-sharing with Claire. Spending far too much time moderating the Engineering Lobby. This university had given me so much.

I gulped down the last of my coffee. "I'll have to think about this. I don't know if lecturing is the best position for someone quite as noncommunicative as I am."

"When it comes to engineering concepts, you're brilliant at it." Professor Hahn grinned and finished her coffee. "And if you want it, I'm sure it's yours. The dean's been a huge fan of your research."

We both opted for another coffee, entertaining the possibility of me working here, of furthering my research, of helping her with hers. We'd have spoken through the night if my phone hadn't buzzed.

Barry Anders (Simucon): You need to come to the office right now.

LINCOLN

[21 weeks ago]

@theanswerisno:
I've put in hundreds of hours on this
game and I'm still not done. I don't
know if I want to keep going. I'm not
enjoying it anymore.

@pancakesareelite:
Then stop

@theanswerisno:
Didn't you hear me?
I put in hundreds of hours.

@pancakesareelite:
I heard the part where you said you're
not enjoying it anymore

@pancakesareelite:
Come on, let's play something else

Knowing Elizabeth would still be locked in to her final test, I went straight to Anders's office, half expecting him to know about the job offer. I knocked once and let myself in.

Anders's head zapped up. "Shut the door behind you."

The door snicked shut, leaving only the sound of Anders's heavy sigh. Heavier than usual.

I slipped into a seat. "What's so urgent?"

Anders ran a hand back and forth over his bald head. "How do I even ask you this?"

On a good day, I'd enjoy seeing him tongue-twisted and panicked, but this was different. The reason hit me seconds before he asked, "Is it true? Are you having…relations with Gordon-Bettencourt? Tell me it isn't." He shut his eyes.

Panic bloomed in my chest, but I stomped it down. I'd prepared for this scenario. "Yes."

"Dammit, Carden. Couldn't you have lied to me?" Anders laid his head on the desk.

The room shrunk in the seconds passing. My fingers found a tear in the leather armrest. "What good would that have done?"

"Well, for one, I wouldn't have to get HR involved. This relationship will need to be disclosed. You're her superior, Carden."

I kept fidgeting with the tear, my eyes focused on a spot on his desk. I turned his words over and over in my mind until my own thoughts burst out of me. "Well, I don't want to be."

I'd planned to chat with Elizabeth about it first, I'd planned to chat with my mom, and I'd even planned to ruminate on it for days, weeks, and months. But sitting here, across from Barry Anders for what felt like the millionth time in a decade, I was sure of my decision to leave.

I shut my eyes, waiting for the world to fall apart at my confession. But it didn't. I glanced at my boss.

"What do you mean?" Anders asked.

"I don't want the promotion. I don't want to manage. I don't want…this." I gestured toward him. "Can you picture me being you?"

With every sure word I spoke, the room seemed to expand back to its usual size.

Anders's mouth dropped open, and he waved me off. "Slow down. Don't make any rash decisions because of Elizabeth. We don't even know if she'll place top two, and even if she does, we could make it work. The policy is there to discourage complications, but there are ways around it."

"I'm not doing this because of Elizabeth." Not directly, at least. A smile teased at the corner of my mouth as I thought back to the late nights we'd worked together and how enthusiastic she'd been. I'd enjoyed going back and walking her through the basics. "I'm doing it for me. If you thought I would be a good manager, you wouldn't have tested me the way that you did."

Anders dropped his head. "I wanted you to be a good manager, but you're right. I wasn't sure you would step up." He looked upward. "But you have. I trust you now. What have they offered you? I'll add fifty percent to it."

"It's not about the money. I'll be pursuing a job in academia." The fabric gave under my fingernail with a satisfying rip.

Anders slapped his palm on the desk. "Those pesky word warriors have had their eyes on you for years." He leaned back in his seat, popped open his drawer, and pulled out a couple of individually wrapped chocolate truffles. "I suppose the heart wants what it wants." He slid one across the desk. "You're making me stress-eat my favorite chocolates. These are handmade with Venezuelan cocoa and rolled in flakes of milk chocolate."

"Thank you." I took the chocolate and rolled it between my fingers. "Could I bother you for a reference? Apparently, I'm the front runner for the job, but having the backing of Barry Anders could only benefit me."

"Of course." Anders chuckled, his teeth coated in brown chocolate. "I'll be sure to tell them how incredibly well you managed your intern."

"Speaking of…" Heat filled my cheeks, and I looked down at my lap. "My evaluations were objective."

"I give you a lot of shit," Anders said, and looked up at the ceiling, "but I have no doubt you wouldn't allow someone to unfairly achieve something at the cost of another. Had it been any of the other managers, I'd have to be a little more concerned. But you, you didn't rate her well enough for me to believe you're biased."

"She wasn't good enough back then. She is now."

"Soon we'll know whether that's true. I'm happy to keep HR out of this, considering your resignation, but I will ask that you step off from the final test's evaluation committee."

"Understood." I dipped my head. "I hope you won't judge her any differently."

"I would if I could, but I can't. The grading on the final test remains completely anonymous." He ran a hand across his head. "If I had any hair left, I'd have lost it because of this. How the hell are we going to run this department without you?"

"With great difficulty and regret, I imagine." I stood and tucked the truffle into my pocket.

Anders laughed. "I'll miss your interesting sense of humor, Carden. I wish you all the best in academia and with your"—he paused—"personal life. Elizabeth has quite the reputation, and I would hate to see a man like you end up entangled in a web of drama. Be careful with her."

All the playfulness dropped from my voice. "Be careful how you talk about her. Not only is she very important to me and deserving of your respect, but also she may very well be your newest hire in Roads and Transportation—and I hear the department could use a hand."

"Touché," Anders said. "So, what happens now?"

"Now I have to call my mom and break it to her that her son won't be the first manager in the family, but he will likely become the family's first professor."

51

ELIZABETH

[18 weeks ago]

@pancakesareelite:
Are you sure?

> **@theanswerisno:**
> No

@pancakesareelite:
What aren't you sure about?

> **@theanswerisno:**
> I don't know

@pancakesareelite:
What's that supposed to mean?

> **@theanswerisno:**
> I've never been sure about anything

@pancakesareelite:
Gaaaaah, you're infuriating

By hour five, my brain felt as though it would leak out of my ears. But at the same time, this test was exhilarating and reminded me of all the reasons I went into engineering.

Every late-night crying fit over a difficult revision, every minute spent studying Lincoln's final drawings, even the fundamentals of designing by hand, all came back and guided me through this process.

If I didn't get this job, I knew without a doubt that I'd grown as an engineer by leaps and bounds. I stood a chance. Nerves and excitement bubbled up at the thought.

The last eight weeks had led to this moment, and I'd done it all in spite of Douglas. For a few blissful hours, while connecting roads and creating open public spaces, I forgot he existed.

And that was a victory on its own.

As the test's timer neared zero, Mr. Anders walked in and his curious gaze settled on me. "Okay, interns. The managers are ready to scrutinize your drawings. I'll give you a few seconds to save your work, and for the sake of maintaining anonymity, send it off to the printers when I say so."

"Now." He made finger guns, and I hit print along with the other six interns in the room.

I exhaled a long breath and laid my head in my arms. Everything ached. I needed food. I needed a bed. I needed Lincoln.

But I also needed to know the outcome.

"Well done, everyone." Mr. Anders applauded us, and while nothing he did ever felt sincere, my eyes still welled up. "You did it."

We did it. Whether we did it well was a different question.

Cedric's hand shot up. "Mr. Anders, when will the scoring begin?"

"Immediately. It'll take the managers and senior engineers at least two hours to work their way through your drawings and accompanying reports. In the meantime, we'd like to invite you upstairs for a few drinks. After all, we're celebrating your new job or saying farewell. Either way, it's a party."

I looked down at my phone. It was already 4:00 p.m.

I shuffled out of the boardroom along with everyone else. Mr. Anders stood at the door, grinning at everyone and slapping them on the shoulder. But when I reached him, he froze. A smile that made me uneasy spread across his face. "Congratulations are in order."

"For what? I haven't gotten the job yet."

"For managing to romance the robot," he said with a chuckle. "You can tell him I said that. He'll laugh."

Lincoln? *Mr. Anders knows?*

My mouth dropped open, and he took a step closer to me. "Please don't parade it around the office. Despite his resignation, it'll still be a touchy topic for now."

"Resig— What?" I choked out.

The regular smirk I expected appeared on Mr. Anders's face. "I better let him take over." He lifted his brows.

I spun around and found Lincoln standing behind me with two foil-wrapped sandwiches in hand. That lopsided smile appeared, and for a moment, I wondered if I had imagined everything or if I really existed in a world where Lincoln Carden brought me a sandwich without asking. Where Lincoln Carden was mine.

He extended both sandwiches. "You must be hungry."

"I'm starving," I whined. "What's what?"

"Grilled cheese." He lifted his left hand and then his right. "Chicken salad."

If we weren't standing in the middle of the office, I'd walk into his wide chest and take a big inhale of his delicious clean and citrusy scent. "I can't pick. Don't make me pick."

"I'm not. They're both yours. I had a feeling you rushed out of your apartment this morning without breakfast, and I know how it goes when it comes to lunch." He grinned and took a few steps closer.

My stomach grumbled. He knew me better than I knew myself. "Aren't you hungry?"

"I've already eaten," he said, and the smile he offered me let me know that, if we weren't around the exact people we were hiding from, he'd lean down and give me a kiss.

He led me to the stairs leading to the roof, where all the other interns were gathering.

"You resigned, and Mr. Anders knows about us. How long was I in there?" I asked, already stuffing a big bite of the stretchy grilled cheese sandwich into my mouth.

"Someone told Anders about us and so he confronted me. I don't like lying."

"And then you resigned? Lincoln!"

He pushed open the door to the roof and held it aside so I could step ahead of him. "I have so much to tell you, but I want to do it when we're alone. I promise I'll tell you everything later, okay?"

I stood on my toes and whispered, "So you can kiss me while doing it?"

A slight redness crept to the tips of his ears. He looked around. "It's no wonder we got caught out."

"Any idea who tattled?" I narrowed my eyes and zoomed them straight in on Cedric.

"No, and I don't care. As far as I'm concerned, they did us a favor. Fewer secrets. Less guilt."

No more secrets. Lincoln had no intention of hiding me. My heart expanded while I finished off the rest of the grilled cheese sandwich.

My beautiful boyfriend unwrapped the chicken salad sandwich and handed it to me. "Can I get you a drink?"

I took the sandwich, and my heart hiccupped as I remembered something Lincoln's mother had said. He fed the people he loved.

Lincoln Carden loved me.

"I love you," I whispered, quickly realizing how impossible it would be to work alongside him knowing how he felt. Every surface in that office would need extra support and disinfectant.

"What are you thinking about?" he asked. "Your cheeks are bloodred."

Before I could tell him, I was swept away by one of the senior engineers, who was gathering the interns and wishing us farewell. Without the need to impress anyone anymore, the time passed in easy conversation.

Mr. Anders eventually walked out onto the roof, followed by a few of the other managers. "Okay, the results are up. Boardroom Two has each drawing stuck underneath a number. Feel free to look through the designs and claim your position."

My mouth went completely dry. If I had been chewing, I'd have choked. I scurried downstairs with Lincoln following.

Cedric practically leaped to the lower floor and sprinted toward the boardroom. His cheer cut something in me. "Number one!"

As soon as I reached the doorway, I froze, but Lincoln's strong body nudged me across the threshold. I surveyed the room for my familiar design and found it underneath a large printed 3.

My stomach dropped, and I squeezed my eyes shut for a second.

Lincoln released a long, low grumble beside me. "I'm so sorry."

I leaned in and scrutinized my own design, reading the comments scribbled across it. Not all were critical. There were so many positive notes too. I grinned and spun around to look at Lincoln. "Number three ain't so bad."

He smiled. His eyes sliced toward numbers 1 and 2, and I knew he wanted to check them out. We walked over to Cedric's design, and honestly, I had no idea how he managed to do this much in the time we were given.

"Good job," I said.

"Thanks." Cedric seemed to resist his natural inclination to snarl and said, "I'm impressed you went from seventh to third. That's quite the feat across eight weeks." After complimenting me, he looked like he may throw up.

We moved over to number 2, but before I could get a proper look, my phone buzzed in my hand. Eight weeks ago, I'd set an alarm to call my grandmother so she could celebrate or whine with me.

I hit dial. She rejected my call. I sent her a text instead, letting her know she could call me back when she had a chance.

"I better pack up my office," I said, my heart a little sore at my loss, but I was not nearly as devastated as I had anticipated.

"Oh crap," Lincoln mumbled. "Packing. I'm supposed to be packing up my childhood home." He grimaced and ran a large hand across his face. "New owners are moving in on Monday, and the cleaners are coming over the weekend. I promised my mom I'd have everything out by today." He shifted on his feet and then met my gaze. There was a heaviness in his deep brown irises that wasn't there a second ago. "Is there any chance you want to come with me?"

52

LINCOLN

[14 weeks ago]

> **@pancakesareelite:**
> Do you have any major regrets?

> **@theanswerisno:**
> Starting a chat with you that one time.

> **@pancakesareelite:**
> That is SO mean

> **@theanswerisno:**
> My regret is not starting it sooner.

I don't know why I invited Elizabeth along with me. Well, I knew why. I was in love with her, so it was actually all very simple. But I hadn't thought about it long enough to figure out what state I'd be in while packing up my father's study.

I didn't need her to see me unravel. Not now. Not when I've only just earned her love. Not when she'd had such a major disappointment to deal with.

She ran downstairs to my truck with her backpack and small box of belongings. I had the white divider in my arms and threw it in the bed of my truck.

"I brought my laptop so if you don't need my help, I might get some job applications done. You don't have to worry about me at all. I don't even need to be in the same room as you."

My heart dropped right out of my chest because, without me having to say anything, Elizabeth knew. She knew when I was sad or worried. She knew when I was trying to hide it, and even though I managed to fool almost everyone else, I couldn't fool her.

Like I could never fool Lily. Elizabeth and Lily had morphed into one person. My person. I couldn't believe I didn't see it sooner. But with every touch and joke, I could barely tell where Elizabeth started and Lily ended. Everything I craved to know about my online crush, I now knew about Elizabeth.

Her mouth pressed against mine as I lifted her into the truck.

With all the confusion and doubt I often experienced, there was one thing I knew for sure: I was the luckiest man in the whole world.

•   •   •

I unlocked the door, slid my hand around the corner, and turned on the light. The house was empty—naked. A strange feeling stretched across my chest as my fingers grazed against the fading wallpaper.

I gestured to the small open space, aware of how tiny it must appear to someone like her. "This was the living room." I pointed in the other direction. "Kitchen, bathroom's there if you need it."

I turned to face the only room that still had anything in it.

Wordlessly, Elizabeth came up to me, her hands clutching her backpack straps.

"My dad's study," I said.

She didn't say anything. She only dropped one of her hands to find my fingers. And somehow, that simple gesture had me turning the brass doorknob and pushing open the heavy door to reveal the almost-untouched room.

Time was up. Tonight it would go. It had to.

"You can set up over there." I pointed at the desk at the back of the room.

Elizabeth's pretty eyes widened. "At your dad's desk?"

She gulped, almost frozen in place. I took a quick step toward her and lifted her chin, placing a soft kiss on her lips before removing her backpack from her grip. She watched me in complete silence while I undid the zipper and set up her workstation.

"When I started high school, my mom refused to buy me a desk and made me do my homework here." I turned on her mouse. "I think it was her own version of exposure therapy. It was mostly effective."

Elizabeth came around the small desk and rested her hand on my forearm. "The job applications aren't urgent. I'm here if you need help with anything, okay?"

I nodded and swallowed, the hard lump in my throat immovable. I pulled open the drawer and scooped out the stacks of files he'd kept there.

"What did your dad do?" her soft voice asked from behind me.

"He was a construction worker. But he kept far too many notes and made copies of everything." I flipped through the invoices and bank statements. I took out one of the garbage bags I'd brought along.

These are just papers. They're not him. Just papers.

I blew out a long breath and started dumping them one by one. A strange pinch started in my chest but worked its way upward and out as I did it, leaving light in its path. With this newfound feeling, I tackled the bookshelf.

My dad had spent many hours in here reading. Some of those hours I had spent with him.

"He was a sci-fi and fantasy reader with political thrillers sprinkled in between," I said. To my surprise, a smile curled onto my face at the memory. It wasn't often I could speak about him like this. It hurt my mom. It hurt me.

Elizabeth hopped up and came toward me. Even while my focus was on the books, it was easy to see she hadn't been working. Instead, she had been studying me from above her laptop screen. "Did he have a favorite book? Author?"

"This one." I picked up the worn-out copy he and I had both read countless times, written by an author no one else seemed to have heard of. "It's a satirical fantasy with a corrupt government so it somehow ticked off everything he enjoyed."

She watched me leaf through the pages. The blue ink in the margins made my chest flutter.

"Was this him?" She dragged her finger across one of the notes. "Looks like your handwriting."

A laugh escaped me. "It is mine."

She raised a brow. "I've had to study your handwriting to make any sense of the comments you've scribbled onto my drawings."

She said nothing further, allowing me to continue talking about my dad if I wanted to. And I did want to. I leaned down and kissed one of those bloodred cheeks. There was no way she'd ever know how much this moment meant.

"He read it first, loved it, and gave it to me to read. I annotated it and then I gave it back to him and he annotated it, but it was mostly him replying to my notes."

The book was cracked open on one of the fight scenes near the middle. I'd underlined the sentence that didn't make sense to me. The logistics of the fight weren't working out. My dad had left a note to say: *Don't you dare point out errors in this scene, Link. It's perfect. In all of its chaos and disorder.*

My throat tightened, and yet I still laughed, blinking away the tears threatening.

We fell onto the couch and read through all the comments, the conversations recorded in between the stories I'd escaped in.

"I think I'm going to keep this copy." I turned it around in my hands.

"You absolutely have to," she said. "You know, if you wanted, you could keep everything. No one would judge you for it."

"Maybe I should keep this couch. It's really comfortable," I replied, curling an arm around her and pulling her as close as possible.

"It is." She tilted her head up and kissed my cheek.

The act was so soft, so out of the blue that my heart skipped.

Before us, the TV and console lay waiting. With the burst of strength her kiss gave me, I leaned forward and picked up one of the controllers. I turned it around in my hands. The remote for the TV lay beside it, but it didn't work. I reached around the TV and found the dip of the button. I was surprised that after all these years it turned on.

"Is this your old PlayStation?" she asked, and reached for the other controller.

My dad's controller.

"Technically, yes. But also, no." I found myself grinning. "My dad convinced my mom that it was a present for me, but he stuck it in here. We caught him playing when I wasn't around."

Elizabeth giggled against my side.

With shaking hands, I turned on the console, wondering whether it would even work, whether it would still have the saved game stored.

It did. The game loaded, and on the screen, up came the last scene we'd played together in *Return of the King*. Transported back in time, I was given a chance to do what I didn't do back then.

My throat all but closed up after I got the next few lines out. "Lily, do you want to finish this game with me?"

53

ELIZABETH

[10 weeks ago]

> **@theanswerisno:**
> Hey, Pancakes?

> **@pancakesareelite:**
> Hmm?

> **@theanswerisno:**
> Thank you for always being around

> **@pancakesareelite:**
> Anytime. Every time. All the time.

"I thought you'd never ask," I said.

Lincoln slid off the couch and onto the cushion near the TV. I joined him on the other cushion, wanting to be as close as possible. Soft vulnerability came off him in waves.

"I haven't played this before," I said. But I'd seen the movie, so at the very least the concepts weren't entirely foreign.

"You'll catch on quickly," he said, his voice an echo of what it usually was. "I've seen you jump headfirst into far more complicated games."

The half smile on his lips tempted me, but I stayed put.

As if reading my mind, he kissed my shoulder but then turned his attention back to the game. "My dad was my first Player Two. He was the first person who introduced me to games, and when he was around, I didn't need anyone else. I didn't need friends." He swallowed, his eyes fixed on what was happening in the game.

I kept moving too. Slashing. But my focus was on Lincoln.

"My dad was always there and ready to play a game with me. Even when he was tired or stressed."

Like Link was for me.

"And this was the last game we'd played. This was the last thing I'd done with him before we went to the store and never made it there." His voice broke. "If we'd played a second longer. If we'd left a second earlier…" He dipped his head, his knuckles whitening around the controller. "Maybe he wouldn't have been standing there when that driver lost control. Maybe if I hadn't gone with him, he wouldn't have worried about me. Maybe…"

I hit pause and took the controller from his hands before wrapping his big figure in my arms. His tears dampened my clothing and sank into my skin. I tightened my grip, pulling him closer. For a few minutes, I could barely tell where I ended and where he began because Lincoln's pain became my own as my heart cracked open, letting all of him in. All of his grief. All of his love. All of the things he didn't like about himself.

I loved all of Lincoln Carden, and I always would.

He straightened, apologies slipping from his mouth. I shushed him and used the back of my sleeve to dry his face.

"I'm not usually like this." He cleared his throat.

It was as though I could see the mask being pulled over. The one he used when he thought he was being too much. I leaned my forehead against his. "You can be however you want, whenever you want. I'm here. And if you want to pack this up, I'll help you. If you want to play it, I'll beat you."

"It's not a competitive game." A laugh huffed out of him, and he shook his head. "You are so perfect."

My heart fluttered pathetically. This man could say anything to me, and it would flutter. But he wasn't just any man saying anything. He was Lincoln, the kindest, smartest, most handsome man in the world.

"Hey, Lily," he said, handing me the controller, "I'd like to finish it. With you."

"And as I've proven time and time again, my answer to you is always *yes*."

The last bit of the game didn't take too long, but with every step, with every arc of his virtual sword, Lincoln unfurled. His shoulders dropped, his smile returned, and there was a lightness surrounding him that wasn't there before.

At some point, we paused and opened the chips he'd brought along. The controllers became a little greasy, and our laughter grew more frequent.

And this went on and on, until the game credits rolled. Which was when he gave me one long look. A look that struck my heart. Held it. Fixed it. A look so soft that I was glad he didn't say anything because no words would match the amount of value he'd given me with that one look.

Slowly, he packed up the console.

"Are you keeping it?" I asked.

He shook his head. "Nah. Donating it, along with the games and most of the books. Maybe some other kid can play on it with their dad or find their Player Two." He lifted my hand and kissed my fingertips. "I've been lucky enough to find mine. Twice."

• • •

At some point during the night, which was slowly edging into morning, Lincoln and I moved boxes of books to his truck.

I took a moment to explore what had been his childhood home. It was so much smaller than the house where I'd met his mother. But this place was lived in and worn down with memories that were scratched into every surface. Sometimes, literally so.

I moved my laptop, still open, even though I hadn't done a single application. The desk and chair needed to go next. I flopped onto the couch while he moved the last of the boxes.

Lincoln's hand dropped to his stomach. "I'm starving."

"Me too."

He whipped out his phone. "There's a twenty-four-hour pizzeria, and while the Google reviews average at 2.7, it is the only place that's still open."

"What's a little food poisoning between lovers?"

He chuckled. "Favorite pizza?"

"Anything with cheese."

"Girl of my dreams," he replied, sitting beside me, bumping my mouse.

My laptop screen woke up, opening my inbox. There were two unread emails. Both from Mr. Anders.

The first email told me what I already knew. Cedric and Peter were the top two interns this year, and I followed closely behind.

The next email was also about the internship.

[UPDATED] INTERN POSITIONS

I glanced at Lincoln as I opened it. Cedric was still number one, but number two had changed. Number two was no longer Peter. Now it read Elizabeth Gordon-Bettencourt.

At the bottom stood a single line: Peter has taken a job in the United Kingdom. We wish him all the best.

My mouth dropped open. "Does this mean?"

"I think so," Lincoln said with a chuckle. "Lily! You got it."

"I got it?" I said, my voice cracking. "I…can't believe it."

"I can." He pressed his lips against mine. "Congratulations, gorgeous girl. Simucon is the best place for you to learn. You'll get all the experience you need to really tap into the skills you're already developing, provided you're willing to deal with a few jerks."

Joy and nerves prickled across my skin. "I can handle them."

He nodded, grinning. "They're in trouble. They have no idea what they've gotten themselves into."

I crawled closer to him, already thinking of all the things we could do to celebrate.

But then the doorbell rang, and Lincoln held up a finger before going to the front door. He returned with the pizza.

He sat down and placed it between us before opening it to reveal the super cheesy perfection. I grabbed a slice and bit into it, gesturing for him to speak. Finally, he told me all about his meeting with Professor Hahn.

I swallowed the food before it was ready to be swallowed. I coughed. "You'll be a lecturer?"

His frown returned, but there was a smile playing there too. "Yeah. I'm gonna try. I don't know if I'll be any good at it."

"If you were my professor, I'd either have passed everything to impress you or failed everything because you're gorgeously distracting."

He burst out laughing.

"Lily," he breathed, and shut his eyes, "you're not helping."

I reached out and pinched his chin. "Link, you're the best teacher I've ever had. During games, with road design and traffic analysis, even on-site. You're patient and kind, even when I thought you didn't like me."

"You thought I didn't like you?" His dark brows pulled together.

"Uh-huh." I took another slice. "You were so angry around me."

"I couldn't think clearly," he said with a long sigh, and I knew he was about to give me one of those toe-curling compliments. "Elizabeth, I enter a black hole of focus, and it helps my productivity, but it's not always easy. Then you were there, shimmering and shining. All I wanted to do was look at you, make wishes upon you, bottle you and take you everywhere."

There it was.

I lifted the pizza box because I couldn't handle the separation. Lincoln pulled me closer until I was on his lap.

"I can't wait for you to take me everywhere."

"I will." He offered me a kiss. "But for now, can I take you home? To my home?"

54

ELIZABETH

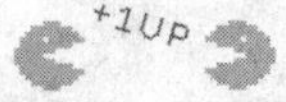

[8 weeks ago]

@pancakesareelite:
Wish me luck

>   **@theanswerisno:**
>   For what?

@pancakesareelite:
I'm starting something potentially
life-changing tomorrow

>   **@theanswerisno:**
>   Good luck, Pancakes. Maybe after you've
>   changed your life, you can change mine

Lincoln loaded everything into his truck, including me. I curled up in the passenger seat and watched him close the door to his childhood home for the last time. He couldn't hide his feelings from me anymore. I could see the heartache, but there was something else too. Some inkling of peace.

My head lolled to one side and shot upright as he climbed in beside me. He turned the heater on and laid his jacket across my legs.

"You can sleep," he whispered. "I'll drive gently and avoid potholes."

I wanted to make a joke, but exhaustion stopped me. Today had been too much. The last eight weeks had been too much.

At some point, the seat belt was peeled off me, and I was pulled into Lincoln's arms.

"I can walk," I slurred.

"I know," he replied, holding me even tighter.

I wanted to exist only in this moment with the man I loved in a way I'd never loved anyone else.

And as soon as he got me into his apartment, I wiggled awake. "Want to shower." I pointed at myself. "Join me."

Again, Lincoln scooped me up, and then he carried me to the bathroom.

When the water temperature was perfect, we stepped into the shower together and washed off the day. I washed his chest, kissed it too. He lathered my hair with shampoo, taking care to rinse it all out.

It was like a fever dream in the best of ways.

"Do you really love me, Lincoln?"

He nodded.

"Forever?"

He nodded again and emphasized it with a kiss. This was what I'd been waiting for. A moment when I had stopped worrying about this job and he had stopped worrying about everything else. A moment that was only about us. About solidifying all the emotions I had when it came to him.

"I'm not going anywhere. I promise," he whispered against my mouth. "Nothing you could do, or anything you have done, can scare me off. You're stuck with me because I'm sure of one thing, Lily—I was always meant to be yours."

My heart felt like it may pop out of my chest. I leaned into him as we made our way to his bedroom. "Lincoln, I would like nothing more than to mount you but I have to sleep. Don't touch me. Don't even look at me with your gorgeous face." My eyes were already closing. I smiled and stroked lines across his damp chest. "Besides, we've gotta worry about your back."

"You're so full of nonsense," he teased, and then winced. "To be honest, it is cramping a little." Still, he scooped me up and placed me on the bed.

I wriggled my fingers. "Let me massage you and show you what I am really capable of. I held back last time."

"Tomorrow." He kissed my nose. "You need sleep, love."

I curled into the curve of Lincoln's body. "Who would have thought Link and Lily would lead to this?"

He chuckled. "Link dreamed of it."

"Lily too."

• • •

The next morning, after Lincoln proved, yet again, that he was the perfect lover, we went to my apartment.

I walked over to my closet and made a show of grabbing my laciest underwear. Lincoln's breath hitched before he dropped his head back.

"Um…" I started. Despite feeling sure about our relationship, I didn't want to overstep. "Will I be spending tonight with you? I just want to know what I should pack."

"Lily, if I had my way, I'd take all your stuff and throw it in the back of my truck right now."

A wide grin stretched across my face. This was what happiness felt like.

"So what are we doing today?" I asked.

"I'd like to take you out on a date. Somewhere nice and fancy. I haven't figured out where yet." He curled an arm around me and kissed my cheek. "But first, breakfast."

"Pancakes?" I teased, despite knowing he preferred eggs.

"For you, I'll eat pancakes. Every day. For the rest of my life."

I hoped he would. But before I could say that out loud, he pulled me in for a long kiss. "You were about to say something filthy with that sweet mouth."

I giggled and went in for a slow, luxurious kiss. He slipped his tongue between my lips, and my body prickled with desire.

I pulled back, sucking in a deep breath of air. "You could kill me with those kisses." I leaned in for another. "But it is a worthy way to go."

There was a knock at the door. My chest sank, and panic swirled in my belly. No one had this address. Except my gran, who didn't drive, and Alistair.

Noticing my inability to move, Lincoln opened the door.

"Hi," a woman's voice said. "I'm looking for Elizabeth?"

A voice I knew. A voice I'd missed.

"Mom?" I asked.

Lincoln stepped aside as my mother ran toward me and pulled me into a tight hug. I wrapped my arms around her small frame and squeezed, afraid I might break her. Her floral scent took me back years, through good and bad times, but I couldn't let go. "Mom," I whispered. "Mom."

"My love, my Lily," she said, her voice muffled by my hair. "I've missed you so much."

"I've missed you," I said, and loosened the hug, but I didn't release her. I was afraid if I did, I'd lose her again. "What are you doing here? You haven't replied to any of my texts."

Her red hair was pulled back into a stern bun. I hadn't seen her hair up in years. Douglas preferred it down.

She ran her hands down her royal-blue shirt. "I know. I was busy with something very risky. Something I once asked you to trust me with."

I stared at her, afraid to say the thing I was hoping for.

"I left him, Lily."

Tears sprang to my eyes, matching hers. "Are you sure?"

She nodded. "It took me so long, and I had to keep so many secrets because I needed to make sure that, when I left, he understood that if he ever came after us or dared to write about you again, he would regret it. It took me years to dig up enough evidence of his schemes. I may not be able to bring down the entire GB empire, but what I have is enough to scare him into submission." She lifted her chin, and I finally saw the brave woman my grandmother always spoke about. "We are free of Douglas Gordon-Bettencourt and all his henchmen."

I couldn't believe what I was hearing. My heart was racing. "Mom, it must have been so scary doing this alone. I could have helped."

"I got us into this mess. I wanted to get us out. And I wanted you to focus on your life, on your career, on…" She glanced at Lincoln and raised an eyebrow before leaning in. "Is this the gorgeous boss my mother's told me about?"

Lincoln cleared his throat and shifted on his feet, looking anywhere but at us. "Hello," he said with a small wave. His lopsided smile came out, and the spark of joy in my chest spread through to the tips of my fingers and toes, setting everything alight.

"Mom, this is Lincoln Carden, the love of every life I've lived."

LINCOLN

[Yesterday]

@pancakesareelite:
Don't go to bed yet, I just need to
finish drafting this email and then we
can play

@theanswerisno:
I waited a lifetime for you. I can wait
a little longer.

I knocked on the bathroom door. "Lily, come on. We're going to be late. William made me promise I'd help him set up Thunderstruck's booth. Didn't you promise Rose you'd help her over at Fun&Games?"

"Uh-huh," she replied. "I'll be done soon. Rose'll totally understand when she sees this."

Elizabeth stepped out of the bathroom wearing the maroon leather pants I'd dreamed of. They hugged her curves and hung low on her hips. My mouth dropped open.

"You like?" She ran her hands down the black corset, tight around her waist. "This is because you made me watch *Star Shield* three times. I was inspired."

"Oh no," I groaned, then nodded. "I mean yes, yes, obviously yes but oh no, no, no. How am I supposed to…?" I couldn't even finish my sentence.

She spun around, obviously enjoying my pain.

"Maybe we can be late." My eyes dipped to her cleavage and got stuck there.

She pressed a soft kiss on my mouth. "Nope. Rose asked me to be there early, and I agreed. We have no excuse."

"But this is an excuse." I gestured to her outfit. "Like you said, Rose and William will understand."

"I like to keep you waiting." She winked, knowing it would drive me up the wall, and before I could grab her and have my way, she swayed her hips and escaped, making sure I'd get a good view before adding a cape and completing her costume.

We hopped into my truck and drove down to where Comic-Con was being held. I read the directions off the special-access tickets Rose had given us. "It's supposed to be here. Which is weird. It's not where the main con access is."

We parked. Beside us, Claire, Dean, and Hannah climbed out of their car. Claire gave Elizabeth the tightest hug.

Shaun, Neema, and their brand-new baby arrived. Elizabeth practically teleported toward them.

"Lincoln," Claire called, and pointed at Elizabeth, "it was the secret identity trope all along."

"Fated mates, maybe," I said, that familiar heat filling my chest.

Claire clapped and nodded before asking, "How's work? Any regrets?"

"None at all. I love it there." My cheeks ached from all this smiling. I wasn't used to this. But my new job was good, and after all these years, I didn't feel so frazzled every morning.

Elizabeth, on the other hand, seemed to thrive under pressure, and she gave Anders a run for his money on the daily. It was as though she was avenging me for every trouble he'd ever given me. I'd be lying if I said I didn't enjoy that.

"William sent a text," Shaun yelled over at us. "He said to hurry and stop chitchatting."

We walked through the entrance, and the doorman stopped us. "Are you here for Rose and William?"

We nodded, and he took a quick look at the tickets Rose had emailed us. He led us inside and pointed to the board game area. "In you get. Pick one costume off the rail. Your names are on them."

"No way," Claire said. "She was being serious about us dressing up?"

"But I like my costume," Elizabeth said.

"I like it too." I slipped my hands around to her backside underneath her cape and nearly glitched. That was dangerous.

The stillness of the empty venue was eerie and somehow exciting. I'd been here before, but it was filled to the brim. I had never returned.

Shaun located the costumes and wasted no time finding his name. "Hey! I'm an elf! Look at this epic wig." He lifted his clothing and a few smaller outfits. "There are costumes for the kids too." He handed Hannah's outfit, which looked like a hobbit's costume, to Claire. He handed an even smaller version to Neema and then walked into the changing booth.

Shaun stepped out fully dressed, and his excitement was almost enough to get us moving, and if that didn't do it, well, the person who walked out from the board game area did.

"Legolas!" Rose's mother yelled at Shaun. "You look marvelous.

Come on, the rest of you need to hurry. We need to be done and packed up in fifteen minutes."

"Done with what?" Claire asked. Although by now, I think we all had an idea of what was coming next.

"With the wedding, of course."

Shaun and Neema high-fived. "Knew it!"

Claire squealed with Dean hugging her from behind and swaying from side to side.

While my heart exploded with joy, Elizabeth's hand slipped into mine, fitting perfectly. I tugged her closer, and she spun against my chest, kissing the underside of my jaw. The nonchalant public display of affection had heat spiraling through me.

I dragged her into a booth, where I had the honor of peeling off her incredible costume. It wouldn't be the last time I'd do that.

Main quest: Watch friends get married. Side quest: Think about marrying Elizabeth.

By the time we made it out, everyone was ready and waiting. We walked into the board game area and found Rose, dressed as a hobbit and scattering white rose petals everywhere. Her face was emotive on a regular day, but now she looked like the sun.

"You're here!" she squealed, and we went in for a group hug. "Mom! Let's get a move on. I'm ready."

William was at her side in an instant. He pulled her into his arms and spun her around in the air. "I'm ready too. I've been ready."

Elizabeth shifted closer to me, close enough for me to smell her delicious scent. It was different now, knowing I'd get to taste her later. I took a moment to stare at her, admiring her pink-tinged cheeks and her copper hair framing her face. Her eyes. Those eyes. I couldn't look away.

"What do you think about when you look at me like that?" she whispered.

"Nothing."

"Nothing?" She curled an arm around me. "Not even something…naughty?"

I grinned. "Honestly, I'm not thinking about anything except how good it feels to look at you. And I know that's not the cheeky answer you expected but…Lily, do you know that nothing has ever silenced my brain the way you do?"

Her beautiful eyes widened.

"I know peace when I look at you," I said, and added a disclaimer. "Well, as much as my brain allows me to have."

She giggled, but her eyes were shining. "I can't wait to marry you. Scenario four won out. I don't know what you're waiting for."

My eyes widened, and I thought she may have triggered my fight-or-flight response again, which I've since come to understand as being a rush of emotion. "Are you proposing to me now because I've been slacking?"

"If I was, what would you say?" She pulled me aside.

Scenes of our future together flashed across my mind.

Waking next to her.

Hosting game night together.

Visiting our moms.

Lily'd come in for the occasional lecture just to tease me.

I'd consult on her projects to tease her.

Gaming with my Player Two and maybe future little gamers.

There was nothing I wanted more.

I leaned down and kissed her on the mouth. "To you, my Lily, the answer is always yes."

ACKNOWLEDGMENTS

As always, I would like to thank my parents for raising me the way they did. Thank you for your support and love. My dad is waiting for the movie, and yes, Mom, I'll still cover my eyes when they kiss on-screen.

Next, to my husband: Thank you for giving me the time to write and recognizing how important this is to me. Thank you for having my back and for buying me many, many cappuccinos.

To my perfect daughter, I can't wait to read more of your brilliant words. *Oh No, Cat* is my favorite book.

Cathie, my agent, thank you for being my cheerleader even when I feel I've lost my way.

Alex, thank you for jumping on a call to chat about Lincoln and Lily. We had an adventure with these two, but it was all worth it.

Caroline, your enthusiasm with *Playing Flirty* was a delight.

Yumna, the SpongeBob to my Squidward, I can't do this without you.

Somehow, I got lucky and landed myself a friend like Nuhaa. I write for you. You write for me. It's equal.

Zoë, your late-night feedback saved me. Come back to South Africa, please.

Rushdiyah, Muneera, Natheefah, Gwendolyn, Keisha, Nadine, Kate, Jessie, Robin, Haley, Arini, Potty, Marilize, Michaela, Hannah, thank you for helping me through a really difficult rework and for keeping a close eye on the ADHD representation.

I'd hate to forget anyone. If I do, I am so sorry. Off the top of my head, these are the names that come to mind: Kauthar, Jamy, Tams, Rebecca squared, Kelly, Zayaan, Shannon, and Marizaan. If I missed you, please tell me, and I'll definitely remember for the next one.

Jo Watson, Charlotte Stein, Swati Hegde, and Abbi Waxman, your words and blurbs for *Playing Flirty* are forever appreciated.

Maria, I hope you enjoy Emily Ann. 🖤

To all the readers and authors who gave *Playing Flirty* love, I wouldn't be able to continue this journey without you. Thank you.

Thank you to my sisters, my cousins, and friends for the constant love and encouragement.

This book was hard. It was (re)written during a difficult time, but by the blessings of the Almighty, I've done it.

I hope this book heals you like it did me.

And as with anything I write: Don't try this at home. 😉

ABOUT THE AUTHOR

Shameez Patel was born and raised in Cape Town, South Africa. She lives there with her husband, child, and three cats. During the day she juggles her time between parenting her daughter and working, but at night, she escapes to new worlds that often include magic and monsters and always have someone to fall in love with. Shameez became obsessed with fiction at a young age. Her parents fondly recall receiving her first handwritten story before the age of ten, titled "The Treasures of Zombie Island," which surprisingly featured no zombies at all. She has been writing ever since.

RAISING READERS
Books Build Bright Futures

Thank you for reading this book and for being a reader of books in general. We are so grateful to share being part of a community of readers with you, and we hope you will join us in passing our love of books on to the next generation of readers.

Did you know that reading for enjoyment is the single biggest predictor of a child's future happiness and success?

More than family circumstances, parents' educational background, or income, reading impacts a child's future academic performance, emotional well-being, communication skills, economic security, ambition, and happiness.

Studies show that kids reading for enjoyment in the US is in rapid decline:

- In 2012, 53% of 9-year-olds read almost every day. Just 10 years later, in 2022, the number had fallen to 39%.
- In 2012, 27% of 13-year-olds read for fun daily. By 2023, that number was just 14%.

Together, we can commit to **Raising Readers** and change this trend. How?

- Read to children in your life daily.
- Model reading as a fun activity.
- Reduce screen time.
- Start a family, school, or community book club.
- Visit bookstores and libraries regularly.
- Listen to audiobooks.
- Read the book before you see the movie.
- Encourage your child to read aloud to a pet or stuffed animal.
- Give books as gifts.
- Donate books to families and communities in need.

BOB1217

Books build bright futures, and **Raising Readers** is our shared responsibility.

For more information, visit **JoinRaisingReaders.com**

Sources: National Endowment for the Arts, National Assessment of Educational Progress, WorldBookDay.com, Nielsen BookData's 2023 "Understanding the Children's Book Consumer"